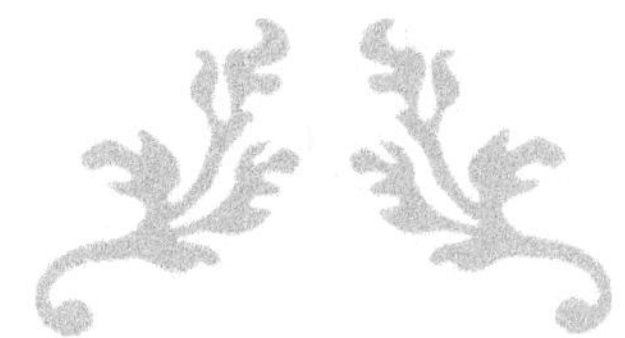

PHOLUS REBORN

absman420 writing as Austin Miller

Respectfully dedicated to FANTCDUDE, the greatest of us all

"Those who cannot remember the past are condemned to repeat it."

GEORGE SANTAYANA (1905)

1. "Pholus"

When I got the call that my Grandfather had passed, I felt an odd mixture of disappointment and relief. I'd just seen him a month ago, when he'd turned 92, still as spry and troublesome as ever. He'd been a landscaper and gardener since coming to America in his youth -- he claimed it tied him to the old country, the old ways. The fact is, he knew plants and he knew how to love them -- shame he never learned how to treat people the same way. Oddly, it was people he objectified and plants he felt emotion for. His garden had been lush and inviting, alive and ready-to-burst, even up to the end, when his heart had burst. I'd inherited that from him -- not the bad heart, the green thumb -- though I only grew marijuana in the basement of my house.

They'd found him in the garden, dead. It was the Executive Manager of the Home who felt the need to inform me that my Grandfather, apparently, had been masturbating when he'd died. "And in the garden, of all places!" he'd said with indignity. I shrugged -- what should my reaction have been? It was the Home's Resident Mortician who'd pulled me aside and informed me quietly that my Grandfather had been "remarkably blessed" with "prodigious equipment" and that the erection he'd had when he'd died hadn't yet gone down. "Hopefully, it's genetic," the Resident Mortician said to me with a wink. Sadly, I'd not inherited that from him -- mine was more pint-sized than prodigious -- but I reacted as if it were. You know, bro code.

It was no secret that my Grandfather was the bane of the old folk's home -- the sexually-forward, inappropriate old man who wouldn't leave the ladies alone. Or the nurses. Or the staff. Although they had a soft spot in their hearts for him -- everything else was about his hard spot, the one he was constantly playing with, often in the most public and inconvenient of places. I can't tell you how many calls I'd gotten over the years because my grandfather had been "at it again" — try having that conversation with your grandfather! All in all, they were not sorry to see him go.

While in his room, gathering his few personal effects -- the things worth anything -- another old man came in, one of his fellow gardeners, and presented me with a towel-wrapped object, saying, "Big Red wanted you to have this."

I'd never felt like I'd connected with my Grandfather -- "Big Red" -- we both shared the same red hair, and the nickname -- though I was just plain "Red" (worse, "Little Red" when I'd been a kid) to his "Big Red" -- but that was all. I'd always assumed it was because I was gay -- his generation had their old-school outlooks -- and he believed in big, hearty masculine expressions. Potency with him, above all -- fertility. His garden had been a reflection of that.

But he wanted me to have something — and that made me happy. He'd thought of me! Even in death, there's hope!

Rolling back the towel, I was surprised to discover a clay garden gnome, about twelve inches long -- but at least not the cheap, Disney-fied version with the goofy red hat and cheeky smile. That would've probably made me leave it behind. This was significantly older, a hand-painted terracotta statuette of a disheveled old man dressed in rags with a lusty half-smile on his face. The only other noticeable detail about the sculpt was that the gnome had an obvious bulge — you don't see that on the modern-day Wal-Mart gnomes!

"He wanted me to have this?" I ask the other old guy, trying not to sound ungrateful, like I wasn't suspicious of a joke. "A garden gnome?"

"Gnomes are powerful symbols of fertility," the old guy said -- just my luck, my Grandfather was pals with a professor — then he added, "Look it up. You've got The Google" and I felt a lot better about my Grandfather's friends. "It's been in the garden long as I can remember," he continued, tapping it with his finger. "Your Grandpappy said he'd had it his whole life!"

"His whole life? Wow... Thank you," I said. "I have the perfect place for it." -- (Ironically, I did!).

"You got a garden, boy?"

I smiled, thinking of marijuana, my basement hydroponics. "I grow stuff," I said.

And after I'd gotten all the business and paperwork and payments at the Home complete -- my Grandfather safely in a box being shipped to the family site, his eternal erection hidden by pine.

I headed back to my house, a few hours away, the ancient Gnome with the Big Bulge resting in a box in the back seat.

I DID have the perfect place for it -- my little basement grow. I put it down at the head of a row of a hybrid I was developing. I aimed its little bulge at the marijuana plants and said, laughing, "Okay, Gnome, let 'er rip. Show me the fertility!"

And then the strangest thing happened. For the next year, it did just that.

****

My mother was largely inconvenienced by her father's funeral, taking her away from something of greater value to her -- Botox and charity fundraisers, the court of public opinion. Upon entering the funeral home, she hugged me because she was required to, then immediately pulled away, muttering, "I'm mortified that you're stoned for your grandfather's funeral!"

I shrugged. "We all medicate our own ways, mother."

"I disapprove. And so would your grandfather."

I snorted. "Big Red liked plants better than people."

"Don't be smart -- you know what I mean."

I looked around. "Where's Dad?"

She made it about her. "Your father's still on the coast. Apparently the big case they're working on is more important than supporting his spouse in her time of mourning. He sends his love, by the way -- and wants to know when you're starting law school?"

I smiled at her disbelievingly. "Really? That's a lot of words for Dad to string together about me."

She shook it off. "Well, I'd like to know when you're starting law school," she said, still speaking sotto voce, as if people would overhear. "It would thrill me to learn you're doing something with your life."

"Mother, please don't start. Not here -- not now."

"You're nearly thirty years old, Red!" she said, stepping closer to me, speaking even more intensely in her whisper. "Your grandfather is dead and you still float along thinking about nothing more than your needs in the moment -- how proud he must be, looking down on you from Heaven! You sit around in that dorm-room of a house and smoke marijuana all day with your even bigger loser-of-a-friend, Jack-Apple!"

As many times as I've heard this speech, or variants of it, I chuckled despite myself. "AppleJack," I said, laughing. "You know his name, mother. We've been friends our whole lives." I chuckled again. "Jack Apple…"

"Jack-Ass, more like. You know, honey, you're no better than the company you keep," she said, scolding. "And I don't know why you keep him." She was silent for a moment, then asked, snidely, "You're not… *boyfriends*, are you?"

I snorted a loud laugh, completely inappropriate in the funeral home -- everyone looked. "No," I said, smiling. "Mother, he's straight."

She grunted disbelievingly, granting us another awkward silence. Why couldn't I be like her rich gay friends on the coast? With their money and looks and lack of educated opinions -- she understood them. Finally, she asked, "Did you collect your grandfather's things? His army trunk?"

I nodded. "Yes," I said. "I have it all back at my dorm-room of a house. Would you like to come over later and go through it?"

She shook her head. "Sadly, I can't. I'm flying out as soon as this is over. There's a gala tonight that I'm co-chair for and I must attend. You can look after it, can't you, Red? I'm sure there's nothing of any real value."

I laughed inadvertently.

"What?" my mother asked.

I shook my head-- my mother had no space in her heart for sentiment. "Nothing," I said. "He left me a garden gnome…" I held out my hands in an empty gesture.

If the Botox had allowed her the capability, she would've scrunched her eyes. "An ugly old terra-cotta thing?" she asked.

I nodded and nearly smiled. "Yes!" I said. "You know it?"

She looked like she was weighing whether she'd answer, when she finally said, "I tripped over the damn thing playing hide and seek as a little girl and twisted my ankle!" She looked away, pursing her lips. Then she added, "He was more concerned about me almost breaking his stupid statue than he was about my injury!" She shook her head. "I swear to God, the things he chose to care about…"

I shrugged yet again -- a common gesture with my mother -- and said, "He went out of his way to make sure I got it."

She waved it off. "You can have the stupid thing!" she said, as if I'd needed her permission. "Do you even have a garden?"

****

I started growing pot in college, a little closet set-up. I failed miserably at first, until I learned how to time the lights, control the temperature, deal with the watering -- my roommate AppleJack and I took a course in hydroponics our senior year that was inspiring, quite frankly! By the time we graduated, we'd gained a bit of a reputation around campus for the quality of our bud. (We called it "Jack'd Red.")

When I bought the house -- which my parents insisted on calling my "starter house" -- I transformed the basement into a hydroponic farm. I did it right along with the renovation of the upstairs master bathroom -- no fuss, no muss -- all the plumbing I could want.

It was just a hobby, but I loved the routine of it -- it was relaxing. In a weird way, it made me feel closer to my grandfather. Look, we both had gardens, just mildly different philosophies -- I was sure the same god oversaw both. The garden god -- the god of pot. The fertility god.

Well, maybe not a god, exactly, but that ugly Gnome oversaw everything. He and his massive bulge lorded over the grow room from a shelf above the younglings.

And the oddest thing happened -- my yield increased by over 65%. At the time, I wasn't sure I bought into it, either. However, it's not that hard to link cause and effect when the only thing I did differently was add the Gnome. The fact was, the plants were growing quicker and stronger and their yield made me start to wonder if fertility gods weren't real.

Until one day I carelessly knocked the little Gnome off the shelf and broke it.

And that's where the story really started.

****

According to "The Google":

The Ancient Greeks had a God for it -- act surprised -- a God of Fertility: Priapus. Apparently his power was manifested in his oversized genitals, creating fertility in males, females, and the land -- but with the Christian invasion (and the way that particular religion embraced the forbiddance of sexual expression), Priapus and his penis became a demon, or represented as a withered old man with an uncontrollable erection, often pushing his giant cock before himself on a cart. Religion made genitals and their symbology a punishment, a curse -- act surprised.

So… Gnomes. Little old men with massive genitals -- a European ode to the Ancients. Little clay gods of fertility for your garden -- Priapus through the ages. The fact is Gnomes didn't become "cutesy" until the release of "Snow White and the Seven Dwarfs" at the beginning of the 20th century, when Priapus became Dopey.

I find stuff like that fascinating.

****

Ultimately, the Gnome didn't matter because it was just a delivery device.

I mean, literally.

Just as I was about to buy into the idea that a fertility icon in your garden increases yield, I went and knocked the fucking thing off the shelf while tranferring a tray of younglings. Fucking stoner thing to do, honestly, and I hate talking about it because it makes me look stupid. I tried to "catch" it with my foot -- or at least soften the impact. All I managed to do was scratch myself as it bounced off my sandal -- Don't laugh! It drew blood -- and then shattered on the cement, missing the floor mat because of my interference. Fucking idiot.

And I was hoping, you know, maybe some glue? While at the same time thinking, doesn't destroying it wreck the mojo? Doesn't breaking it stop the voodoo that it do so well? Isn't that the folklore? Immediately I pictured my Grandfather, Big Red -- now a year in his grave -- he managed to get through his whole life without breaking it! Ninety-one years more than me! Maybe some glue….? Idiot.

So I knelt down next to it and gingerly lifted it up -- the front wasn't cracked, but collapsed from age, barely more than dust -- glue wasn't going to help. Fuck.

And then the discovery.

There was something inside the hollowed-out middle, wrapped in what seemed to be very old cheesecloth -- very, very old, like great-grandma's linen that never came out of the box, faded and brittle and delicate beyond possibility -- someone had planted something INSIDE the Ancient Gnome.

Eagerly -- nervously -- I carried the whole mess to my work-table and clicked on the bright, overhead light. I was more afraid of ruining whatever was inside than anything else, especially if it was some sort of message or something. (This was why I wasn't an archeologist -- the stress!) Should I be wearing gloves?

I had to break the Gnome a little further to get the package to come out freely. I was a nervous wreck, suppositioning all over the place -- had my Grandfather known about this? Was it my Grandfather who'd planted it? Was this why he wanted me to have the Gnome in the first place?

What could it possibly be?

The rag or cheesecloth or whatever the hell it was that wrapped it nearly dissolved away, turning to dirty dust even as I tugged on it. Pieces of it came off intact, but it was nothing more than wrapping, no message or clues. Just old -- insanely old -- hundreds of years old. If my Grandfather had known about this, he hadn't changed anything -- he hadn't wrapped it in anything new.

It was two objects wrapped together. One was an icon, about four inches long, a crude stone carving of an overly muscular man with an enormous phallus -- his dick went practically to his chest -- his eyes dark jewels. The other was a tiny, dark bottle, like a perfume bottle, heavy glass, deep blue, a small stopper with a wax seal. Holding it to the light, I couldn't see through the thick glass, but I could feel its age.

I spent a few seconds cleaning the bottle, dusting it off and wiping it down gently. Even if there was nothing inside it, the bottle itself was spectacular -- I'd never seen anything like it. I picked up the statue and did the same, wiped it down, cleaned it up, blew off the dust. When I rubbed and blew on his disproportionate phallus, I made a dumb joke like, "That's the best blow job you've had in a while" -- something like that.

I was looking in his jeweled eyes when -- I swear -- they lit up, bright red. Not just "caught the light", not just "sparkled", they LIT UP and -- I'm not kidding. I'm not making this up -- I had a vision. I heard it speak to me.

It said, "PHOLUS"

I dropped the little muscular stone like a scorpion -- like a venomous fang. I looked at it in horror as it balanced on its side by its big penis, staring helplessly at the table.

What in the name of God?

"Name of God!" I thought. "That's IT!"

I pulled out my phone.

****

From The Google:

*In Greek mythology, **Pholus** (Greek: Φόλος) was a wise <u>centaur</u> who lived in a cave on or near Mount Pelion.*

Are you kidding? Pholus is really a thing?

A centaur? Weren't they half-horse?

Well, I guess that little statue is partially-horse, at least.

And this Pholus lived on Mount Pelion…? That was familiar. Where had I heard that before? Hadn't my grandfather mentioned he came to the US as a boy from some valley near Mount Pelion? In Greece? I was pretty sure...

But there was something else.

*In astronomical terms, **Pholus** (from Φόλος) is an <u>eccentric centaur</u> (an object classified somewhere between an asteroid and a minor planet) in the outer Solar System, approximately 180 kilometers (110 miles) in diameter, that crosses the orbit of both Saturn and Neptune. It was discovered on 9 January 1992…*

Wait. What? -- I was born on 9 January, 1992. Pholus and I were twins… which wasn't funny. It was getting weird.

Nicknamed "Big Red," its orbit around the sun takes 92 years and one month…

92 years and one month… my Grandfather -- Big Red's exact age when he died!

Okay, I was fucking freaking out by this time! Too many coincidences. A centaur -- an eccentric planet -- my birthday -- my grandfather's orbit -- but that still wasn't everything. There was one more.

*When **Pholus** (from Φόλος) appears in an <u>astrological reading</u>, it represents a spark, a start, grand events set in motion from something small, like shooting oneself in one's foot, the butterfly effect. When Pholus appears, an unexpected adventure follows.*

Fuck you, the Google.

****

I leaned against the wall and stared at the work-table for a while, at the askew little icon and the blue-glass bottle.

I sat on a stool, smoked a joint, and stared at the stone man, released from his prison, forever erect. How did he talk to me? How had that happened? I'd never heard of "Pholus" before -- I couldn't have made that up. And even if I had -- there were too many coincidences… there were three different versions of "Pholus" and all of them applied to me! I couldn't have known about that and "forgotten" -- I didn't smoke that much weed.

No. I'd had a vision -- the icon had spoken to me.

Assuming that to be true, I thought, I shouldn't fear it. If this icon was meant for me -- and it seemed like that was the only conclusion -- then I had no reason for fear.

Sadly, by the time I worked up enough brave-energy to touch the icon again, nothing happened -- it was just a piece of cold stone. No more flare -- no more sparkle -- no more insight. The little stone dude had a pretty amazing cock... and he seemed so proud... but he'd stopped talking.

So, the bottle then.

What could it possibly be? Perfume? Wine? Magic Potion? Poison? I mean, it's ridiculous. I should have it analyzed -- I should find out what it is -- I should know before I unleash some disease, some demon, some genie. Maybe ingesting whatever was inside would transform me into a centaur -- well, being gay, maybe My Little Pony?

I couldn't see through the deep blue glass, so I didn't even know if anything was inside at all. I was so busy playing mind-games with myself that I hadn't realized how much time had passed, even.

Sigh. Another joint.

Anyway, when I finally got around to opening the stupid thing, it was nearly midnight. The stopper, which was also glass, was sealed with what appeared to be a thick wax. I used a tiny screwdriver to flake it off. It took a little back-and-forth to completely break the seal, but once I did, the little stopper eased out quickly.

The Scent.

The Scent alone.

My cock was rock hard immediately, just on the scent alone -- sex and leather and sweat and metal, the smells of masculinity, from the playful snips, snails and puppy-dog tails of youth to adult desire, dominance, and desperate need. The rut of the thrust, the spreading of the seed, it was fertility, the deep, moist earth. It was the Essence of Man.

I was compelled to taste it -- I didn't think twice about it -- it wasn't until long after the moment that I thought there may have been danger. In the moment, there wasn't any thought at all, just need -- driving masculine need. Whatever was in that bottle I needed in me.

A drop was all -- and barely enough to qualify for the word "drop" -- it rolled lazily out of the bottle like a thick, congealed syrup -- but when it hit my tongue...

Orgasm!

Immediately, my cock shot -- overwhelming! Like this huge, savage, I've-never-felt-it-like-this-before orgasm! Out of nowhere -- like, so incredibly all-encompassing that every cell of my body was my cock and they were all shooting at once. And then as the flavor spread across my tongue, I was able to taste it -- battle and strength and muscle and sweaty maleness mixed with earth and flavored with fire, the taste of heroes and prowess and sweet, hard-won victory. Horse flanks, battle songs and flasks of wine, wrestling naked for sport and the tight, sweet holes of olive-skinned apprentices -- it was everything dark and earthy, meat and marrow, savagery and strength. It was gloriously masculine.

And the aftertaste was dirty, and sexual, and rutted, the nasty, shit-flecked maw of the satisfied fornicator -- the flavor of lust.

I was oh, so horny -- I needed to fuck, cock-driven, unapologetic, just lay-in and pound kind of fuck. Not love-making, no gentleness -- playfulness, yes; powerful, definitely -- fucking male on male sex! Then came the mental run-down of my fuck-buddy list, too few and too far between, the usual Grindr stall, the seedy bar -- any option. All options. Need to fuck.

It was a stranger whose name I sort of remember -- I didn't care -- all that mattered was the hole. By that time, crazy, stupid needy lust. My wee cock was flared and strong, flexing beyond its norm -- serve it, suck it, take it, fuck it. Pholus has started his adventure!

****

I woke the next morning in a stranger's bed, crusty and sweaty, the smell of sex on my breath -- glorious! My cock immediately hardened. He slept on his side, my unknown partner, his back to me, a little blond thing -- his hole was red, swollen, smeared with my dried cum and his ass juices.

It smelled glorious -- earthy, sexy -- raw. It was impossible to resist, so I didn't, licking his hole, loving the taste, digging in and eating. Gripping around his balls, I felt his cock harden with his morning's piss. Fuck, I wanted that, too. All of it.

He woke moaning. "Ohhh, man... stop. I can't... I'm sore and I gotta pee..."

"You taste so fuckin' good," I mumbled, slurping his hole. "Lemme just eat it awhile..."

"That's gross," he said, pulling himself away. "I'm gonna pee -- I don't wanna... you should go. Call an Uber or something."

I was laying there with this hard-on -- a big hard-on, too -- I showed it to him. "Aw, c'mon, baby, you can't leave me like this..."

"You got an okay dick," he said, pulling himself out of bed, "and you sure know how to use it. You fucked me every which way sideways last night -- I'm sore as hell right now. But you should be gone when I get done."

"Aw, fuck," I said, with this impossible hard-on, and these blue-ass balls. Cold little bitch.

Where the fuck were my shoes?

****

The Uber driver could smell me -- I could tell. And I know it made him uncomfortable -- he shifted himself in his seat several times. After a while, I realized it was because he had a hard-on, too.

That was fucking hot.

Cocks were fucking hot.

With my fingers, I squeezed mine through the material of my pants while we drove. I knew he saw me -- I didn't care. It felt too good.

Everything felt good.

In the shower, I noticed it more in my balls than in my cock -- the growth, I mean -- but also from the undeniable rush of testosterone. The way it felt. I was a man -- all man. I felt like a man -- and I fucking loved it!

I gave very little thought to the idea that whatever was in that bottle had adversely affected me -- just the opposite. Whatever was in that bottle had changed me for the better! Somehow, it had awakened something in me -- it had connected me to something greater than myself -- MY masculine essence.

I shot off a load in the shower, praising Priapus and Pholus (and Phallus, too!) -- I could phuck them all! Who could deny the power of the cock?

Who wouldn't want this?

2. "Nonischemic Priapism"

From "The Google":

__Priapism__ is a condition in which a penis remains erect for hours in the absence of stimulation or after stimulation has ended. Most cases are ischemic. Ischemic priapism is generally painful while nonischemic priapism is not. In ischemic priapism, most of the penis is hard. In __nonischemic priapism__, the entire penis is only somewhat hard.

****

Aw, fuck man -- that was me in one bold chapter heading -- *nonischemic priapism*. My dick hadn't been flaccid in over two weeks. The only reason it didn't concern me was because it didn't hurt -- so I figured why shouldn't it show itself off? It was a damn nice cock -- it was just putting itself out there. As a matter of fact, it was kind of hot.

Fucking EVERYTHING was kind of hot! That my sex drive was stuck in high gear was kind of hot -- finding out I have *nonischemic priapism* was kind of hot. But hottest of all? My dick was getting bigger.

My dick, my balls -- bigger. It didn't help that my cock was semi-hard all the time, it just kept me from noticing it right away. But in the last two weeks, my hard cock had shot up to eight inches! And not in Grindr inches, either -- ACTUAL inches!

And my testosterone production was up, too, like a thousand percent, thanks to my growing balls, over-producing to make up for their past. My workouts had been fucking crazy -- they would just go on and on and I'd never lose energy -- two, three hours. The harder I trained, the hornier I felt, my big cock jutting out before me, struggling against the compression-anything I wore. I swear, I was shooing the guys off like flies -- I think my smell attracted them. I think my sweat was becoming some kind of pheromone or something. I was fucking them in the steam room, the shower, one guy in the janitor's closet -- I was a fucking beast! A beast with big, low-hanging balls.

****

Wow, look at you!" the doctor exclaimed as he entered the examination room. "You found the gym, I see."

I smiled. "Just trying to get into some kind of shape before I turn thirty," I lied. "I've always wanted to be a little bigger." The little paper exam outfit I wore left little to the imagination, but I flexed my bicep anyway -- it was about the size and hardness of a baseball.

He sat in the chair across from the examination table and opened my chart. "Your numbers look good across the board. Your blood pressure had been borderline high, but that seems okay now. I'd been concerned about your prostate, but the numbers aren't weighing it out anymore. Everything is good, except..." He made eye-contact with me. "...your testosterone levels are off the charts. Are you on something you want to tell me about?"

"I'm not on anything, doc. I promise."

He smiled in that way that said he knew my response was bullshit, but he didn't care. "You have to make sure when you're cycling to use the proper safeguards or your balls will atrophy -- I'm just expressing concern."

"My balls are quite juicy," I laughed, fearlessly (and shamelessly) pulling the paper dress away. "See?" They hung off the side of the exam table, heavy. My cock -- still in its state of *nonischemic priapism* -- enjoyed the exposure, too, nearing its new nine-inch max.

The doctor stared, slightly open-mouthed. "Yes, they..." He breathed in deeply, discovering my scent. I found myself able to release it directly, like an invisible spray. "Something's happening," he said quietly, drawing more of it in.

"Yes," I said, pulling him closer. "This is why I came to see you -- I've been having this effect on guys lately. Maybe you should examine it more closely?"

He took my cock in his mouth, unable to resist. He was tentative at first, uncertain what was going on, even though this was clearly fulfilling some deep-held fantasy of his, some bad porn plot.

But as soon as he got a dollop of my precum on his tongue, he lost all of his inhibition, sucking me with gusto.

I let him enjoy himself -- his desperation turned me on, but his lack of technique didn't sustain it -- finally, I planted my cock as deep in his throat as it could go and gave him a load. Honestly, I was bored -- and he was behind schedule anyway.

He choked it down, spilling some on the exam room carpet. I don't blame him -- it was a lot. But I knew that my orgasm triggered his. I saw it pass through his body -- I love when I have that effect on guys. I saw him shudder and reflexively thrust his hips -- I knew what that meant.

I smiled. "Wow. Thanks, doc."

He sat up quickly, embarrassed. "I've... I've never done anything like this before! I don't know what came over me..."

I chuckled. "Well, I know what came IN you. Does that count for something?"

He stood -- he's suddenly nervous. "I'm so sorry! It was so unprofessional of me..."

I laughed again. "It's not your profession, doc. You did fine."

He's breathing heavily, full of guilt, trying to figure out his next move -- he wore his confusion and shame like a life-jacket. "Look, I... thank you... I swear, I've never done anything like this..."

I stripped away the paper dress, revealing myself entirely to him, and began to slip my clothes back on, scanty underwear first. "Well, now you can say you have!" I laughed, patting him on the shoulder. "It's all good, doc -- I promise. Just tell me everything's okay with my chart and my heart and my blood pressure and stuff -- that's all that concerns me."

What about the nonischemic priapism? Isn't that what brought me here?

(Ha! That's not a problem -- look at my bulge!)

The doctor was looking at my bulge, too -- he saw me catch him and reddened. "You?" he asked, tucking the chart under his arm and reaching for the doorknob.

"You're as healthy as a horse."

****

I was getting muscular -- not huge, not like one of those bodybuilders -- but BIG, you know? Commanding. Six months after I'd been blessed by the gods, I weighed a solid 235 at 6'1", carrying almost no body-fat -- way different from the skinny-fat 190 where I'd started. I learned (from The Google) that testosterone was a natural leaning agent -- the more I produced, the leaner I got. So, at 235, I looked fucking awesome, even bigger than I really was! I looked like a superhero!

I started getting hairier, too. At first, a thicker pelt on the chest, a scruffier beard -- sexy -- but then I began having to trim my shoulders, my back, and my pubic bush or it would've taken over. I became the King of Manscaping. I ended up with a rough beard -- I gave in on that, otherwise I was shaving two or three times a day. Apparently, the boys liked the way it felt on their holes, so I didn't sweat it. The hair grew thicker in the grooves of my abs, too, emphasizing them even more.

I was so… fucking… manly!

By then my cock was nearly 11 inches long in its constant semi-erect state, displaying itself proudly before me. People REACTED to it -- no matter how I tried to hide it at first, once someone saw it, they couldn't stop looking. And to be honest, I discovered I liked the attention. I thought I would've been freaked or embarrassed by having such an obvious member, but it was the opposite -- the bigger it got, the greater my pride and eagerness to show it off.

****

"So let me get this straight," AppleJack said as he hit the bong, "You're not on steroids."

"No."

"No. Instead, you drank a magic potion that you found…?"

"In the garden gnome willed to me by my Grandfather," I finished for him, taking the bong.

While he chuckled, he exhaled a surprising amount of smoke. "Well, at least you're not on steroids." He smiled playfully.

"Thanks, AppleJack," I said, taking a hit.

"Dude, don't call me that," he said, reaching for his beer. "We're not five anymore."

I released the hit. "I just like getting a rise out of you, man," I said, refilling the bowl with more of the sweet hybrid we'd been working on.

AppleJack and I had become best friends in college, but we'd known each other most of our lives -- we come from the same small town in Upstate New York. His unfortunate baby-nickname permanently settled on his shoulders when his mom made the mistake of shouting it aloud at the playground one day. Ah, the brutal Fates...

He thought he'd be able to leave it behind when he went to college -- at least, I was the only one who knew it and I tried to use it privately (and sparingly) -- but he told it to this girl he'd been dating, who'd delighted in it, and the next thing he knew, everybody on campus was using it. He's tried to embrace it, using it as a screen name and online identity, but I knew he'd always secretly hated it.

Aside from his name, there was nothing particularly appetizing about him. I mean, here I was transforming into a creature that craved all kinds of cocks, but I still wasn't turned on by AppleJack -- I'm not sure he'd be pleased about that or not. Straight guys could be weird -- they didn't want to have sex with you, but they wanted to make sure that you wanted to have sex with them. The cool ones would let you crush on them, and most were simply a drink or two away from letting you suck their dicks.

AppleJack was kind of pasty and soft. His job was mostly in tech -- he was a money-market manager -- so he could dress like a slob, sit at his impressive computer setup, and nobody ever saw him. He was on the heavier side of hefty -- in all the years I'd known him, I'd never seen him naked (and we've roomed together since college!) and I was always sort of glad about that.

I liked the guy a lot, don't get me wrong -- he was my best friend -- but he was not a beautiful man.

"I remember the gnome," AppleJack said, taking his hit on the bong. "It was on the shelf -- ugly fucking thing. You say your grandfather willed it to you?"

"Yeah, some old guy gave it to me when I went to pick up my grandfather's effects -- said ol' Big Red had wanted me to have it."

He took another hit. "Do you think your grandfather knew what was in it? I mean, it's kind of a weird thing to will to someone, don't you think?"

I shrugged, accepting the bong back. "My grandfather was very 'old country,'" I said. "I'm willing to believe he sincerely wanted me to have the gnome itself, not knowing anything was inside it -- or maybe he did. I don't know. If he knew what was in there, why didn't he take it himself?"

AppleJack grunted, picking up the little stone icon from the coffee table. Examining its muscular build and its prodigious cock, he asked, "So you were cleaning the dirt off this guy, his little jewel eyes light up and you hear the word 'PHOLUS' -- that's what you said, right?"

I release my hit. "I'm not making this up, AppleJack -- it happened. PHOLUS -- clearly and distinctly. I'd never heard the word before. Ever. I had no idea what it even meant. So I looked it up and found out it meant three things: it was a centaur…"

"A centaur," AppleJack repeated. "A half-man, half-horse, right?"

I nodded. "Right. But it's also a small planetoid, called an 'eccentric centaur,' whose orbit crosses the path of Saturn and Neptune in the outer solar system." AppleJack took a hit. "Here's where it gets weird," I continued. "It's nickname is 'Big Red,' which was my grandfather's nickname."

"Okay," he said. "Coincidental, for sure…"

"I'm not done," I said. "It's orbit around the sun takes ninety-two years and a month, the exact length of my grandfather's life."

He was quiet for a moment, slowly exhaling.

"And the weirdest of all?" I said, reloading the bowl. "Pholus, the eccentric centaur, the planetoid, was discovered on the day of my birth."

He made a little "mind-blown" motion with his hand and said, "Pfffffft…"

"I know!" I said, gesturing big. "And that's not even all! It has an astrological meaning, too -- when Pholus appears in a reading, it means a person will have a great adventure based on a small gesture!" I sat back into the chair. "You know, like breaking a gnome on your foot and discovering a magic potion."

AppleJack snorted and pursed his lips like he was about to speak, but instead leaned forward and grabbed the bong. He took a long, considered hit before he finally said something. "Do you want my honest opinion?" he asked, leaning back into the sofa.

I nodded. "Yeah," I said. "That's why I'm telling you all this."

"Okay," he said, making eye contact with me. "I think the Pholus-thing is bullshit."

"WHAT?!?"

He held up a hand. "Relax. Lemme explain. Do I think you're on steroids? No. Knowing you and your work ethic, it is much more likely that you drank a magic potion than it is you took steroids."

"Thanks," I said dryly.

AppleJack shrugged it off. "But… the point is, I BELIEVE you about that part, okay?"

"But you don't believe the thing about Pholus."

He frowned and turned his head to the side. "I believe it's something, but let's put it aside for a second." He picked up the muscular icon by the waist, dancing it around the little glass bottle like it was a GI Joe action figure (with that cock, a REAL American Hero). "These two things came wrapped together, so it's more than likely that the message intended was 'Drink this and turn into THIS guy' -- right?"

"I… I guess…"

"Look, you're not turning into a centaur, are you? I mean, you're not getting hooves or anything, are you?"

I smiled. "The DOCTOR told me I was as healthy as a horse!"

AppleJack gave a sarcastic "haha," then said, "Not what I meant. What I meant is, it looks like you're transforming into THIS guy, not some horse-guy."

"So, what do you think the Pholus-stuff is?"

He shrugged and reached for the bong. "I don't know," he said. "It's something -- it's weird -- but I'm not sure it's all related."

"So what do I do?"

"I don't know," he said, playing with the icon. "But if you end up with a cock the size of this guy's, you should definitely consider porn."

****

I loved comic books -- I'd collected them most of my life -- heroic drama that all had some weird psycho-sexual backdrop to play against. Clark loved Lois, but Lois didn't like Clark -- Lois loved Superman, who was really Clark in disguise, but Superman wanted Lois to want him as Clark -- a love-triangle with two people, that kind of silliness. Batman and Robin required the approval of the comics code authority, for gods' sake -- and in early issues, they slept in the same bed! Truthfully, they had the most classically Grecian relationship of all the modern superheroes: an adult man raising a youthful ward and teaching him the ways of society. All that was missing -- thanks to the comics code -- was the classically Greek sex.

To me, mythology had the same basic feel to it as comic books -- and the tale of Pholus was an "insert" story, "retro-fitted" into the established continuity by later story-tellers.

In comics, the hero has Adventure One followed immediately by Adventure Two. Everything's fine -- there's an established continuity. Later writers (usually lazy writers) would come along and say, "Here's a story that happened BETWEEN Adventure One and Adventure Two" -- an "untold tale". That was the story of Pholus in a nutshell.

Heracles (the less-popular, less-friendly Greek version of the Roman Hercules) in an effort to win his immortality, had performed twelve labors -- actually, ten labors, but he'd cheated, so had two more added on. Somewhere between his fourth labor, stopping a monsterous boar, and his fifth labor, cleaning the dung-filled Augean Stables in a day, he found the time to squeeze in killing all the centaurs. Apparently, he went to meet his friend, the civilized centaur Pholus, at Pholus' cave in Mt. Pelion and they dined together. Heracles then used a bottle of Pholus' special wine to lure the centaurs out of hiding -- centaurs couldn't resist wine -- and when the centaurs attacked, driven crazy by the scent of the wine, Heracles slew them all with poisoned arrows. Pholus, shocked that something as small as an arrow could fell something as magnificent as a centaur, accidentally dropped the arrow on his foot, where it pierced his skin and killed him.

Moral: Don't shoot yourself in the foot.

Seriously. That was Pholus' story.

In a comic book, it could get stretched to an entire issue -- maybe -- if the centaur battle was included. But it still had that lame, Aesopian feel to it. I was the reborn version of the "don't shoot yourself in the foot" guy?

Were all the changes I was going through worth that?

****

It became too difficult to continue with my normal life. My co-workers? Well… at first, they were supportive. Goin' to the gym! Good for you! That kind of stuff. Then they saw the changes -- and they didn't know I'd taken some magic potion -- so they were a little uncomfortable. Everybody expected quitting and failure -- the weight-management empire was built on that predictable arc -- so when they saw ME "succeeding" at the gym, they automatically suspected I was "on" something. I must've been doing steroids -- that's the only way I could've gotten so big. Success means cheating.

And what the hell was going on in my pants?

It was hard NOT to notice the size of my bulge, the way it just filled my crotch, which I, personally, was loving. The heft of my balls alone -- goose-eggs now -- the way they pulled so heavily, gravity's continual yanking -- it felt so good. It did nothing to diminish the *nonischemic priapism*, sadly, which led to several uncomfortable meetings with HR. Apparently, my continuous hard-on was threatening, not medical.

Six months since the start of the transformation, I'd gained almost fifty pounds of muscle -- unnatural even for a guy on steroids, frankly -- and because there was no way to logically explain it (I mean, I couldn't tell them the truth, that I'd taken some magic potion), my co-workers simply avoided me, or displayed a strange mix of moral superiority and base sexual desire. Same with my friends and family. It was getting more and more difficult to be around the people that knew me, but didn't like the new me.

****

@applejack: HR told you to wear a tighter jockstrap? Hahaha
@applejack: Red, you're never going to be able to reconcile your old life with your new one.

@me: this is my first time with a new life -- I lack experience
@me: getting plenty of secret exec-washroom cock, tho

@applejack: Haha
@applejack: Best to just cut the ties and start fresh.
@applejack: unless you want to tell them all you drank a magic potion

@me: I told you and we're still friends

@applejack: Yeah, well… I'm antisocial
@applejack: It doesn't matter
@applejack: I got an idea

@me: ?????

@applejack: but I want 10%
@applejack: Trust me, my friend -- this is genius

@me: 20% — that's my final offer! Haha
@me: okay. What?

****

I became a Brand.
PHOLUS REBORN!
AppleJack had this crazy vision! (Well, honestly, I had the vision -- he just figured out how to exploit it.) "It's all about angles,"

he explained as we did our daily maintenance on the hydroponics. "The only people who ever get any traction have great angles!"

"Gimme that wrench." He did -- I tightened the joint. "Now tell me about angles."

He took a hit off the joint he was working on, watching me work. "You're a god reborn -- literally! We've already got all the exposition: the Gnome, the magic potion in a bottle, the figurine, all of it -- the truth -- right? You drank a magic potion and it literally transformed you into Pholus, with his incredible body and mind-blowing phallus and insatiable sex-drive! An Old God in a New World! It's fucking BRILLIANT!"

I stood up and took the joint from him, bumbling it a little in my ever-thickening fingers.

"We create a website -- a social media presence -- tons of content and over-exposure. We build the brand, cultivate a following -- we book appearances, interviews. You come on-stage, parade that big dick around like you like to do so much…"

"And pick up all the dollar bills people throw, right?" I interrupted with a snark, passing him the joint back.

"God. Damned. RIGHT!" he said. "Do you know how much people will pay you just to look at that thing?"

Actually, I already did. I got PLENTY of desperate offers at the gym -- the hungry stares, the locker room stalking. The problem was that I enjoyed that attention, too -- and if I allowed myself to… "go there" and started fucking around, well… it was very hard to stop. I mean, I was horny all the time -- hell, I had a fuck-buddy lined up for later after AppleJack went to bed -- but I was still able to be me. I was still a normal geek into comic books and hydroponics. When I allowed myself to indulge in my "bestial" side, I didn't know who that guy was -- he was just sex and indulgence.

But I was really starting to like him!

I had to adjust my cock when AppleJack mentioned it.

"See?" AppleJack laughed. "Your dick likes the idea!"

I shrugged, often my gesture of capitulation, and asked, "So… what do we do?"

****

AppleJack created an Instagram account (@PHOLUSreborn - *"an old god in a new world"*) while I finished the daily slog. "Post as many selfies as you want," he said, "the racier, the better. Right now, it's about exposure -- except, don't expose the goods. Let's keep an air of mystery for a while. That way we can create a reveal when we've built a big enough audience."

I took a hit. "This is hysterical."

We put up a slow-motion video of me jumping rope commando beneath a pair of loose gym shorts, and within two days, it had gone viral, with just over eleven million views. AppleJack orchestrated this whole inter-connected social media presence, so I would upload across all platforms simultaneously. I became an "Influencer" on IG so fast I had to look it up on The Google to find out what an Influencer was. Only Kylie Jenner had gained followers faster -- little bitch.

And I hadn't made a single movie yet!

AppleJack took the reins, booking me photoshoot after photoshoot, which for my part, I loved every second of! First, I discovered my fetish for underwear and gear, jocks and thongs -- with this body, this incredible package, everything I wore looked amazing.

I loved the camera and the camera loved me right back. There was a freedom that came along with that release of fear -- a willingness to experiment and play. I would dress up or dress down, shave sometimes, buzz sometimes, clothed, unclothed, barely clothed, inside, outside, upside down (the fact was, this new body was incredibly flexible and I seemed to have lost my inhibition).

My IG and Twitter would go crazy every time I posted new content. Who was I? Who was I wearing?

Finally, we put up my first video on OnlyFans. It was literally just me sitting in my computer chair, facing the camera. You could only see me from about mid-thigh to the tip of my nose, exposing my scruffy chin and my snow-white smile, my incredible muscle with its gruff, auburn body hair, my flexed, impossible abs, my highly-developed adonis belt running beneath the band of my jockstrap. As the video began, I was sliding my jock down, revealing my cock to the camera for the first time. I exposed my trim, auburn bush, then the base of my thick member.

There had been some commentary and speculation on the internet about whether I pumped, or whether I injected silicone. Apparently, that was a "thing" with some people — whatever. One of the purposes of this video was to finally show the beauty of my all-natural, magic-potion-induced cock! It was all real!

It was like the opening scene of STAR WARS when we first see the bad guys' spaceship and it keeps coming and coming on-screen, forever being revealed — my cock was like that. The waist band went down, showing more and more of my thick shaft. Finally, with a little tease, I exposed the glans itself -- I'd always been cut, but I'd noticed lately that the foreskin had been growing back, so I guess Pholus was natural.

With a quick shift of my hands, I slipped the jock's waistrap behind my balls, lifting them slightly -- taking steroids didn't leave a man with nads like these, big and heavy and full of cum. After that, I put my hands behind my head and just let my cock get hard.

It stretched down over my balls then rolled over onto my hip, forever swelling as it went. I couldn't help but flex the muscles of my pelvic floor -- making me do a kegel -- which caused my cock to bounce up onto my abs. For a moment, the glans settled in my navel, but then its own growth pushed it beyond.

Fully hard, it was nearly twelve inches long, as thick as a coffee cup at the base -- the funny fish-eye of the iphone exaggerated it even more. I was breathing deeply and comfortably, clearly horny, but purposely not touching it. I took a deep breath and squeezed -- a pearly-white glob appeared at the tip, about the size of a marble.

I smiled, bent forward and -- making sure the camera could see me -- I gently put the entire glans in my mouth, sucking down my own tasty juice.

The video ended with me kissing the tip of my cock and smiling at the camera, whispering, "Pholus is reborn." Cut to black.

****

It wasn't even two minutes long, the video, but within a week, money was no longer an issue in my life.

Like I said, we hadn't even made a movie yet and my personal bookings were going through the roof! I mean, I dug doing live cam shows where I'd flex and tease and demand worship. Guys would pay "tributes" to me, cash tips to get my attention, and I totally got off on that.

And this was the weird thing: the worship… empowered me. I mean, it… it made me… more than I was. As I did cam shows and live shows and as my audience grew, I grew, too. Not just muscularly (where I was steadily improving), or scrotally (where I was pushing boundaries), I mean spiritually. Can you imagine what it does to your psyche to have guys pay you obscene amounts of money just to touch your cock? To have them beg you to suck it? To love it the way you love it?

I accepted it -- I welcomed it. I had been blessed by the gods -- I was something more-than-man. A demi-god -- a demi with a semi. A demi-semi-god!

Sex was easy, constant -- I was either seducing or fucking. Wherever I was, whatever I was doing, it was a prelude to sex. I couldn't have enough -- there was never a moment when I was satisfied, when I wasn't eager for more. And men fell under my spell -- whether it was my smell, or my aura, or the obvious swell of my cock -- they all gave it up for me, they all became eager bottoms.

It was the way of men to worship gods.

And all men worshipped the god of the phallus -- and now Pholus, who seemed the god made flesh.

****

Each of the doctor's three examination rooms were crammed full of framed PLAYBILLs or posters from every Broadway show in the universe. He'd seen way more than me -- shows I'd never even heard of -- and I doubted I was the first patient to pass time waiting for the doctor by reading them. Today, sadly, I was in the Andrew Lloyed Webber room -- he must be punishing me.

I wasn't wearing the paper dress they'd provided me, but instead pulled off the oversized t-shirt I was wearing and stood there in my baggy athletic shorts and sneakers. I'd already seen the resident who'd measured me -- I was now 6'3" -- weighed me -- I was 271. He had a tough time getting the blood pressure gage around my bicep and I could tell he was fighting a throbbing erection, but I enjoyed the antics. Now I was in the interim between him and the doctor and reading show posters to avoid playing with myself.

Finally, the doctor came in and said, "Whoa!" when he saw me. "My resident wasn't kidding…"

I smiled. "How are you, doc?"

"Right this moment?" he said. "Stunned." He sat down in the chair opposite the exam table and opened my chart. "So… you gonna tell me what you're on? I mean, you've gained nearly forty pounds since the last time I saw you three months ago and… you've gotten taller by an inch-and-a-half. What the bloody fuck are you taking, Red?"

I sat in the little plastic chair next to him. "I'm gonna be honest with you, doc," I said, drawing a deep breath. "And I'm not sure you're gonna believe me, but the truth is… I drank a magic potion."

He gave me a curious look, which I interpreted as an invitation to continue, so I told him the rest of the story, the gnome, the bottle, the whole thing. It felt surprisingly good to confess -- maybe AppleJack was right. Maybe the truth was the best bet.

At the end, the doctor sat there a second, absorbing my story, when he finally said, "Yokumberry Tonic."

"I'm sorry -- what?"

"Yokumberry Tonic." He tsk-ed. "And you call yourself a Theatre Queen! LI'L ABNER... the show? Turns out the reason Li'l Abner is as big as he is is because his Mammy makes this special Yokumberry Tonic. One sip turns a normal man into a huge bodybuilder..."

"I know it, I know it," I said, smiling. "But after they take the stuff, don't they lose all interest in sex?"

The doctor laughed. "Yeah, but it gives us that great eleven-o'clock number..." He sang, "PUT 'EM BACK... THE WAY THEY WUZ..."

I joined him, and together we sang, "OH, PUT 'EM BACK THE WAY THEY WUZ!"

We laughed between us for a minute. Finally, I quietly asked, "So... you believe me?"

He sighed. "Well, medically speaking, of course, it's impossible. But if you hadn't grown an Inch-and-a-half in three months, I'd be quicker to disbelieve you. I'd like to get a hold of that bottle and see if we can get a sample..."

"Oh, no," I said, holding up my flat hands. "No science. I don't want to be anybody's experiment. I just want to make sure I'm healthy."

"Oh, you're healthy," he said, waving my chart. "Aside from an abnormally high testosterone level, you're the healthiest man in America! That's one of the reasons I believe you're not on some kind of weird steroid -- your chart doesn't bear it out."

"...'ONE of the reasons'..?"

He crossed his arms before his spindly chest. "Well, c'mon, Red. I've known you for almost ten years, both professionally and personally. No offense, but you're not the kind of guy who seems willing to put that kind of work in -- you know, to get like THAT." He pointed to my pecs. "Magic potion is way more reasonable."

I snorted. "My best friend said the same thing -- I'm a little hurt that everyone thinks that of me."

He smiled, leaning back in his seat but still with his arms crossed. "So why are you here today?"

I shrugged. "I just wanted to tell you the truth, I guess -- have someone on my side. Someone smart and disconnected. All these changes I've gone through have been surprisingly challenging for my psyche, you know? And I'm just worried that..."

He reached out and touched my hand -- it was an unexpectedly gentle gesture. "What?" he asked quietly.

I looked him straight in the eye. "What if it doesn't stop?" I asked. "What if I keep on growing and growing and my cock gets so big, I… I have to push it around on a cart?"

"I'm not trying to be snide, but I think that's one of the reasons you shouldn't drink magic potions."

There was a moment of silence between us as we studied each other -- it was way easier to manipulate AppleJack.

That wasn't very helpful," he said. "I'm sorry. Maybe that's just a bit of leftover bitterness from the last time you were here and used your powers on me."

"I'm sorry about that, too, doc," I said. "I was just realizing I could do that pheromone-thing, then -- I wasn't completely in control of myself. You can see I'm not doing it now, right? No oral sex in the exam room today!"

He made a little cheerleading motion. "Woohoo…" he said sarcastically.

"So, what do you think I should do?"

He sighed and stood. "Come back and see me in three months," he said. "Don't worry until we have something to worry about. And don't drink any more magic potions!"

"That seems fair."

3. "Centaurs"

More from "The Google":

*A **centaur** (/ˈsɛn.tɔːr, -tɑːr/; Ancient Greek: κένταυρος, kéntauros, Latin: centaurus), or occasionally **hippocentaur**, is a creature from Greek mythology with the upper body of a human and the lower body and legs of a horse. Centaurs are thought of in many Greek myths as being as wild as untamed horses, with a weakness for Dyonesian Wine, and were notorious for being lusty, overly indulgent drinkers and carousers, violent when intoxicated, and generally uncultured delinquents. The centaurs were slain by Heracles after using the civilized centaur, Pholus' wine as bait to lure them to Mount Pelion.*

****

"You got a package!" AppleJack sang as I came downstairs into the basement Grow Room.

"I sure do!" I called back, fondling my big dick through my baggy gym shorts.

He made an "Ew!" face as he continued to prune some of the big plants. "No, at the post office. There's a slip there on the desk -- you gotta sign for something."

"Oh," I said unenthusiastically. I'd just gotten home from the gym and I was looking forward to a shower, some food, and smoking a bowl (or two) with AppleJack. I didn't have any clients on the books and I was anxious for a night off. If I got too horny later, I could always go live on my OnlyFans page -- and I had at least two dozen fuck-buddies I could call who'd drop everything if I wanted them. I wasn't stressed.

"Is it five o'clock yet?" he asked. "They're still open."

"Geez, AppleJack, why you bein' such a nag?"

He laughed. "First, fuck you for the AppleJack. Second, cause I wanna see what someone sent you from Greece that you gotta sign for!"

"Greece?" I asked, examining the notice.

"Yeah," he says, snipping some leaves. "Who you know in Greece?"

I shrugged. "Nobody that I remember."

****

At nearly 6'4" and almost 285, I was big, but I still felt realistic. I mean, there were football players and professional wrestlers who were way bigger than me, but I still got attention when I came into a place, no doubt about it. My standard public outfit was a pair of extremely baggy gym shorts -- a person would make a joke about them looking like a skirt, if they were brave enough -- and usually a loose, zip-front sweatshirt or a hoodie over an oversized t-shirt, baseball cap and sunglasses. My cock -- in its permanently priaptive place -- was nearly eleven inches long "soft," but it was my balls that made things difficult. About the size (and weight) of fresh avocados, there was no place for them to hide, my big quads kept everything up-front and on display, compensatory baggy shorts or no.

Because I'd been at the gym before coming to the post office, beneath the baggies, I had on a tight pair of compression shorts trying vainly to hold everything in place -- pity the limited strength of spandex!

Fortunately, it was the post office, so sexual stimuli was unlikely.

When I entered, the only person who looked at me was the little old lady waiting her turn. As she scanned over my body, her eyes focused on my crotch and widened like saucers. When I said, "Hi," she quickly turned her back to me. I smirked, then I pulled out my phone. I was posting some of today's workout vids to IG when the old lady went to the counter.

I shuffled to the "Wait Here" line just as someone came into the store. I glanced up to see this beautiful boy who legit looked like he'd just gotten off the bus from Hooterville, he was so new to the city. Like he'd just gotten his Associate's Degree from his local farmtown community college and now he was here in the Big City to set the world on fire in his clean, pressed jeans (belted with an oversized buckle) and stark white t-shirt! A beautiful thing, maybe twenty-one -- twenty-two or three at most -- 5'10", probably 180 or so, so lean, I'd have said skinny if he hadn't had the muscle tone he had. (Maybe a swimmer?) But so sexy.

He'd probably been blond as a child, but his hair was more tan now, buzzed short on the sides, the rest hidden by his trucker's style baseball cap that had a cartoon unicorn on it. He had lengthy scruff on his face, all the parts of a beard -- sideburns, cheek fuzz, chin scruff, mustache -- but none of them connected, so it was a fill-in-the-blanks beard. Bright blue eyes and a big pink lower lip that looked like it needed to be kissed to tell how soft it was.

There was an angelic sweetness to him that made me want to throw him on the counter and fuck him hard and raw right then and there.

That was not the thought I needed to have -- my own monster came to life in my shorts.

For his part, he gave me the up and down, licked his lips, and whispered, "Damn!"

I gave him a gentle, flirty smile. "That's funny," I said. "I was just thinking the same thing."

And as those moments go when you meet someone you're attracted to, they opened a second window at the counter -- (the old lady at the first window was caught up trying to choose the stamps she wanted -- they clearly knew it would be a process) -- and the attendant called me over. "Sir?" she called. "I can help you here!"

I waved to her and looked at the boy. "Package," I said to him, like it was a bad excuse, waving my notice as I stepped away.

He glanced at my cock, fully obvious. "Yeah, I reckon it is," he said, impressed.

I smiled like I was embarrassed and we made eye contact again. Damn, he was cute.

At the window, I greeted the woman, sliding the package notice and my ID under the glass partition. She checked the notice, then glanced at my ID, then looked up at me suspiciously, then down at my ID again. "This ain't you," she teased, a smile on her face.

"Yeah, it is," I said.

"Oh, really?" she said. "You six-foot, a hundred-ninety pounds? I don't think so, baby."

I shrugged, making a face like you-caught-me. "I've… I've gained some weight since I got that license."

"Baby, it was just issued last year."

"I swear to God it's me," I said. "I have my passport, too!" -- there was some reason I carried it around in my fanny pack, something AppleJack said about being prepared for anything -- whatever, I had it. As I fetched my passport and slid it under the partition, the old lady left the other window and I saw the hot boy sidle up -- did he walk slightly bow legged? He glanced at me before he began his transaction -- God, he had a nice ass, look at that profile, tight little bubble butt -- no way he could take my cock.

The attendant looked at my passport photo and up at me. "This one looks MORE like you," she said. "But I don't know..." She leaned back in her chair and called toward the back room. "ROGER!"

A middle-aged man toddled out of the back room, slovenly in his uniform, heavy black-framed glasses. He looked at me with a deer-in-headlights expression then turned his attention to her. "What's up?" he asked.

"Look at this," she said, handing him my ID's. "He's sayin' this is him."

"I swear to God it's me," I said. "Why would I pretend to be someone else? To get a package?"

The man looked at the ID's, then looked at me, then back, then up. Finally, he said, "You put on some weight."

"Well, in fact," I said, gently flexing my arm. "I drank a magic potion."

A beat, then the two of them broke out in laughter. I laughed, too, even though I didn't know why. Why do people always laugh at the truth?

He put my ID's back down in front of the attendant, nodded, and said, "You should get your ID updated, before it gets you in trouble."

"Thanks, buddy."

"You got any more of that potion?"

The attendant broke out laughing. "Ha! That's the only thing that'd get you that big, Roger -- magic potion! Don't nobody get that big without taking some kind of something!" She got up to retrieve the package. The two of them continued their verbal spar as they went into the back.

I looked over at the boy, only to see he'd gone.

Damn.

A few seconds later, the woman came out of the back with my package. About the size of a shoe box, a little bigger, but that shape -- she handed it to me and gave me back my IDs. "You should get those updated, baby," she said. "And don't drink no more magic potions!"

We laughed, but I was anxious to get out of there.

Although wrapped in an Airmail envelope, I could feel the box beneath was made of wood -- what the hell was it? The stamps --

"Fragile!" "Handle with Care!" "Contains Spirits" -- and International Inspection stickers covered most of the front, but there was my name (with "PHOLUS" written beneath it) and my address in clean block letters. No return address.

I stepped outside into the warm, Spring sunshine, turned toward the small parking lot, and there stood the boy, leaning against the building with one of his legs bent casually under him, as if he had nothing better to do in this world -- he looked like he should have a piece of straw in his teeth. "Howdy," he said.

"Well, look at you," I said, smiling.

He smiled back. "I'm a-feelin' something 'tween us, right?" he asked, which was when I noticed his twangy accent, that slurry drawl of someone who barely moved their lips as they talked. "I ain't wrong, right?"

I took a step closer to him -- I was easily a head taller. "Oh, there's something between us all right," I said with a smirk. "You aren't wrong."

"That's awesome," he said as he pushed himself away from the building, nearly into my arms. "I'm Pokey Dakota. Wanna fuck?"

****

"I reckon I wasn't sure I wanted to move to the city," he said, as he got out of the car at my place -- the cheerful babble had accompanied us the whole way. "But my buddy Donny talked me into goin' 'n I agreed that the timin' was right."

"Where you from, Pokey?"

"Oklahoma," he said, which would've made me do a spit-take if I'd been drinking. "Pokey Dakota from Oklahoma. My real name's Patrick, you know, but I's the youngest of four brothers, 'n they called me Pokey -- I reckon it just stuck."

I just thought he was fucking adorable!

"This your house, Red? This is nice. I live downtown with, like, six other guys 'n I 'preciate y'all got someplace we can go that's more private."

We entered and I threw my keys down on the little table by the door and put the package on the island separating the living room and kitchen.

Pokey was impressed, whistling his approval. "This is nice," he said leaving his shoes by the front door. "I reckon it smells like marijuana in here."

AppleJack came upstairs from the Grow Room, smoking a big, fat J as he walked into the kitchen. Spying Pokey, he exhaled some impressive smoke and quietly asked me, "Are you seriously picking up guys at the post office now?"

I snorted and said, "Well… yeah. Special Delivery."

Pokey seemed confused. "I'm sorry," he said. "Is this your boyfriend?"

We both laughed, though AppleJack was louder.

While he kept chuckling and hit the joint, I answered. "No, no -- housemate. We've known each other all our lives, but we've lived together since college -- he's straight, tho, isn't that crazy? Pokey, meet AppleJack… oh shit, I'm sorry!"

"DUDE!"

"I'm sorry, man! It was out of my mouth before I even realized what I'd said."

Pokey was laughing. "AppleJack. How 'bout that?" he said. "Horse that throwed me was named AppleJack."

That got AppleJack's attention. "What?" he asked suspiciously.

"I used to work the Rodeo Circuit til I got throwed and hurt my hip, 'n AppleJack was the name of the horse that throwed me -- i'n't that funny?"

AppleJack gave him a dry look, then turned to me and said, "I hate this kid."

Pokey wasn't to be discouraged. "Oh, no, AppleJack -- No! Don't be like that! The thing to do is embrace it, you know? I mean, ain't nothin' worse 'n Pokey, right? But I decided to own it instead of being ashamed of it and I swear, it changed everything."

AppleJack took another hit. "Thank you, Pokey. I… will consider your wise and learned thoughts." He turned to me and added, "I love when you bring your playmates home" before he disappeared into his bedroom and shut the door.

Pokey quietly said, "I reckon he sure acts like your boyfriend."

"You got off easy," I said, putting my hand on Pokey's shoulder. "I think you scared him."

He turned to face me. "I'm sorry, Red. I didn't mean…"

And then I kissed him.

"Damn," he mumbled when it broke. "You a good kisser." He went in for another, more serious this time, wrapping his arms around my neck.

"C'mon," I said. "Let's head upstairs."

"What about your package?"

I smiled -- he made it too easy. "That package can wait," I said, pressing into him. "This one can't."

He said, "Oh, I get that. I reckon that's a joke, right?"

I pulled him after me. "C'mon…"

****

"You gotta let me fuck you," Pokey growled. "With that cock, you prolly never get fucked as good as you should. Lemme show you…"

Not surprising that Pokey was verbal in the sack, but damn he was dirty! He licked out my pits and worshipped the cantaloupe-sized peak of my biceps -- he was getting off on me, for sure -- but I soon realized that he wasn't treating me with the reverence and awe of my normal partners. He was treating me like a piece of meat, a plaything.

His confidence level far exceeded his experience, but I loved that he was willing to go for it. When he ate my hole, he won me over -- fuck, I had to reward an enthusiast -- especially the way he buried his face in my hairy, sweaty crack, like he couldn't get enough. "Galloping God, you taste good," he said from deep between my ass cheeks. "You taste like a BEAST!"

His tongue was assertive, confident in its exploration -- his little scratchy beard felt so good against my skin. "You ready for my dick?" he asked. "I reckon you need my dick real bad."

I was lying forward on the pillow, on my knees, my ass in the air, a nearly 300lb demigod submitting to this young little rodeo twink with his perfectly flat tummy and his spatter of chest hair -- I was so in this scene! Ride me, cowboy!

He tapped the head of his cock against my hole. "Turn over," he said. "I reckon I wanna look at you while I fuck you."

I'd forgotten how good a dick up inside me felt -- I hadn't bottomed since before my blessing -- and I gotta say, Pokey Dakota wasn't bad -- he knew how to fuck.

On my back, my huge legs spread wide, he stood next to the bed and pounded my hole, my own hard cock resting at the top of my abs, scant inches from my chin, fairly leaking my pheromone-laden pre-cum -- even I was under my own spell. "Damn, you tight," Pokey muttered, using every bit of his eight-inches, burying himself deep.

"Not damned," I panted. "Blessed."

"I reckon I'm gonna cum in your blessed hole…"

"Yes," I moaned, placing my hands on his chest and pinching his nipples. "Yes. Give your offering…"

When he shot, driving his dick deep into me, his eyes rolled back in his head. In that moment, I felt -- not only my own orgasm -- I felt this energy leave me through my hands and enter him. I wish I could describe it better -- I was still relatively new to magic. It wasn't like he took something from me -- it wasn't like I gave him power -- it was more like I awakened something in him, something akin, related to me. I felt that change in his energy -- I was the cause of it. The catalyst. It formed into this link, this bond -- I could… feel him -- his soul. It was so weird, significantly more intimate than the sex we'd just shared. Whatever else my powers had done to Pokey Dakota, I could feel the reins that connected us now.

When he opened his eyes, there was something there that hadn't been before -- a glint, a lust. The corner of his mouth curled into a devilish smile and I felt his cock re-harden inside me, even harder than it had been, and he just started lust-fucking me.

What an incredible fuck that was -- the sudden power, the masculinity, the determination -- we were sweaty and breathless and oh, so hungry for each other. This… bond we suddenly shared amplified our sexual connection and we lost our sense of restraint. Such… a good… fuck!

The cock he pulled out of me was nearly twelve inches long, with heavy, obvious balls to match. Twice as big as it had been before, thick -- it looked magnificently out-of-proportion with the rest of him.

He loved it!

"Look at me!" he joyfully yelled, like he'd won the lottery. "LOOK AT MY COCK! Oh, my God, it's HUGE!"

He turned to the mirror and got the full picture -- it wasn't just his cock. His whole body had changed. He was still lean, though you wouldn't describe him as skinny anymore. He was muscular, like a swimmer or a gymnast, not an ounce of fat on him, every single muscle separated and defined -- ripped to shreds. His abs were utterly spectacular, rivaling even mine, and that sexy Adonis Belt that just drew the eye to his… well, his horse-cock. That's the only way to describe it -- and probably the only way fitting for a centaur, too -- human on top and horse on the bottom.

He was flexing for himself in the mirror, shocked and amazed -- awed. "Holy fuck, Red. What'd you do to me?"

"I don't know," I said, sitting up and watching him, casually wiping up my cum as I did. "Something happened when we came -- I felt the energy change."

"Yeah, me too!" he said excitedly. "I reckon it felt like my soul connected to my balls." He laughed. "Holy fuck, Red." His cock started to harden again. "I'm still horny!"

"Pholus is a centaur," I said, shrugging. "Maybe you're a centaur now, too?"

He stepped into my arms and started kissing me. "If I turn into you, I'm all for it," he said. "If I stay like this forever, I'm all for that, too! Either way, I'm fucking horny as fuck! Let's go out -- what do ya say? Let's go out and fuck some boys! I'm randy!"

I chuckled. "First things first," I said, reaching around him and smacking his hind quarter. "I'm gonna tag that pretty little ass of yours. I bet you can take me now."

"I reckon I'm willing to try!" he said, laughing as he rolled onto his back. "Look at me -- first week in the city and I get turned into a freakin' centaur! Ain't they gonna laugh on the rodeo circuit?"

4. "Dionysus"

Dionysus (/daɪ.əˈnaɪsəs/; Greek: Διόνυσος) is the god of the grape-harvest, winemaking and wine, insanity, ritual madness, religious ecstasy, festivity and theatre -- the frenzy he induces is Bacchanalia. <u>Dionysian Wine</u> was said to be a weakness for Centaurs, driving them into fits of uncontrollable drunken debauchery. (See Heracles /ˈhɛrəkliːz/ HERR-ə-kleez; Greek: Ἡρακλῆς, Hēraklês -- Fourth Labor) Unlike the other members of the Twelve, Dionysus preferred to walk among men rather than reside on Olympus.

****

I fucked the little bronc buster in the shower.

We fought over who'd get the good light, flexing in the bathroom mirror -- ripped as he was, I still had him by over a hundred pounds. Our cocks were nearly the same size, which, given the outline of the bodies they were mounted on, his looked significantly more out-of-proportion than mine. "Look at this," he said, gripping himself. "I reckon I can't even put my hand all the way around it!"

"It's hot as fuck," I said, turning the shower on -- a walk-in. The best thing I did when I bought this house was have it gutted and modernized. The second floor was almost entirely the Master Suite -- AppleJack's room was on the first floor, off the TV room. (And of course, the Grow Room was in the basement.) Anyway, the Master Bath was tiled, mirrored, and glassed -- almost as if I'd anticipated turning into a Centaur. So as he leaned against the glass of the shower wall, he could clearly see me fucking him from behind.

I was amazed that that tiny, tight bubble-butt of his could take a cock the size of mine -- yet there I was, balls deep, my foot-long cock completely buried in him. Fucking magic, man!

The fact was it was rare that someone was able to take my cock — mine started scaring guys when it passed ten inches — much less with the vigor and unselfish desire of my new fuck buddy. I'd have to say I was enjoying it as much as him -- it was nice to let go and be an animal.

For his part, if I'd thought Pokey was verbal when he was topping, it was nothing like the noise he made when he was being fucked. Loud streams of verbal filth -- it was so hot. "Fuck me with your centaur horse-dick" stuff. I don't know how he did it -- it was some rodeo trick -- but he suddenly spun around and ended up facing me, his legs wrapped around my waist, leaning back into the shower wall, working his own rock-hard erection.

He looked me in the eye and pursed his lips. "You can't throw this cowboy!" he yelled. "Ride hard, Red! Harder! HARDER!"

Holding him up with one hand, I grabbed his cock and started stroking it with the other -- he howled. Then I leaned over and put the head in my mouth -- I felt him cum from the inside, seconds before he filled my mouth with his horsey-spunk, and that made me shoot my big load.

When I finally pulled him off my cock, it leaked out of him as he leaned against me and caught his breath. "Hot damn," he said, licking some cum off my pec. "I stayed on THAT horse!"

I kissed him and gently lathered him up. "Set a new in-house record, too," I said.

"God damn right I did!" He said as he began washing me. He laughed. "First week in the Big City and I turn into a Unicorn!"

I laughed and rinsed. "You mean centaur!" I said, kissing him.

"What's the diff? They're both horses. I reckon a unicorn is just a little gayer -- like me." He kissed me playfully on the lips. "And I do have this magnificent horn..." He wagged his big cock at me.

"You're incorrigible," I chuckled, turning off the water.

"What's that mean?" he asked sincerely. "I got plenty of courage! I reckon I fucked you, didn't I?"

I shook my head slightly and wrapped my big arms around him, pulling his wet, naked body close to mine. "You better watch yourself, Pokey Dakota from Oklahoma," I said quietly. "You could become my favorite real quick." We kissed a little more deeply that time, maybe even romantically? I could feel his cock start to get hard… again.

"God damn, I'm horny!" he said. "Looks like this unicorn's ready to fuck again!"

****

AppleJack poked his head out of his room when he heard me rummaging around the kitchen for something to eat. "Is he gone?" AppleJack asked, looking around.

"Oh, stop it, you big baby," I teased, waving him off. "He's a nice kid."

AppleJack snorted a laugh. "He's a frisky colt!" he said sarcastically. "A show pony with a stupid name! Pokey Dumbass Dakota! And I bet you're gonna fall in love with him just to piss me off."

"Would that piss you off? Me falling in love with someone?"

AppleJack sighed, crossing his arms in front of his chest. "Don't destroy our burgeoning porn empire over love, Red. That would be what would piss me off -- and break my heart."

"Aw," I said, pursing my lips. "You're so sweet." I laughed. "Have no fear, AppleJack -- I'm not falling in love with Pokey Dakota. However," I said, grabbing my dick beneath my loose bed shorts, "it is nice to have a fuckbuddy who can take this whole thing."

"Ugh… Jesus…" He spun around, changing the subject. "So, what's in the box?" he asked, pointing to the unopened package still sitting there on the counter.

"Oh, yeah -- the box! I almost forgot." I grabbed a knife and went to the counter. As I cut the tape sealing the airmail wrapping, I story-told, "This is funny -- at the post office, they didn't think my ID was me. It still has me as six-foot, one-ninety -- I'm a hundred pounds heavier and three inches taller now. And who the fuck knows where I'll be next year at this time? What if I'm six-eight, four-hundred?"

He was chuckling, producing a joint from seemingly nowhere. "We'll get it updated," he said casually, sparking up. "And everytime they don't believe it's you at the post office, we'll do it again. No one said fantasy was going to come without bureaucracy, Red." Chuckling, he took a hit. "Real life has paperwork."

I laughed, tearing the paper off the box. "Yeah, well, I'm a creature of fantasy, now! I live in the Magic World -- what the fuck? This is a CRATE!"

The shipping box was made out of slats of balsa wood, strong but light, obviously meant to protect its delicate contents. It didn't have a latch or a lid -- we literally had to pry the top off of it with a screwdriver. Inside was a bunch of stuffing and filler and layers of delicate unspun cotton wrapping something.

A card on top -- a rich vellum, heavy weight. The envelope said "PHOLUS".

"A card!" I said, taking a hit from AppleJack's joint before opening it.

Same thing, beautiful heavy paper stock -- it reminded me of hemp -- and written by what seemed like a fountain pen or a quill. Neat and flowery, like calligraphy.

I read aloud:

You've been reborn!
The Fates spun a realignment of the stars
to bring you back to me, my favorite.
To prove my veracity, I include a gift --
one of your very favorite things --
Dionysian Wine!
A Warning: Beware leaving the bottle uncorked --
it will attract Beasts.
All of my love -- anxious to see you --
Chiron

"Who's Chiron?" AppleJack asked.

"I don't know. There's something familiar about it, but..." I shrugged. There was a moment of silence between us as I dropped the card on the table and reached into the box -- AppleJack took a hit as I unwrapped the exaggerated layers of cushioning to expose a wine bottle, unlabeled, made of what seemed to be the same ancient glass that had held the elixir that had transformed me, frosted and dark blue. It was sealed the same way -- the stopper covered (dipped?) in wax.

"How old do you suppose that is?" AppleJack asked. "How many hundreds… thousands of years old do you think that is?"

"It looks like the same kind of bottle I found in the gnome."

"Well," said AppleJack, taking a hit, "a gift from Magic World! Do you suppose what's in that bottle will turn whoever drinks it into you?"

Realizing that I'd already turned Pokey into something like me, I doubted I needed an elixir. "No. This Chiron who sent it says it's Dionysian Wine... one of my favorite things!"

AppleJack grabbed the note and looked it over, then he looked up at me, confused. "You can read this?" he asked.

"Yeah. It's all fancy-formal, but the calligraphy is beautiful, isn't it?"

"No, I mean, this isn't in English."

"What? Yeah, it is -- I just read it. Don't fuck with me, AppleJack."

"I'm not. Look..."

He handed me the note and I looked at it again. AppleJack was right -- it wasn't in English. It was Greek.

Έχετε ξαναγεννηθεί
Οι μοίρες γύρισαν μια αναδιάταξη των αστεριών
για να σας φέρω πίσω, το αγαπημένο μου.
Για να αποδείξω την αλήθεια μου, συμπεριλαμβάνω ένα δώρο -
ένα από τα αγαπημένα σου πράγματα -
Διονύσιος κρασί!
Προειδοποίηση: Προσέξτε να αφήσετε το μπουκάλι άβολο -
θα προσελκύσει τα θηρία.
Όλη η αγάπη μου - ανυπομονώ να σε δω -
Χείρων

I didn't know Greek -- except now I did. I could read it easily. *"All of my love -- anxious to see you -- Chiron."*

I didn't know Chiron -- except I did. Somehow. I pulled out my phone and pressed the "assistant" button. "Siri," I asked, "who is Chiron?" A few electric 'bings' and I had my answer.

"Chiron is the wisest and justest of all the Centaurs."

I sighed. "Of course he is."

AppleJack exhaled. "Wisest and Justest. So, is he supposed to be, like, Head Centaur or something?"

"I don't know," I said, wrapping the bottle and putting it back into the box. "Maybe this is my buzz talking, but did you ever wonder if there was any truth to the old stories, the myths? Do you think it's possible there are mystical beings on Earth, wandering immortals, or old gods?"

"Who knows?" he said, drifting into his thoughts. Just before he took a hit, he said, "But thanks to my brilliant marketing campaign, they know you're here!"

Pokie Dakota took to his powers like a pony to a pasture -- he ran with them. He'd fine-tuned his pheromone powers before I'd even fully explored my own -- he taught ME about our abilities! He hadn't been a centaur for a month yet and he already had all the muscle daddies at the gym under his spell -- they paid him what he called "tributes". The term the kids were using was "cash-master" or "fin-dom" (financial domination) -- guys would fall all over themselves to give Pokie Dakota money, and they got off while they did it.

He was irresistible. Forget about his powers, the kid was simply beautiful! This lean, spectacularly defined body, these tiny little hips, and this tight, round bubblebutt -- and then his face! If you could tear your eyes away from his body, or his cock, you would lose yourself in his bright blue eyes and his smooth, youthful skin. And those lips…!

He insisted on the Shaggy Doo beard, but even that wasn't a flaw -- it seemed to physicalize his childlike sense of hope. As a matter of fact, the mousey brown-blond of his hair was the only dull thing about him.

Pokey was able to get whatever he wanted without paying a dime. His body, his charm, his pheromones, it was kind of impossible for his target to deny him. He became a member of my gym by seducing the owner, but he had memberships at several other gyms that were sponsored by his many cash-daddies. The kid loved to fuck, I'd give him that, and he seemed to be always ready, but he never seemed to have to. To be fair, he always seemed to want to.

He was already at the gym when I came in, training at the pec deck with an older guy. The older guy was on the machine and Pokey stood directly between him and the mirror, so the guy was forced to look at the lovely boy. (Not that the guy seemed to mind.) Pokey wore a sleeveless spandex top and a pair of Jed North shorts that just seemed to emphasize the surreal size of his basket. (He must've been wearing something strong beneath it and I was just as curious as everybody else about what that could've been.) His cock looked magnificent.

The old guy was completely hypnotized by him -- I was sure from a different angle I'd see the guy's erection. Whatever. We all had our kinks.

Pokey and I approached the gym in very different ways. I liked to work out -- I didn't NEED to, it seemed. I would just keep growing and getting bigger regardless of training, but I really enjoyed it! I had no desire to compete -- as much as I liked flexing in front of an audience, it turned me on so much that an erection was inevitable. That had no place on the competition stage -- though it had found its way onto gay bar go-go boy platforms a few times. (Pokey's idea.)

Regardless, the pumps this body was capable of now made working out almost sexual -- I wouldn't trade this aspect of my transformation for the world! Me and my body doing amazing feats of strength and feeling powerfully male, sweating hard and driving men wild with my scent.

I wore a pair of white leggings with a thong beneath, holding MY perpetual *nonischemic priapism* in place. I wore a XXXL t-shirt and a baggy, sleeveless hoodie over it -- the base of the t-shirt almost reached the base of my package, teasingly showing a little something-something, hinting of what must be.

As I walked to the leg area, I passed Pokey, who waved at me like a kid on the playground. I air-kissed him and kept walking, adjusting my headphones over my ball cap. The leg area was surprisingly busy, so I set myself up at the deadlift station, loading up the bar with 135 and warming up with some easy reps. Just as I broke a sweat, Pokey showed up.

"I reckon I could smell you from over there," he said. "You gotta learn to control that or you're gonna give every guy in the gym a hard on." He smiled and laughed. "Myself included!"

"How you doin', Pokey?" I asked, smiling back. We hugged. "Workin' the daddies, I see."

He shook his head. "I don't know why you wanna have some pretext about working a real job," he said. "All the modeling and flexing and clients and movies, it ain't none of it necessary. I ain't paid for anything since you made me a unicorn!"

"A centaur," I said, smirking.

He shrugged. "Yeah, yeah. That's what you say. I reckon I identify as a unicorn."

I laughed aloud. "I love you, Pokey," I said. "Fuckin' nut."

"Point bein', you ain't gotta work for shit. We're magical beings now -- we're above it"

"You know what, Pokey? We're each experiencing this fantasy our own way."

"Fair enough." He smiled. "With that in mind, I reckon there's someone I want you to meet, friend of mine. What are you doin' tonight?"

"I got a live show on OnlyFans at nine -- otherwise, I'm open."

Pokey began to prance excitedly. "Oooh, can I be on it with you? Can I be a guest star?"

I knew what an appearance from Pokey did for my numbers. "Of course!"

"My buddy, too? Trust me, Red -- he's a porn star already. You've heard of him."

I doubted it, but I shrugged. "If you vouch for him, why not? I mean, he's not under your chemical control, is he? Like all these daddy-slaves you got goin' on?"

"No… but I want you to think about him maybe becoming one of us."

"Really?"

He nodded sincerely, biting his own lower lip. "Trust me, Red. Trust me."

****

On a nice Spring day like this, I preferred to walk home from the gym. It gave me a chance to strut my stuff in public, which I loved, and cruise the men — Pokey had taken to calling it "hunting." As civilized a centaur as I was attempting to be, our nature was our nature, it seemed — debauchery was in our genes.

I would be lying if I said I didn't like what I was becoming, the muscle, the incredible cock. Some people seek celebrity status and then hide from it — I preferred the tease. I loved the looks, the gawks, the jaw-drops, the double-takes — it tickled me. Yes, I ended up sort-of forced to wear mirrored sunglasses, so I wouldn't make eye-contact, but that wasn't terrible, either. (Eye-contact seemed to be an invitation for conversation, so I avoided it -- only using it on my prey. When I was hunting, I mean.)

It was my height that made the difference. I was six-five -- I was a freakin' giant to most people. Bodybuilders tended to be shorter guys, who could really stack on the weight. Guys over six-feet had a whole different journey with mass -- guys my height had long muscle bellies, so putting on size was a challenge, calorie-wise and training-wise. That's not even discussing supplement-wise-- unless their supplement was a magic potion they found in a garden gnome. That changed the playing field.

So I was tall AND built -- I think that alone made me stand out -- but I was also hung like a fucking horse! (If that didn't tick a guy's top three buttons, he wasn't a very honest gay man.)

I was still in my gym clothes, sweaty, knowing full well that my scent was pervasive, but just enjoying its effect on people, when I passed by the Hipster barber shop: Dunn's. The horse-pun made me laugh and I felt a pull to go in -- so, trusting my gut, I opened the door.

It was a nice space, tricked out to be sort-of retro-masculine -- lots of metal floorboards and leather -- it smelled great! Six old-school barber chairs and a waiting area, black-and-white tiled floor, the whole thing. It was Monday, so there was only one guy working -- and he was sexy, even if not my type.

Just a bit shorter than me -- maybe six feet even -- no particular kind of build, but easy to hang clothes on. Dark brunette interspersed with silver, his hair was cut in a high fade, long quiff on top but slicked back -- his beard fanned out to his upper pecs, an iron gray mixed with a black undertone and flecks of gray, meticulously groomed. His septum was pierced with a small silver hoop that matched his earrings -- his wrists adorned with bracelets and beads and several heavy silver rings sat on the wrong fingers. He wore a thermal three-quarter sleeve undershirt beneath a short-sleeved plaid shirt beneath an open leather vest. Jeans with a heavy leather belt, a chain leading to his wallet and black chucks completed the look.

He was sitting in the barber chair reading a paper and smoking a pipe when I came in. "Well, damn," he said, hopping up and putting the paper aside. "Please tell me you're here to let me fix that beard!"

I laughed. "I am here to let you fix this beard."

He looked up at the ceiling. "Thank GOD," he said. "You are so much hotter than… whatever this look is."

Was I defensive? "Well, I knew it needed some attention…"

"Believe me, my friend, I will give you all the attention you need. I'm Dunn," he said, offering his hand. "Dan Dunn -- I own the place."

"Hey, Dunn," I said, shaking his hand. "I'm Red."

That was the first moment he actually smelled me -- I could see him catch my scent. "What are you wearing, Red?" he asked. "It's musky and deep…sexy." He inadvertently touched his cock. "Is it Dior?"

"No, it's…"

"Tom Ford?"

"No…"

"Don't tell me," he said, putting his hand on my shoulder and leading me to the chair. "I'll figure it out before we're done -- it's familiar."

He did a dramatic flourish with the barber cape and wrapped it around my neck. "I'm more concerned with the beard than the haircut," I said, "honestly…"

"I got you, Red," he said, misting my hair with his spray bottle, wetting it down to cut, "but I'll be the stylist, okay?"

I laughed. "I'm liking you, Dunn."

"Good," he said, combing out my hair. "I'm definitely liking you. But I'm sure you get that all the time."

I smiled. "Yeah," I said. "But I like it when it comes from hot guys."

He chuckled devilishly. "You're gonna get me in trouble, Red," he said, clipping my long red hair on top and beginning his cut, "with that kind of talk. God you have a beautiful mane -- thick and gorgeous!"

"Don't give me any thick and gorgeous straight lines…"

"Thick and gorgeous?" he laughed. "Please don't be straight."

I'd had my hair cut a million times, so I could only say that he was confident and quick, but I'd never had my beard groomed by someone else before -- it felt indulgent and oddly sexual. My beard wasn't terribly long, but he straightened it with a hot brush, trimmed it up, and oiled it for me. Feeling him do his work got my cock hard -- it felt like worship, after all. And we all knew how much I liked worship. At the least, I knew I was putting out the pheromones -- I could see the effect on him.

He'd had a hardon since I'd sat in the chair, but it was raging by the time he was trimming my beard. His breathing was ragged as if he were losing control.

"Figured out who I'm wearing yet?" I asked quietly. "Why not get another whiff?" I lifted my arm out from under the cape and put my hand behind my head. He looked at my armpit for a second, still damp from the gym, then made eye contact with me, questioning. "Go ahead," I urged.

He put his face into my armpit and inhaled deeply -- I saw the effect on him.

"Do you like that, Dunn?" I asked quietly.

"Yes," he mumbled, pressing his face into the wet material. "Oh, God, yes!" He sniffed deeply and licked.

"Good," I said, boldly. "Shave the back of my neck and I'll let you blow me."

"Yes, yes, of course," he said suddenly, standing and prepping his tools -- reaching to the hot lather machine and getting a dollop. "Anything for you," he mumbled. "Anything…"

"Good man."

Pokey had been right -- why pay for services when these men were so happy to tribute me? I got a great haircut, my beard groomed, my neck shaved, and a blow job thrown in for nothing. He was even willing to come to my house and do a private appointment next time, if that would please me -- all he wanted to do was please me. I did love that.

I tipped him. I reached out and laid my hands on his package, feeling his rock hard cock beneath his jeans and I said, "You can cum now, Dunn" and he shot so hard he fell to his knees before me, where he belonged anyway.

"Thank you, thank you, thank you," he mumbled from his knees, leaning forward and hugging my massive leg. "You're a god!"

"Your god," I said, stroking his slick black hair. "Say my name -- my true name. Pholus."

"Pholus…" he whispered with fervor. "Praise be to Pholus!"

5. "Dionysian Mysteries"

As if The Google ends:

*The **Dionysian Mysteries** were a ritual of ancient Greece which sometimes used intoxicants and other trance-inducing techniques to create ecstasy, remove inhibitions and social constraints, liberating the individual to return to a natural state, shifting their perceptual emphasis from a chthonic, underworld orientation to a transcendental, mystical one, with Dionysus changing his nature accordingly.*

****

AppleJack had some big project he was working on -- "I'm coding," he said when I saw him in the kitchen. "Even now when I'm wasting brain energy on this conversation, in the back of my mind I'm coding. I'll see you in a couple of days -- and debut a whole new website!"

I was finishing up the dinner dishes at the sink, chuckling at his hyper-seriousness. "Will you need food or anything?"

"I'll surface for Red Bull and Cheetos as needed."

"Okay," I said as he headed back to his room. "Hey, you might want to wear your noise-cancelling headphones tonight while you work -- Pokey's coming over."

"Oh, Jesus," he said, stopping in his tracks and shaking his head. "Thanks for the heads up." He snorted. "Pardon the pun."

So I did the daily maintenance on the hydroponics (shirtless) and spent some time admiring my new look in the bathroom mirror. As a redhead, I'd always kept my hair relatively short because it was wavy and difficult to control. Now, with this shaggy quiff over a medium fade, the auburn curls resembled a mane -- maybe I'd grow it out a little more and do a man-bun?

The drama was the beard, though -- all straight and neat and slick with product, I looked like a successful business man and not a lazy college student. What did they call that -- casual elegance?

I was starting to look like what I was, I thought -- a demigod. I entertained myself modeling, squeezing my oversized cock into little outfits and underwear, flexing and posing, thinking maybe my growth wouldn't ever stop. Maybe someday I'll be a giant with a giant cock?

Wouldn't that be fucking awesome?

Pokey showed up about an hour later -- as if he'd known I'd just ordered pizza -- along with his buddy. He hugged me, stroking my buzzed head. "Well, look at you!" he said, giving me a kiss. "You didn't have to get all done up for us!"

I smiled. "You like?"

He shrugged and said, playfully. "I reckon I'd do ya."

I looked over at his buddy, handsome guy -- built! -- clean shaven with hair buzzed down to the nub. A long, aquiline nose and sleepy, bedroom eyes gave him a Mediterranean look, dark and dangerous. Taller than Pokey, but not by much -- maybe six feet.

Keeping my left arm around Pokey, I offered him my right. "Hey, I'm Red!" I said -- he immediately shook my hand.

"I know who you are," he said, smiling broadly. "You're Pholus Reborn -- I follow you online! I'm Sean…"

Pokey interrupted him. "No… I told you -- no real names." Pokey looked up at me. "He's got the best porn name in the business!"

When I looked at him, he acted like he was embarrassed, but it was obvious how proud he actually was. "Colt Cavalier," he said, maybe surprised that I hadn't known it.

"Clever," I replied, smiling.

Pokey was lost in his kid-like enthusiasm. "It's a horse joke!" he said.

I smirked at him, kissing his forehead. "I get it," I said. "C'mon in, you guys!"

I'd been in the main room watching TV -- the bong on the coffee table -- before they'd arrived, so I directed them there. Pokey and his buddy sat on the sofa -- I was in the lounger. "What do I call you?" I asked. "Do you like being called Colt…?"

"No," he said, chuckling uncomfortably. "I actually prefer 'Cav', 'Cavalier', or my real name, 'Sean.' 'Colt' is a little too porn-formal."

"I feel the same way about 'Pholus,'" I said. "Do you guys want a bottle of water or something?"

"Yes," said Cavalier. "And a hit off that, maybe?" he asked, pointing to the bong.

I smiled. "At least one. Pokey, there's bottled water in the fridge -- why don't you go grab some for us?"

"Okay..." he said suspiciously, getting up off the sofa. "Don't ya'll start having sex till I get back..."

Both Cav and I laughed out loud, but looked at each other like we'd been caught with guilty thoughts. He was a beautiful man -- there's no two ways around that. I mean, a little over-groomed for my taste, almost too perfectly smooth, but undeniably hot. He wore a loose pullover that didn't even begin to hide his muscular body, the square expanse of his pecs and the coconut roundness of his medial delts, a pair of joggers and shower sandals.

"You a bodybuilder?" I asked, loading the bong.

"Physique," he replied, accepting the bong when offered. "I'm an athletic model, almost too big now -- that's what I keep hearing -- but I like myself at this size." He hit the bong like a champ, casually exhaling. "This is good shit," he said. "Tasty."

"Home grown," I said. "It's my new hybrid! Glad you like it. Be careful, it'll fuck you up fast."

"Home grown?" he asked.

"It's a hobby," I said, taking the bong back and refilling the bowl. "Genetic -- I'm from a long line of growers."

He smiled. "Not show-ers?"

I reached down and adjusted my cock, suddenly lively. "Oh, I think I show pretty well..." I took the hit, trying not to be competitive by taking more than he had.

Pokey reappeared, carrying three water bottles in one hand and the box I'd gotten from Greece in the other. "Hey," he said, plopping back down on the sofa. "Is this the package you got that day at the Post Office? What is it?"

I set the bong down and took the box from Pokey. "Yeah... careful. It's a bottle of old wine." I put it on the coffee table.

"Who's Chiron?" he asked.

"What?"

"The note. It says, 'All my love -- anxious to see you -- Chiron.' Who's Chiron?"

"You read the note?"

He's instantly apologetic. "Oh, I'm sorry. Shouldn't I have? I reckon it was open and sitting there -- I didn't think it was personal."

"No, I mean. You can read it? It's in Greek."

He was quiet for a second -- suspicious. Was I playing him? "No it ain't," he said. "I can't read Greek."

I pulled the card open and handed it to Cav. "Well?"

"Pokey, my boy," Cav said, "it isn't in English, that's for sure."

Pokey grabbed it from him, ready to be defensive, and then studied it for a second. "Holy cow," he whispered. "I c'n read Greek!" Interesting that after going through the physical transformation he did, Pokey was astounded by the linguistic growth! He'd gained a foot-long cock, and that was reasonable, but to read Greek...? "How 'bout that?"

I handed the loaded bong to Cav, who gratefully took it.

"But that don't answer my question," Pokey said, studying the card. "Who's Chiron?"

I shrugged, opening my water bottle. "Well... what little I've read..."

"Chiron is the wisest of all the centaurs," Cav said, exhaling a huge hit. Then, when he saw the confused expressions on our faces, he continued. "What? You don't have Google? Dude, you're portraying yourself as Pholus... REBORN -- don't you think you should know your own story? Research your character, man! Talk about shooting yourself in the foot!"

I took the bong back and did a hit. "I prefer to let the universe unfold," I said, smiling. Cav smirked.

"I reckon you c'n tell me," Pokey said, sidling up next to him. "Tell me all about this Chiron."

As I cleaned and loaded a new bowl, Cav talked. "Chiron was a great teacher," he said, leaning back into the softness of the sofa cushions. "He famously taught Achilles, Perseus, Heracles and a bunch of others, including Pholus, his most beloved student. He and Pholus were 'civilized' centaurs, they say," said Cav, making air-quotes. "And in classic art, the two of them are depicted with fully human bodies and the back end of a horse where their butts should be, not the 'bestial' centaur, with a human torso and a horse bottom."

"I'm impressed," I said, offering the bong to Pokey, who took it, but clearly lacked experience with it, clumsily taking a small hit and coughing up a storm.

Cavalier shrugged. "I'm a civilized porn star," he said, smiling.

"And you want to be a centaur," I said, which caused him to smile slyly. (Damn, he was sexy...)

He crossed his arms before his chest. "I do," he said. "You know, when you first came on the scene, I noticed you. Not just your body or your crazy cock, I mean, your angle -- the whole Pholus-thing -- it's fucking genius, man! The story, the magic-potion, the transformation, the centaur imagery, it's everything! But I just thought it was clever marketing -- I didn't think it was real. Then last week, Pokey here put the whammy on me at the gym and after helplessly… and thoroughly... getting fucked in the posing room, I got him to confess how he'd done it, seduced me like that, turned a total top into an eager bottom, which was when I realized your story was real. And here we are."

I retrieved the bong from Pokey and took a hit.

Cav leaned forward. "Listen, Red. I have an idea... how we can work together -- synergize. Like, hear me out: a HERD of centaurs -- eight, ten, a dozen at most -- crazy hot, sexy guys, all with your brand! We film together under your label, make personal appearances at Prides, Conventions, and Circuit Parties, dressed in sexy pony gear -- think of the publicity! We can make a fucking fortune! With your powers and my knowledge of the business, we can completely dominate the market!"

"I want to be the pink pony!" Pokey said, affectionately squeezing Cav's thigh and kissing him on the cheek.

The porn star/ physique model put his hand flat against the side of Pokey's head and playfully pushed him away -- Cavalier could handle horses. "Let the adults talk, Pokey."

Pokey giggled and fell away to the far side of the sofa. "I reckon I'm high already," he said to no one, then he laughed again.

"Listen," Cav said to me, sincerely, "I've been in the industry for a good long time, you know, and I love it! Don't get me wrong, I love doing movies and competitions and modeling and fucking for money, but I'm almost thirty-five years old, you know? My metabolism is changing -- I can feel it. I gotta WORK now to maintain this — not to mention what it costs to feed it and 'supplement' it! And I don't wanna be some washed-up porn star who ends up as some bitter real estate agent. I wanna do what I love -- forever. I wanna be a centaur. What do you think, Red…?" He corrected himself. "Pholus?" He sat forward, forearms across his knees.

I snorted. "You were the one making fun of me for allowing the universe to unfold as it should, you know?"

Cav smiled a gentle, relaxed smile and leaned back. "Not everyone knows the Desiderata…"

We both laughed and I passed him the bong.

Pokey sat up. "Wait, I reckon I'm confused. Is he gonna be a centaur or not?"

I confess, I had some misperceptions about porn stars. I had this idea that guys did porn because they had to, not because they wanted to. All their other options had to have been blocked, I figured, so they were forced to do it, trapped in the lifestyle. Or maybe they thought it would be easy money, or a quick road to fame and fortune? Or maybe drugs? Or maybe their egos were bigger than their cocks?

Like, who would aspire to be a sex worker? I could only imagine what my high school guidance counselor would've said. (But who knew? Maybe Colt Cavalier's high school guidance counselor was a client of his...?)

Cav was calculated and smart -- I liked that about him already -- and he genuinely liked what he did. He liked that his body was his money-maker, that he knew how to use it, and that people were as attracted to it as he was.

Clearly, here was someone who had never in his life been awkward, never had been an Ugly Duckling, never known gangliness, or heftiness, or skinny-fatness -- he only stood out for his consistent physical superiority. As a high school Varsity athlete, as a model, as a bodybuilder... and now as a porn star, he moved with the confidence of someone who knew how good his body looked from every angle.

I was way bigger than him -- in every way -- but I was still kind of intimidated.

"The kid wasn't happy about being left out," Cav said after I'd shut the bedroom door. He didn't notice I'd locked it, too -- that's how much I trusted Pokey.

"No, he wasn't," I said, taking Cavalier in my arms and kissing him.

As a matter of fact, Pokey had pitched a bit of a fit. "That ain't right!" he'd said. "Why can't I play? He's MY friend..."

"Pokey," I'd explained, "I'm not entirely sure what I did to transform you. I need to concentrate on it with Cav, and you can be... a distraction."

"Can't I just watch?"

Cav had laughed too. "You can't keep your hands to yourself now, kid -- and we're not even naked!"

He'd grunted. "Well, what am I supposed to do while you two is transformin'? Sit here jerkin' off listenin' to y'all?"

I'd pulled a ten out of my wallet and handed it to him. "Well... pizza guy is due any minute, remember? Someone's gotta tip him," I'd said, smiling.

"I ain't givin' anybody money!" Pokey'd said with indignation. "Sorry, that ain't how this works! I'm a unicorn now! If anything, pizza guy will be tippin' ME!"

I'd swatted his cute little butt. "Don't seduce the pizza guy," I'd said, kissing his forehead and starting up the stairs, Cav behind me.

Pokey'd fallen back in his seat, arms crossed, insulted. "I reckon we'll see what I do," he'd mumbled, reaching for the remote.

Cavalier had dangled a carrot for him then -- he'd turned on the stairs and said, "Pokey, I promise, as soon as I'm a centaur I will fuck you the way you pretty unicorns like!"

That had shut him up.

In the bedroom, Cav broke our kiss. "Is what you said to him true?" he asked, stroking my arms. "Do you really not remember how you transformed him?"

"I remember," I said, kissing him again. "I just wanted it private -- personal."

"The kid's pretty irresistible. I mean, he's not even my type and there I was letting him fuck me in the posing room, desperate for his cock. I never felt anything like that."

"He's not your type?"

"Red, I fuck little twunks for a living -- after a while, they just become one pretty-boy's hole after the next. No, he's not my type," he said as he pulled my loose t-shirt up over my head, exposing my massive torso. "You are."

"Oh, yeah?" I said, gently flexing for him. "You like?"

He buried his face between my pecs and licked my hairy cleavage. "Oh, fuck yeah, big fuckin' beast. You're fuckin' everything."

I stripped him of his clothes, awed by his incredible body. Hairless from head to toe, tanned and sanded smooth, his skin was flawless and soft.

"I've never kissed someone so much taller than me," he said. "So much bigger…"

"You gonna be able to fuck me?" I spun and showed him my overdeveloped glutes — I knew the pheromones were pumping hard.

He snorted. "I'll find the motivation," he said as he stuck the index and middle fingers of his right hand into his mouth. Before he gave me a chance to prepare, he jammed those thick, wet fingers into my ass. He immediately found and skillfully stimulated my prostate.

I moaned a little.

"Yeah, big horse-daddy likes that," he growled. "His tight horsey hole..." He smacked his left hand flat on my ass. "Prance, pony..."

I started flexing my hips, fucking myself on his fingers -- he put another in. It felt so good.

"Damn, don't nobody fuck this demigod enough, do they?" he whispered. "I bet everybody wants that crazy cock and nobody pays attention to your hole -- that changes with me, baby."

Cav had a nice dick -- a little over eight inches, thick and impressive -- as far as porn stars went, it was middle-of-the-road, but attach it to his unbelievable body and you could see why he stood out in the crowd. If his dick had been the equal of the rest of his physique, he'd have been a superstar.

He would be when I was through with him.

His right hand still inside me, Cav hocked some spit onto his cock, spreading it with his left hand. Slipping his right hand from my hole, he used my pheromonic ass juices to lube himself completely. "Fuck," he moaned, licking his fingers. "You taste so good..."

"You gonna eat me out or are you gonna fuck me?" I asked, so ready. "Put something in my hole, Cav!"

He smacked around the outside of it with the head of his cock. "Are you gonna turn me into a centaur?" he asked, smacking me with his dick. "Are you gonna turn me into a centaur if I fuck you real good?"

"Yeah," I said, desperately. "You're gonna lead the herd."

"Goddamn right I am. Herd Master!"

He slammed his cock into me, forcefully, mercilessly -- I gasped.

"That's the way," he said, balls deep, as he slowly started to thrust. "Look how good that feels. Let the Herd Master ride you, horsey."

Between the two of us, we developed a rhythm -- I was impressed that he didn't just shift to high gear and start power-fucking me. It wasn't just business to him, and that made me feel a lot better. He seemed eager for me to enjoy it as much as he was, but it still didn't feel like an audition.

He slapped my ass. "Turn over," he ordered. "I want you to see who's breaking you."

"Mmmm..." I said as I rolled over, "you DO know how to train horses..."

He shrugged. "I'm a Cavalier -- that's what we do." I spread my legs and allowed him back inside, much preferring this angle. I squeezed my own nipples while he thrust, squeezing his hips with the inside of my thighs. "You are so tight," he moaned. "I don't think I'm gonna last much longer…"

"Fine by me," I said. "Sooner you cum, the sooner you're a centaur -- and then the real fucking can start!"

He flexed like he was prepping to do a big set at the gym. "Fuck, that turns me on!" He started to thrust at the tempo of his words. "I'm. Gonna. Be. A. Mother. Fucking. CENTAUR!"

Just as I could with Pokey, I could feel Cav's orgasm coming -- I could feel the way the energy built inside him, because it transferred to me, triggering my own. He held his arms out to his sides, flexing his torso as he released his load. And as my physical orgasm let go, I felt the magic release as well -- that's what it was, energy, magical energy -- I felt it channel through me then enter him.

And then I saw it change him.

He could feel it change him, too. And because Cav was expecting it -- unlike Pokey -- Cav was open to experiencing the changes, not just being surprised by them later. He stepped back from me, pulling out… and pulling out… and pulling out some more, revealing this foot-long thing of beauty, this magnificent phallus magically in place of his previous cock. His balls swelled behind it, churning out new levels of testosterone and ejaculate, beginning their constant, weighted, never-ending pull on his groin.

Cav was ecstatic. "I can feel it!" he yelled, stroking his incredible new cock -- he couldn't get one hand all the way around the base. "Oh my sweet Greek gods, it's happening!"

He spun to the wall mirror, breathless at what he saw, a smile growing wider and wider on his face. He began flexing and posing, his stage routine, glued to the mirror. "Look at this shit," he said, flexing his abs. "Look what's happening to me!"

I already knew -- the visceral fat was disappearing, dissolving -- his waist was tightening on its own. At the same time, his musculature thickened as his subcutaneous fat dissolved, too, shredding his build -- he'd obviously gained some muscle weight, but the extreme loss of body fat was what was remarkable. His abs, like Pokey's -- and mine -- were just this side of impossible. He was competition-ready, but glowing with health.

And when I finally spared a second to look at his face, I could see the changes there, too -- the improvements, the tightening of skin, the loss of bags, the shimmer of immortality. Cav's eyes now had the same devilish sparkle that Pokey had -- that I had -- that lusty, needy, playful look.

I didn't think, when I first laid eyes on Colt Cavalier, the porn star and physique model, that there was much that could be improved with him -- yet here he was, somehow elevated over the mortal he'd been just minutes ago. Believable only because he was standing there before me breathing, otherwise I'd think him a product of exaggerative story-telling, wishful thinking, or serious air-brushing.

Cav was so happy, he reminded me of Pokey, the way he pranced and skipped around, like the excited Colt he suddenly was. "You did it!" he sang. "Oh, Pholus -- you really did it! Thank you! Thank you! This is so awesome!" He ran into my arms and kissed me, genuinely reeking of love (and male pheromones). I knew he was bonded to me -- I could feel that, too.

Then he broke the kiss and said, "We gotta fuck! Oh gods, I'm so fucking horny right now! Where's the kid? Let's get the kid in here! Fuck!!!"

As I sat up in bed, I watched the halves of his ass flex as he strode to the door -- a thoroughbred. Glutes of a god.

He threw the door open and was calling, "Hey, Poke..." when he stopped, frozen in place, and quietly asked, "What's that smell?"

"What?" I asked from the bed.

"That smell..." he mumbled, his cock rising. "Can't you...? It's so fuckin'... HOT..."

"Cav?" I asked, but he ignored me, beginning to stroke his cock. "CAV!"

He shuffled out of the room, distracted, playing with himself.

I ran after him without thinking and by the time I got to the door, I could smell the scent he was talking about: sweaty muscle and lusty maleness mixed with earth, flavored with fire, sex and leather, oil and metal, muddy horse flanks and sweet, juicy holes -- it was familiar to me. I'd smelled it before…

I held my breath and walked to the landing. From here I could see the living room from above.

And I understood.

Pokey had opened the wine.

The ancient bottle sat there open on the coffee table, next to the pizza boxes -- Pokey had peeled the wax seal back and the stopper laid next to the bottle. Pokey was collapsed on the floor next to the coffee table, leaning against the front of the sofa, helplessly masturbating with an expression of poppered-bliss on his face, drooling slightly as he looked at the bottle while his hands ran up and down his massive cock.

Cav had made it to the bottom of the stairs before he'd fallen to his knees, now unable to move but for the need to jerk off -- like Pokey, he stared into space and played with his new huge member.

I ducked back into the bedroom and released my held breath.

I had to save them -- my centaurs! -- but I couldn't fall victim to their fate! I had to act fast.

I took another deep breath and charged out of the bedroom. Leaping over the railing on the second-floor, my new body landed easily, if not noisily, on the living room floor, about two feet away from the coffee table. Without breathing, I strode over, stepped over Pokey and put the stopper back in the bottle. Then I reached up and pulled the chain to start the ceiling fan.

Only then did I exhale.

Cav orgasmed a couple seconds later and only then seemed to come to his senses. Poor Pokey had been hit much harder -- and who knew how long he'd sat there before we'd found him -- but, like poppers, the smell seemed to clear and Pokey was able to bring himself to climax. He sighed in relief, collapsing and catching his breath.

"Are you okay, Pokey?" I asked, kneeling down next to him.

"I am now," he said breathlessly. "You saved me -- thank you! I couldn't stop… I just couldn't… and I couldn't cum…"

Cav knelt down on the other side of him. "Why did you open the wine, Poke?"

"To let it breathe, I reckon," he said. "So we could celebrate you becoming a…" He looked at the naked Cavalier in all his glory. "You done it," Pokey said, smiling, his cock suddenly jumping back to life. "Damn, Cav, look at you…" He leaned up to kiss Cav, but Cav pushed him playfully away.

"Don't you worry, we're gonna fuck like beasts," Cav said, wrapping his arm around Pokey's neck. "But first, I think we should drink that wine."

"What?" Pokey and I said together, but for different reasons.

I was slightly more defensive. "Did you see what just happened?" I asked as Cav reached for the card that had come with the bottle. "The smell alone tranced the two of you -- and it might've gotten me, too if I hadn't been so damn slow to follow. And now you want us to drink it?"

"Well, yeah," Cav said, standing, looking at the card as he spoke. "Chiron said this was Dionysian Wine, one of your favorite things! Why would he lie about that? Besides, there was a warning, wasn't there? -- here it is: *A Warning: Beware leaving the bottle uncorked --it will attract Beasts.* Doesn't that sound like what just happened to us?"

I crossed my arms before my big pecs. "So now you can read the card, too?" I asked.

He shrugged -- whatever. "I think Pokey's instinct was right, Red -- I think we should drink the wine. Look, we're centaurs now -- and the wisest and justest of all of us centaurs has sent you a gift -- doesn't it make sense that maybe there's some perceptual experience we're supposed to have? Maybe our bond will be strengthened by imbibing this? Maybe we'll just like it and it'll make us super horny! We won't know till we try it. Look, Red, whatever else is true, we aren't human anymore, so we need to stop limiting ourselves with human weakness and hesitation."

Pokey gave a singular nod. "What he said," he said.

God damn, Pokey was adorable -- and Cav was irresistible.

I sighed. "Pokey, go get three brandy snifters out of the china cabinet."

"Why do I always gotta get stuff?"

Cav snorted. "Cuz we're both bigger than you, now go!"

We watched him leave and I joked, "Herd Master."

Shrugging, Cav chuckled. "I'm a natural," he said. "C'mon, I'm starving." He opened the pizza and took a slice.

"You really think this is the right thing to do?" I asked, grabbing a slice myself. "The wine, I mean?"

That derisive snort. "Yeah," he said, his mouth full. "What's the worst thing that could happen?"

****

I'm running through the forest, my hooves thundering, the trunks of trees flying by my flanks, the light of the moon reflected in my nighttime eyes. I can hear the others behind me -- I can feel them as well, their presence -- as we run through this dreamy reality, this magical landscape. The trail weaves and dips, which might confuse a lesser scout, but I follow it with ease -- and they follow me -- meeting the physical challenge with an athletic proficiency, leaping ravines and fallen trees. Everything smells earthy and delicious, distinct and savage.

The sense of freedom and movement is overwhelming! Running at full pace is nothing short of blissful joy, the peak of equinion ecstasy. This is what I am made for -- to run! My powerful lungs heave, my heart beats faster, my hooves pound out their cadence. Like crossing a finish line, I break through a line of trees only to find myself in a moonlit meadow, open and grassy, everything colored in the monochromatic hues of the moon -- the stars twinkle and tell their fortunes. Artemis calls for the Hunt.

I rear up on my hind legs, showing my hairy white fetlocks to the light. I am thick, and big, a workhorse, an auburn-haired beauty with a cream colored belly. I am strength and unstoppable power. At eighteen hands high, my bestial self easily supports my human torso. Nature is coated with a thick, dripping layer of magic -- I can perceive the lights of faeries and the movement of dark beasts. I am the bridge between worlds.

Gods, I can still taste the wine!

And at that moment, Cavalier crashes through the tree line, entering the meadow at full gallop. Where I am a workhorse, Cavalier is a thoroughbred, a race horse -- he is sleek and muscular, so dark black he blends with the night, but for the moon reflecting off his sweaty coat. He is almost as tall as me, at seventeen hands, but his bestial self is as toned and athletic as his human half. He slows himself to a canter and circles me, smiling broadly -- he is playful, frisky with his new body. His eyes have the same glowing appearance as my own -- we can see in the dark, in the light of Selene.

"Look at us!" he sings, he whinnies. He leaps through the air and kicks his rear legs. "Pholus, do you feel it? We must hunt!"

I circle with him, pressing against each other -- we rear up together, to display our heights. We are playful, youthful. He's right -- I do feel it. I want to run. To hunt.

"Yes," I say with a quiet confidence. "Gather Pokey."

Cavalier sets out a call and we wait for the young colt to arrive -- I can feel him approach from the west. "He's frollicking," Cavalier mumbles. "He plays with the faeries. He will never be a hunter, that one."

I smile. "He follows his nature."

Cavalier chuckles, another whinny. "I will build you a herd of hunters, Pholus, warriors mighty and proud. We will take back our rightful place in the world."

His words are sexy, his voice is grit -- Cavalier has found his purpose. I hold his hands in my own as we face each other -- he smells like sweat and old sex. "With you leading this herd, we will only know glory -- and strength! I am full of love for you, my centaur! My headstrong Cavalier! Your true form leaves me nearly breathless in its beauty!"

He smiles. "I have dreamed my whole life of this, hoped to escape the limits of humanity, hoped to expand my perception beyond reality. I love you, too, Pholus, my creator and brother, and my gratitude and devotion are eternal. Look at us!" He yells at the heavens, rearing up on his hind legs. "LOOK AT US! The centaurs are back and the gods will take notice!"

It is that moment when Pokey Dakota enters the meadow -- he trots, a fancy step, almost as if dancing. He breaks into a gentle lope, still in rhythm, strutting over to us. Pokey is whiter than snow, his coat twinkling in the moonlight, each strand of hair a spun diamond, leaving a trail of glowing, sparkly glitter that dissipates into the dark behind him. He is barely fifteen hands high, little more than a pony, but he's got the high rump of an arabian, strong and sound. Pokey's tail resembles bright blue cotton candy, spun and whipped light -- it's the same color as the hair on his head, his flowing blue mane.

He holds himself up proudly until Cavalier laughs, "You look like some mortal girl's childhood toy!"

Pokey smiles slyly. "I reckon I can feel your jealousy, Cavalier -- it's so negative. I told you… I'm a UNICORN!" He spins around, kicking and showing his less-than-beastial bestial form. "I will bring beauty to our herd. And DANCE..." He begins his dressage routine -- Terpsichore is his muse -- the moon is his spotlight.

"Be still, little one," I say to him gently, taking his hand in mine. "You act like a yearling."

He smiles and kisses my hand. "I can't help it!" he sings. "I'm so happy!"

"It is the Bacchanalia," Cavalier says. "And in this state, we must be true to our nature. We must be what we truly are!" He slaps his own chest with his open palms. "We must hunt!"

He closes in on Pokey, brushing up next to the sparkling beauty. "Do you feel it in you, Pokey? Close your eyes. Reach beyond the appearance, beyond the physical -- you are a spectacular beast, yes, but you are still a beast! Do you feel it, Pokey? Do you feel what you are?"

Pokey Dakota, his eyes closed, mumbles, "Yes…"

Cavalier kisses Pokey deeply. "We hunt."

We are running through the woods again -- I have my bow in my hand and can feel my quiver across my shoulders. It is all familiar somehow -- I've wielded this weapon before, it's mine by rite. I've shot thousands of arrows in my time -- I'm a skilled shooter. I've been trained in archery by…

Cavalier distracts me -- he has a scent. He carries a cudgel, but has a spear strapped across his back -- his weapons glimmer, as if made of magic. We slow ourselves to a trot and he shares the smell

-- a buck, by the water. Pokey catches up to us, a look of serious determination on his face. He carries a sling, a small pouch of rocks strapped around his withers, and he has his bow across his back. None of us, in this dreamlike, magical place, questions why we have something we didn't have before.

We bring ourselves silently to the river's break -- the buck is unaware of us, lowering his head to the water. In a single move, I step out from behind a tree and raise my bow -- the arrow glows, reflecting the light of the moon, almost magical itself -- and easily put the shaft through the buck's neck. It's then that Pokey, revealing himself, looses an arrow of his own, piercing the animal's breast.

In pain, the beast reacts, trying to flee. Cavalier is upon it before it can even right itself, striking it in the back of its skull with his cudgel, the bone-breaking crack echoing through the woods, sending the tree-bound birds aloft into the night. The buck falls to the ground.

It's our first kill as a herd, and we don't know all the rituals. At the moment, there is nothing civilized about us -- we are beasts. We tear at the flesh and bathe in the warm blood and taste the tender guts -- we howl at the moon while we dance to our good fortune and offer the gods their sacrifice to thank them. We share the kill with the other predators of the night -- there is no waste -- it is simply another death in the chaotic realm of nature. We are beastly slaves to chaos.

It's in that moment, lost to my bestial side, completely and utterly reveling in the animal, that I hear it, far to the east. "Pholus!" a voice calls.

I follow it, leaving my brothers and my sons behind, racing toward this voice.

"Pholus!"

I leap from the top of one hill to the next -- distance passes beneath me in an impossible way -- I fly through the night, my hooves barely touching the ground. And suddenly, I'm on the shore of a great body of water -- an ocean! -- and I'm fairly sure I can run across the surf and leap from wave to wave if I want. I have only to believe…

"Pholus, you're in the Realm!"

His voice is on the other side of this sea. Familiar.

My teacher -- my master -- my love.

It is Chiron.

"Erastês!" I yell -- another word I don't know, but I know I'm not loud enough to hear over the roar of the surf. "I will find you! I will come to you!" The waves crash on the rocks.

He is so near -- and so far away. But then everything collapses upon itself -- reality drains down the disposal -- the dream ends. There is only comfortable blackness -- silence, the surf fades away.

And from this deep, dark place, Chiron's voice finds its way free.

"Pholus... BEWARE!"

****

I woke as a big spoon.

I was in my own bed -- I was certain of that -- the familiar feel of the mattress, the way the mid-morning sunlight shone in through the drapes I never remembered to shut. Even with my eyes closed, I knew where I was.

Just as I was certain that my little spoon was Pokey.

The smell of his hair, the size-difference -- I snuggled him close. The body I felt on the other side of the bed, the one my back was up against, must've been Cav. How the hell did we all end up here?

Didn't matter. The moment -- enjoy the moment. The Present was eternal.

Pokey rubbed against me, which started to get me hard. He could definitely feel that against his tight little ass. "Mmmm," he mumbled. "Gotta pee first..."

I chuckled sleepily and felt him slip away. He didn't shut the bathroom door so I could hear his heavy stream of piss -- the noise woke Cav, who shifted his weight and exhaled. "What the fuck happened to us?" he asked quietly, his back against mine.

"I'm not sure," I replied, touching my legs to make sure they were human legs. "Was it a dream? Some kind of shared dream?"

"No," he said. "A dream-like quality, for sure -- but I think it was real."

"Did we..." I swallowed involuntarily. ".. eat a deer's heart?"

I felt him nod slightly. "I believe we did." He snorted. "Wasn't it awesome?"

But before I could answer -- and to be honest, I wasn't entirely sure what my response would have been. My civilized-side was repulsed, yet my bestial-side wanted to do it again and again and again, and make it even bloodier still -- before I could articulate that, we heard Pokey yell from the bathroom.

"Oh my God, LOOK AT ME!"

He came into the room, naked and beautiful, that incredible body and sweet, fat, dangling cock. "You guys!" he screamed, forcing us to turn our respective ways to face the foot of the bed. "Look at me! Look at my HAIR!"

The hair on Pokey's head was the exact same shade of cotton-candy blue it had been when he'd transformed into a centaur, wavy and wild, choreographed, long enough to be a mane. When he shook it, glitter fell out. His beard -- that thing he called a beard -- and his body/ pubic hair were still the same tannish, dirty-blonde color they had been, but the hair on his head was bright bubblegum-blue! Violet Beauregard blue! Smurf in heat blue! There could not have been a more unnatural shade in the spectrum than the blue that colored his hair.

It was undeniably cartoon unicorn blue.

Cav snorted and laughed, falling back into the pillow, covering his face with his arm. Even I couldn't help but smile -- yet somehow, the kid still looked sexy. If you wanted to fuck a sno-cone.

But for Pokey, the greatest realization of all. "You guys," he said. "I reckon it was all real. We really are what we are."

"Yeah we are," Cav said.

"Welp," Pokey summarized, decidedly happy. "Ain't we just ridin' a gravy train with biscuit wheels? Now, who wants to fuck?"

"In the shower," I said. "I don't want you getting glitter in the sheets."

6. "Apotheosis"

Not the last time:

__Apotheosis__ (from Greek ἀποθέωσις from ἀποθεόω/ἀποθεῶ, apotheoo/apotheo "to deify"; in Latin deificatio "making divine"; also called __divinization__ and __deification__) is the glorification of a subject to divine level and, most commonly, the treatment of a human like a god. In theology, apotheosis refers to the idea that an individual has been raised to godlike stature.

****

The Hipster Barber Shop, Dunn's, was more-or-less on the way to the gym, so it wasn't hard to steer Pokey in. "This is my guy," I told him. "He'll clean you up."

"I like the smell of this place," Pokey said as we went inside. "The leather 'n such -- I reckon it's sorta manly."

There were a few more people in the shop than when I'd been here last, a second cutter in the back corner chair -- another hipster with a beautiful beard and a top-knot smoking a cigar. He and his client were deep in it, chatting away, completely ignoring the rest of us.

Dunn had just finished at the register so was there to greet us. "Pholus!" he exclaimed, unconsciously touching his package, bowing slightly. Clad only in a leather vest and two heavy silver necklaces, leather gauntlet on one wrist and assorted beads and bracelets on the other, the same black jeans and sneakers as the last time I'd seen him. Once again his beard and hair were manicured to perfection. "I'm honored! What can I do to be of service?"

"Hello, Dunn," I said, smiling, hitting him with a wave of pheromones. (Pokey reacted dramatically, leaning into me and whispering, "Go, Captain Overkill," as he teasingly poked me in the side. I barely glanced at him.) "Something I hope you can help me with," I said to Dunn, pulling the baseball cap from Pokey's head, releasing his cascade of uncontrolled azure locks. "This."

"Oh, my!" Dunn said.

I smirked. "Yeah... it needs..."

"Some style," Dunn finished, studying it academically. "I mean, the color's gorgeous -- whoever did it did a spectacular job." He put his hands through Pokey's thick hair, examining it -- I hope Pokey found it as erotic as I did. From the smell coming off him, he did. "I mean, it's got highlights, lowlights, beautiful tone... why didn't they cut it? What's wrong with you kids today?" He looked Pokey straight in the face. "Fear not, I can make your boy beautiful," Dunn said, glancing from him to me.

"He's not my boy," I said, handing Pokey his hat. "But he is part of my tribe, so he needs to look his best."

"Got it." He turned to Pokey. "First, let's go wash this good. It looks like there's some glitter or something in it."

Pokey laughed and cast a glance at me before heading back with Dunn. Dunn turned to me as they were walking to the sink and I made a motion to my beard and mouthed, obviously, "LOSE THIS!" Dunn frowned and turned away, back to his project.

One guy sat in the waiting area, clearly perturbed that I'd cut him in line -- I could read it coming from him. Only in entitled hipster barber shops would a guy think to give attitude to me, a six-five, two-hundred eighty-five pound musclebeast, but that was the world in which we lived. "Some of us were in line," he said.

I smiled and hit him with a heavy wave of pheromones. "Thank you for letting us in," I said, gently touching the head of my cock through my tight gym shorts -- they kept no secrets. "Your generosity pleases me."

"Um..." He sniffed the air curiously. "You're welcome?" he said, crossing his legs in an attempt to hide his sudden, swollen erection. "I mean, anything." He bowed his head in shame, but couldn't keep himself from looking at me, now that I'd made him infatuated. "Anything for you."

I smiled -- weak-willed mortals. "Exactly," I said, winking. "Anything for me." Then I moved to the far side of the waiting area, where I could keep an eye on Pokey, but have some privacy while I texted AppleJack.

                                   @me: You still mad?

@applejack: I'm not mad.
@applejack: Not exactly.
@applejack: I guess I'm disappointed.
@applejack: We've been friends our whole entire lives, Red.
@applejack: I can't believe you'd think you had any better ally.

                   @me: There's nobody I'd rather have at my side
                                  @me: you know that!

@applejack: Yeah, except you won't make me a centaur.

                         @me: C'mon, AppleJack. That's not fair.
                         @me: It's not that I don't want you to be.

@applejack: You make that dimwit kid a centaur!
@applejack: You make some porn star you just met a centaur!
@applejack: But your oldest friend…
@applejack: who, coincidentally, CREATED your whole brand…
@applejack: no, he gets to stay human

             @me: To make you a centaur, we have to have sex.

@applejack:...
@applejack:...
@applejack: Like, what do you mean?
@applejack: What specifically?
@applejack: You don't have to FUCK me, do you?
@applejack: Is that why you only pick porn stars and rodeo clowns?

                                      @me: Haha

@applejack: I mean, I think I could do anything OTHER than that.
@applejack: You know, get super-high…

                       @me: Actually, it's just the opposite.
                           @me: You'd have to fuck ME.

@applejack:...
@applejack:...
@applejack: I think I could do that.

@me: hahaha
@me: Except...
@me: It's not just mechanical.
@me: We have to be "into" it for the mojo to work.

@applejack: I think you owe it to me to try.

@me: But what if it turns you queer, Applejack?
@me: Have you considered that?

@applejack: So what great things am I doing as a straight man?
@applejack: When was the last time I even dated someone? College?
@applejack: Women don't want me, Red. They never have.
@applejack: so what if it turned me queer?
@applejack: to have a cock like that...

@me:...
@me:...
@me: Okay. We'll try.
@me: But I can't make any guarantees.

@applejack: Thank you, Red. This means everything to me.
@applejack:...
@applejack:...
@applejack: No pressure.

@me: We'll talk when I get home. Find some good flower
@me: something that will fuck me up

@applejack: I have the perfect thing. TTYL
@applejack: Wear something sexy. Haha.

@me: Hahaha

****

His words echoed through my mind. "Why not me?"

In all the years I'd known AppleJack, I think we've had two fights -- and I'm not even sure I'd call them "fights," maybe arguments at best -- and even those were from our early days of sharing a living space, when we were both learning our boundaries. The closest we got to arguing now was sarcasm -- we're so codependent on each other that we might as well be married. I couldn't even imagine a time when we wouldn't be together -- he called it my "Golden Girls" fantasy.

"Why not me?"

I'd never seen him so genuinely hurt like that -- so raw.

And he'd been right -- I'd done nothing to deserve what was happening to me. I'd won the lottery. I'd drunk a magic potion, not gotten Odysseus back to Ithaca. What right did I have to deny anyone?

It just kept coming back to the ugly truth: I didn't find AppleJack attractive. His horse-face and his dumpy body -- I think the reason we'd remained friends as long as we had was because I wasn't attracted to him. Lusting for AppleJack would never be a chapter title in the book of my life.

That said, wasn't I supposed to be some rutty-sex demigod? Shouldn't I have been, like, "Yeah, cock!" and just… found the inner drive?

"Why not me?"

Because I love you, but I have no lust for you.

But I could never say that to him.

Because I loved him -- and I didn't want to lose him.

****

I looked up and noticed that Pokey and Dunn had disappeared -- they'd been nearly finished so it didn't take a genius to figure out why they'd gone to the office, or the back room, or wherever the hell they were. Pokey was no doubt "letting" Dunn suck his cock -- that was what Pokey considered tipping.

I was actually sorry I wasn't getting to watch, frankly -- Dunn could suck a good cock.

I'd almost gotten distracted by my phone again when they emerged, Pokey leading the way, jubilant. Dunn had done a hard fade on the sides and back of his head and pulled the rest of Pokey's blue cascade back into a ponytail. He looked like a European Soccer player or a super-hip lower east side douchebag.

It wasn't just the haircut -- Pokey'd had his septum pierced, and a big silver hoop hung from the base of his nose, a small blue bead decorating it. His ears, too, matching hoops and beads.

"Well, look at you!" I said, smiling.

"Look at me!" he said, spinning and posing. "Ain't I gorgeous?"

Dunn, a dizzy smile on his face -- and if I didn't miss my guess, the taste of cum in his mouth -- opened the cash register, removed all the money and offered it to Pokey. "Your tip," he said, tears of joy in his eyes. "I know cutters don't usually tip the clients, but it was such an honor to work with you. I want you to have it."

"Aw," Pokey said, reaching for the money. "You're so sweet…"

I admonished him. "Pokey," I said quietly, "not appropriate. Release him."

"No, it's okay," Dunn said to me, as if explaining. "I want him to have it!"

"No you don't. He's doing something to you to make you think that."

"Red!"

"Let him go, Pokey…"

There was a moment -- but with a dramatic sigh, Pokey obeyed, and I could almost feel the reins lifted from Dunn. "Spoil sport…" he mumbled.

"You got a beautiful haircut, boy. Be grateful." I looked at Dunn, who seemed to be wondering why he was standing there with the contents of the till in his hands. I hit him with my own wave of pheromones. "Put the cash back in the drawer, Dunn," I said to him, "Forget it happened."

Dunn whispered, "Yes, my Lord," as he swiftly obeyed, his erection renewed in his tight black jeans.

"Ohhhh," Pokey said, knowingly, "I reckon I get it now! You want him for yourself…"

I chuckled. "Not just for me," I said. "For US… get me?"

Pokey hadn't put two and two together -- I needed to be more obvious.

"A Dun IS a kind of horse," I said quietly.

Pokey got it. "I reckon it is," he said, nodding while considering. "That's about as right as rain. So… you gonna make him an offer or do you reckon we should talk to Cavalier first?"

Talk to Cavalier first? I thought. *Why?* I didn't need his permission to create centaurs. I mean, I knew we'd had this "Herd Master" thing we'd thrown around during sex, but was that serious? Did that take away my power to make my own choices?

But before I'd had the chance to voice my thoughts to Pokey, Dunn interrupted.

"Make me an offer?" Dunn asked, suddenly curious. "You like his hair that much?" He reached over and began stroking Pokey's head affectionately. Pokey, like a good pony, leaned into it.

"I do," I said, smiling. "You're a helluva groomsman."

He laughed. "Always taming the beasts," he said, playing with Pokey's ponytail, pulling on it gently until Pokey leaned his head back. "And so you guys want me to be a centaur? That's cool."

"How'd you figure that?" Pokey asked, pulling slightly away from Dunn, but still keeping an arm around him.

Dunn shrugged. "I looked you up after you did your voodoo on me last time," he said to me. "You're Pholus -- reborn! -- I read your story on your website, magic potion, transformation. It's super-hot. And then you and the kid here show up today and he's got blue hair -- no shit blue hair. It's totally real -- it's not dyed, it's not affected -- it's porous and healthy… and blue. And then he hits me with the same smell-thing that you had -- pheromones? -- and I realized it was all true. You're magical beings -- you're no-shit Centaurs." He opened his arms in a welcoming gesture. "So make me an offer! Transform me! What do we gotta do?"

****

Turned out there was a massage table in the back room of the barber shop where Dunn did piercings. It was a tiny room, barely enough space for the three of us -- I'd tried to send Pokey off to the gym, but he'd insisted on watching this time -- the same smell of leather and old smoke that hung comfortably throughout the shop was here, mixed with alcohol (shaken, not stirred) and nervous sweat.

As soon as he'd shut the door, Dunn and I began kissing. He was playful, skilled -- I'd never kissed a man with a pierced septum before, the weight of the jewelry on my lip was sexy. I sat on the edge of the table and he pushed his way between my legs while we made out. I unbuckled his belt and opened his jeans. Commando, which pleased me, Dunn's impressively thick cock sported a PA, silver and heavy -- he shaved his balls, but his bush was groomed very naturally. Otherwise, I could see his trail leading up under his leather vest with the same black with flecks of gray that decorated his chest, his upper pecs hidden by his beard.

"Lemme eat you out," he mumbled. "I'm dying to get a taste… dying… let me pleasure you before I fuck you."

He slowly dropped to his knees, sliding down my muscular torso, stopping briefly to suck my nipple ("We're gonna pierce these," he whispered.), then slid his tongue and the tip of his nose down the center groove of my abs. But instead of continuing to my cock, he spun me round so I faced the table and then yanked my shorts down, exposing my big, muscular ass, but trapping my cock.

He spread my cheeks wide, breathed in deeply, losing himself in my scent, and then got to work, lovingly -- skillfully -- pleasing my hole. I leaned on my forearms, feeling my cock get hard somewhere out of my reach. I'd never experienced someone as talented as Dunn eat me out. I mean, I'd met guys who were into rimming and ass-play, enthusiasts, but they were weekend warriors compared to Dunn! Even Cavalier, with all his professional experience, couldn't evoke the feelings I was having now -- this was a man born to eat ass! I was starting to believe he was going to give me an oral anal-orgasm. An oral analgasm.

My inability to access my own cock was killing me, adding to the excruciating pleasure.

And there was Pokey, as predictable as a porn plot, climbing up on the head of the table, pulling his big, hard cock out of his shorts and slapping me in the face with it until I took it in my mouth. "I thought you were gonna watch," I said, allowing the whole of his plum-sized glans in my mouth, tasting the salty-sweetness of his pre-cum.

"I am watching," he responded, forcing me to take more.

Dunn had me so open and sloppy wet that when he dropped the heft of his PA-enhanced thickness into my hole, it just slammed against my prostate in big, solid reverberations, a weighted log pounding into me. He slapped my ass cheek. "You like that, demigod?" he asked roughly. "Say yes."

I pulled my mouth off Pokey's cock. "Yes," I said, breathing heavily.

"Good," he growled in my ear. "Suck blueboy's cock and get ready for the best mortal fuck you'll ever have."

He wasn't just talking. Cavalier may have been a professional, but his fuck had been all-business, a bit of "these are my standard moves and now it's your turn with them" -- I mean, I'd enjoyed myself, but it was nothing compared to the fucking I was getting from Dunn. Here was a guy who wasn't only skilled, he was passionate -- he loved the act. And Dunn was clearly experienced. A young top could learn a lot from him -- I'd hoped Pokey was truly paying attention. I knew I was.

"You ready for my cum, demigod?" he asked. "You ready for MY offering?"

"Give it to me," I said, removing my mouth from Pokey's cock and masturbating it. "It's the price of apotheosis!"

He paid that price in full.

The energy was so great, even Pokey shot his load, filling me from both ends with my favorite filling. I was curious if Pokey could feel the transfer of energy that changed Dunn from human to beast. From the way Dunn was reacting inside me, he could definitely feel something -- our bond was forming.

"It's happening," he said, slapping my ass with both hands. "Oh fuck, Pholus, this is incredible!"

Pokey laughed. "I reckon the incredible's just starting," he said. "Look at your body!"

Dunn hadn't been in any kind of real shape -- he'd moved with the grace of someone who'd known some sort of athletics at some point in time in his life, but he clearly had no regular gym routine now. He was someone you could hang clothes off of, though, and he looked like a model with his slick hair, his massive black beard, and all that silver jewelry. He was the kind of guy you'd look at and say, "Man, with a body, he could be unstoppable!"

Well, now he was unstoppable.

Like Pokey, he hadn't gained much muscle mass -- he retained his leanness, his lanky build -- but now he was more like a swimmer or a Greek statue, ripped, tight, every striation visible, every muscle sculpted to perfection. He opened his vest and revealed his abs to us, flat and smooth, again, not an ounce of fat, but hairy and tempting, eight-pack or not.

His cock -- I'd used the word "log" to describe it earlier, but now it actually was, thick and heavy, the foreskin holding on as best it could. The PA seemed small now compared to how it appeared before. We all watched his cock grow to its new full size, rock hard, rivaling Pokey.

"Your turn," he said to the boy, that familiar glint in his eye.

Pokey smiled, stripping his shorts off as he slid down the table. "Yee-haw," he laughed. "Show me what you got, big daddy. Let's see how long you stay on the ride."

He ate Pokey's ass while I ate his, losing myself in his hairy crack, his scent -- I felt like I could identify any of my centaurs by smell alone, each was unique and individual. And while he fucked Pokey, I fucked him -- and he was amazed at being able to take my cock. Physics be damned -- we were magical beings now!

We'd been loud and shameless -- we'd been beasts -- grunting and screaming and unapologetically fucking in the backroom of the barber shop. They could definitely hear us -- they could probably smell us over the after-shave. But damn that had been a nice way to spend the morning -- and Pokey'd gotten a great haircut!

When we went back into the shop, nobody was there -- even the other cutter had taken off. "Looks like we scared 'em all away," Dunn said, flexing his arms in the wall mirrors. "Damn! This is fucking awesome!"

"You just wait," Pokey said, redressed and ready to go.

Dunn kissed him lovingly. "Anytime you want a good fuck, boy, you just drop in." He patted Pokey on the ass and sent him toward the door. Then he hugged me. "How can I ever thank you for this? This incredible gift?"

I winked. "Just keep my beard looking neat," I said.

He smiled. "That's the price of immortality? I'll pay it." He kissed me and I could taste Pokey's cum on his breath. "Thank you, Pholus. I'm yours forever."

I snorted. "In a thousand years, I'll remind you you said that."

****

"Why not me?"

AppleJack's words echoed in my head throughout the rest of my day, even over the music I had playing on my headphones at the gym. I had no real answer to them. The same thing had happened with Dunn that had happened with Cav that had happened with Pokey before him -- I'd been in a frenzied state of lust, we had a shared orgasm, and the transformation had just happened. How was I supposed to duplicate that with AppleJack?

I wasn't even sure I owed it to him to try, given that the chances of success were so small. I wondered which might hurt our friendship worse: that I wouldn't do it, or that I couldn't do it? That was what I had on my mind when I got home late that afternoon -- the resolve to let my friend down as best I could.

The last time I'd seen him had been this morning's awkward Breakfast of Shame for my new centaurs -- just bacon and scrambled eggs -- when blue-haired Pokey had let it slip that I'd transformed them before AppleJack had even had his coffee.

Without speaking, he'd just shuffled back to his room with his cup.

It wasn't until later, after Cavalier had left and Pokey had gone upstairs to take a shower and get ready for the gym, that AppleJack had come out of his bedroom and hit me with the hard line. "Can I ask you something?" he'd asked. "Those guys, those guys you… transformed. Was there something special about… I mean, that made you… pick them? Pokey Dumbass Dakota and that Porn Star guy? Why them and… not me? Why not me?" He'd taken my silence, my inability to answer, as permission to continue. "You gain the power to change people into what you are and you don't even consider me -- after everything I've done for you, and with you. That fuckin' hurts, Red."

I'd tried to blame the wine -- tried to explain how the fumes from the bottle acted like super-poppers, driving us mad with lust. He wasn't having any of it.

"Don't lie to me," he'd said. "If you don't want me in your club, fine, but don't lie to me."

That was how we'd left it, unresolved, so I didn't know what I was going to be coming home to.

Happily, I entered to the smell of a really sweet strain -- AppleJack was smoking the good stuff. He was sitting in the great room, *Judge Judy* playing on the TV, in the same spot where Pokey'd almost OD'd last night. "Hey," I said, tossing my gym bag down. "What's this?"

"This is some amazing indica I scored from Benny, over at the dispensary. You gotta taste this shit."

"Gladly," I said, taking the chair across from him. "I haven't even caught a buzz yet today."

He leaned forward to load the bowl. "Well, you've been busy…" He stopped himself short. "I'm sorry. I'm sorry -- I promised I wouldn't be bitter. I'm trying to be an adult about this…" He was lost in his internal thoughts for a long second -- probably stoned -- then he said, resolved, "I have to take a leak -- I'll be right back. Load yourself up."

He ducked out of the room and I began fixing a hit -- this bud was gorgeous, still freakin' wet, little rust-colored tufts squatting like Whoville atop tiny, tight turquoise buds -- sweet little Mary-Jane Who here was putting out way more pheromones than I did on my worst day. I could just sit here and snort the bud itself and never smoke a leaf and get high. I'd been getting off on scents a lot, lately -- what was up with that? Since I'd been a beast, actually…

It was like smoking menthol, that's how smooth and cool the hit went down -- what was that flavor? Was it laced? The aftertaste was even nicer, hanging on my exhalation like a friendly ghost. Oh, sweet Mary-Jane. I didn't even cough -- me!

AppleJack reappeared with a couple of bottles of water. "Good, isn't it?" he asked, handing me a bottle and flopping back on the sofa. "I've been holding this for a couple weeks, waiting for the moment." He took the bong from me and finished the bowl, loading another before he'd even exhaled. "You've got some catching up to do."

"What's the moment?" I asked, taking the fresh bong from him. This hit was just as nice as the previous.

He smiled a devious grin. "This is the day I seduce you," he said, cracking open his water. "And that's a day none of us saw coming."

I snorted my exhale, shaking my head. "AppleJack..."

"Look, I'm even gonna let you call me that, just to show you how important this is to me. As a matter of fact, you can even let that be my centaur name! Let everyone know it -- Pholus and his trusty steed AppleJack!" he laughed, loading me another bong.

"Are you sure you want to be associated with the dimwit and the porn star?" (And the barber now, too? Best not to tell him about that.)

He handed the bong to me. "Ah, I was mad when I said that. Maybe I'm a little jealous. How's that for honesty, my lifelong friend?"

"Wow," I said, exhaling. "You really ARE trying to be an adult."

He smiled and made eye contact with me, motioning for me to finish the bowl, so I did. "I told you, I'm gonna seduce you if I have to, but one way or another, I'm gonna be a centaur before the sun sets. I'll bet you the rest of this bud."

"That you'll seduce me?" I laughed and took a drink of water. "That's a bet I'll take."

He offered me his hand -- such a straight-boy thing to do -- and we shook on it.

"Well, all I gotta do now is resist you till sunset," I joked, "then that sweet bud is mine and I can let the vampires have you!"

"Take another hit," he said, reloading for me, "then I wanna show you something."

"Your dick?" I asked. "Not interested." Laughing, I took the bong from him and did the hit, already feeling this shit, the edges of perception getting kind of soft -- the only thing that did get soft lately. The continuing joys of *nonischemic priapism*, not that I wanted him to think he was getting anywhere.

"Not my dick," he said. "On my system -- something guaranteed to seduce centaurs!"

I looked at him skeptically before I exhaled. "Are you gonna try and hypnotize me or something, AppleJack? You got spirals on your screen? Dude, I love you and you know that -- you're my best friend -- but I don't feel that way about you, you know?" I sighed. "I'm afraid of letting you down."

He stood, taking a sip of his water and setting it down on the table. "I feel the same way," he said, offering me his hand. "But I'm gonna be a centaur. Now, c'mon -- leave the bong."

I took his hand and followed him to his room, a curious smirk on my face. Anyone witnessing this pear-shaped fatboy leading this hypermasculine stud toward the bedroom would conclude a transaction had just been accepted, not that the stud had been seduced. What was he planning?

He stopped at his bedroom door, getting between it and me.

"What?" I asked.

He smirked. "This is where we test my theory," he said, opening the door and forcing me quickly inside. Before I'd even had a chance to react, he was shutting the door behind us and locking it.

This was maybe the third time I'd been in AppleJack's room in all the years we'd been in this house. His huge computer workstation dominated the far wall -- multiple screens at all angles -- sadly, none displayed hypnotic spirals. The living area was kind of a disaster -- as it had been since we'd lived together in college, so I wasn't shocked.

Then the smell hit me.

At first, I thought maybe it was AppleJack's dirty laundry -- the undertone of sweat and shit -- but when my dick started to get hard, I knew immediately what I was dealing with. I searched around the room, glancing this way and that, trying to find... THERE! The nightstand on the far side of the bed -- the Dionysian Wine, uncorked and breathing!

Warning: Beware leaving the bottle uncorked -- it will attract Beasts.

I reached for my cock -- I couldn't help myself. "What are you doing, AppleJack?" I mumbled as I took a step toward the bottle -- my cock ached. I could barely stay on my feet.

"Springing a trap," he said matter-of-factly. "I mean, not in a villainous kind of way -- I have heroic intentions, like Magneto!" A human, he approached the bottle easily. "And you told me your weakness."

He picked up the ancient thing as I forced myself to take another step toward him. Masturbating furiously, I couldn't support my weight and I fell to my knees -- the scent was overwhelming. He took a washcloth and poured a tiny amount of wine on it, like it was chloroform, then he walked to me and held it under my nose -- it drove me insane. He moved it around and I followed it like a dog.

"Yeah, you like this, don't you? You need it."

He stood behind me and brought the washcloth to my face, covering my nose and mouth with it.

"Breathe in deep, Red," he whispered in my ear. "Let the beast out."

I couldn't form a coherent thought -- too much. The scent, magic mixed with cotton -- pervasive. My cock -- I needed sex. So. Fucking. Horny. He held the cloth in place, like I was even strong enough to push it away -- no, I was too busy trying to suck the drops of wine out of the material.

"Fuck," I moaned, rolling my head but unable to escape the smell.

"What's the matter, Red?" he whispered in my ear. "What do you need?"

"Wine… makes me... horny," I growled, snorting deeply. "You... fucker…"

"I'm gonna be a centaur, Red," he said, pushing me to my hands and knees -- well, elbow and knees. My other hand was working hard on my cock -- why couldn't I cum? I just needed to cum. "And rape is kind of a centaur thing."

I felt his fingers on my asshole and I wanted to do anything but be turned on by them, but I couldn't -- I just got hornier! I moaned loudly, hating myself for it. I felt lube, wet and cool, sloppy on my hole. Oh, gods… fuck me! Plug MY bottle!

"You've had man-boy cocks and porn star cocks," he said, awkwardly fingering me. Poor technique -- I didn't care. "Now you're gonna have a straight guy cock -- trifecta, Red!"

He shoved something in my hole -- his thumb? No, too big for a thumb -- it was his cock.

His straight guy cock -- the trifecta.

It's size didn't matter. Whatever other magical abilities I had seemed to be the ability to find pleasure from any cock, even the smallest, most disappointing straight guy cock. My ass could tighten enough to feel him, milk him, tease him to the brink of ecstacy -- I was a magical being and I could elevate sex for anyone.

"Yeah, gimme the pheromones, Red. You're making it all easier."

A toy jackhammer -- a rabbit -- sloppy and unpracticed, arhythmic and uncomfortable, he wanted to get through the mechanics and straight to the orgasm. I could feel that in every thrust of his selfish little cock. No wonder he failed as a straight guy -- this was no way to satisfy a woman.

Not that it mattered -- the fucker had me and he knew it. I was on the edge of Bacchanalia, dying to enter the abyss, desperate for release. And he was close -- so close.

"Gonna cum," he said, speed-fucking me.

So was I, gods help me.

And then he did -- I felt his tiny shot, his wee spurt, but that was enough to trigger me. My orgasm exploded as if by magic, emanating in waves off of me like ground zero -- the power threw AppleJack from me. It happened so quickly that I was worried the magic hadn't worked and we'd have to go through this scene again.

Honestly, at that moment, I had only one thought: put the stopper back in the wine bottle. In that moment during the post-orgasmic crash to normalcy but before the fumes from the wine could ensnare me again, I held my breath and took the two steps it took to reach the canter, then I corked it.

Then I breathed again. I could still smell the scent in the air, but it was already dissipating.

AppleJack moaned from the other side of the room, next to a pile of dirty laundry. "Oh, fuck," he mumbled, beginning to move. "I can feel it!" He started laughing -- that sort of out-of-control power-mad laugh that misunderstood comic book villains had -- like Magneto. "I'm a fucking centaur! I did it!"

In all the years we'd known each other, including being roommates in college, I'd never seen AppleJack naked. I'd only seen him shirtless a handful of times -- AppleJack was one of those overweight guys who wore a t-shirt when swimming -- so even though I thought the physical change he'd gone through seemed dramatic, I had no idea of the entirety of its scope.

The others had been lean before their transformations, so they had little body fat to lose, and they ended up looking "ripped" enough to walk onto any competition stage or modeling runway they chose. AppleJack didn't have that, not exactly, the shapes an artist would use to construct him would still be curves, but not fat -- thick without definition, mass with shape. He looked like an old-school bodybuilder from the 50's, before the veterinary-grade horse testosterone and the equipoise. His legs and his ass were lineman thick, huge and powerful. Big, round pecs with coconut shoulders and a belly that resembled a roidgut more than he'd probably like, but he was lucky the flab was gone.

His cock was thick, if still a little ungenerous in length -- especially compared to the others in the herd -- but his balls were huge. Filled with so much chutzpah, they'd have to be.

Still the same dirty-blond, pink-skinned, unremarkable face he'd always had. Without the fat, his jawline was slightly more defined, his cheekbones seemed more noticeable, but he was still the same horse-faced guy he'd been, not handsome, not ugly -- filler in a lineup.

Maybe a beard…?

But he didn't care -- he was all about the muscle. He was celebrating his body -- he wouldn't look at his own face for quite some time, though I doubt he'd be disappointed.

He had no idea how to show himself off -- he didn't know any poses, so it was a lot of spinning for angles. His cock was rock hard, all nine inches shamelessly displayed before him. "Holy fuck, Red! We did it!" He laughed again. "I seriously didn't think you were gonna be able to come through for me -- but you did! You DID! Thank you, my friend! This is fucking amazing!"

I stood there, stunned, holding the stopper in the bottle, just staring at him. "You just raped me," I said.

He snorted. "No, I didn't," he said, crossing to me. "You were the one who didn't think you were gonna be able to do it. You didn't think you were gonna be able to get off on your fat friend. Well, I figured out a way for you -- like I ALWAYS do! Like I've always done for you our entire lives." He pulled back the curtain on the window. "And look, the sun is still up! So my winning ass is gonna go smoke MY bud and then maybe go get this new dick sucked someplace."

He'd almost gotten to the door when he spun back and said, "Oh yeah, I brought you in here to show you the new website. Click on my mainscreen there and check it out, then come join me for a bowl."

When I didn't respond, he added, quietly, "Don't be upset, Red. Seriously. I love you, man. Our friendship means the world to me. Now come get high." He wrapped his muscular arm around my shoulders and led me out of the room.

I brought the wine with me -- I'd keep it under lock and key from now on.

7. "The Agoge"

*The **Agōgē** (Greek: ἀγωγή in Attic Greek, or ἀγωγά, agōgā in Doric Greek) was the rigorous education and training program mandated for all male Spartans. The training involved cultivating loyalty, military training (e.g., pain tolerance), hunting, dancing, singing, and social preparation. The aim of the system was to produce strong and capable warriors. Discipline was strict and the males were encouraged to fight amongst themselves to determine the strongest member of the group.*

****

Meeting Cav and the Four Seasons' Bar gave me an excuse to wear clothes, which I rarely got to do anymore. I spent more time in posers and sexy lingerie than I did in clothes -- whatever the clients wanted. Most of the time it was posers, especially the muscle-worship scenes, or a jockstrap. Often I would give it to the client at the end of the session, wet with my sweat and his drool, so he had a reminder of me to sniff and jerk off to until the next time he saw me.

Unfortunately, I'd now been having to get my posers custom-made to fit my enormous genitals, so I didn't give them away as much anymore. I would usually wear those beneath a designer tracksuit or joggers when I'd show up at the mark's hotel and allow the client to lower my pants (while kneeling before me). Pokey thought the whole thing was ridiculous and beneath me. A guy would be honored enough to pay me tribute without me having to perform at all, why lower myself?

Gods forbid that I actually liked it!

The fact of the matter was that I really got off on guys getting off on me. As I said to Pokey, we all defined our post-human lives however we chose -- there were no rules anymore -- so if I wanted to let rich guys worship me for a grand an hour, I would. I thought Pokey's whole cash-master thing was a little impersonal and unfeeling -- the guy didn't even GET anything for his money... just the satisfaction of giving it?

He didn't need to lecture me.

So it was nice to walk into the Four Seasons wearing actual clothes, not something meant to be torn away to get to the goods. I was wearing a cotton collared pullover on top, salmon colored, tight across my bulbous pecs and shoulders, over a pair of cotton/spandex bluejeans, made to compliment bodybuilders and their out-of-proportion proportions. I had my Ferragamo loafers and belt on -- it was so much fun to wear something other than flip-flops or horseshoes!

Entering the bar, I removed my sunglasses and put them on top of my head, helping to hold back the locks of my shaggy, auburn hair as it continued to grow out. Cav's presence was so powerful, I spotted him immediately, seated on the far side of the bar, his aura glowing. He wore a pair of gray slacks and a white collared shirt with the sleeves rolled halfway up his forearms -- meticulously tailored, his outfit showed off his incredible body without revealing anything. He had on a Gucci belt and loafers, giving him a slightly stereotypical mob look with his bald head and clean-shaven everything.

He stood when I approached, a smile on his face, and we hugged. "Hey, handsome," I said, taking the stool next to his. "Look at you!"

"Look at me? Look at you," he said, giving me the up-and-down. "It's nice to see you can dress up."

"Is that why we're meeting here?"

He snorted. "No. I got a client upstairs in a little bit and I'm taking advantage of the atmosphere. You never know who you'll meet..."

The bartender appeared, a nice-looking woman in her mid-twenties, together and professional. I ordered a vodka martini (with a twist) and Cav tapped his rocks glass, looking for another. She smiled lovingly at him when he blew some pheromones her way, then she disappeared to make our drinks.

"Does that work with women?" I asked.

He laughed. "It works with any sexual being. Women like to have sex, too."

"Do you do women?"

He made one of those "I can't believe you just said that" snorts and said, "Do I 'do' women. No, I'm gay. But sometimes… a mouth is a mouth."

Laughing, he slapped my knee -- smiling, I brushed his hand away. The bartender appeared with our drinks, as well as two shots of Ouzo (on her), so we toasted ourselves. "*Yamas!*" Cav exclaimed, clinking my glass.

"*Euoi euan,*" I replied, not really knowing what I was saying -- the words just tumbled out. We tapped our shots on the bar and then downed them quickly. I had a soft spot -- perhaps genetic? -- for Ouzo.

"You continue to surprise me," Cav said, settling back with his drink. "How do you know that toast?"

I shrugged. "I don't know," I said, sipping my excellent martini. "It just came out of me, like so much does." I chuckled. "Why? What'd I say?"

"It's the ancient toast of the Satyrs," he said. "It means 'good sons' -- like, good job, boys!"

"Of course it does!" I laughed, taking a healthier drink. "How do you know this stuff?"

He swished his drink around in the rocks glass and chuckled. "I have been into Greek mythology my whole life. When I was a kid, I had one of those picture books with all the Gods and Goddesses and their stories and rivalries and schemes -- the men were all huge and buff and the women were beautiful. I deep-dove into it when I was a teen, fascinated by the 'rutty' sex gods, the Satyrs and the Centaurs, who just drank and fought and fucked their immortal days away. If I'd gone to college, I probably would've ended up with a degree in Classical Antiquities or Art History, which would've proved as useless to my current career as not. So I ended up saving a lot of money and now I'm a centaur!" He laughed. "Go figure."

I smiled. "I'm glad it's paid off," I said, enjoying my drink.

"It has," he said. "I love where I am, and I love what I am. And I hope I spend my immortal days together with you drinking and fighting and fucking." He finished his drink and signalled for another. "But you and I have a problem and we need to talk about it and get it solved."

I was confused and crossed my arms before my big chest. "I don't have a problem with you," I said.

"No, I have a problem with you!"

The bartender came over and took Cav's empty glass, replacing it with a fresh one and then dropped two more Ouzo shots before us. Cav picked his up and handed me mine. "*Euoi euan,*" he said. We clinked glasses, tapped them on the bar, and downed the shots.

"Now, what are you talking about?" I asked, dropping the empty glass on the bar. "What problem do you have with me?"

"I got a text from Pokey this morning. He said that you made a new centaur."

I nodded silently. "Yeah…" I confessed quietly. "I hope Pokey took the time to explain how it happened…?"

"Oh, no -- he sent videos. I saw the whole thing. The guy's hot -- it's not that." He sipped his drink. "You and I had an agreement and my understanding of that agreement was that I was Herd Master. Yes?"

My instinct was to be defensive, which I knew was a mistake with someone as sharp as Cavalier. "Yes," I said simply. "I thought about notifying you at the time, but honestly, the moment was upon us…"

"Right, I understand about 'the moment' being upon you, but I want to go back to that first phrase, where you said, 'I thought about notifying you…' See, the inference there is you knew you were doing something wrong, but you went ahead and did it anyway, prepared to blame 'the moment' instead of taking responsibility and living up to your agreement with me and your word."

I took a big gulp of my martini and sighed, saying, "Harsh." I allowed a moment of silence between us, then I quietly said, "It wasn't my intent to disrespect you, Cav."

"Maybe not," he said, finishing his drink. "But you did." He signalled to the bartender for another round, making a smooth circular motion with his finger then giving her the thumbs up. Then he turned back to me. "So, how are we gonna make this better between us?"

"Cav, I'm really sorry, man. Honestly, I didn't mean…"

I held up his hand flat to me and shook his head. "It's over -- it's forgiven," he said. "What I wanna know is, what are we gonna do to make sure it doesn't happen again? I don't want any more surprises."

I sighed and dropped my head.

"What?"

"Let's have the shots, first."

****

So I told him what happened with AppleJack. ("Wait," he interrupted. "That fat straight-boy you live with? The one who was so rude to us?") I didn't hide any of the details -- I didn't try to make myself a victim, or a tragic hero, just point-to-point narration -- this was what happened.

"So the guy raped you," he said, sipping at his drink. "At least, slipped you a roofie…"

"I'm not sure I'd use those words, exactly," I said. "We'd agreed to try."

"Why did you agree to try? Let me understand that, first."

I nursed my second martini -- it was nearly gone. "We've been friends our whole lives," I said. "There's a lot of history there. I owed it to him to try…"

"Why?"

"See, here's the thing: you've been beautiful your whole life. You were athletic and popular growing up -- you had a great body and a crazy dick -- you've earned what you've gotten, don't get me wrong -- but you've never known anything else. Not quite a year ago, I was barely six-feet tall and a scrawny one-ninety -- a guy like you would've overlooked me without even noticing I was there. The only person in my corner was that fat straight-boy, you know?

"Then I drink a magic potion and suddenly I'm six-five, nearly three-hundred pounds of muscle and hung like a fuckin' horse, but my best friend is still the same fat straight-boy. What do I do, leave him behind? Cast him off? That'd be pretty shallow of me, wouldn't it? I'm a demigod and I'm turning all these other guys into demigods, but not you, best friend of nearly thirty years! You get nothing for your investment in me!"

"Still," Cav said, putting his empty glass on the bar, "I don't like the way he handled it. He and I are gonna have a conversation about that. You want another?"

"No, I'm feeling kind of toasty right now -- it's been a while since I've had THIS many -- what do you mean, 'conversation about that'?"

He smirked, playing with the ice in his empty glass -- he signalled "check" to the bartender. "Well, again, I'm the Herd Master and he's part of the herd -- unless he gets some special pass on that, too?"

I shook my head, wondering where he was going.

"Then he needs to learn some respect -- and I'm gonna teach it to him." He turned his attention to the bartender. "No, no," he said when she offered the bill -- he pulled his black Amex out of his wallet. "Use this."

When he saw me smiling, he said, "What?" defensively.

"Nothing," I said, brushing him away. "Just glad to see someone paying for stuff for a change."

He chuckled. "I leave great tips," he said. "Watch." The bartender came back and handed him the bill folder to him. When they made physical contact, Cav leaned forward and whispered in her ear. Suddenly, she breathed in deeply and shuddered, losing her balance and falling slightly against the bar. She couldn't help herself, moaning as a second orgasm went through her.

Cav stepped back, a knowing smile aimed at her. When she made eye contact with him, even I could see the lust and desire there -- even Cav's dick was starting to plump up. Cav turned to me and winked, gesturing for me to follow.

"Thank you," the bartender said breathlessly after us.

Walking through the lobby of the Four Seasons, I could feel everyone's eyes on us, these two incredible specimens of manhood. I forgot how much I fucking loved it -- how it energized me.

"One last thing," Cav said, as we walked toward the private elevators on the back side, "I think you owe me a blind pick."

"What? What do you mean?"

"I mean, you've let two guys into the herd without consulting me and to make that up to me, you're gonna give me a blind pick. I get whoever I want, no questions asked. What do you think? Then we're square and I can work on molding this team into what they need to be."

"Wait -- 'what they need to be'? What are you talking about?"

"That, my friend, is our next conversation." The elevator arrived -- he pulled out his special access key. "I got my client. Do you wanna join? This guy's an actual movie star -- an Avenger!" Cav winked at me and playfully bit the end of his tongue. "Come play -- what are you gonna do instead, sit home, get stoned, and watch TVLand? Isn't that a little too civilized? Does that sound like something a centaur would do?"

"Well, when you shame me like that…"

Smiling, I stepped into the elevator with him. We made out the entire ride to the penthouse, kissing, but trying not to wrinkle each other's shirts.

Then we got worshipped by the God of Thunder… but I signed an NDA, and even that's more than I can say about that. We'd joked about transforming him -- he'd be gorgeous as a beast -- but ultimately decided he'd be too high profile.

Cav said he had somebody better.

****

AppleJack laughed out loud -- literally -- when Cavalier first used the term "Herd Master."

"Are you kidding?" he snickered. "Dude… I'm not into roleplay."

"Excuse me?"

"The Pholus-thing, the centaur angle -- it's all marketing bullshit." AppleJack pointed to me, casually loading the bong. "Red drank a magic potion, yes, but it turned him into a Hypermasculine Superstud, not a horse. Now he's found a way to do the same thing to us -- and not a one of us is really a horse! Except maybe our cocks…"

His joke didn't land, but that didn't deter him.

"I'm totally not looking to be a part of your little club." AppleJack offered the bong to Cav, who silently took it. "My interest in this was purely selfish and physical -- I wanted the body and I wanted the cock. That's as far as I go with being a centaur."

Cavalier had insisted on coming home with me to confront AppleJack. We'd just finished up with his client -- where I got to growl "Hulk Suck Cock" in an impassioned way -- and it was barely 10pm. "Do you suppose your housemate is up?" Cav had asked in the elevator from the penthouse -- he'd left his shirt untucked.

I'd laughed. "He's a computer programmer. He just GOT up! He's probably playing Warcraft even as we speak."

He'd nodded, thinking. "Good," Cav had concluded. "I wanna talk to him."

Apparently, the doormen had seen him coming and had his car waiting for him -- a Porsche 911 Turbo, silver-white with a black interior. He'd handed the guy who'd opened his car door a hundred. "Thank you, Mr. Costin," the guy'd sung, making sure to politely shut the door. "See you soon!"

"They all know who I am," Cav had confessed. "They all know who I am and they all know what I do for a living and instead of judging me, they scramble to open my car door for me. They respect me. Your boy AppleJack will respect me, too."

But it didn't seem like AppleJack shared that view. The entire time Cav had the bong, taking the hit and holding it, he didn't break eye-contact with AppleJack. Then, after exhaling a huge cloud, he spoke calmly. "You say you don't want to be part of our little club, but you sure forced your way in." He handed the bong back. "Maybe you should've learned what you were getting involved with before you raped your best friend."

"Whoa, whoa, whoa there, pony," AppleJack said. "You don't get to talk to me like that, smoking my weed, not in my own house."

Cav remained calm. "This isn't your house," he said. "Keep it honest. It's HIS house -- you rent a room from him."

"Oh, so this is where I get judged by the porn star? Are you fucking kidding me?"

"No," Cav said, leaning forward, not increasing volume, but increasing intensity. "This is where you're judged by your Herd Master and punished for your disrespect."

AppleJack laughed again. "I don't know who you think you are, dude, but I'm pretty much fucking done with you thinking you're better than me."

Cavalier inhaled deeply and slowly, controlling himself, then he turned to me. "Get the wine, Red," he said. "It's time to open this fool's eyes."

I started to question him, but he cut me off with such a look that all I could do was obey -- he was Herd Master. Here he was trying to make a point to AppleJack and I was the one showing bad behavior. Instead, I went quietly and got the wine from its hiding place in my room, then I got three brandy snifters from the cabinet.

When AppleJack saw me with the bottle, he was immediately suspicious. "What's going on?" he asked. "What are you doing with that stuff?"

Cav grunted. "I see you're respectful of the wine…"

Dryly, AppleJack responded, "I've seen what the wine can do…"

Cavalier smiled coldly. "You're about to see what I can do."

AppleJack looked at Cav in a way that showed me his fear for the first time. "No," he said, standing. "I think I'm done."

"Sit down, AppleJack."

AppleJack reached for his bag of pot. "Fuck you," he said.

Cav stood, putting him face-to-face with AppleJack. Height-wise, Cav had him by maybe an inch or two, but they were pound for pound pretty evenly matched, each around 235/ 240. Of course, there were significant differences between the way they carried that weight -- Cav was a ripped bodybuilder and AppleJack seemed ready for off-season rugby, beauty or the beast, but they weighed in the same. Not that AppleJack knew how to use that weight.

More, I don't think AppleJack had ever been in a confrontation in his life where he wasn't safe behind a computer screen and an avatar. He was clearly out of his league.

"SIT!" Cavalier commanded, absolute fury hidden behind his calm demeanor.

AppleJack sat.

Cav continued to stand, looking down at my humiliated housemate. "Now, we're gonna do this the easy way or the hard way, but we are gonna do this. I am the Herd Master and you, you disrespectful motherfucker, you will learn your place. Pour the wine, Red."

I uncorked the bottle, immediately aware of the scent -- so were Cav and AppleJack, who'd never smelled it with his centaur senses. He immediately reacted. As I started to pour the third snifter, Cav said, "No -- not you, Red. This is just gonna be the two of us, him and me."

I knew now was not the time to be questioning him, so I merely restopped the bottle and held the snifters.

"You just gonna obey him, Red?" asked AppleJack from his chair, angry and hurt. "Just gonna do what the porn star says? Was his dick that good?"

Cavalier slapped AppleJack then, hard across the mouth -- AppleJack nearly fell out of the chair. Cav shook his head. "Disrespectful."

"WHAT THE FUCK?" AppleJack yelled, holding his hands to his face. "You fuckin' HIT me! Lemme up -- I'm callin' the cops! What the fuck...?"

Cavalier slapped him again on the other side. "Disrespectful," Cav said. "Again."

"RED!?!" AppleJack looked to me like I was a lost ally -- he didn't understand.

I shook my head, holding the two snifters. "Drink the wine, AppleJack," I said. "He's right -- you need to know what you've gotten yourself into." I offered one glass to Cav, who took it, the other to AppleJack, who looked at me with a crushed, bruised expression, then knocked the snifter out of my hand, sending it sailing across the great room. The crystal crashed and shattered.

Cav shook his head. "Disrespectful. Again and again and again." He sighed. "Pour another, Red." I went to do just that, using the third glass I'd brought for me. Cavalier crowded AppleJack into the chair. "Now, listen... you will drink this if I have to force you to -- and I will. And you know I can. So just fuckin' do it. Take responsibility for what you've done and fuckin' man up."

Reluctantly, AppleJack reached up and took a glass -- the fear in his eyes was obvious.

"Sniff it," Cavalier ordered, bringing his own to his nose. "Do you smell that -- that scent? That's what magic smells like. That's your beast-self calling. You can't imagine what you've gotten yourself involved with."

Even in the depths of his fear, AppleJack had an obvious hardon.

Cavalier clinked glasses with him. *"Euoi euan,"* he said in toast to the satyrs. "Drink up."

Ultimately, curiously, helplessly, AppleJack raised the snifter to his lips and threw the wine back in one shot. He swished around in his mouth a little bit, tasting ecstasy, rolling his eyes, then he swallowed.

Cav meanwhile, drank his down and set the snifter on the table, an eager smile on his face as he faced AppleJack.

Sighing, I sat down in the other chair, and immediately realized I was sitting there alone.

AppleJack and Cavalier were gone.

I glanced around the Great Room, shocked. "Guys?" I asked, like maybe they were behind the couch, about to jump out at me. Cav's snifter was on the table where he'd left it -- AppleJack's was on the floor in front of his chair, like he'd dropped it.

They weren't in the kitchen, or hiding in AppleJack's room -- I felt like I was sneaking around in a horror movie, the tense sustanado of strings following my every move. They were nowhere to be found -- although the more I considered it, and tossed away the impossibility of it, the more I knew exactly what had happened and where they'd gone. I'd been there myself.

The Magic Realm wasn't just a shared dream -- it was a real place. Drinking the wine somehow transported us to that other place, or changed our perooption enough that we could experience it. Either way, that could only mean one thing:

We were really centaurs. We were really no-shit, back-in-reality centaurs.

And I was really Pholus reborn!

****

I woke the next morning on the sofa in the great room, the sun streaming in across my face, warm and comfortable, to the bubbly sound of someone taking a bong hit. I opened my eyes slightly, not terribly surprised to see AppleJack sitting there, exhaling smoke. "Hey," I said, rubbing the sleep from my eyes and sitting up.

He offered me the bong -- I waived it away -- not before coffee -- so he set about taking another hit himself.

We studied each other for a moment. It was still a little disconcerting to see AppleJack with his new body, all that muscle --

this was what it must've been like for him to see the changes I'd gone through. That body... and I still didn't find him sexy.

"So," I said, breaking the silence, "what kind of horse are you?"

He snorted, exhaling in a huff. "I'm an Appaloosa," he said, as if trying to hold back tears. "I'm golden brown with a spotted butt -- I'm BEAUTIFUL!" He broke down and wept then. "I'm sorry, Red. I'm so sorry!"

"No, buddy, it's okay..."

"No, it's NOT!" he said, falling forward out of his chair until he was on his knees at my feet. "All our lives, I've treated you like shit, just glommed on and taken advantage of you. And when I saw you become Pholus, I was so fucking jealous -- why you? What have you ever done to deserve a fate like that? You're the most unambitious person I've ever met in my life -- and then when I saw you could transform other guys, and you weren't picking me, I went a little crazy." His words caught in his throat -- he sobs continued. "I'm so sorry, Red!"

I couldn't think of what to say as he knelt there, crying against my knee, so I just stroked his hair.

"I promise you," he mumbled, "I will bring honor to your herd. I will transform our friendship as you have transformed me. I will make you proud... Pholus."

He made eye-contact with me and I saw the truth of his intention, so standing, I pulled him into a hug. "I love you, AppleJack," I said plainly. "You're my best friend."

I felt him nod against my shoulder. "I am," he said, still a little teary.

I could feel his cock getting hard against my hip. He tried to pull it away, but I wrapped my arm around his lower back and forced him back into position. "Don't," I murmured. "I don't mind."

We held the hug -- with his uncomfortable erection -- for nearly a minute. Then I kissed him gently on the forehead and said, "I'm gonna make coffee, then you're gonna tell me what happened with you and Cav."

"I promised him I wouldn't," AppleJack said, following me into the kitchen. "It's between me and the Herd Master. Is that okay?"

I nodded, smirking. "I guess I don't have much of a choice," I said. "I suddenly feel as unnecessary as royalty. How about you and I spend the day together working our basement farm? We haven't done that in a while."

He laughed. "The plants won't recognize us."

"So let's farm shirtless!"

8. "Gymnasium"

*The **Gymnasium** (Greek: γυμνάσιον) in Ancient Greece functioned as a training facility for competitors in public game(s). It was also a place for socializing and engaging in intellectual pursuits. The name comes from the Ancient Greek term gymnós meaning "naked". Only adult male citizens were allowed to use the gymnasia. Athletes competed nude, a practice which was said to encourage aesthetic appreciation of the male body, and to be a tribute to the gods. Gymnasia and palaestrae (wrestling schools) were under the protection and patronage of Heracles, Hermes and, in Athens, Theseus.*

****

@Cavalier:
HERD MEETING!
Saturday Night (Full Moon) @ Red's
- 7pm Socialize
  — meet the new meat/ have a glass of wine
- 8pm Forum
  — Agenda: Training/ Publicity Shoot/ Pride Float?
- 9pm Hunting

Please text confirmation. Thanks!

@PokeyDakota: Yee-ha! Can't wait! Should I wear something special or something that comes off easy?

@Dunn: Confirmed -- excited to meet everyone!

@AppleJack: Okay, only cuz it's at my house…

                                        @me: It's what I was reborn for...

@6092011964: Got it. Confirmed.

@PokeyDakota: Wait a minute 609… who are you?

@6092011964: This is Gambit.
@6092011964: I'll be teaching hand-to-hand combat
@6092011964: and weapons training.
@6092011964: I'm a buddy of Cav's.
@6092011964: Excited to make warriors out of you!

@Dunn: I'm even more confirmed than before! Haha.

@PokeyDakota: Are you hot?
@PokeyDakota: Or are you one of those guys
@PokeyDakota: who's taken too many hits to the face?

@6092011964: I'm hot.

@Cavalier: Can confirm -- he's definitely hot.

@PokeyDakota: Are you gay?

                                        @me: Pokey…

@PokeyDakota: I just wanna know...

@6092011964: Yeah, but probably not as gay as you.

@Cavalier: LOL

@Dunn: Hahahaha!

@AppleJack: <burn> I'm gonna like this guy.

@PokeyDakota: Screw all of you --
@PokeyDakota: You're lucky to have me!
@Pokey Dakota: I'm the sweet kid brother of the group.

@Dunn: And I'm the slutty sister.

@AppleJack: I'm the emotionally distant step-dad.

@6092011964: I see I have my work cut out for me.

@Cavalier: Okay, boys. I'm already over this group text.
@Cavalier: We'll see everybody on Saturday.
@Cavalier: Don't forget: the floor is open for nominations
@Cavalier: for our final core member.
@Cavalier: I want someone in place before Pride next month
@Cavalier: You know what I'm looking for

@6092011964: I got somebody. I'll drop you a DM.

@Cavalier: Awesome!

@Pokey: Is he as gay as you, 609?

@6092011964: Gayer…
@6092011964: But still not as far down the spectrum as you.

@Cavalier: All right -- enough!
@Cavalier: See you on the Full Moon, my warriors!

@AppleJack: Finally!

@PokeyDakota: Peace out, ya'll!
@PokeyDakota: Even you, 609

@Dunn: Anyone needs a haircut, cum see me.

@me: see you, guys!

****

On the Friday before the Full Moon, I showed up at a South Side gym that seemed to be some weird combination of dojo, rock-climbing, and American Ninja Warrior training facility. Everywhere were hoops and ramps and obstacles stacked on other obstacles, braced with mats and only accessible by swinging ropes and rock walls. It was like a gymnastics graveyard -- it was like the place you went when your sport was eliminated from the mainstream and you had to throw your equipment somewhere and you couldn't afford a trip to the dump.

There was a guy doing cleans in the far corner -- when he saw me in the reflection of the mirror he faced, he dropped the bar and headed over. If this was Gambit, then Cav wasn't kidding -- he was fucking gorgeous! I'd put him at six-three, six-four -- just a bit shorter than me -- maybe two-hundred thirty muscular pounds. He was hour-glass shaped -- tight in the waist, but blowing up into colossally wide shoulders with arms that could either tear your head off or hold you securely (depending on his mood) and thighs that would be the envy of any professional rugby player on the planet. He was shirtless, wearing only a pair of spandex fight shorts with a pair of chess-piece knights (one white, one black) over the crotch, socks and flip-flops, a sweat towel around his neck, adding to the illusion that his neck was thicker than his head. He wasn't hurting in the crotch department, either. (And that's coming from me!) Both arms were covered in tat sleeves and he had a giant "GAMBIT" in Olde English across the base of his traps, the same white knight chess-piece on his left shoulder blade and the black knight on his right.

He was handsome in a totally masculine kind of way: sharp, square jawline and a strong, clearly broken nose. Dark Brown eyes, heavy, sculpted brows, each pierced with three hoops. His facial hair was a day's growth away from a beard, featuring a thick mustache that could be a Fu Manchu if he seemed to be trying, which he didn't. The hair on his head was buzzed to the same length as his nearly-beard, but he sported a tiny mohawk -- a cock comb -- across the top of his head, his ears pierced with black discs. He looked like the playground's ten-year-old bully grown to manhood.

"You gotta be Red," he said, putting his hands together in front of his heart and slightly bowing. "Or do you prefer Pholus?"

"Red's fine," I said, transferring my gym bag to my left hand so we could shake. "You must be Gambit -- you an X-Men fan?"

We shook -- firm grip, no testing. "Sure," he said. "Though I think I've made the name my own."

"This your gym?"

He shrugged, looking around as he spoke. "Nah," he said. "It's owned by a bunch of guys -- rock climbers, Ninja Warriors -- they're never around in the daytime. They just let me train here."

"That's cool."

Again, the little shrug. "Ah, it's a shithole, but it doesn't cost me anything. C'mon back." We started walking toward his cross-fit platform -- one side was all weights and bars and gadgets, the other was an open, matted area. "It's not often I get to train with a guy taller than me," he said quietly as we stepped onto the mats. "Throw your shit there."

I did -- I dropped my bag and took off my hoodie. "You should know," I said, "despite my build, I'm no athlete. I didn't exactly earn this body -- I drank a magic potion. I'm just sayin'."

Gambit smirked. "Yeah, Cav said. But I'm here to teach you how to use it, not build it. Take your shirt off." I did. He nodded slightly. "Nice -- good pecs. Great abs. Shoes and socks, too. What are you wearing under your dress there?"

My gym shorts? Yeah, they were baggy enough that if they were plaid, they could be mistaken for a kilt -- I got his joke -- but I wore them for a reason. "Compression shorts," I said, "nothing fancy like yours."

That smirk -- it promised devilry -- "Take 'em off -- I don't wrestle guys in dresses." When I did, he whistled in an impressed way. "Damn. The cock's amazing, but your balls are HUGE! Cav wasn't kidding. We're gonna have to learn how to work with those things!"

We met at the center of the mat, face to face -- I was a good two inches taller and at least fifty pounds heavier, but there was no question about who was the better athlete. The Alpha Man.

"Down to the mats," he said, dropping himself. "This is what you're gonna do: get your body into a tight little ball and just roll around. I don't want you to land, or be flat on your back, or stop motion, or flop over or whatever." He did it next to me, bringing his knees up to his chest and wrapping his arms around them -- I mirrored him and we started rolling on our backs. "Don't straighten your spine," he said. "No flat-back. Always curve and roll."

I felt like I was in Primary School PE, learning to somersault and log roll -- it was silly and fun.

"The secret to wrestling is always rolling, never being flat to the mat." He was on his knees beside me, rolling me around like a ball -- he was playful, then he tapped me twice on the lower back with his open palm. "Up to your knees." I uncurled and knelt facing him. With one hand, he grabbed the back of my neck and brought me forward until our foreheads touched. "What I just did there -- I tapped you." With his free hand, he double-tapped the side of my hip. "In wrestling or grappling, that means STOP -- it often means surrender

-- so when someone taps you or taps the mat, you release IMMEDIATELY. Respect the tap and no one gets hurt. You've learned the first two rules of wrestling, Red. What are they?"

"The secret to wrestling is rolling and always respect the tap."

"Good," he said. "You're doing well for a guy who hasn't earned his body."

I snorted. "Asshole," I said, smirking.

That little shrug. "You probably shouldn't have told me that, then, cuz I'm gonna use it against you now that I see it bugs you. C'mon, we're gonna roll together -- same idea, though. I want you to follow the motion -- if you feel it going one way, go with it that way -- don't fight it. I want you to feel me, feel where I'm going, feel my weight change. Okay?"

"Okay."

We went to the mats. Still holding the base of my neck with one hand, he rested his head in the crook of my neck on the other side, wrapping his substantial legs around my waist -- I mirrored him as best I could, tucking my legs between us. We began rolling around the mat together, a big human ball. It was wonderfully simple and erotic and evocative of a past memory, hazy and long forgotten, learning to wrestle as a youth, with an older, muscular, white-bearded man -- sucking him off in gratitude for the lesson -- my *Erastês*...

When Gambit and I broke, my dick wasn't exactly hard, but it was interested -- his was the same way.

"Whatever the fuck smell you guys put out," he said, adjusting his cock, "it drives me fuckin' crazy. I just want to bury my head in your pit and lick it clean, you know? Jesus! Am I gonna smell like that? You know, after...?"

I nodded. "Yeah," I said. "We've all got it."

"Then can we do this thing? Can we get through the transformation first and then wrestle? I mean, right now I'm barely able to think, much less teach. And I don't want this lesson to be just foreplay -- I'm actually looking to teach you to grapple. But it ain't gonna happen if I just wanna fuck you."

"I like you, Gambit -- you're all business."

He smirked. "Liking me has nothing to do with business. You gotta learn to keep your mouth shut and keep your feelings to yourself."

"All right, all business," I said, pulling down my compression shorts. "You gonna fuck me here on the mat or you wanna hit it in the locker room?"

Gambit smiled. "Good answer, Red," he said. "I think I'm gonna be able to learn you a lot."

I hit him with a big wave of pheromones as I lowered his shorts -- his cock came springing out, beautifully long and straight, like a ski slope, nearly nine inches with a cone-shaped glans, pierced with a very large PA. "Damn," I said.

"Just get it wet," he said, brushing the tip across my lips. "I don't need your compliments."

I grabbed it around the base and spit on it, cause that's what I felt like doing, spitting on him. Then I got busy on his glans, taking the head in my mouth and soaking it with my tongue. I'd only barely started on the shaft when he put his hand behind my head and pushed himself all the way in, tickling the back of my throat in a way that would've gagged the old me, but excited the new. I could feel the heavy metal of his PA as I gently squeezed my throat around him.

"Show off," he said. "This is business, not pleasure -- just get it wet."

His gruff bluntness was a weird turn-on for me -- I'd always been a passive guy, for sure, but never submissive. It was strange enough that all these guys had to fuck me to join my herd -- I would've rather been biblical and simply washed their feet -- but now Gambit was challenging my beliefs about being a top at all, even a passive one. Something about Gambit's attitude had my juices flowing.

"That's enough -- get on your hands and knees."

I did, releasing his cock and letting it slowly roll out of my mouth, soaked with my spit. I spun around, presenting my ass to him. He stuck his thumb in his mouth then pushed it into my hole. "Open up," he said. "Relax." He was stretching my hole with his thumb, dropping a long line of spit down onto it, getting ready to press his ring through. "You're gonna like this," he said. "Just gotta let me in, Red."

I couldn't help but moan -- he was so rough.

"You're giving yourself away," he said. "Now I know you're ready..."

He shoved his cock boldly in, balls-deep in seconds, his nearly-nine nearly filling me -- had I NOT been a rutty demigod, it might've done more than surprise me. As it was, he seemed glad at my abilities. "No need to hold back," he said. "I learned that with Cav."

He just got to work, pounding deeper and deeper. This was only the second guy who'd fucked me with a PA and I loved the way it smacked its weight against my prostate. Intense or not, Gambit was hitting all the right internal buttons.

He was as unapologetic and powerful in his fuck as he was in everything else, walking a fine line between too much and ecstasy -- Gambit remained impassive. He just fucked like a piston, selfish enough to think his pleasure gave me mine. Unfortunately, in this case he was right.

He didn't really take any breaks, though he varied his pace from time to time, chasing whatever lustful spark that would lead to his orgasm. He slapped my big, muscular ass with his open palm. "Gonna cum," he said. "Get ready with the magic."

As it had with Pokey, and Cav, and Dunn, and AppleJack, his orgasm triggered mine and the magic flowed out -- I felt it penetrate and change him, even as I faced the floor, looking at the puddle of my own cum.

"I feel it," he said. "Fuckin' yeah, I feel it!"

As before with the others, I could feel him grow while inside me -- I knew exactly what was happening to him.

He pulled out, standing, turning to face the mirrors. "Fuck yeah," he growled. "Now we're getting someplace." I stood up next to him, smiling, and he did a Most Muscular in my face -- I did one back in his.

Unlike most of the other centaurs, Gambit didn't just lean out -- he put on some serious muscle. Size-wise, Gambit was now second-only to me -- only two inches shorter, only twenty pounds lighter -- but he looked significantly more intimidating. I looked approachable -- Gambit looked dangerous. His cock hung two-thirds of the way down his thigh in that same unforgiving arch. He was gonna need a bigger ring.

We flexed together in the mirrors -- standard poses, playful poses -- lots of getting in each other's faces. "I can't even tell you how great I feel," he said, a smile barely breaking his facade. "I feel like I'm on coke mixed with super-steroids mixed with trimix! No wonder Cav raves about this."

I snorted. "You wanna fuck or you wanna talk?"

A sly smile crept onto his face. "You can fuck me when you can pin me," he said. "So let's roll..."

We locked a hand behind each other's neck and started circling, looking for a take down, naked as proper Greek wrestlers should be, sweaty and semi-hard -- the battle bulge -- like men seeking dominance. Gambit lunged and easily grabbed my leg behind the knee and pulled me off balance. We went to the mats, my body slamming loudly on the ground.

My body was learning as we went along -- I was becoming a better wrestler with each move he used. My body would learn it, understand it, counter it -- all on instinct alone. I was loving this physical freedom!

We were both so involved with our match, we didn't realize someone was standing there watching until we almost rolled over him. A tall guy, long and lean, ripped to the bone, his blond, over-treated hair piled on top of his head in a sloppy man-bun, matching fuzz on his chin. When he realized we'd become aware of him, he stopped recording and put his phone away.

He could easily be Pokey's older brother, except for the beakish nose. He wore cargo shorts, a muscle shirt, and climbing shoes -- WAY too much hemp-based jewelry. At least he didn't have any ink.

"Lickety," Gambit said, holding me to the mat while he spoke. "Glad you made it."

The guy laughed, a big bray. "Dude, this is some real ancient Greek shit you got going on here -- naked wrestling? Can I tag in?"

"Absolutely!"

That laugh again, then the guy started enthusiastically pulling off his clothes. He had a great body, ectomorph or not, and it made me think back to when I was this skinny/ fat nothing and wondered why I never trained harder. I had to drink a magic potion to make something out of myself.

Gambit released me, which allowed me to come up off the mat -- I sat on my heels next to him. "Red, this is one of the owners of the gym -- this is Lickety Split..." A look of admonishment from the guy and Gambit continued, smirking. "I mean, the Infamous Lickety Split, who will be competing in the finals of American Ninja Warrior later this summer!"

"Congratulations," I said to the guy as he pulled down his shorts.

"Thanks, dude," he said, exposing his cock -- a nice piece of meat, long and lean, like him, but he had some really big balls, too. "Red, right?"

I felt a wave of pheromones come off Gambit, untrained -- very strong -- and Lickety Split moaned, "What the fuck, dude?" and fell to his knees, his cock instantly beginning to harden.

"That's cool," said Gambit. He did it again, this time with more accuracy. "I see how to do it."

Lickety Split started stroking his cock. "Dude, what are you doing to me? That smell..."

"Just stroke yourself, Lickety, think about how hot you feel and don't pay attention to our conversation for a few minutes, okay?"

Fap, fap, fap -- "Sure, dude."

Gambit turned to me, indicating Lickety Split with his thumb. "So, this is the last candidate."

"What do you mean 'last candidate' -- for the herd?"

Gambit nodded. "Yeah. He's what I want -- he's super-fast, he's agile, he can think his way through an obstacle, and he has absolutely no fear. He's everything we need."

"Maybe," I said. "Have you talked to Cav about this?"

Gambit shrugged slightly, giving me a look like "duh". "Yeah," he said. "Days ago. Cav said bring him in today. I think I timed the whole thing out pretty damn good!"

"He didn't say anything to me about it."

He held up his palm flat to me, like he was taking an oath. "I promise, Red -- he cleared it."

"Do you mind if I text him?" I asked. "Not because I don't believe you, but because this is starting to feel like a test to me."

"A test?"

I rolled my eyes. "I promised Cav I wouldn't create anymore centaurs without telling him, that's all. I feel like I gave him my word."

He nodded. "THAT I understand. All right, have fun." He looked at the enthusiastically masturbating Lickety. "I'll keep myself entertained."

****

@me: Hey, Herd Master!

@Cavalier: Pholus! I was hoping I was gonna hear from you today!

@me: Then this IS a test.

@Cavalier: Of course it's a test!
@Cavalier: Have we met?
@Cavalier: Are you finally starting to understand me?

@me: I passed?

@Cavalier: You did indeed.
@Cavalier: Thank you, Red.
@Cavalier: What do you think of Lickety Split?

@me: He could be Pokey's older brother!
@me: Lots of fearless energy...

@Cavalier; Glad you approve.
@Cavalier: OK, boss, see you tomorrow night!
@Cavalier: Have fun with the boys…

****

Back at the center of the mats, Gambit was on his knees, flexing his biceps as Lickety Split licked his sweaty armpit. The long, flat tongue of a guy looking to suck the color from a shag carpet, Lickety lapped like a dog. He slid under Gambit's pec and took the whole tiny nipple in his mouth, roughly nursing. Gambit grabbed the back of his head and forced him to take more -- he was nearly suffocating in the mass of Gambit's pec, but he loved it.

As I approached, I knelt next to Gambit and hit the boy with a subtle wave, just to get his attention. Lickety leaned over like a lost little lamb and helplessly buried his nose between my pecs. Gambit snapped his fingers, getting Lickety's attention, and flexed his bicep for him -- Lickety went to it like a fish to a lure. Grabbing the mass of it and worshipping -- Lickety's cock was hippety-hard..

Just to be an asshole, I made the same move -- I snapped my fingers before Lickety's face and flexed my own bicep for him. Lickety fell on it like he'd never seen one before.

I smiled at Gambit -- he knew the game.

Within a minute we were standing face to face, with poor Lickety crushed between us. We were flexing our pecs for each other as Lickety slid down our sweaty torsos until he knelt there and sucked our cocks, one in each hand. He worked mine for a minute, swallowing it as deep as he could, while he masturbated Gambit -- then he'd switch, gagging on Gambit's weighty PA. I was afraid Gambit was gonna chip the guy's tooth, he was pounding Lickety's mouth so hard.

Lickety was so turned on -- so far beyond rock hard that his dick looked like it was gonna explode at any second. He was so deep gone on Gambit's pheromones that he didn't know what end was up -- or what end he wanted up.

Lickety Split was ready to cum -- he had to. We could all feel it -- he just needed to know where.

Without waiting, I took him to the ground, his back slamming into the mat, then I squatted on Lickety Split's cock, just in time to catch his load, which, for whatever reason, triggered my own unmotivated orgasm, spraying all over Lickety's pecs.

He screamed, arching his back beneath me as I felt the power leave me and enter him, changing him.

"I felt that," said Gambit. "I felt that happen."

"So did he," I said as we watched Lickety Split morph beneath me into a lean, muscled superhero instead of a skinny rock-climber.

Lickety Split threw off the effects of the pheromones within a minute or so, regaining his composure and his wits. Like Gambit -- like all of us, frankly -- he was delighted by the changes in his body, the growth of muscle, the ampleness of cock.

Flexing in the mirror, he laughed. "Dudes, let's see what these new bodies can do."

We did the ramp wall first, easily beating the fourteen-footer, and then twenty-footer, me and Gambit scrambling up the side like we didn't weigh nearly three hundred pounds each. We vaulted and climbed and swung on ropes and did press-ups, scaled walls, cleaned huge weights and had a hanging sit-up competition, which Lickety easily won. I'd never experienced movement in this way before -- I never felt so free and confident, so strong and able. I felt like Captain America, or Spider-Man, or… Gambit.

"Oh, man, I can't WAIT to get into the ring with some clown and tear him up," Gambit said, flexing in our faces. "I feel fucking amazing!"

Lickety raced up the rockwall on the far side of the mats, moving with ease across the ceiling -- he made a breath-taking leap over to a retaining column, catching it like Tarzan on a coconut tree, feet first. "Look at this crazy shit," he said, dropping with a front flip to the mats in front of us. "I'm fucking Spawn!"

I smiled. "It doesn't wear off," I said. "This level of energy you feel right now is the norm -- this level of horniness you feel right now is the norm. My dick pretty much stays hard twenty-four-seven -- *nonischemic priapism* they call it. Get used to that."

Gambit held his arms out to his sides, his beautiful nudity on display. "Get used to being this?" he asked. "Why would I ever want to get used to being this? This is to be celebrated every moment of every day. I'm gonna fuck my way through the world and dominate those who stand against me -- stand against you -- US!" He knelt on one knee before me. "I'm your knight, Pholus. And I will make our herd a fighting force worthy of your name. This I swear."

Lickety Split danced around the mat. "I wanna make an oath, too!" he said. "What do I get to be?"

"You're his scout, his fleet-footed messenger, his spy, your speed and your loyalty are your gifts to him and your herd."

Lickety smiled and dropped to his knee. "I'm that," he said. "I'm anything you want! I'm yours. This I swear!"

And there on the mats, the real fucking lasted until the moon had well risen. And I felt content and strangely complete.

9. "Heracles"

***Heracles** (/ˈhɛrəkliːz/ HERR-ə-kleez; Greek: Ἡρακλῆς, Hēraklês, Glory/Pride of Hēra, "Hera"), was a divine hero in Greek mythology. Trained in the arts and the arts of war by the civilized centaur Chiron, he was the greatest of the Greek heroes, a paragon of masculinity, and a champion of the Olympian order against chthonic monsters. Heracles slew the centaurs after they attacked him in Pholus' cave, drunk on Dionysian Wine. His iconographic attributes are the lion skin and the club.*

****

The caterer showed up around 4:30pm on Saturday, the day of the full moon, to set up, surprising AppleJack, who was in his underwear doing bong hits in the great room, casually jerking off while watching baseball on the flat-screen TV. Like most straight guys, he still lacked any kind of style or panache with his undergarments -- boring boxer briefs in seemingly endless supply. I was happy to see him have more freedom and confidence with his physical body, but what good was having a great dick if you packaged it so poorly? (He needed a fairy godmother... maybe Dunn could help him out?)

Anyway, the caterer (the chef -- Adrian) and his assistant (Mahmood, maybe? -- I didn't quite catch it) brought their load into the kitchen and then got to work while AppleJack went to hide in his room -- they seemed friendly, but driven, always acting like they were behind.

@me: Caterers, too? Fancy...

@Cavalier: Did Adrian get there? He's amazing!
@Cavalier: We're gonna eat like the gods we now are!

@me: I was expecting some snacks
@me: Maybe a charcuterie plate...?

@Cavalier: Centaurs are not grazers.
@Cavalier: It's a night of Fellowship! That means meat.
@Cavalier: I worry about you sometimes.
@Cavalier: What did you think of Gambit?
@Cavalier: He said he had a good time.

@me: I'm surprised by how much I like him!
@me: He makes you look humble!

@Cavalier: He said his dick is amazing now.

@me: Can confirm.
@me: You got a little man-crush on him?

@Cavalier: Who doesn't?
@Cavalier: HE'S got a man-crush on him!

@me: He owes me his ass.

@Cavalier: You'll never take it.
@Cavalier: No one has.
@Cavalier: Ever.
@Cavalier: Not even me --
@Cavalier: (and I used my super powers!)

@me: Challenge accepted.

@Cavalier: Yeah, you...
@Cavalier: The most passive top ever.
@Cavalier: Good luck, my friend.
@Cavalier: I'll be over around 6 or so
@Cavalier: Wanna smoke some of that good bud
@Cavalier: before the rabble arrives
@Cavalier: See you soon.

@me: Peace, my friend.

I felt like a teenage girl with wardrobe anxiety -- what should I wear?

It was an evening with the boys, for fuck's sake, what difference did it make to me, the freakin' Daddy God to all these ponies? Yet here I was, going through every shirt in my closet like it mattered which one they tore off me.

I ended up in one of AppleJack's stupid Brand Wear t-shirts, heather gray with the words PHOLUS REBORN in carved marble letters across the chest -- it made my pecs look amazing! Besides, cheeky or not, it finished this stressful moment. I wore a custom jockstrap beneath a pair of stretch jeans shorts, rolled part of the way up my thighs, showing the base of my quads, the impossible mass of my bulge -- barefoot otherwise.

Downstairs, I did a bong hit with AppleJack, who wore the same sloppy sweatpants he always wore and a brown, ill-fitting t-shirt from before his transformation (now tight in the pecs and shoulders, loose in the gut) which sported a computer power logo on the front, then I went to finish setting the table. As was his knack, Cavalier showed up just as the work was ending.

"Hail, Pholus," he said, hugging me. He wore a simple cotton pullover and a pair of gray dress shorts, belted by Gucci, but a different pair of loafers -- a huge, ostentatious Rolex.

"Hail, Cavalier," I echoed and we kissed each other's cheek. "Quite a thing you got goin' on here tonight."

He made a surrendering, what-can-I-do gesture. "It's fellowship," he said, passing me and heading to the kitchen. "It's the first time we're all together -- that merits a celebration!" Passing through the great room, Cav said, "Hail, AppleJack," who replied by flying the peace sign back, so he didn't have to release his hit.

"He needs a stylist," Cav said to me, under his breath. "Let's see if Dunn can whip him into shape."

"Ha! I was thinking the same thing!"

Then he was in the kitchen and he and Chef Adrian greeted each other like lost friends from the old neighborhood. It was a whole lotta "How's your mama?" and "Look at you!" and "Whatever happened to..?" -- old friends resparking. Chef Adrian talked through the menu, letting Cav and me sniff things and taste. He'd also opened a bottle of wine for us -- a South-African cabernet -- and we each toted a glass into the great room.

"He's fucking amazing," Cav said to me. "You talk about you and AppleJack being friends your whole life -- I've known that guy since we were both in middle school." He laughed as we sat on the sofa. "Hey, AppleJack, you gonna load me one of those?"

"My pleasure," AppleJack said, handing Cav the bong.

As AppleJack did, Cav gave him the up-and-down. "That what you're wearing?" Cav asked, taking his hit.

I was happy to see AppleJack was his usual, defensive self. "Why?" he asked. "You want me to put on pants?"

Cav raised an eyebrow and released the hit. "It's a dinner party, friend," he said. "Show some class."

Huffing, AppleJack strode toward his bedroom -- but he didn't say anything.

"How'd you do that?" I asked, taking the bong from Cav.

"Do what?"

"Get him to do what you wanted without bitching…?"

Cav looked toward AppleJack's bedroom, then back to me. "We have an understanding," he said, winking. "Take your hit."

Pokey -- Dunn in tow -- was the first to arrive, officially. "He didn't know where he was going," Pokey said, indicating Dunn with his thumb, "so I reckon I showed him the way."

"It wasn't that hard to find," Dunn said, hugging me. "He just wanted to ride around in my truck and suck my dick." Dunn freeballed beneath a pair of gray casual slacks and sandals. A v-neck sleeveless thermal shirt with a gray vest over it, his many statement necklaces, bracelets and rings -- Dunn wore so much silver, you could melt him down and make a fine tea set from him. His black and white beard was meticulously groomed and oiled -- his hair slicked back on top, shaved on the sides, yet a strand or two still fell into his face. His septum ring and his earrings were the same size heavy hoops.

Pokey, on the other hand, wore his usual straight-leg, pegged jeans so low on his hips that his oversized rodeo buckle rode the base of his dick like a bucking bronc, the cowboy boots he seemed to never take off and a bright blue t-shirt -- the same color as his hair -- with a white, sparkly unicorn on the front. I'd forgotten that Dunn had pierced Pokey's septum -- it was actually pretty sexy on the boy.

It was the first meeting between Dunn and Cavalier and they hugged like they'd known each other their whole lives, as well. "The Herd Master," Dunn said, smiling. "Finally -- I've been having such fantasies. I'm a big fan of your work."

"Thank you," Cav said. "It's a little something I do. You should film with me."

"Right now?" Dunn mocked. "I'd love to, but I don't have my good harness on."

Cav chuckled. "Maybe after a glass of wine…"

We took them into the kitchen and the Chef's Assistant (Mahmood, I think?) got them drinks before we sat in the great room, where AppleJack was back at smoking -- he'd changed from his sweats into a pair of tan cargo shorts with a cheap webbed belt. "I thought I smelled weed," Dunn said, reaching into his vest pocket. "I brought a couple joints with me in case anyone smoked." He dropped them on the coffee table, big phat things. "I've been at gay parties where nobody smokes but me -- it's depressing."

"Let me introduce you guys to AppleJack, he's the brains behind the tech stuff and the hydroponic grow we've got going on downstairs."

AppleJack waved sarcastically.

"Well, I'll be dipped in shit," said Pokey excitedly. "Look at you, AppleJack! Why, the last time I seen you I reckon you were a pork-pie rolled in pig grease! Damn, boy! Pull that shirt up -- let's see what AppleJack the Centaur looks like!"

He acted embarrassed, but it was easy to see AppleJack's pride and excitement to be in this moment with the guys -- he stood, lifting his shirt and showing his torso. Compared to the fat boy he used to be, AppleJack's body was amazing. He lacked the unbelievable definition that some of the others had, but his curves all worked together in a complimentary way.

The boys wolf-whistled and hollered -- AppleJack waved them off, but he did squeeze his basket seductively before sitting back down.

"You've got a good body," Cav said, grabbing the bong, "but you show it for shit. You're a stylist, Dunn. What do you think?" Cav hit the bong.

"Well, I just met you," Dunn said to AppleJack, taking the bong from Cav, "but I am a gay man, so, naturally, I'm going to critique you. And I'd start with that haircut. It makes you look like a lazy straight boy."

I snorted.

"What?"

AppleJack let Dunn take the hit, then said, "Well, I AM a lazy straight boy…"

"Oh, honey," Dunn said, exhaling. "I'm so sorry…"

Pokey sat on the arm of AppleJack's chair. "Wait," he said, "turning you into a centaur didn't turn you gay? Not even bi? Not even curious?"

AppleJack loaded a bowl for himself. "I'm always curious," he said. "I'm just not labeled."

"Have you fucked a woman since you became a centaur?"

"Pokey…"

"What?" he asked me sharply. "I wanna know. How come you always treat me like I'm a little kid?"

"Cuz sometimes you act like a little kid and I don't want your impulsiveness to get you in trouble." I took the bong from AppleJack and prepared my hit.

"I reckon me and my impulsiveness will be just fine, thank you." He made a sour face at me.

I blew Pokey a kiss and took my hit -- he rolled his eyes.

"To answer your question," AppleJack mumbled, looking down, "I haven't."

"What?"

He looked like he was struggling with his confession. "I haven't slept with a woman since I became a Centaur," AppleJack said. "But hey, it's cool, I haven't slept with a man, either. I've beat off five billion-fucking times in the last five days, but that's about all. Do you think it's my haircut?"

There was silence, until Dunn reached out and put his hand on AppleJack's knee. "I think it's okay to be whoever you are and desire whatever you want, sexually. I don't care who you fuck or how you fuck or if you fuck at all. I'm not gonna judge you or define you, honey -- I'm just gonna support you, okay?"

AppleJack was stunned -- there were very few people who'd ever said supportive words to him before, so he wasn't quite sure how to react. Finally, he said, "Okay."

Dunn slapped his knee and said, "Good -- but you do need a better haircut."

Everyone laughed -- even AppleJack.

That was when the doorbell rang, announcing our last arrivals. Cav and I walked to the door together, leaving the others behind to stare curiously from the sofa. "Look at you," I whispered to Cav. "You're giddy like a kiddy. You DO got it for this guy."

"Shut up," he said. "You don't know nothin'. Do I look okay?"

"Yeah, except that big zit on your forehead."

"What?" He started to reach for it, then realized I was joking. "Asshole."

And there was Gambit in all his glory, Lickety Split standing behind him, nearly blocked by Gambit's width. He was almost my size, so the two of us weren't gonna fit in the doorway together any time soon, but Cav hadn't seen him since his transformation, so he was mostly shocked. "Holy shit," he said, breathlessly. "You got it good!"

The corner of Gambit's mouth curled up. He wore a sleeveless plaid shirt over a pair of black jeans and sandals, showing the entirety of his tat sleeves. Like Dunn, he'd strapped leather gauntlets on his wrists which caused the veins in his arms to pop. The silly cock-comb across the top of his head was perky and inviting comment -- it was only a matter of time before Pokey said something.

Still, at six-three, two-seventy something, Gambit was naturally intimidating. Here I was yet again, bigger than him in literally every way, yet feeling smaller. I had to find out how he did that.

He and Cav did a "bro hug", shaking hands and hugging at the same time -- maybe Cav was just trying to avoid touching him? All good -- I'd be happy to do it for him. "I can't believe how fucking big you got," Cav said. "I'm fucking jealous."

Gambit smirked. "As it should be, Herd Master. And you remember Lickety Split?"

That same stare -- the same bit from last night. "I mean, the Infamous Lickety Split, who will be competing in the finals of American Ninja Warrior later this summer!"

Cav held his hand out to Lickety to shake. "I imagine you'll tear it up," he said. "Especially with your new abilities."

Lickety broke six feet -- his lean structure gave the illusion he was taller than that, the sloppy man-bun heightening it. He wore fitted cargo shorts, leather sandals, and a straw-colored three-quarter sleeved Henley that added to his bleached, left-out-in-the-sun-too-long look. Lickety Split ignored Cav's outstretched hand and hugged him instead. "Gonna kick some ass, Herd Master," he said, laughing that braying honk.

Meanwhile, Gambit turned to me and said, "Hail, Pholus!" before hugging me, wrapping his strong arms around me and pulling me close.

"Hail, Gambit," I said, squeezing him back. "No grappling tonight, tho -- I don't wanna get wrinkled."

"Whatever we do tonight, we're doing nude -- right, Cav?"

Cav sighed dramatically. "You read my mind."

"You said not to wear underwear..."

Cav laughed. "Come in. We got food and drink."

As Lickety and I hugged, he added, "And a fuckton of marijuana by the smell of it."

We stepped into the great room and since all eyes were on us anyway, Cav announced, "Guys, this is Gambit. He's a buddy of mine that I recruited to teach us self-defense and small-weapons tactics. He's your drill sergeant, so treat him nice or face the consequences."

Gambit smirked his usual smirk and nodded. "Guys."

"The guy next to him is Lickety Split…"

"Dude…!"

Cav was confused. "What?"

Gambit chuckled and said, "It's the Infamous Lickety Split, who will be competing in the finals of American Ninja Warrior later this summer! It's a dumb joke we do at the gym."

Cav gave Lickety Split the side eye. "I'm not doing the whole joke -- guys, this is the Infamous Lickety Split!"

"Happy to join you," Lickety said, making a B-line for the bong. "Are these for anybody?"

Cav continued to introduce and identify for Gambit. "Okay, the guy with the beard is Dunn, the guy with the blue hair is Pokey, and the other guy is AppleJack. This is your team."

Gambit looked them over quickly (and quietly) then said, "I got my work cut out for me."

****

Chef Adrian was glad we were all there, at least -- he had *hors d'oeuvres* ready for us, little smoked shrimp things and a bruschetta duet that we wolfed through like untamed animals starved to near death. He'd had to have been either flattered or horrified.

Centaurs had never been known for their manners at parties, so I let their enthusiasm roll off my back. It was nice to have friends in the house.

Pokey had somehow blue-toothed his way into our stereo system and had taken over the music, running some playlist on his phone -- the music took a considerable turn from coffeehouse jazz. Dunn rolled his eyes. "House music and pop-star divas," he said, shaking his head. "Fucking kids today."

The party moved toward the food, as parties do -- everyone found themselves around the kitchen island, waiting to formally sit and eat. The chat was lively and largely friendly, a group of guys getting to know each other with the help of alcohol and pot. (My favorite overheard line was from Lickety Split. "I dig the dick," he said, pawing at it through his shorts. "I can handle that -- but my balls totally get in the way of everything. What the fuck do you do with them?") Only Gambit, who didn't seem to drink or smoke, and

AppleJack, who drank and smoked too much, were the standoffish ones.

"Sit, sit!" Chef Adrian insisted. "Timing matters!"

Cavalier and I sat at opposite ends of the table, AppleJack on my left and Pokey on my right, putting him next to Gambit on his other side. "Between the muscle daddies," Pokey said. "Right where I wanna be, I reckon."

Gambit turned his head slightly toward the kid and quietly said, "You touch me before I give you permission, boy, and I will beat you as blue as your hair." Then he winked.

Dunn, across the table from Gambit, on the same side as AppleJack and Lickety Split, flipped his hand open like a fan and waved it at his face, saying, "Boys, you're getting me all hot over here. No making porn at the dinner table!"

Mahmood (I think?) filled our wine glasses with the South African Cabernet, then they presented the appetizer. "Tuna Tartare in Ginger Sauce," Chef Adrian announced, "paired with a really distinctive cab. Enjoy!"

Everybody clapped and a round of "Thank you's" followed from the more civilized.

I stood and raised my glass, beating Cav by seconds. "My centaurs," I said. "My tribe, my… chosen herd, I know that this is Cavalier's meeting and I'm not looking to step on his toes, but I wanted to toast you all, and thank you, and welcome you to my cave -- I hope you're all here a lot. I'm excited about the adventures we're bound to have. *Euoi euan!*"

"*Euoi euan!*" they echoed, though probably only Cav knew what the toast meant.

The tartare was delicious! It was almost impossible to eat with restraint. Even AppleJack, who could be finicky about fish, ate with a zeal. Mahmood (pretty sure) cleared quickly and efficiently just as Chef Adrian presented the main course.

"Filet Mignon," he announced. "With a reduced red wine, garlic sauce. Does anyone NOT want rare?"

Gambit chuckled. "If anybody doesn't, I'll eat it."

But everybody did, because nobody was a fool. To pretend this was anything other than an exceptional piece of meat -- and I knew I was overusing the phrase "exceptional piece of meat" lately, but in this case, it was warranted -- would be a disservice to the animal that gave it to us.

Nobody spoke. That's how good it was.

"I reckon I've eaten a lot of steaks in my time," Pokey said, setting down his utensils, "but that was the best piece of meat I've had in my life!"

"Filet Mignon," Cav said, drinking his wine. "You ever had a piece of meat *without* a bone in it, Pokey?"

A gentle laugh from the table, but Pokey didn't take the bait. "I reckon I like to suck the marrow out of a bone." He threw a quick glance to Gambit. "It's where all the good stuff is."

Gambit smirked. "You don't stop," he said.

AppleJack threw back the rest of his drink. "What do you think you're gonna get, good jokes from the rodeo clown?"

That got a big awkward silence from the table -- it was meaner than most gay dinner party jabs — but it was Cav who admonished him. "Hey, AppleJack," Cav said, "I thought you and I had a conversation about being respectful. These are your brothers now."

AppleJack sat back in his chair petulantly, crossing his arms before his chest. "I'm sorry," he said to Pokey. "I'm kind of fucked up."

"You're a lot fucked up," said Gambit, putting his hand on Pokey's shoulder while he addressed AppleJack. "Maybe you should lighten up on that stuff."

AppleJack stood, a little uncertainly. "Yeah, maybe I should," he said. "Maybe I should do a lot of things. Thanks, coach." He started to walk away from the table.

"AppleJack," I said. "Don't…"

"I'm gonna go out back and start the fire pit," AppleJack said, interrupting him. "I'll be okay…" He indicated everyone and everything. "This… is all hard for me."

His leaving only upset Chef Adrian, who said, "But I have a special dessert -- marijuana infused ice cream!"

Lickety Split got there first. "I'll eat his!" he said.

Everyone laughed, and the mood lightened again.

"I'm worried about that one," Cav said. "AppleJack."

Gambit glanced at him then went back to his dessert. "He'll be okay," he said. "He's never been on a team."

It was Dunn who said, "He doesn't know who he is. Give him room to discover himself." Then he added, as an aside on *Golden Girls*, "And tell him to get a haircut."

We all chuckled and ate our desserts. Then there was coffee and much ado about Chef Adrian and maybe Mahmood, applause and thanks. We decided to retire to the backyard and do the "meeting" portion of tonight around the firepit. The guys started heading out as I clucked around the kitchen after the Chef, telling him not to worry about clean-up -- apparently, Cav had already scheduled a cleaning service for tomorrow morning. He knew how to do it right, that Cavalier.

It didn't stop me from tipping Chef Adrian a few hundred dollars extra (which Pokey would probably take from him before he got out the door, but whatever) -- I was pretty sure that Cav did the same thing. The Chef shook my hand. "You guys are all huge!" he said. "I was afraid I wasn't going to have enough meat for you!"

"One thing we got around here," I said, "is plenty enough meat." We laughed.

I gave him a little dose of pheromones before he headed out the door -- he wouldn't forget us anytime soon

****

If I'd made my backyard seem fancy in the narrative previously, it was a mistake -- I'd renovated the house, but had done nothing to the yard. Mine was a regular, boring city backyard, barely five-hundred square feet, bordered by a six-foot slat-wood fence decorated with a string of Xmas sparkle lights. A big Crepe Myrtle dominated one end -- the rest was open lawn centered around the fire-pit -- not even a patio, just a cement slab. I had a cushioned bench and a couple folding chairs set out and around. The sun had gone down just enough that there were only colored streaks left in the sky -- the full moon was rising.

The fire was blazing by the time I got outside. AppleJack sat on one end of the park bench, Gambit on the other with Pokey on his knee. Gambit had one arm around Pokey's waist and the other across the back of the bench, behind AppleJack's shoulders. AppleJack seemed to be okay with that. Dunn had lit one of the joints he'd brought and they were passing it back and forth between themselves and Lickety Split, who sat on one of the cube seats next to the bench, Dunn standing between them. Cav smiled from the nicer lawn chair when I came out and he asked, "All good in there?"

"It is indeed." I smiled. "They're cleaning up. Thanks for an amazing dinner, Herd Master." I settled in the empty chair. The other guys echoed this sentiment.

"My boys deserve it," he said. "We gotta keep our strength up." He clapped his hands for attention. "So guys, before the moon rises and we go hunting, I want to have a quick meeting." Everyone shifted themselves into comfortable listening mode -- the dinner-fun was over, now it was time to pay for the meal.

"When I first came to Red," Cav said, enjoying the spotlight, "it was with a scheme to expand his centaur-themed porn empire with a herd of hot horsemen. We'd find and recruit these crazy hot guys and turn them into sexy supermen -- we'd raid the other porn houses of all their best tops -- we'd own the industry. That was my original plan. It wasn't until we discovered our bestial selves that I realized we were here for so much more." He paused for a second and sipped his coffee. "Regardless," he continued, "I still want to cultivate the brand. I think we owe it to ourselves and our soon-to-be grateful public. With that in mind, the Pride Parade is coming up next month and I have booked us a float."

There was a stunned silence amongst us, until AppleJack dropped a dry "What?"

"I think it'll be good for us," Cav said, casually pointing at AppleJack. "Especially you. Listen: Pholus is up there, all his hugeness dressed as a Greek God, and the rest of us are in these scanty 'My Little Pony' meets the leather-scene costumes, you know? We prance around and douse everybody with pheromones -- when we get to the judges' station, we jump off and do this Magic Mike meets Samoan Haka dance..."

Gambit interrupted. "Wait. We dance...?"

Cav looked at him like he was crazy. "Yeah, we dance. Are you fucking kidding? We're gonna seduce this whole fucking town!"

"I'm in," Dunn said, exhaling a cloud of smoke. "I'll make the costumes!"

"I want it rainbow themed," Cav said to him. "You know, it's Pride. Pokey, will you choreograph something for us?"

Pokey was like a Hollywood-wannabe who'd just scored their first gig. "Yes!" he said, with jazz hands.

Gambit shook his head. "I don't know, man..."

"Hey, if I gotta learn to fight then you gotta learn to dance," Pokey said, poking Gambit in the pec. "It's equity."

Cav was devilish. "Singing and dancing were a big part of Spartan military training," he said.

Gambit dropped his head back over the bench, looking up at the sky. "Fuck," he mumbled.

AppleJack sat up straighter. "Oh, finally -- YOU have to do something you don't like to do!" He turned to Cav. "I'm In," he said, "I'm in just for that!"

"Me, too!" said Lickety Split, nearly giddy. "I've been waiting a long time to see Bruiser Boy step outta his comfort zone. This dream keeps gettin' better, dude!"

"So that's almost everybody," Cav said, looking at me.

"Are you kidding?" I said, smiling. "I'm totally in! Isn't this what centaurs should be doing?"

"If History is to be believed," Cav said, "it'll be the biggest orgy this town has ever seen." He twiddled his fingers before him, like a mad supervillain. "I'm such a horny little devil." He laughed to himself for a second. "Anyway, that's four weeks out, so we don't have a lot of time -- especially cause I'd like to get some publicity shots taken. I really want to shoot a calendar, but I don't think we can get it done. We can at least get pre-orders going... So, group shots for sure and solo shoots -- we'll schedule it out this week, okay? I want to get moving on this. We good?"

General assent with reluctance from expected quarters, but we were moving forward.

Cav smiled. "All right then, boys -- looks like it's time for us to be beasts!" He looked at me and quietly asked, "Red, would you get the wine?"

"Beasts?" asked Dunn. "Is this the part where we get naked, dance around the fire and sing to the moon? Cause that's my favorite part of any party."

I left them there, joking loudly -- and drunkenly -- and stonedly -- it did my heart good.

I went inside, only to discover that Cav had already set the tray up -- the ancient bottle of Dionysian Wine and seven small rocks glasses. I couldn't help but smile -- he had way more of a plan than I did.

As far as I was concerned, the universe was unfolding nicely, thank you.

By the time I got back outside, the boys were all shirtless, dancing around the firepit, laughing and silly. Even Gambit, I was happy to see, was loosening up a little -- tho, for the exceptional athlete that he was, he seemed to completely lack rhythm. It would be interesting to see who'd be more successful with the other, him teaching Pokey to fight, or Pokey teaching Gambit to dance.

I set the tray down on the little metal side-table next to Cav's chair and joined them in their dance -- Lickety and Dunn helped me pull my shirt over my head, the cool evening air on my freckled skin. And their hands -- and maybe mouths...

Cav had gone over and began filling the glasses while we danced -- and just as it was getting a little more serious in the body contact and dry-humping departments, Cav dinged his glass. "Guys," he said loudly, "before this gets out of control, let's get to the reason we're here." He passed the glasses out quickly. As soon as Gambit sniffed his, I could see something come over him, surprise mixed with lust. I'd forgotten that he and Dunn -- Lickety Split, too! -- hadn't done this, yet.

All the guys were enjoying the wild, uncontrollable, perfumed lust of the wine's scent. I saw several hands adjust cocks.

"Before we hunt tonight, I want us to take some time to train and do some proprioceptive learning -- it's important that we really understand our bestial bodies and how they work."

"What the fuck are you talking about?" Gambit asked. "Hunting? Bestial bodies? Aren't we just gonna drink and fuck? I thought that's what 'hunting' meant. I thought it was code."

Cavalier smiled and held up his flat palm. "You haven't had this experience yet," he said. "Neither you, nor Dunn, nor the Infamous Lickety Split."

"Thank you, Herd-Master Dude," Lickety chimed in, his arm around Dunn's shoulders.

Cav held up his glass. "Trust me, boys, this shit is about to change your world."

"Literally," Pokey quipped. "I reckon."

"What is it?" asked Dunn. "It's smells like the promise of great sex."

"That's the best description I've heard of it," I said. "It's Dionysian Wine -- it's thousands of years old. Our centaur ancestors probably drank this!"

"Can we just drink it and get back to the action?" Gambit asked. "Our centaur ancestors would expect us to be fucking by now." He smirked, holding his wine in one hand, the back of Pokey's waistband in the other.

"This is better than fucking," Cavalier said, which got a snort out of Gambit, but that was all. "I'm serious, my friends -- run free, meet in the meadow, explore and train... THEN we hunt!" He raised his glass. "*Euoi euan!*"

"*Euoi euan!*"

I watched as everyone threw their glasses back, tasted, and swallowed.

And then disappeared.

"*Euoi euan!*" I said to no one and drank mine.

And I felt my perception change.

****

As before, I'm aware of motion first -- running, the pounding of hooves on the earth -- then speed, the wind against my chest, my flanks. The dark forest, the blacks of tree trunks flying by, the brush of leaves, yet the confidence of my step, my direction -- there is no fear.

The others are behind me, around me -- I can feel them, their location to me, my sons and brothers -- there is ecstasy in their movement, joy in their abilities. We are speed and agility, we are free from the constraints of humanity and their limited reality. We see the world through magical eyes now -- the same eyes that see so clearly in the dark, that see the truth of our existence, the plan of our rebirth.

I can feel Gambit closing in on my right at a full gallop, his hoof-falls as heavy as my own -- his weight must be astounding. Lickety Split is on my left, easily keeping pace with me -- it's clear he wants to break out in front, but stays in position for the moment. There is a race between Cavalier and Dunn happening behind me -- Dunn is feeling his oats, his joy is palpable.

We break into the meadow, surprising both Lickety Split and Gambit, who slows himself down to a canter. Lickety continues to run the border of the meadow at full gallop, circling and enjoying his freedom of speed, arms outstretched playfully like he's an airplane. Lit by the light of the Full Moon, it would be easy to see even if we didn't have our Centaur eyes. It's my first time seeing Gambit in his bestial form -- his, too. He's a massive Shire, a workhorse like me, easily nineteen hands high, powder gray with black fetlocks and bushy black tail. If Gambit had been hot as a man, he's something greater as a Centaur -- he's a dangerous beauty.

He stops before me and rears up on his back legs, playfully punching his front legs toward me. I didn't think Gambit could smile so widely. "What is this?" he asks. "Is this real? It feels like a dream."

"It's not," I say, frollicking with him, pushing our weight against each other. I'm a Clydesdale, eighteen hands high and one hundred-sixty stones, but Gambit has me beat in pure mass. "It's just something about the way we perceive this realm. Cavalier thinks it's because it's ruled over by Magic."

"So it's real? We're not just sitting around your backyard drunk on ancient wine and mass hallucinating?

I smile. "No -- It's real."

He is elated. "Fuck… YEAH!" he screams at the moon, flexing his arms for Selene to see. "This is fucking amazing! The power!" He's dancing, prancing around the meadow. "Fuck YEAH!" He's stroking his bestial form, feeling his coat, his rough hair. Even his horse cock has unsheathed.

Lickety Split comes galloping toward us at a breakneck speed -- with ease, he leaps over Gambit's back, landing effortlessly on the other side. He trots around us proudly, tail up. Lickety Split is a Pinto, straw yellow with white blotches and a light brown tail. Lickety's long torso on a Pinto's squat body, not quite fifteen hands high, looks slightly odd in proportion, but his speed and agility are second to none. He and Gambit double high-five, then he turns to me and we make the same move, if not a little more awkwardly. "This is fuckin' awesome," Lickety says, smiling. "This is the best thing that's ever happened to me in my life -- better than Mt. Fujiyama by way more!"

It's then that Cavalier and Dunn come breaking into the open space. Cavalier is a black thoroughbred, invisible and deadly, sleek and fast, but Dunn is a Mustang, just a hair smaller than Cavalier at sixteen hands, his body steel gray, gunmetal gray, though his legs, chest, and tail are black, with odd white stripes on his forelegs. Even if Cavalier is considerably more aerodynamic, Dunn is no also-ran. As he trots to us, his hair and beard flow in the air -- he, too, revels in his bestial form, his smile just as wide as Gambit's.

"This is worth everything," he says, joyous, hugging me. "I've waited my whole life for magic to happen! Thank you for bringing me in! I've never felt like this -- never seen the world like this! I'm not enough of a poet to do it justice!"

It seems impossible to stand still -- gentle canters, trots, lopes, leaps -- our bestial selves play and rear up, showing our height and our power. Gambit isn't the only one with his sheath opening, the head of his shocking cock adding its own ripe smell to the air -- Dunn, as well. And their raw, exposed cocks were exciting me.

AppleJack breaks the tree line, running at a quick canter, not quite a gallop, still reserved, but clearly joyous in movement. An Appaloosa, AppleJack is fifteen hands high, a solid golden brown, except his bold white rump, spotted with dark brown dots, the same color as his tail. He's beautiful!

"AppleJack!" I call, opening my arms wide to him. We hug openly and lovingly, raw and real. "You're beautiful!"

His smile splits his face. "I AM," he says, holding his arms out to his sides. "I am BEAUTIFUL!"

But by then it's time for Beauty's true entrance, and Pokey Dakota does not disappoint. He leaps into the meadow, high and proud, his sparkly white coat reflecting in the moonlight like a drag queen's disco ball, his tail matching the bright blue hue of his hair. He lands, immediately rearing onto his rear legs and spinning around -- he's a show pony, a lead horse in the circus parade, one of the mounts on the merry-go-round. He's the beauty and the beast. (If the beast were a kiddie villain, cute and cuddly but lacking morality.)

He stops before the group and bows, kneeling on one foreleg. The guys smile and clap.

Except Gambit. "What the hell are you supposed to be?" he asks.

"I told you," Pokey says, hitting a pose. "I'm a unicorn!"

Gambit bursts out laughing. "Are you fucking kidding me?" he asks. "Think so? A unicorn? Well then, where the fuck are your wings?"

"My wings?"

"Yeah, your unicorn wings?"

Cav, standing next to Gambit, half-whispers, "Pegasi have wings, not unicorns."

"Pegasi? The fuck is that?"

"Winged horses."

"Right!" He returns his attention to Pokey. "Where the fuck are your Pegasi wings? Show me some wings, or you're just a centaur like the rest of us!"

Pokey glares at him, but at the same time, I can see him thinking, hoping, praying. He breathes deep and squeezes his body like he's about to scream or shit (or both). "I'm not like the rest of you," he says, eyes closed, imagination running. "I'm not…"

"You're a centaur," says Gambit. "You're pretty, but you're a centaur. Just. Like. Us."

"No. I'm. NOT!" Pokey rears up on his hind legs, infuriated. "I'm DIFFERENT!"

And his wings unfurl, just like that -- huge, white, feathery wings with sparkly blue tips, dove's wings, they span across wider than he is long. As shocked as the rest of us, he lands on his four feet and gently flaps, trying to get the feel for his new appendages.

There is a stunned silence across the herd. Then, suddenly, Pokey begins laughing -- he hits a quick gallop and takes off into the sky!

"What the fuck…?" mumbles Gambit, crossing his arms before his massive chest.

Cav gives him the side-eye. "Looks like he's a unicorn, don't it?"

Gambit snorts derisively. "That kid's full of surprises."

The herd cheers Pokey as he glides and dips and floats and flips through the air. He lands awkwardly, not quite having the mechanics figured out, but anyone can see he's suddenly eager to practice.

Pokey struts up to Gambit with a smirk on his face, his wings folding against his sides. Without saying anything, he puts his hand behind Gambit's head and pulls him in for a kiss. Gambit happily reciprocates.

Hoots and hollers.

As their kiss breaks, Gambit quietly says, "I knew you could do it."

"Bullshit," Pokey says, poking him in the chest. "You're a bully."

Gambit smiles. "Sure am, unicorn," he says, wrapping Pokey in his arms and kissing him seriously.

Cavalier claps his hands, pulling focus. "All right, the rest of you, welcome! I wasn't kidding, was I? Look at what we are and look at where we are -- do you understand now why I thought we should have some kind of training? Figure out our abilities when we're in our Bestial Forms?"

General assent from the Herd -- they are distracted by everything, seeing sites with new eyes.

Cav trots a quick circle around himself. "This meadow seems to be our landing spot in this Realm, so let's think of this as home base. If you get lost or separated somehow, find your way back here -- you'll discover you have a kind of homing signal built in. At least, I have -- this is only my third time in the Realm, so I'm still learning, too."

"How long are we here?" Dunn asks.

"Until we go back," Cavalier says, shrugging. "Time is weird here -- it doesn't move the same way. Enjoy it while we got it, you know? Live in the moment. So I want us to play around a little bit, learn about our new bodies. And one thing I want you all to try is manifesting weapons. We can create weapons for ourselves, I've discovered, by thinking WEAPON and reaching for it. Suddenly you'll find it in your hand. Watch."

He closes his eyes, breathes deeply and suddenly there's a quarter-staff in his hand, about six feet long, two inches in diameter -- it glows with a golden energy. "I'm able to make this quarter-staff," he says. "I can make it a spear." The quarter-staff quickly morphs into a cruelly-tipped spear, the same golden glow. "And I can make a club." He does. "In this Realm, I don't think technology exists, so we're limited in what we can make to hand-held weapons. And I think we're all gonna be different. Like, Pholus can make a bow and I can't. So I wanna see what you guys can do. Go get 'em!"

There is the playground spirit of boy scout camp. They work alone initially and share their discoveries with each other as they make them -- Cavalier tours around like a teacher at recess, trying to contain the explosions.

There are immediate successes. Dunn is able to make a whip, which he wields with a Catwoman-like accuracy, delighting him. Lickety easily makes a bow -- which turns out to be the only weapon I can manifest -- but he can make a sling, too, as well as this weird thing called a bolas, a long leather cord with a hard ball at each end. He throws the bolas, it wraps around the target, messing up legs or whatever, and takes them down -- it's a cool little doo-hickey. Gambit seems able to create whatever he wants, a bow, a quarterstaff, a whip, a lasso, a shield, but the spear comes first, obviously his preferred weapon. Only AppleJack seems unable to manifest anything but a club.

"I feel like fucking Charlie Brown at Halloween," he says.

"A club's a good weapon," Cavalier says. "You can smack that bitch who pulls away the football with it."

"I can build a fucking computer system in the real world," AppleJack observes, "but here I can only imagine a club."

"This is a magical place, not a technological one," Cavalier says. "A mythical place. Don't you think, Pholus?"

I nod in assent. "There's something strange and familiar about it all at once. We should explore it... in the daytime."

"Explore in the daytime," Cavalier agrees. "Hunt at night."

"I'm ready to hunt," Gambit says, inserting himself into the conversation. "I'm starting to… desire it."

Cavalier nods. "The longer we spend in our Bestial forms, the harder it is to control those instincts."

"Why control them?" Gambit asks. "Why not just follow them? We are beasts -- we are magnificent beasts!"

"My brother, I completely agree! HERD," he called, "HUDDLE UP!"

We gather in a tight circle, flank to flank -- there is a nervous pawing of hooves on the ground, small stomps and digs -- we are excited, anxious. The scent of blood and the prospect of violence dance before us. "We are powerful and strong and magnificent!" Cavalier cheers. "We are smart and crafty and clever! We are the balance between animal and man, the bridge between the civilized and the bestial. We are back in this world and have learned from history. We will now own it!"

"YES!" screams the herd in a powerful unison.

We begin stomping in a circle beneath the moon. "We are savage!" Cavalier chants.

"SAVAGE!" we answer, and stomp!

"We are superior!"

"SUPERIOR!" Stomp!

"We are the beasts of Pholus!"

"PHOLUS" we chant, loudly. We dance in this way -- we put ourselves in a state of frenzy. "Pholus! Pholus! PHOLUS!!!!" We shout loud enough to wake the gods, screaming blood-curdling screams, building up the courage to run into the night and find prey.

"We HUNT!" yells Cavalier, directing us in a Northerly direction. We are at a full gallop across the meadow, Lickety Split is out in front, but not much further out than Dunn or Cavalier. The largest, Gambit and I should be the back, but even we are faster than poor AppleJack, bringing up the rear. Pokey soars overhead -- I have a feeling he'll never run again.

And just as we're about to hit the forest, an animal leaps out from the tree line, charging us. A gigantic lion -- male with an oversized mane, and oversized balls, the same golden glowing nimbus that surrounded our weapons -- roaring a deafening cry, showing its teeth, lands directly before me, maybe ten feet away.

I can see the Herd react, manifesting weapons, but before they can move to action, the Lion stands on its hind legs like a man. It shifts and morphs -- growing, anthropomorphizing, what had been a lion is now a man. No, a god! He is easily eight feet tall, hyper-muscular, hyper-masculine, thick black hair covers his bloated muscle. He wears a leather battle skirt, sandals, and a lion-skin draped over his shoulder, the lion's head biting its own foot to create a cape, otherwise bare, exposing his magnificence, his physical, masculine perfection. Short black hair in oily curls and a long, thick black beard that rests upon the shelf of his upper pecs add to his dangerous beauty. He is fantasy made flesh.

But then, so am I.

He looks me dead in the eye, incredulous, shocked, awed -- but it isn't until he says my name, "It cannot be -- Pholus!" that I truly recognize him for who he is -- that I remember him.

I remember everything.

I remember him trashing my cave -- my home -- demanding wine, of all things. I remember the jealousy and the fury, the childishness and the arrogance, acting as if falling in love had been my fault! No civilized dinner, no breaking bread and sipping wine, no pleasant conversation -- the myth lies.

Instead, he beat me with his club, brutal and bloody, leaving me to die while he slaughtered my brethren and children with his poison arrows. And then, to humiliate my memory, concocting the "shot himself in the foot" story.

Yes, I remember him -- I remember him well.

"Heracles," I say. "It's been a long time."

"This cannot be," the demigod Heracles says, his voice deep, gravelly, bass-intensive. "Thou art slain -- by mine own hand! How didst thou survive?"

I shrug. "How doesn't matter," I say. "All that matters is I'm back. Pholus is reborn!"

He scoffs. "So I see. And, like vermin, thou begins already to spread thy plague and create an imbalance in the Magical Realms. How comes thee here, Pholus, to this place where only the gods art allowed? Where didst thou get the wine?"

"The wine? We haven't seen each other in thousands of years and the first thing you do is question my character? Don't worry, old friend, we came by the wine honestly," I said, smiling devilishly. "We raided no weddings."

He scowls. "As always, thy sense of humor eludes me -- it borders on disrespect. Thou acquired no Dionysian Wine in the modern world honestly. I sense another hand in this. If thou lives, Chiron must live, too. Tell me where he is, Pholus."

"Since my rebirth, I haven't seen Chiron. As far as I know, he's still dead."

"Thou art a liar!" he spits. "In thy heart, thou knowest the lie in thy words. Tell me where he hides, Pholus!"

"I don't know where he is."

Heracles is enraged. "LIAR!" he screams, manifesting a club, a monstrous thing that only a man of his size could wield -- the thing that killed me. "Unless thou tells me where Chiron can be found, by my hand, thou whilst die again -- thou and thine kindred herd -- I will slay all of thee gladly... "

Suddenly, unexpectedly, a spear pierces Heracles' upper left chest where it meets the shoulder -- Heracles screams in sudden pain, sounding like the roar of a lion, blood gushing from the wound. He tries to pull it out, but the point of the spear sticks out his back, unable to be drawn for its own barbs.

I see that Gambit has made the opening move. "You will not find us so easy to kill," he shouts.

Enraged, Heracles raises his club. "Thou shalt be the first!" he threatens Gambit, readying to strike.

As he prepares to swing, the tip of Dunn's whip lashes around Heracles' wrist, restraining him. It takes most of Dunn's strength to hold the demigod --barely at that, he braces his hooves for the struggle.

Heracles looks to see what's holding him, but before he can do anything about it, his torso is pierced multiple times by golden arrows, loosed from Lickety Split's bow. Heracles screams in frustration as much as pain -- his club disappears from his right hand and he begins to manifest a shield in his left.

But even that's interrupted as Pokey's lasso catches Heracles' left wrist. Pokey and Dunn have him, but are barely able to hold Heracles' massive arms. Heracles looks eager to pull Pokey from the sky.

Gambit enters Heracles' space, raining body blows and uppercuts -- painful pressure points -- he hits the entrance wounds of the arrows multiple times. He is just trying to distract -- but he knows how to punch for pain.

"NOW!" Cavalier shouts, as he and Lickety Split begin to charge. Lickety spins his bolas in a lasso-like windup, while Cavalier manifests his quarter-staff. Cav goes high, leaping over Heracles' right shoulder as Lickety goes low, launching his bolas to wrap around Heracles' legs.

As Cavalier flies past the demigod, he swings his quarterstaff, cracking Heracles in the back of the skull. Stunned, Heracles goes to the ground, face first in the dirt, barely holding on to consciousness. AppleJack is on him first, beating the demigod with his club, striking him with all the ferocity of a feral horse until Gambit pulls him off.

Heracles is bloodied and beaten -- still he tries to get up, noble warrior that he is. "Thou shalt pay for this mistake," he says, through the spit of blood. "But then, Pholus, thou hast a history of shooting thyself in the foot."

I close in on him. "You are asleep in your hidden world on Mt. Olympus, Old God, dreaming of being Chiron's favorite. How horrible it must feel to wake and be reminded of the truth."

"Curse thee, Pholus!"

I smile coldly. "Yes, curse me, Old God. Say my name, for no one even remembers you anymore -- you're forgotten!"

"But you will remember us," says Cavalier, menacingly, standing over Heracles' body. "You will remember the defeat we handed you tonight. And if you attack us in the real world, the result will be the same. We have learned from history, Old God, and we will not repeat it."

Cavalier manifests a huge, cruel spear. He points it straight down at Heracles. "I know you're just a dream-self, or a projection, or something magical -- I know you're not really here. But in your dream, you will die by Cavalier's hand," he says. "Remember it."

But just as Cavalier drives the spear into Heracles' back, through the ribs, piercing the Old God's heart, there is... an explosion of light, soundless -- like Heracles is a bomb, and there is only sight to perceive it. We are all blown back from the force, the stunning silence -- even Pokey is knocked from the sky.

It only takes a second or two to recover, to regain balance and restore sight. There is still a body lying where Heracles fell, but it is no longer the Old God -- it's the battered and bloody corpse of an adult male lion.

We approach, forming a loose circle around the dead thing -- is it a prayerful moment? A respectful one?

"We. Fucking. Killed. A GOD!!" shouts Gambit to the heavens, a joyful grin breaking out on his face.

"We didn't kill him," I say. "He wasn't really here -- there's no way we would've taken the real Heracles down so easily. At best, we can say we killed a lion."

"Bullshit!" Gambit argues. "You think that was easy?"

Cavalier nods his head. "I agree with Pholus," he says. "It might've felt real, but I don't think..."

"You're wrong," Gambit says, hands up before him in a stop motion. "It's Gambit one -- Heracles zilch!" He kneels down on his forelegs and soaks his hand in the blood of the Lion -- he wipes the blood across his own chest. "I'm a fucking Warrior." He goes from centaur to centaur, leaving a bloody handprint on their chest, labeling them all. "We're all fucking warriors!"

Cavalier and I watch -- I can't help but feel a certain amount of pride. I'd put this group together on instinct alone, no battle plan, and here they are, celebrating victory together. I accept my bloody handprint when it comes -- and I see the joy in Gambit's eyes.

I wish I were as confident.

I put my arm around Cavalier's shoulders as he drops his around my withers. "What have we just set in motion, Cav?"

He smiles and leans into my ear. "History," he says. "Only this time, we win. You and me -- we'll win."

"Guys! Guys!" interrupts AppleJack. "Look what ELSE I can manifest!" He holds up a leather sling-bag full of wine! "I can make wine!" he laughs. "I'm Jesus!"

"You're Dionysis," Cav corrects him, laughing.

"Whatever. Taste it."

Sure enough -- Dionysian Wine -- but not the ancient stuff we had bottled at home. This tastes fresh from the vineyard -- it's incredible, vastly more complex than anything in the modern age. I slug it back.

"Hey, hey, hey," says Cavalier. "Save some for the Killing Blow!" I hand him the bag and he begins drinking.

AppleJack says, "I'm working on manifesting a joint!" He makes a motion like he's pinching a joint with his fingers -- nothing. "I'll get it," he says.

We drink and dance and sing and revel in our equinian fraternity. As the moon sets finally, so do we, falling like big lumps of exhausted horse-flesh against the base of trees, or each other.

As we pass out, we exit the Realm one by one, until all that's left is the ruined corpse of the beast, already discovered by the scavengers of the night.

10. "Orgia"

*In ancient Greek religion, **Orgia** (ὄργια, sing. ὄργιον, origin) were ecstatic rites characteristic of the Greek and Hellenistic mystery religions. Orgia (orgies) were part of the Dionysian Mysteries, which involved a frenzied trance. Orgia are popularly thought to have involved sex, but, while sexuality and fertility were cultic concerns, the primary goal of the orgia was to achieve an ecstatic union with the divine.*

****

I was Red.

Until recently, I was pretty certain of that.

I remembered Red's life, his parents -- both of whom must've had the recessive hair gene -- I remembered his Grandfather, whose genes were dominant -- (and apparently a dominant hard-on in his jeans, too) -- whose nickname, "Big Red," was the progenitor of my own. I remembered Red's lame little skinny-fat body, his weakness, his sad genitals. I remembered college with my life-long friend AppleJack, the adventures, the disappointments, the sexual dissatisfactions, the regrets -- I remembered Red. I was Red.

Except I was Pholus.

I remembered Pholus' life, leaving my parents -- different parents than Red's, but still mine -- to become *erômenos* for the centaur Chiron -- an honor, they said. Wrestling, archery, music, philosophy, in all the arts I excelled, even the arts of war. As was the way in ancient Greece, this was a sexual relationship -- but we'd moved beyond the societal boundary of sexual favors to pay for education. We fell in love -- a scandal. I remembered Chiron being an incredible, giving lover. A young man, I was always eager to get to the orgasm, but Chiron taught me to slow down, to enjoy the moment, to breathe…

I remembered my initiation into the Centaurs -- I remembered the first time my *Erastês* Chiron bade me fuck him, when I felt the power enter me. Change me. He'd not transformed any of his other students: not Perseus, not Heracles, not even Achilles, who he claimed so much love for. No, he'd elevated ME -- Pholus. I remembered that.

As Red, when I drank the magic potion that I'd found in the garden gnome, I guess I'd just assumed that I'd gained Pholus' powers and abilities, but I was still fundamentally Red, just some souped-up, hypermasculine version of him. I hadn't realized it'd actually transformed me INTO Pholus!

But Heracles recognized me! He looked right at me and he knew me as Pholus. He wasn't seeing my immortal essence or anything so hokey, he looked at my face (and my body) and knew me as Pholus. And in that moment, I remembered being Pholus -- I remembered everything about him. Me.

So the question really was: who was Red?

Was Red a real person or had Red been just... holding space for the rebirth of Pholus?

Did Red's life still matter? Had Red's life EVER mattered?

This had been the question worming its way around my brain in the week since we'd beaten Heracles in the Magic Realm -- which I realized was a surprisingly easy victory. The Heracles of legend couldn't possibly have been brought down by seven untrained centaurs (well, six centaurs and a unicorn). He'd killed dozens of us in one battle alone -- the battle I'd caused, speaking of shooting myself in the foot.

It seemed more and more that the only solution was to find my former *Erastês*, the wisest and justest of all the centaurs. If there was one being who would have the answers, it would be him.

Chiron.

****

@LicketySplit: CENTAUR FUN FACT: Centaurs worshipped Dionysus, the God of Wine!

@Cavalier: FYI, Dionysus was also the god of plants and vegetation, so he was Pot God, too!

@AppleJack: HAIL, DIONYSUS!

@me: We could use some Dionysian Love in our basement grow!
@me: You're all welcome to cum by and pray.
@me: Or at least kneel.

@Dunn: AppleJack is too busy playing w himself
@Dunn: to care for his basement babies

@Gambit: These text chains annoy the fuck out of me!
@Gambit: Is there any business, or just CENTAUR FUN FACTS?

@Lickety Split: CENTAUR FUN FACT: "Centaur" is short for "Hippocentaur"

@Gambit: When you show up at the gym, I'm gonna kick your infamous ass.

@PokeyDakota: Hi, guys! I got some business!
@PokeyDakota: I got us a rehearsal space for tomorrow night.
@PokeyDakota: I'll pin you all.
@PokeyDakota: Bring your good attitudes!
@PokeyDakota: (and your dancebelts)

@Gambit: What the hell is a dancebelt?
@Gambit: Is that like a weightbelt? I got one of them.

@AppleJack: Can we hail Dionysus afterwards?

@Dunn: My friend, we're gonna in-hail some Dionysus beforehand…

@PokeyDakota: You guys…

@Cavalier: We're all excited about it, Pokey
@Cavalier: It's gonna be fun!

@Gambit: Great! Now would you all get the fuck off my phone
@Gambit: I'm trying to train people here!

@PokeyDakota: You still got a job?
@PokeyDakota: I'll never understand you guys.

This part of the story would work better as a video montage.

One of those hokey, time passes while the characters learn/ practice/ hone their skills over the heavy, driving beat of some inspirational yet overproduced earworm by the latest up-and-coming chart climbers. The music video would convey a ton of visual exposition, so all a lazy writer had to do was list the events covered and the director and editor would be responsible for the work.

The first sequence would probably be at one of Pokey's dance rehearsals, early on, when we looked like a pornographic version of *A Chorus Line* standing there watching Pokey demonstrate complex moves with these incredulous, disbelieving looks on our faces, awkward attempts at simple step-touches. A sad lot.

Cut to the interior of Lickety Split's gym where Gambit would be training AppleJack, teaching the proper form for cleans, initially with just the bar. AppleJack would appear frustrated, but determined.

A shot of Dunn working on costumes in a studio, several male mannequins fill the background, all in similar states of undress, leather, spandex, gold and silver lame shine as Dunn pins and cuts, working like a man with a vision.

Next the photo shoot -- another studio, another time of day -- a giant white backdrop that runs from the ceiling to the floor -- big lights. Our boys pose as a group, wearing only their jeans. The mood is light and there is much laughter as the guys become competitive while posing.

That would probably get us to the end of the first chorus of the song that drives the video. Now, in the second verse, we see slight improvements in the learning/ practicing/ honing of skills. A shot in the Magical Realm -- during the day, so the colors are extraordinarily real -- practicing archery in our Bestial Forms, me and Gambit working with the other bowmen, Pokey and Lickety Split. It takes most of Gambit's skill to keep Pokey focused, his ADHD only intensified in his bestial form. Still, the two of them hit the bullseye. All the watching Faeries clap their wee hands together! Even Gambit cracks a smile.

Back in the dance studio -- different day, different rehearsal clothes -- the routine is already in motion when Pokey stops it. He walks up to Gambit and shows him a move, a particularly hip-intensive one -- there's some initial tightness, but Gambit gets it. Pokey dramatically sighs and starts the routine again. Success! Encouragement!

More at the photo shoot -- company in white thongs, harnesses, and cowboy hats. Slutty and funny, like right before a porn movie shoot.

Cut to the interior of the gym. This time, AppleJack cleans 135. With a huge smile, he drops the weight to the floor and hugs Gambit.

Interior of our basement. AppleJack and Lickety Split tend to the plants, practicing their dance moves as they do. They share a phat joint and blab like old friends.

Back to the dance studio -- another sequence, *Magic Mike*-like, sexual and taunting, the camera moves freely through the bodies. The dancing doesn't jibe with the beat of the song driving this montage, but it looks great, all flexing and slutty poses -- sweaty smiles from even the least.

Then, during the bridge, the camera cuts away to a seemingly incongruous shot -- quiet compared to everything we've been seeing, even if that's not reflected in the music -- interior of a coffee shop. The camera rises from floor level to discover an open laptop on the counter -- as it continues its sweep, it reveals Cavalier, sipping an espresso and intensely reading. The camera shows us, over his shoulder, that he's reading about Heracles.

Another shot in the dance studio as the final chorus rolls around. The company, mostly shirtless and sweaty, moves with confidence, expressive faces, clearly enjoying themselves.

A quick shot of AppleJack jumping into Dunn's barber chair. Dunn, with a flourish of the cape, looks to the heavens and mouths "Thank you!"

A short vignette of Cavalier and me looking at photos on a table, choosing ones we liked and eliminating some. The camera shoots straight down and we see dozens of hot pics of the Herd in various stages of undress -- it could be the layout of a porn mag.

Finally, the last moves of the dance routine, some hips, some changing positions, and then hit the final pose. Hold…

Release as the last strains of the soundtrack play out. High fives. Hugs.

Fade to New Scene as heartfelt laughter continues to echo…

****

So far, the summer had not been as oppressively hot as it had in years past, but even so, I was glad the parade had been moved to the evening -- it was the smartest thing the Pride committee had ever done, in my opinion. There was still plenty of light to see and it kept everybody all in one place for the night-time festivities. We had to be on-site a little earlier than any of us would've liked, but given the size of the crowds forming, we probably wouldn't have gotten there if we hadn't.

It was a Cavalier Production, so everything was anticipated and overdone. The float itself was an eight by twenty-four flat trailer about three feet off the ground towed by a Dodge Ram. It was decorated with astroturf grass and a long bench in the ancient greek style running up the middle. The sides were decorated with columns (Doric, I was happy to say) and oversized bunches of grapes. There was a pedestal at the front end for me -- as Pholus -- to stand on, and even that was decorated with vines and grapes.

There were several large "terra-cotta" pots (they were in fact, plastic) along the edges of the float that contained candy, pins with the Pholus Reborn logo, rainbow bead necklaces (branded the same way), and condoms.

"Really?" I asked him, pulling out a handful -- they were rainbow colored. "Condoms?"

Cav snorted. "For the fans," he said. "I didn't get anything that would fit us."

The bed of the truck had a tri-corner stand displaying a wrap-around banner with our Logo and hash-tag elevated by poles. Beneath that were the amplifiers for the music. A big cooler at the tail held many iced bottles of water and gatorade. Otherwise, supplies and snacks. "You think of everything," I said to Cav. "How much did you pay for all this?"

He looked at me curiously. "Pay?" he asked. "I thought we decided we weren't gonna pay for anything anymore...?"

I sighed heavily.

He laughed. "I'm kidding, I'm kidding," he said.

But when I met the driver (and presumably owner) of the truck, I saw immediately that he was under Cav's pheromone power, aching to obey his smelly master, willing to do anything for just another sniff... maybe a lick...?

I wondered if Cav had been kidding or not.

Well, as Pokey so often argued, we were no longer human -- there was no reason to continue to live as humans. We should USE these new gifts we've been given -- it was senseless not to.

Had I really been reborn to work an hourly job? Had the Fates woven me back into the fabric of reality because the world needed one more OnlyFans page?

AppleJack, Dunn, and Lickety Split showed up together, so over-baked, they'd lose any British cooking show. "You've been playing in that new strain," I said, hugging AppleJack.

"Does it show?" AppleJack asked. "Dude," he said to Lickety Split, "Mom can tell we're stoned!"

"Oh, shit," said Lickety Split. "Sorry, mom!"

"Chill," said Dunn, opening his vest and showing me the joints in his inner pocket. "We brought enough for everybody."

I kissed Dunn's cheek, putting my arm around his shoulder. "See?" I said to AppleJack. "Someone's thinking of me, not just smoking my stash!"

AppleJack snorted and said, "I was thinking of you while I was smoking your stash…"

Lickety Split put his arm around AppleJack's shoulder. "It's true -- he did!" he said. "He thought of you the whole time. He said, 'This is Red's stash, I think,' then we smoked it."

They laughed -- gods, Lickety Split brayed like a mule.

"You two are dangerous together," Cav said, stepping into the group and offering water.

Lickety's smile couldn't have been wider -- he was so excited. "Dude, we're gonna have so much fucking fun tonight!"

Cav agreed. "We're gonna show this town a thing or two about centaurs, that's for sure."

That was when Pokey and Gambit came strolling up. They'd come from the other direction and had clearly been checking out the competition. "The ManHunt float is about five in front of us," Pokey said. "They've got a DJ and some hot gogo boys, but they're right behind the marching band, so it won't be easy for them!"

Behind us was the Coldwell Bank float and then the Lesbian Softball League after that. What was the world coming to -- bank floats at Gay Pride? Commercializing Bacchanalia…

We were able to store our personal items in the truck -- most everybody had underdressed the white thong. (Whatever the fuck cottony-spandex material they were made from, we might well have been wearing nothing -- they gave that little support -- but the way they displayed our big ol' baskets could not be denied. They held us like water balloons in a cotton sack.) The rest of the costume consisted of a white elastic banded chest harness, that had a short, over the shoulder white cape with a colored Grecian border, attached to the harness with big, golden disks, golden gauntlets, and a laurel wreath around the back of our heads. On the bottom, lace front sandals and chap shorts made from white (p)leather. Attached to the belt of the chaps, each of us had a long-hair horse tail in a different color. "It would be better with the white cowboy boots," Dunn mumbled.

"Too out of period," said Cavalier -- he had the red tail.

Gambit snorted. "Yeah, the harnesses are super-Greek." (His tail was orange.)

"Horses wore harnesses in ancient Greece," said Dunn. (Blue tail.) "Modern centaurs wear them for fun." When he shook his ass, his tail wagged.

My costume was the same as theirs, underneath, (my tail was green), but I had some additional decoration -- I had, well, this sort-of toga over it. I mean, it was like a "sexy halloween" version of a toga, scant and revealing, meant to show more than it hid, but someone looking at me would guess Greek God of Gay Porn, so it was successful like that.

Especially for the hungers of Pride, which were certainly souped-up from any other Saturday night. And we were looking to let people know we were here.

"Here's the plan," Cav said as we loosely huddled around the side of the float. We were already getting wolf whistles and woofs from the forming crowds lining the sides of the road -- it was hard not to react to that energy. "It's about getting up in people's faces. Give 'em some candy or whatever, plus a little dose of our magic, a little taste of centaur -- get 'em hooked. Rev 'em up. If you want to take a break and be up on the float, that's cool. But the float's about flexing and sexing -- you're always engaging, not taking a break. This parade's about two hours long, so you can make it. We're gonna end up at TRADE tonight, so invite guys you like there. Everybody good?"

Everybody agreed, laughing or playing -- the energy was exciting.

Cav clapped his hands, like he was dismissing us. "You guys look sexy as fuck."

Dunn bowed with a flourish. "Thank you," he said.

AppleJack (yellow tail) jumped in. "I just found out what yellow means to gay guys, by the way! So I'm the Pee Horse, am I?"

Lickety Split and his purple tail brayed. "Pee Horse!"

Gambit, under his breath -- "He's the Pee Horse."

Even Dunn was laughing. "You guys fucking suck!" he said with a smile on his face. "Someone's gotta be yellow... Nobody ever wants to be yellow."

Pokey shook his pretty pink tail. "I'm loving mine!" he said. "I reckon I was skeered you were gonna give me blue."

Gambit chuckled, wrapping his arm around Pokey's neck and pulling him in. "Yeah, now -- blue hair, pink tail -- you're in baby colors."

Pokey corrected him. "TRANS colors," he said.

Smirking, Gambit shook his head as he looked Pokey in the eye. "You..." he said and pulled Pokey in for a kiss.

Cav was right there. "Boys, boys, don't waste it on each other. We have a city to corrupt."

Dunn pulled out a joint. "Do we have time for a quick prayer to the Pot God?"

"There's always time for prayer," Cav said.

"Hail Dionysus!" said AppleJack. "Isn't that who you said?"

"They learn!" said Cav, looking to the heavens, taking the joint from Dunn.

It had gone around the circle more than once when one of the city cops walking by came over to tut-tut us. Of all people, AppleJack faced him, taking a few steps out of the circle. "Hey, officer," he said, launching a heavy-hit of pheromones. "We're just having a pre-parade prayer. That's cool, isn't it?"

The officer stood there, staring at AppleJack in a confused way -- he didn't understand why he was sexually stimulated all of a sudden, just that he was. "No," he said, trying to clear his head. "Prayer's fine."

AppleJack leaned over and kissed the officer's cheek -- the officer shuddered in bliss. "Happy Pride," AppleJack said. "Continue on, nothing to see here."

The officer's erection fought the confines of his uniform shorts. "Sure, continue on," he mumbled, walking away -- his hard-on displayed for all to see. "Nothing to see here." He waved. "Happy Pride!"

When AppleJack turned back to the herd, we cheered him. "Dude, I'm doing that the next time I get a speeding ticket," said Lickety Split, high-fiving AppleJack. "Go, Pee Horse!"

"Go, Pee Horse!" we echoed.

"Do you guys see how easy it's gonna be?" asked Cav. "So let's start this parade!"

****

Even after the parade started, it took a good fifteen minutes before we actually moved. Costume-wise, we'd added these tear-away white joggers that gathered under the knee -- no one liked them, but we acquiesced when we realized they actually enhanced our packages, not hid them. (Dunn was all "told you so.") Besides, the "reveal" of our chaps was during the dance routine at the judges' stand -- these joggers snapped up the side of the leg, ready to be ripped off at a crucial moment -- and we didn't want to give everything away!

Once we were in motion, the whole thing was a sort of blur -- not because of our speed, certainly, but because of the interaction with the public. So, of course, the streets were lined with people -- packed with people, really -- and the energy was palpable. Ripe and horny and communal anyway, they embraced the centaurs! How many selfies? How many live shots on IG and FB -- our hashtag was trending almost immediately -- how much exposure could we get? How much exposure later when we were truly exposed?

I was standing on my pedestal -- the music blasting from the amps in the bed of the truck. "PHOLUS IS REBORN," the deep-voiced announcer said, then the dance mix (sampling the word "reborn" at unexpected moments). I would raise my arms and wave -- such penny drama.

Turning to my right, I saw Cavalier posing for pics with a group of guys, letting them stroke his abs -- on my left, I saw Gambit's back-piece (his name with the white and black knights on either end) as he flexed a double-bis for the crowd. They screamed as he allowed someone to come up and feel his arm -- the guy licked it instead.

I knew what Gambit's pheromones were doing to that guy, already -- poor thing couldn't hide his hard-on if he'd thought to -- and the crowd was loving It!

All six of them were releasing their scent -- it surrounded us like an invisible fog, moving with us down the parade route. Pity the poor Coldwell Bank people and the Lesbian softballers behind us, continually breathing our fumes.

Pokey jumped up on the trailer suddenly, leaping on the bench just as the announcer said, "PHOLUS IS REBORN!" Pokey pointed at me -- I raised my arms -- and when the beat broke, we danced together. Pokey motioned me to join him on the bench -- I jumped down, straddling it and Pokey thrust his junk in my face, weaving his hips before me. It was all I could do to keep myself from grabbing his swaying hips and sucking his cock. Gods, Pokey even had ME under his spell!

That kid was a natural.

Finally, bored, he pushed me off the trailer, saying, "Be with your people," while he took over dancing on the pedestal. He was no question better than the professional go-go boys way up in front of us on the Manhunt float -- I'd no doubt they'd be tributing Pokey by the end of the night.

Admittedly, it was a lot of fun street-level, too!

It wasn't hot, but we were all breaking out in a light sheen of sweat -- and pheromones. It was all about getting touched, getting stroked, smiling for selfies, giving them a taste for free. At six-five, three-hundred pounds, I was something they'd never seen before, an example of a man they'd likely never have access to -- it was all very heady. One guy came up as I was flexing my bicep and buried his face in my armpit -- the crowd went wild. That guy would find me later -- guaranteed. He could with his eyes closed.

I tried to have interaction with each member of the herd, not just to check in with them, but to enjoy them as well. This whole event was the most public foreplay I'd ever had the pleasure of engaging in -- I wanted to be inclusive. AppleJack surprised me the most. I expected him to be a little overwhelmed and intimidated by the crowd, but I saw no evidence of it. He was smiling and laughing and giving stuff away. He and Lickety Split stayed within each other's range -- whatever was going on with their blossoming friendship, I wanted to encourage it. Gambit had been right -- AppleJack had never been part of a male group-dynamic before. Seeing him thrive in one thrilled me. Lickety Split took in everything with the same goofy sense of humor he always displayed, shamelessly shaking his purple tail and laughing that stupid laugh.

I ran into Dunn as he was resupplying himself with goodies to give away -- we danced together, slowly grinding our hips. I reached up and pinched his nipples, pulling them toward me until Dunn leaned forward and we kissed. Cheering crowd. "Hail, Pholus," he whispered in my ear.

"PHOLUS IS REBORN!"

Dance dance dance dance.

Gambit, the MMA fighter, had been in front of crowds before -- they didn't intimidate him in any way. As a matter of fact, he was a brilliant manipulator of an audience -- he could practically read their energy and answer it, or lead it, or whatever the hell he was doing. He and I grappled playfully, wrapping our muscular bodies around each other -- no ground work, I was happy to say -- but plenty of takedown attempts. It was super erotic, of course, two guys our size -- he allowed me to put him in a full-nelson, holding his exposed torso to the crowds, his beautifully hairy armpits, my cock jammed between his orange tail and his hard ass. There wasn't a man within our view who didn't want to step up to Gambit and feel him, lick him, worship him, suck his magnificent cock.

When he tapped, I released him, and we flexed "Most Musculars" at each other -- just for the reaction. "This is a fuckin' blast!" he said -- that smirk. "Best thing that's ever happened to me in my life! Killing gods -- getting worshipped by crowds -- I fuckin' love this, Red, I mean, Pholus!"

"And they haven't even seen us dance, yet!"

He shuddered. "Don't remind me."

I laughed. "You're gonna be great, Warrior!"

"Yeah, duh I'm gonna be great," he said, heading back into the crowd. "Just don't remind me."

Cav was sitting on the end of the bench on the float, doing leg-ups and flexing his abs for the crowd, posing like the bench was a chaise lounge. "Watch this," he said as he gripped either side of the bench, pressing his body up, pointing his legs out before him like the letter "L". Without bending his legs, he rolled up into a handstand, in perfect alignment even balancing on a moving vehicle. The crowds yelled.

"I tried gymnastics in high school," he said to me as he landed his feet and stood up, waving to the crowd in acknowledgement. "I was terrible at it. Imagine if I'd been a centaur twenty years ago?" He lowered the waistband of his pants, flexing his abs and his magnificent Adonis belt, sticking his tongue out -- the crowd loved him. "They recognize me," he said. "As COLT Cavalier, I mean, porn star."

"You're famous!" I said, smiling. He rolled his eyes. "Is that a problem?"

"No, not at all," he said, shaking his head. "Of course, I haven't made any new content since I transformed, so they all think I have the same old cock! Surprises coming!"

I chuckled. "Many people cumming, too."

He smiled slyly. "MANY people."

"PHOLUS IS REBORN!" the amplifiers reminded us.

And that was how it went, small personal interactions against the canvas of this living crowd. They'd touch me and stroke me and pinch me and lick me -- I let one hot boy suck my nipple but I had to stop him cause I was losing control of my cock, my *nonischemic priapism*… I almost had to pry him off of me.

Gambit didn't even care -- I could see the slope of his cock from this side of the street, pressing against the little resistance offered by his joggers and cotton thong. Lickety Split was hard, too, his erection up by his hip. Even AppleJack was plumped up.

No one said being a centaur was gonna be easy.

Then there was Pokey with his frantic calls of "Judges' Stand! Judges' Stand! It's coming up!"

Dunn clapped his hands. "Everybody move your cape down to your waist," he said, unsnapping his own and demonstrating. "See? It clips on your waist here and here. No, no, go underneath your tail, Pokey -- there you go!"

We were only supposed to have (up to) ninety seconds to perform -- that was the rules for marching bands and dance troupes -- but of course Pokey had choreographed a two-minute piece. We all doubted they'd cut us off.

As the narration played, the six of them got into position -- I was off to the side (I got to have an "entrance") -- Pokey, Cavalier, and Lickety Split in the front row, AppleJack, Dunn, and Gambit behind them in their windows. "It was the time of myth," the narrator said, underscoring beneath it, "a Dionysian playground."

AppleJack stepped up behind Pokey, Dunn behind Cavalier, and Gambit behind Lickety Split -- they each reached forward, flipped up the guy's cape before him and stepped under it, becoming "the back end of the horse" to put it bluntly. Pokey, Cav, and Lickety Split were "centaurs"!

"A land where centaurs played…"

The three of them (the six of them) danced together, a sort of hybrid tap dance thing that would delight any three-year-old at a birthday party. Naturally, the crowd ate it up.

At one point, they reversed, Pokey, Cav, and Lickety Split spinning around and dropping beneath the capes, making AppleJack, Dunn, and Gambit the "centaurs", facing the opposite side of the street. The "back end" of the horses, butts toward the judges, did an exaggerated hip dance, ending with a quick twerk. Huge laugh and cheers!

"But they lost their way…"

The centaurs broke into front halves and back halves again, six individuals, walking sadly to their spots -- it was time for my entrance.

I ran in from the side and vaulted over Gambit's back, -- a mid-air flip and I landed in the midst of them, arms up over my head.

"Until... PHOLUS IS REBORN!"

The music grew, mixing, mixing, a huge crescendo of sound till it reached a peak, and on cue, we all ripped our breakaway pants off, exposing the chaps and the white thongs that barely covered our giant genitals. We held the pose until the reverb played out, the audience silent and awed as we broke into the Haka section of the dance.

Fully masculine stomps and thrusts, everything was about flexing and projecting masculinity -- and of course, emitting pheromones -- stomp, clap, clap, stomp, clap, clap, GRUNT!

"Hunh!" Stomp!

"Hunh! Hunh!" Stomp!

And we formed a tribal circle, dancing as we had around our kill -- the drums re-entered, pounding out a rhythm. We picked it up and we broke into a line.

It was the burlesque section, as masculine as the Haka, but slinky. Lots of abs, lots of posing, out-sexing the guy next to you, slower moves -- ass and hips. We were able to open up and work the crowd, spread our scent, flex in guys' faces. My dick got grabbed a couple times -- I didn't mind. I dosed them harder.

Then, in our last bit, Gambit, Lickety Split, and I stood next to each other, facing the judges. We held each other around the shoulders. Dunn and Cavalier approached from behind us and on cue, easily hopped up onto our shoulders, nothing for our super-bodies, but getting a gasp from the audience -- cheers.

AppleJack and Pokey had been working the wide ring downstage, each of them on pheromone overdrive. Pokey stayed by the Judges' Table, lulling them with his cute little ass and tail while AppleJack approached us, faced front, and squatted down about three feet in front of Lickety Split, the center base of our pyramid. In a sumo squat, AppleJack interlaced his fingers and held his hands ready for a boost.

Pokey ran up to AppleJack, stepped onto AppleJack's hands, and AppleJack "cleaned" him, standing up and throwing Pokey high. Pokey did a front flip/ half twist, landing as lightly as a dove on Dunn and Cavalier's shoulders, complete centaur-pyramid. Pose.

A cheer from the crowd, not even realizing we weren't quite done!

Pokey dove off the top, doing a slow flip before landing in AppleJack's arms. Dunn and Cavalier echoed him, flipping easily off the bases' shoulders and landing effortlessly on the ground. We did one more dance sequence -- the one that had been highlighted in the montage music video earlier, clever viewers would connect that -- then we hit a final Final Pose (one that centered around me this time) as the DJ announced the familiar, and hopefully unforgettable, "NOTHING WILL BE THE SAME NOW THAT... PHOLUS IS REBORN!"

Pose!

Beat of silence.

Explosion of approval from the audience, cheers and screams -- applause from people who aren't holding their phones -- whistles and shouts. It felt like the end of one of those Variety Shows where we're standing there holding the pose, smiling, breathing heavy, sweating until we finally broke.

We hadn't planned on it, so we had to improvise a bow.

Everybody was going crazy, but they were already behind, so we had to move on fairly quickly, leaving the poor Coldwell Bank folks in front of the Judges' Stand with nothing to show for themselves but wet spots on their khaki shorts and hard-ons. And the lesbian softballers? I hesitated to think…

We all rode the float for a few minutes, having bottled water and sharing another of Dunn's joints. We were sweaty and satisfied, fraternal, but it wasn't long before we were back at it, driving the crowd crazy and enticing them to follow us.

Nobody wanted to miss the next part of the evening.

It wasn't just Pholus -- centaurs themselves had been reborn.

And soon people would see what that meant.

****

TRADE was one of those 80's dance bars that converted an old warehouse into a gay haven. In the old days, the neighborhood was considered "off the beaten path," or "sketchy," but within the last ten years, the area had undergone a lot of development. I didn't think someone from the 80's would even recognize it anymore. The parade ended a block away -- it was clearly the intention that everybody should go to TRADE afterwards -- that should say something!

There were two bouncers working the front door, neither were big enough to be a threat to us -- the chunky Italian guy looked at my ID, then looked at me with a disbelieving expression. "I drank a magic potion," I said, hitting him with a dose of pheromones. "I'm sure you understand."

He smiled, handing me my ID with one hand, adjusting his dick with the other. "I get you," he said, dreamily stamping the back of my hand. "I take a lot of shit, too."

I slid my ID back under my gauntlet -- the way Dunn had shown me -- and waited for the others to get through so we could enter together. I figured our outfits would make us stand out from the crowd, white harnesses, thongs, and chaps with tails -- but I hadn't realized what a costume-fest Pride was.

We were not alone!

"This is glorious," Cavalier said to me as we waited together. He put his hands behind his head and stretched his torso -- I could smell him from here. "It's everything I imagined!" He sighed. "I feel like we're on this side of destiny and we just have to take a step…"

Pokey hugged Cav from behind. "Hey, hot herdmaster," he said, stroking Cav's beautiful abs. "I gotta tell ya, I reckon your ass looks fuckin' spectacular right now!"

"Get in line," I said to Pokey. The three of us laughed.

The gang assembled in the anteroom, where the coat-check would've been in winter -- we huddled in a tight circle. "We're here as centaurs, my brothers," Cav said, smirking. "Let's show these humans their place." He held his hand out, palm down. "Satyr toast on three…" The guys each reached out and stacked their hands in the center. Cav counted, bouncing the stack, "One… two…"

"*Euoi euan!*" we all yelled, throwing our arms up.

Then we entered the interior of the club.

The place was immense -- there's just no other word. I mean, it was a warehouse, but all the openness and space seemed larger on the inside than the outside, somehow. The main floor had a huge bar on the North Wall -- some booths and such -- but the space was mostly given to the dance floor. A large balcony encircled it, the South Wall dedicated as a DJ booth. There was a muscular guy there spinning even this early, well before midnight. Cav pointed to him and said, "Former porn star."

There were go-go boy platforms set in each corner and I'm sure the main bar had seen a dancer or two in its time. There was a smaller bar upstairs, but that had a significantly limited selection.

TRADE was all theatrics -- amazing sound system, expensive lights, effects -- hell, even the dance floor lit up and did tricks. Perfect for any drugged-up Mary who wanted to dance reality away.

Tonight they'd get their chance.

It was pretty busy already but filling up fast with the parade crowd. Gambit boldly walked up to the service bar, to the dismay of the waiters -- when the hunky bartender came over to give him shit, Gambit grabbed him by the back of the neck and kissed him. It wasn't even two seconds of struggle before the bartender submitted to him. "He's ours now," Gambit said to us with a handful of drinks, indicating the bartender. "If you need anything, go to the service bar — he'll prioritize you."

We were already trending on social media. Pokey showed us several IG posts with our dance routine from various angles -- we were super sexy, for sure. Pokey was watching it over and over, until Cav covered the screen with his hand. "Later, Pokey," he said. "We have stuff to do."

"I know, I know," Pokey said, sliding his phone into the phone pocket Dunn had made in the side of the chaps. "You reckon I can dance on one of them platforms?" he asked, indicating the go-go boy stands.

"You reckon anyone's gonna be able to stop you?" Cav asked.

It started easily enough, Pokey up on the platform dancing while the rest of us danced around the base. Obviously he attracted attention -- how could you NOT look at Pokey? -- his body was incredible, so lean, so cut, but I'd be remiss if I left out how beautiful his package looked, his swollen balls and his abnormally large cock, looking even larger when compared to Pokey's tight little ass and lean cowboy legs. And then of course, the angle of the viewer put Pokey's crotch squarely in focus.

Pokey squatted down and grabbed his drink. "This is what I should'a done for a livin'," he said. "Fuck the rodeo!"

He drew a crowd. And within moments, they were waving money.

Cav indicated the other empty go-go boy platforms around the perimeter of the dance floor. With a laugh, Lickety Split and AppleJack took one, initially goofing around instead of being serious -- but it didn't take long for them to develop a crowd, either. Lickety Split's cock was thickety-thick and AppleJack's balls were laden with milk. Neither had any idea what he was doing, necessarily, but with junk like that, who cared if they could dance or not?

Gambit didn't even try -- he hopped up on one of the platforms easily and just started flexing. On occasion, he'd throw in a step-touch to make it look like he was "dancing" but in fact, he was simply flexing and showing off. And by the slope of his cock, he was getting off on it, too.

Cav took the final platform, the one under the DJ booth and -- as I expected, I guess, he WAS a professional, after all -- worked it like a pro. Pokey was just dancing, enjoying himself, and that made him sexy. Cav was WORKING the stage, everything he did was designed to get a reaction -- sexy as fuck. And he was loving it.

Gambit offered me his hand and I joined him on his platform. "I wanna do something erotic," he growled, "AND artisitic! Let's grapple in slow-motion!"

I smiled. "Oh, that's hot!"

There was plenty of room on the platform, especially because we were moving slowly and carefully. But we "grappled" in slo-mo -- in fact, we just went through a series of holds and moves, but with a fluidity like we were underwater, almost like it was an out-of-tempo dance, wrapping ourselves around each other like snakes, like the illustrations on the side of an ancient urn.

We were all emitting pheromones, of course, it would be impossible not to given what we were doing. And from the vantage point I had, it was easy to see the effect it was having on the crowd, especially on the dance floor. Not that dancing wasn't always sexual, tonight it was easy to see the tinge of lust that colored the air. The line between dancing and fucking had never been so thin -- poor Terpsichore, seduced by Eros!

But the action actually started with Dunn.

I spied Dunn over on the side wall, in the shadow of the balcony -- and only because he was wearing a white harness and it glowed in the blue light. Dunn knew everybody, it seemed -- the side-effect of owning a barbershop -- and he was right now hanging with a group of leathermen and someone's slave was on their knees sucking Dunn's cock. (I saw the glint of light off his PA while the slave bobbed.) Dunn was kissing the slave's Master while the Master held the slave's leash.

That was the first sex I saw, anyway -- it was 11:05pm.

The place kept filling up.

The dancers were making out, rubbing against each other sloppily, sweaty, spreading the scent of lust to the pounding beat of the DJ, who seemed out of range. I bet Lickety Split could climb up there…

Cavalier was on the platform below the DJ booth -- he was kneeling, slapping guys on the face with his cock as they begged him for attention and humiliation -- money in their hands.

"Let's break," Gambit said. "I feel like getting my dick sucked."

Sitting on the pedestal, Gambit's cock was pretty much at eye-level with someone standing on the dance floor. Gambit pointed to one of the dancer boys in the crowd and said, "You. Suck my cock." The boy happily -- and hungrily -- did, gagging on Gambit's size. Gambit smiled up at me.

I sat down back-to-back with him and found a boy of my own -- hot little blondie -- to suck mine.

One of the bouncers came over to break it up. "Guys," he said. "Guys! C'mon, now, none of that here!"

I pushed the blond off me -- he fell away. "It's hard to keep 'em off this cock," I said, waving it at the bouncer as I dosed him with pheromones. "You don't mind, do you?"

He looked over his shoulder nervously, like he was looking for his boss -- he was sweating, breathing deeply. He couldn't look away -- I mean, my cock was as big as his forearm. "Guys usually go upstairs," he said, touching his growing erection. "Even the hot guys."

"You think I'm hot?" I asked, flexing my abs, displaying myself, bombarding him. "You should suck my cock, then." He was so indecisive for a bouncer. "Look, we're both right here -- why go all the way upstairs?" I touched my erection to his lips. "Suck my cock."

He couldn't help himself -- he did. He worked on it with the desperation of a man who needed to hurry up and get back to his shift. I took the opportunity to program him. "Everything's normal," I said firmly. "Everything you see happening is normal. It's one of those nights -- one of those full-moon nights. Everyone's so horny on a full moon -- it's normal. Just guys being guys, right?"

He bobbed helplessly on my cock, absorbing my every word as gospel.

"Don't let trouble-makers in tonight," I said. "It's a normal, full-moon, hot guy Pride night. No police, though, ok? If police show up, don't let them in -- that would just ruin my night. You don't want anyone to ruin my night, do you?"

"No," he said, desperately, "of course not. No police..." He choked trying to deepthroat me — he could barely get the entire glans in his mouth.

"If police come in here, I'm never gonna let you suck my cock again."

That scared him -- he tried harder. He wanted so badly to please me.

I leaned back and hit Gambit's shoulder with my hand. "I'm going upstairs," I said. "You wanna come?"

He shook his head. "Nah," he said. "I like bein' up here. I'm gonna fuck some ass on this pedestal -- show these fuckers how it's done."

I laughed. "I'll watch from the balcony."

He laughed and fist-bumped me. "I'll wave."

I slid down the platform into the bouncer's arms -- I kissed him for a minute, cementing my hold on him, then I had him walk me to the stairs, preceding me like a celebrity bodyguard. My thong had disappeared -- someone had probably stolen it and would end up jerking off to its scent for days to come -- but I still wore the chaps and the harness, my green tail still shaggy behind me, my sandals and my laurel headband. I walked like a mythical being amongst a crowd of lowly humans -- that was how I felt, my bodyguard keeping my fans at bay as more and more of them became aware of my smell, fell victim to my power.

At the base of the staircase, my bouncer had to go back to the door -- he regretted having to leave me, but he had a job to perform and he didn't want to disappoint me. As I ascended the stairs, my cock bouncing back and forth between my thighs, I distracted just about everybody -- one guy lost his footing and went tumbling down.

I was being followed, of course, multiple sets of eyes were riveted to my glutes as I went up each stair. As I passed guys I thought were hot, I would reach out and gently touch them, acknowledge them, instantly seduce them -- I enjoyed watching them helplessly yield to me, fall in love with me with little more than a glance.

From the balcony, I could see the entire dance floor -- packed with people (and more coming in), the floor was a throbbing, sweaty mass of humanity. There were smaller, separate masses forming around each of the go-go platforms, where the centaurs frollicked -- it fascinated me to watch.

It also turned me on.

"Who wants to suck my cock?" I asked the crowd forming behind me. "Who wants to be first to worship Pholus?"

Quite a number did -- and they were willing to fight for it.

That really turned me on.

****

It went on for hours -- I lost track of time in my lust. It was all a beautiful, hazy, sexual marathon. I'd taken over the corner booth to keep the crowds from pushing me over the edge of the balcony. And right now it was an endless series of holes for me to fuck, so many asses in my face, lined up and eager. They were all sucking and fucking and just as lost in lust as I was, helplessly succumbing.

There were piles of guys collapsed from exhaustion, but unable to stop.

My bouncer approached as I fucked some thick man's ass, whose face I'd never seen, while some heavily mustachioed man ate my hole.

"My Lord," he said, worriedly, "it's four am. We have to close."

I kissed him without breaking my stride. "No," I said. "We'll be here till sunrise, at least. Maybe longer -- until the moon sets. Just stop letting people in."

"Yes, my Lord."

The hairy man behind me stood up, wrapping his arms around my torso -- I could feel his cock against my ass. I was ready for him.

The energy once again built to a fever pitch -- higher and higher, climbing some sexual thermometer, the mercury rising.

And then the strangest thing happened. Everyone around me seemed to slow down, as if someone had turned down the speed of time, slower and slower -- the scene became strangely void of color as well, as if no more than living background elements in a theatrical scene.

I was looking around, seeing this happen across the entire balcony -- maybe the entire bar -- simultaneously. I seemed to be the only living being still in real time and technicolor.

Until I saw Him. At the other end of the balcony -- a young man, beautiful, maybe nineteen, twenty on the outside, his skin youthful and tight, unblemished and golden. Aside from the long golden blond curls falling to his shoulders, he was completely smooth, naked but for a pair of sandals remarkably like mine. His build was lean, unremarkable, yet powerfully beautiful. He looked soft yet firm.

His eyes were a bright purple, the color of ripe grapes, his features classic and handsome.

"Hello, Pholus," he said, his voice dripping honey.

We were the only two people moving in real time, so I slid out of my tableau to address him. "Hello," I said. "You are...?"

He smiled a toothy grin, as playful as Pokey. "An admirer," he said. "You're doing so well."

I answered him with a confused, "Thank you" and he laughed.

He turned and looked over the balcony at the dance floor -- he spread his arms and breathed in deeply. "This is incredible," he said, motioning me to join him. "I haven't felt this in thous... a very long time."

He took my hand and presented the dance floor to me. In the same sort of fluid, deep-sea speed of time, I saw the frantic dancing, the spectacle, the orgy caught in amber fluid. Hundreds of bodies throbbing on the dance floor, rolling amidst each other like a pit of snakes -- where did one human end and the next begin? It was impossible to tell. It was like an erotic relief on marble.

Gambit was on one pedestal, choking some boy in a jockstrap while Gambit fucked him hard -- he was slapping the boy's tattooed face as the boy held his own legs by the ankles, giving Gambit total access. Even at this speed, the slap still looked like it hurt.

I couldn't see Pokey, who was directly below me, but I could see the dozens of men watching him and masturbating, unable to look away. On the other hand, I could see Cavalier, directly opposite me. He's somehow ended up in the DJ booth and he was fucking the DJ from behind as the guy spun the house mix.

I didn't spot any of the others, but I could sense them nearby -- they were all as deep in it, at least.

"This is everything I'd hoped," the youth said, squeezing my hand. "It empowers me." He inhaled deeply. "And I've waited so long."

"Who are you?" I asked him, confused at his familiarity.

He chuckled. "Oh, honey, the reveal doesn't come until the penultimate moment of the story. You should know theatre better than that." Turning, he slowly led me back to the corner booth and the ass I'd been fucking. "All you need to know at this point is that the universe is unfolding exactly as it should." He indicated that I should slide my cock back where it had been, so I started to, feeling the warmth and tight firmness of my eager partner. I couldn't resist fucking him, grooving to the same slow tempo he was in.

"One more thing you should know," the youth said, as he leaned forward and kissed my forehead, as reality returned, color and tempo suddenly existing again.

He whispered in my ear. "Chiron waits for you at home."

I couldn't stop myself from orgasming.

11. "Tulpa"

Tulpa (ˈtʊlpə: *Tibetan*) *a thought form, or independent entity made completely out of their worshipper's belief and faith in them. In Religious Philosophy, it is a largely accepted fact that the power of any given deity is proportional to the amount of belief in them or the amount of worship they are currently receiving.*
The opposite is also true: As a deity's power-base of worshippers shrinks, their divine strength fades -- if all worship of them ceases, they may fade out of existence completely. In a similar manner, the well-being of an Anthropomorphic Personification is often tied to whatever concept they personify.

****

Overnight, we became famous -- or infamous, depending on your point of view. In the modern world, neither were bad -- at least according to Cav. "Any publicity is good publicity," he said, comfortable with cliches. Of course, he had a publicist.

The orgy lasted well into the next day, when the new management shift came to work. By that time, it was mostly exhausted, over-sexed zombies left with barely enough energy to shuffle by. I heard the first thing they did was open the windows to air the place out. I would've used a hose, or diverted a local river to wash the place out.

We left just after the sun had come up but after the moon had set -- not because we were tired, but more because we were bored. We'd pretty much used up this crowd, both for their sex as well as their energy. Besides, we knew it was better to get out of there before reality broke it up, anyway.

We'd gone viral by the time the sun was fully risen -- I mean, we were everywhere online. Our hashtag had blown up -- hundreds of pics and video clips from the parade. Some of these were really funny: multiple closeups of our white pouches or isolated body parts, sweaty selfies of guys with their favorite centaur (lots of these were of Lickety Split, believe it or not -- he had that kind of tongue-stuck-out, YOLO-sort of pose that the kids favored), flexing shots with Gambit, always kissing shots with Pokey.

The dance from the judges' stand made it to the TMZ website! "Chippendales replaced by Centaurs" the click-bait read. "Humans with horse parts!" Sadly, they pixeled out our packages, so if you actually wanted to see our human-horse parts, you had to choose another site. Still, the point was we were getting national attention. We were becoming famous.

On the other hand, the "infamous" videos and pics, the ones from the inside of the bar, were also making the rounds. There were some that were fairly innocuous -- Gambit and I slo-mo grappling on a pedestal, Pokey endlessly twerking with his pink tail, videos of the DJ spinning and the frenetic dancing and the fevered pitch of the place. But then, there were the short porn flicks: me getting my cock sucked while the guy holding the camera says,"That's the bouncer, man!", shots of Dunn with all these leathermen at his feet, worshipping him, his huge boner nearly up to his chest, a big glob of pre-cum dripping off, while some slaveboy sucked his nipple and another licked his armpit -- and this one incredibly well-edited video of Gambit fucking guy after guy after guy in a repeated, GIF-kind of cycle. I was certain Gambit would put that video on his resume.

Shots/ videos of the group orgy on the dance floor, shots of my private party on the balcony, the pile of people being fucked by me, easily-identifiable me. Pholus Reborn.

When we left the bar, the first thing Cavalier had said was, "Now, THAT'S what centaurs are all about: sexual ecstasy! THAT'S what we do in this world! THAT'S why we're back!

"We're starting a new age!"

****

@Cavalier: Gentlemen, the offers are pouring in!
@Cavalier: Do we all have our passports?

@Pokey: I don't.

@me: I need new pictures.

@AppleJack: Yeah. I do, too.

@Cavalier: I need you to take care of it ASAP.

@Gambit: "Pouring in"? Really?
@Gambit: It's only been since Saturday.
@Gambit: What's that, like three days?
@Gambit: Guys, our agent is blowing smoke up our ass.

@Cavalier: I kid you not!
@Cavalier: Social media, baby!
@Cavalier: Little centaurs, we're heading to the promised land!
@Cavalier: We're going to MYKONOS!

@Dunn: Are you kidding? That's AMAZING!
@Dunn: <orgasm emoji>

@Pokey: Where is that?

@Cavalier: Greece

@Dunn: It's where all the rich queens go on vacation.

@Pokey: Howdy! Did someone say "rich"...?

@LicketySplit: Hold on. When is this?
@LicketySplit: I got American Ninja Warrior finals next month!
@LicketySplit: I can't miss that!
@LicketySplit: I'm gonna be the first American Champion!

@Cavalier: When is Warrior?
@Cavalier: Mykonos is around the 20th

@LicketySplit: Ok -- ANW is the first week.
@LicketySplit: 5th through the 10th
@LicketySplit: Sorry for the panic.

@Cavalier: So everyone's cool?
@Cavalier: It's okay to book Mykonos?

@Pokey: Ok by me!

@Dunn: <thumbs up emoji>

@Gambit: <eggplant emoji> <eggplant emoji> <sweat emoji>

@AppleJack: Never been out of the country, so hell yeah!

@LicketySplit: Yeah, but I'm gonna be so jet-lagged.
@LicketySplit: Let's hope I can get it up.

> @me: Really excited about Mykonos, Cav
> @me: works out for me in a lot of ways!
> @me: Well done
> @me: *Euoi Euan!*

@Cavalier: Believe me, it's my pleasure.
@Cavalier: I'm lucky
@Cavalier: My agent works really, really hard for me.
@Cavalier: Pardon the pun.

****

We all thought it was gonna get old hand. We'd do a couple of these appearances and the novelty would wear off and we'd get bored -- familiarity bred contempt and all, right? -- but it didn't happen that way. If anything, the familiarity led us to be bolder. Once the boundaries had been established, the job became to push them. We didn't do anymore parades, but public appearances were very big -- celebrity go-go boys, celebrity go-go boys who could create a sexual frenzy. We left a wake of orgies behind us.

Once the surprise of us wore off, the anticipation took over. And that energy was way more palpable. By the time we got onstage, the crowd had stewed in their juices long enough to be completely marinated before we'd even get to them with the pheromones. It took a lot less to push them over the edge when they wanted to be pushed.

We became… notorious.

As many people hated us as loved us. There were groups that protested us -- these high-moral, religious, anti-gay crusaders who feared their physical bodies so much that they felt the need to stop everyone from feeling pleasure. Oh, we displayed our genitals proudly -- how dare us? We didn't fear the devil, or what they thought was the devil. Pan? Hell, we partied with Pan! I was starting to understand why centaurs were a necessary force in the world again -- someone had to balance this Puritan hysteria. But that didn't stop me from being entertained by the protesters with their signs and their misguided anger.

It would've been easy to have… dosed them, subjugated them, and forced them to do the things they so vehemently protested -- we'd talked about that. Some of the guys wanted to do it very badly. Personally, I believed that would lead to even more anger and problems. It was best to just ignore them. There were plenty of people who wanted to worship.

Chiron waits for you at home.

Those words echoed in my head. Whatever that glowing youth in TRADE had been -- vision? Hallucination? Dream Lover -- his words had been absolutely wrong in their prediction.

Chiron had not been waiting for me at home that night -- AppleJack had been at home, smoking a last bowl before falling into an exhausted sleep. I don't even think he had showered -- he'd still been crusty.

"Did you enjoy yourself?" I'd asked, motioning for him to hand me the bong.

"Dude, I've never done anything like that -- ever," he'd said. "Do you know I had more sex last night than the rest of my life put together?"

I'd chuckled, after hitting the bong. "Let's hope all seven of us can say that."

"Weirder still, man, I feel like I could have sex right now. I'm mean, I'm exhausted, I can barely move, but I'm still horny. What the fuck is that?"

I blew out my hit and handed the bong back. "That's the centaur curse, right?"

We'd laughed lightly as he loaded another bowl. "Some curse," he'd mumbled, playing with the word. "Horrible curse."

"You glad you joined the club?" I'd asked. "I mean... do you have a label for your sexuality yet?"

He'd laughed out loud and lit the bowl. "Centaur," he'd said. "That pretty much covers it."

****

And that's how I found myself aboard a yacht anchored off Mykonos in the Mediterranean Sea, watching the sun set, drinking a domestic red wine and smoking cigars on the aft deck with Cavalier as two locals knelt before us and sucked our cocks. The others were ashore, attending a Tea Party and trying to find playmates for the evening. I wanted the opportunity to talk to Cav, so we hung back, trusting them to bring guys back for us.

Meanwhile, these two local boys were doing a beautiful job. They hadn't come with the yacht, but they seemed to be always around. (I didn't always understand other cultures.) Late teens/ early twenties (younger than Pokey, that's for sure), with flawless olive skin and exceptional oral skills -- we supplied their tireless desire.

"So," Cav asked, puffing his cigar, "how does it feel to be back in Greece?"

"Weird… it's changed from how I remember it." I took a puff on the cigar -- it was hard to remember it wasn't a joint and I shouldn't inhale, so I inevitably coughed. "Remember when you first left home -- for me it was college -- and you came back and everything seemed smaller? Yeah, well, it's nothing like that."

Cav laughed.

"As a matter of fact, I feel this weird sense of… foreboding -- but that implies negativity. Maybe better to say, a sense of weight, like meaning… purpose… you know, destiny kind of stuff. Like, I'm where I'm supposed to be. Does that make sense?"

He nodded and took a sip of wine. "Sure," he said, setting the glass down so he could use his hand to guide the boy's head who sucked his cock -- his other hand held his cigar. "This place has an ancient energy. I'm actually looking forward to hunting here."

I chuckled. "Do you think that's wise?" I asked, sipping my own wine. "Isn't that sort of waving the red flag in the bull's face?"

He smirked, taking a hit on his cigar. "I'm not worried."

I was, so I let that comment hang on the evening breeze and enjoyed the boy's talented mouth on my oversized cock instead. The sun lost its footing on the horizon, streaks of its pink embarrassment filling the sky -- it seemed bigger here than in the States, or maybe the presence of Helios was just more powerful. Maybe all the gods were more powerful here?

"So," Cavalier said after the silence had drifted too long in the air, "what did you want to talk about?"

I finished my wine in one gulp and set the glass down. "After the parade," I began, "in the bar, at just about the peak of the sexual energy -- just as it bordered on religious hysteria -- I had… an encounter. A glowing being… manifested… before me as a young man, beautiful -- breathtakingly beautiful. Time… slowed down and we had this conversation at normal speed while watching everyone fuck in slo-mo, like they were encased in jello. You were pounding that poor DJ pretty mercilessly…"

Cav snorted, hitting his cigar. "He used to do porn… and he dissed me one time in the trades. We did a scene together and he was a fucking asshole. It was fun to put him in his place, make him my slave." He chuckled, thinking about it and smacked his cock wetly on his current boy's face. "So what did you and this being talk about?"

"Well, good news -- he said I was doing everything right. And I felt nothing from him but benevolence. He said a centaur's purpose was to create that exact kind of sexual frenzy -- that it empowered him. He wouldn't tell me who he was -- he made some joke about bad theatre and poorly-timed reveals instead. He was so cryptic and odd -- he had to have been divine."

"No doubt," Cav said, nodding, puffing his cigar and contemplating. "That's all he said?"

I shook my head. "No," I said, "The last thing he said was, 'Chiron waits for you at home.' And then he was gone and I was fucking in real-time again. And… incidentally, Chiron was not waiting for me at home -- AppleJack was. Which I recognize as not the same thing."

"So you came to Greece…"

"Hoping to find Chiron," I said, interrupting. "I figured Greece was probably what he meant by home."

Cavalier turned and looked at me for a minute, puffing his cigar. "I think it may be more obvious than that," he finally said.

"What do you mean?"

"Sometimes the gods put the answers right in our fucking faces," he said, indicating that I should turn my head and look.

The rough coastline of Greece, hued from volcanic rock and the will of the gods. In the foreground was civilization, the mortals who lived on the beach with their technology and ambient light, but Cav clearly didn't mean that. Far up the coast, now lit by the last rays of the evening sun, making its snowy peak orange against the dark blue of the coming night -- a lone mountain. So familiar… on the tip of my tongue.

"There, in the distance," Cav said quietly. "Mt. Pelion."

I gasped.

"My home… Pholus' home."

****

As soon as Cav said "Mt. Pelion," one of the local boys who'd been sucking our cocks, whose English was far better than my Greek, told us that we reminded him of the stories he'd heard about a reclusive sex god who was said to live on Mt. Pelion. An old man with a giant cock -- the stories said he pushed his cock around before himself on a cart -- his smell, like ours, was said to drive men wild with lust, enough to make them impale themselves on his huge penis until they were dead. It was a story locals told for generations, perhaps in an effort to keep the young men from playing in the many caves along the coast.

The boy told us this while impaling himself on my huge penis, so I wasn't sure how much of it was porn-fantasy on his part. But it was worth exploring, so the next morning, we had the captain sail us up the East Coast of Greece toward the Pelion Peninsula. The other centaurs, barely sated, viewed it as sightseeing, an opportunity for fresh meat -- I wasn't ready to share the other stuff with them yet.

And there was something… someone -- I could feel him. The closer we got, passing the spectacular cliffs and inlets of this ancient coast, the more I became aware of him. This feeling reminded me of the bond between myself and the centaurs I'd created -- it had the same longingful pull. The call of sex.

I followed this call. I explained to the herd that I was going ashore in search of an old friend and I would be back before long -- they all figured it was a sex-thing and nobody even blinked.

Going ashore, dressed in linen pants and loafers, shirtless, my hairy beauty exposed to the world, I unerringly led myself up the mountain to the hidden door of a house nearly invisible in the mountainside of Mt. Pelion, as if someone had taken a cave and had Frank Lloyd Wright develop it into a residence -- the old and the new melded seamlessly together.

An olive-skinned beauty opened the door, dressed only in a short linen skirt and sandals. He was spectacular, young and hairless, his pink, puffy nipples sitting atop his tight, muscular chest -- his pink, pouty lips ready to pleasure my cock. But he wasn't the scent I sought.

"*Geiá sou,*" I said in my sorry Greek. "*Eínai o kýrios sas?*"

The boy smiled -- probably because of the way I butchered his language. "He is expecting you," he said in perfect English, opening the door to bid me enter.

Again, walking through the house was like walking through a cave that had been made into a house, all the stone and slate, with the sleek, LCD lighting and hidden speakers piping in some old folk music -- it was the kind of place one saw on the Rich & Famous Real Estate shows, a little too over-the-top to be believed. NOTHING could've been this nice. How much money had this taken? How many years?

The boy walked before me, allowing me to view his spectacular ass, the globes of his bubblebutt peeking beneath his skirt -- it was hard to decide exactly what to look at, the house or the boy. We descended a short stairs and emerged into a grotto. It reminded me of the Ancient Public Baths, a large pool dominating the space, with several types of hot tubs adorning the circumference and a magnificent, raised dais on one end, almost like a pulpit, where a massive bed sat ready for use. This was the biggest-budget porn-set I'd ever seen -- as if Spielberg were shooting a Greek fuck-flick.

As we entered, the boy's Master stood from the hot tub, his back to us, as two other olive-skinned servants dressed him in a white, terry-cloth robe. He was shorter than me -- maybe half a head -- though massively muscular, in proportion with his height, as if someone had taken a super-heavyweight bodybuilder and expanded him proportionally. A mature man -- if I were to meet him as a mortal, I would put him somewhere in his early sixties -- moderately long, curly white hair, he sported a beard that was a bit longer than mine, but oiled and maintained with a meticulous attention mine had never known. The robe didn't hide the fact that he was hairy, but why wouldn't he be? He was a spectacular example of man -- civilized man, anyway.

The robe made no secret of his cock, either. Like mine, it jutted before him like an extra limb, continuously hard and heavy, ready for more. It had to be two feet long, but the way the boys had placed it in the material, it was hard to be sure. I'd hoped to find out. Hardly the image of a withered old crone with his cock on a cart.

When we made eye-contact, he smiled -- and in that moment, I knew him. I'd known him for thousands of years. But that was the moment it all came back, as I'd hoped it would. "Chiron!"
I said.

"Hello, Pholus," he said in English, with a glorious accent, opening his muscular arms for a hug. "Welcome home!"

12. "Chiron"

*In Greek mythology, **Chiron** (/ˈkaɪrən/ KY-rən; also Cheiron or Kheiron; Greek: Χείρων "hand") was held to be the superlative centaur amongst his brethren, as he was called the "wisest and justest of all the centaurs". Chiron was notable throughout Greek mythology for his youth-nurturing nature. He took many erômenoi and taught the art of medicine, herbs, music, archery, hunting, gymnastics and prophecy, including to Pholus, his favorite, whom he rewarded by transforming the youth into a centaur. Centaurs were notorious for being wild, lusty, overly indulgent drinkers and carousers, violent when intoxicated, and generally uncultured delinquents. Chiron, by contrast, was intelligent, civilized and kind, because he was not related directly to the other centaurs due to his parentage.*

****

I couldn't even tell you how long we fucked before we had a chance to talk. It felt like that sexual communication was almost as valuable as the verbal would be. His age was buffered by his confidence and his ability, his skillful love-making knew no bounds.

Our cocks were big enough to be inside each other as we faced one another, each fucking the other while we deeply kissed. "I've missed you," he moaned as he shot yet another load into me. "It's been too long…"

"So why didn't you…?"

"There will be plenty of time for talk," he said, bringing me to orgasm with his talented fingers. "But first, we must be what we are."

It was like having sex with someone you've had sex with a million times but it was your first time together -- everything was familiar and new at the same time. That first sexual coupling lasted nearly the full day and well into the night. We fucked in the grotto, we fucked in his bed, we fucked in a sling that was hung deep in the cavernous depths of the mountain. He showed me more ways to stimulate someone than I'd experienced in at least a lifetime! He was a master at pleasure.

"Well, I should be," he said later, sitting upright against a massive pile of cushions. I sat with my back against him, in the crook of his arm -- we were smoking some of my best bud. "After all, I've been having sex for thousands of years. I've picked up a thing or two."

"Thousands of years," I mumbled, taking my hit. Then, upon exhalation I said, "So are you immortal still? I read you traded your immortality away..."

"That old saw," he replied, chuckling as he took the joint from me. "The stories don't have everything exactly right." He kissed me deeply, sharing the hit he'd taken. Of course, he was a good kisser, too. Making out with him was like kissing a lover I hadn't kissed in forever -- the old rhythms found their way. My *Erastês*.

I texted the herd to let them know I was okay -- I'm sure they were entertaining themselves.

"They're HERE?" Chiron said. "In Mouressi?"

"Yeah, they're on a yacht, moored right in the harbor. We came over for Mykonos Pride -- you haven't seen us online?"

He seemed delighted. "Then I can meet them? Before you all head back to the Americas?"

"Of course!" I said, mirroring his enthusiasm. "I'd be honored!"

He sighed. "Small joys," he said, taking another hit.

****

The myths held some truths, too: Chiron was a teacher at heart. He told me everything. "Surely you've done some research," he said, indicating the computer screen before us -- (when I made a joke about the Batcave, he didn't get my reference, so he didn't know EVERYTHING). "From the story of Pholus, we get the phrase 'shooting yourself in the foot' -- did you know that?"

Yes, I did, though I didn't remember it happening -- but I let him tell it.

"After Heracles finished his fourth labor, killing the boar..." He rolled his eyes. "But before he was made to clean out the Augean Stables, the Lapiths demanded he wipe out the centaurs. Their drunken, sexual carousing was proving too much for the local populace, so Heracles came to Pholus' cave here in Mt. Pelion —

this very cave — to seek a special Dionysian wine to lure the centaurs out into the open. Ultimately, Heracles slew them all with arrows poisoned by the blood of the hydra. After the battle, Pholus, marvelling at the idea that so small a thing as an arrow could kill something as magnificent as a centaur, dropped the poison arrow on his foot, where it pierced his skin and killed him."

"Funny the things I don't remember," I said.

"That's the MYTH," he said, taking another hit. "I love this stuff, marijuana. It's rare that I have any -- I've lost my taste for what passes for wine nowadays." He exhaled and passed back to me. After taking a moment to adjust his huge balls, he continued. "The fact was, Heracles was furious that I'd transformed you into a centaur -- he didn't think you were worthy of… elevated divinity. The irony was his uncontrollable temper was what kept him from being a better student himself -- but he wanted to be ranked with the others: as an equal to Asclepius, or Achilles, or even the noble Jason! But even he knew that was folly -- so he kept taking up these ridiculous 'Labors' to gain popularity and prove his worth. Imagine cleaning out thirty years of accumulated horse shit in a stable by 'diverting rivers' and thinking that's the same as creating the Medicinal Arts!

"He came here to Mt. Pelion to confront you. It was hardly the civilized scene the myths make it out to be. Physically, he beat you pretty badly -- skilled as you are, you were never really a fighter -- and he left you to die as he stole a bottle of Dionysian Wine you coveted to use as bait for the other centaurs. When they came, I was with them -- we were not driven mad at the scent of the wine, as the story would have you believe. We were avenging you, my love -- we descended on Mt. Pelion to honor you.

"But, Heracles wiped us out -- dozens of us with his poison arrows. I'd been hit in the battle and spent the next few weeks curing myself with herbs and medicines." He showed me a scar on his thigh, barely evident after all this time. "Rumor had it I'd died -- that's what the myth said, too, that I'd given my immortality to Prometheus to end my pain -- a ridiculous rumor. I'd just gone into hiding. I WAS too late to help you, though," he continued, rubbing my pec with the arm he had draped over my shoulder. "You were nearly gone by the time I got to you, so I… did what I had to and preserved your essence."

"Excuse me?"

He shrugged. "I'd rather not talk about it, honestly, if you don't mind. Suffice it to say that I took the necessary steps to preserve your essence in the form of your favorite thing: Dionysian wine!" He chuckled then, kissing my head. "I was the one who guarded it for several thousand years, waiting for the Fates to spin you into being again, until it was spirited away from me during one of the many wars of the former century. I'd thought I'd lost you and I mourned for a long time -- then I realized that the Fates held you in their hands and I could do nothing but trust them. I didn't know anything more about it until I stumbled upon you on the internet -- my Pholus, come back to me!"

Kissing, kissing, always kissing.

"Someone sealed it inside a garden gnome," I said. "It was in my grandfather's garden in Europe and traveled with them to the States -- he said he'd had it his whole life. I honestly thought at first that the elixir was meant for him -- his build, his attitude, apparently his huge cock. But after his death, the gnome was passed to me, where it Lorded over a bunch of marijuana plants in my basement until I broke it... and I discovered...'

"Your destiny," he said, grabbing my cock.

"To put it mildly," I said, trying to wrap my hand around his -- impossible. "I had no idea what was going on when I first unwrapped it and the little idol said my name..."

He was confused. "Little idol?"

I kept it in the same ditty-bag as I kept my pot -- my little guard -- the stone icon of a hugely muscular man with his disproportionate penis, erect all the way to his pecs, and his jeweled eyes. "This," I said, offering it to him.

He held his hand up flat and shook his head. "Where did you get that?" he asked.

"Like I said, it was in the garden gnome I got from my grandfather -- it was wrapped together with the bottle in some kind of cloth that fell apart when I touched it."

He seemed incredulous. "They were together?" he asked, stroking his beard.

"Yeah," I said. "It's what started this whole story -- I was dusting it off when the eyes lit up and I heard the word 'PHOLUS'..."

Chiron was contemplative. "That had to have been what woke him," he said to himself.

"Forgive my ignorance, but what are you talking about?"

Chiron indicated the stone figure. "That's a magical icon," he said. "I recognize it -- I know who made it. And it's attuned to Heracles."

"Heracles?" I asked -- I guess the figure could have been a crude Heracles sculpture. "But when I first touched it, it said 'Pholus'."

"It was Heracles, recognizing your energy. How ironic that he should have such a hand in your rebirth -- you'll have to share that with him, when next you meet."

I put the icon down next to the ditty bag and took the joint from Chiron, relighting it. "I'm not planning on running into Heracles anytime soon, thanks."

"You may not be," he said, taking the joint and puffing it, "but the Fates weave as they will. No one is reborn for nothing, Pholus. Not even my favorite…"

Chiron rolled over on top of me, kissing me as gently as he had when I was a boy, when I'd first been given to him by my parents, honored by the opportunity for their child's societal guarantees by becoming *erômenos* to Chiron, the Wisest and Justest, following along the lines of Perseus, Achilles, and Jason (of the Argonauts!).

Along the lines of Heracles, too -- another of Chiron's students -- but sadly not his favorite.

I wondered when we'd stopped being teacher and student, *Erastês* and *erômenos*, and had become lovers instead?

"Now, get your Herd up here," he said. "I'm anxious to meet them."

****

"THE Chiron?" Pokey asked, when I met them at the dock. "The one who sent you the wine?"

That hadn't occurred to me. "Yes!" I said. "The one who sent the wine. And the card -- in Greek! -- that you could read."

"Wow," he said, looking up at the mountain. "He lives in a cave?"

We walked up the gentle slope of the mountainside until we reached the rocky trail that led not just to Chiron's front door, but all the way to the peak of Pelion. The same beautiful boy allowed us in, ready to take us to his Master, but the Herd was blown away by the architecture.

"This is magnificent," said Dunn. "This is Frank Lloyd Wright! Why haven't I ever seen this in the architectural digests?"

I shrugged. "You'll have to ask," I said. "In the old days, this was originally MY cave -- Pholus' cave -- this front section here and what's now the grotto. (Which used to be a natural hot spring, but… it's been expanded.) There's been a lot of… improvement since then."

"It's the fuckin' Batcave," said Gambit, spreading his arms wide in wonder. "It's the honest-to-God fuckin' Batcave! Where's the super-computer and the giant penny?"

"I already tried that joke," I said. "He didn't get the reference."

"My friends," came Chiron's voice from behind us, "welcome to my home -- well, Pholus' home! I am Chiron, the 'civilized centaur', *Erastês*, creator, and ultimately lover of Pholus. It is my honor to meet you."

We turned to face him. He was dressed only in a linen skirt and belt, his magnificent body on display -- his smell irresistible. I don't know what he was wearing beneath it to hold his huge genitals in place, but some kind of strong strap, no doubt. Even in the short time I'd taken to get to the dock and back, he'd bathed and oiled his white beard. A half-head shorter than me, he still seemed larger -- he and Gambit were nearly the same height, though Chiron was significantly more thickly-muscled. Chiron looked like Gambit's wrestling coach.

I began the introductions. "Chiron, this is my Herd Master, Cavalier."

Cav tried to shake Chiron's hand, but Chiron quickly pulled him in for a hug.

"It's an honor," Cavalier said.

Chiron held Cavalier by the shoulders, studying him. "You are brave and head-strong," Chiron said, "excellent qualities in a leader. Even now you want to hunt Heracles down, knowing the danger." Chiron chuckled. "There is a test coming your way, Cavalier -- a test of humility. If you pass it, you'll be one of the greats, like Nessus and Lycabus. I have faith in you -- so does your herd."

Cavalier was speechless, almost starstruck. "Thank you," he said. "I'll make the right decision."

Chiron smiled. "No doubt," he said.

"And this is Gambit."

Chiron studied Gambit. "The Warrior," he said. "I should quite like to wrestle you."

Gambit rubbed his hands together. "Where are the mats?" he asked, smirking.

"Set up downstairs in the gym -- I'll show them to you personally." Chiron smiled and the two hugged -- it was big and brotherly.

I felt like I was working down a receiving line. "And this is Dunn."

Dunn was Dunn. "Your beard is SPECTACULAR!" he said.

Chiron chuckled. "So is yours!" he said.

Dunn waved him off. "Your home is beyond! You have to tell me about its construction!"

Chiron took Dunn in his arms and kissed him passionately. "I will give you a private tour," he said. "Show you all of the secrets."

Dunn pretended to open a fan with his hand and waved it at his face. "It's getting hot in here, Red!" he said.

I smiled. "He is who he is," I said, taking Chiron's upper arm in my grip and leading him to the next. "This is Lickety Split..."

"Dude!"

"I mean, the infamous Lickety Split!"

"The Scout -- the Champion in Another Land!" Chiron said, as if he'd identified some new archetype.

Lickety Split was shocked. "You saw me win the American Ninja Warrior World Championship?"

Chiron smiled and shook his head. "No," he said. "I have no idea what you're talking about. I just read auras. Did your centaur abilities help or hinder you in this... ninja contest?"

Lickety smiled. "I guess a little of both. It helped up here," he said, indicating his arms and shoulders, "but it got seriously in the way down here." He patted his big balls.

"Welcome to being a centaur," Chiron said, hugging him. "They will forever get in your way."

"I love them, don't get me wrong, but they're hell for rock climbing. And mountain-biking..."

Gambit snorted and jumped in. "They're great for wrestling, tho," he said. "They give you something to grip."

"Moving on," I said to Chiron. "This is my... Red's... childhood friend, AppleJack. Our tech guy, he created the website and the whole PHOLUS REBORN theme."

Chiron hugged him deeply. "Then I owe you a great debt," he said. "For you are the reason I found that Pholus lived again! Thank you, brother AppleJack."

"See?" AppleJack said to me. "I told you! I told you the wandering immortals and old gods would get word! Thanks to me!"

Continuing to hug him, Chiron said, "Of all, you have changed the most. The more you love yourself, AppleJack, the more others will love you, too." He kissed AppleJack's forehead. "Open yourself to Eros' message."

AppleJack was near tears and he hugged Chiron back, squeezing the old god. "Thank you," he said. "I'm trying."

Chiron winked. "You're succeeding."

They broke their hug but continued to look at each other -- it was a typically tender gesture from Chiron, and it filled AppleJack with confidence, when Chiron stroked his cheek.

"Last but never least, the irresistible Pokey Dakota."

Chiron stared at Pokey in wonder and awe. "You..." he said, trailing off.

Pokey was becoming concerned. "Me...?"

"What are you, Pokey Dakota?"

Pokey was quick with an answer. "I reckon I'm a unicorn!" he quipped, a huge smile on his face.

Chiron laughed, genuinely chuckling. "No," he said, calming himself. "No. Your power... your natural abilities... I would be quite honored to serve as your *Erastês*. You're a little old for *erômenos*, but one with your level of power needs discipline and training, so exceptions could be made."

Pokey was confused. "I don't understand. What're you talking about?"

"He's proposing to be your teacher and mentor," I said, and began counting on my fingers, "as he was with Asclepius, Achilles, Perseus, Ajax, Theseus, Jason and Yours Truly. It's a great honor."

"You left out Heracles," said Cavalier, crossing his arms before his chest.

"And Dionysus," Chiron said to him. "Let's keep things balanced."

Gambit moved over and put his arm around Pokey's shoulders, possessively. "We're not leaving him here," Gambit said. "That's not happening."

"Calm yourself, Warrior," Chiron said, putting his hand on Gambit's forearm. "I propose no such thing. I merely state that amongst all of us -- myself included -- Pokey Dakota is the most powerful."

"I am?"

"With nothing but faith and desire, you've been able to manipulate your physical form in both the Magic Realm and in this world, too -- it's incredible! Shapeshifting is normally relegated to the gods!"

"I ain't shapeshifted in this world!"

Chiron laughed. "Look at your hair, boy! Is blue its natural color?"

Pokey was silent, taking that in. "Wow," he mumbled, touching his ponytail.

Chiron held his hands out to Pokey, who glanced up at Gambit, then took them, stepping out of Gambit's hold. "Consider it, Pokey,"

Chiron said. "If we survive our current challenge, it would be my honor to teach you." He kissed Pokey on the lips, gently. "Consider it."

Releasing Pokey, Chiron stepped back to include all of us -- he clapped his hands. "I bid welcome to Pholus' Herd," he announced. "My home will always be a safe harbor for you. Let me give you the tour and we can decide if it's the Grotto or the Playroom for our initial sexual expression -- then I should like to see you in your bestial forms." He looked at Cavalier for approval. "Is that all right, Herd Master?"

Cavalier was obviously intrigued by the possibility of a hunt. "Absolutely!" he said.

Chiron smiled (and clearly the lump between his skirt twitched). "Excellent," he said, gesturing. "Come, my new friends and we will descend into the Grotto."

We happily followed him.

****

Gambit and Dunn's Prince Alberts fascinated Chiron. Dunn wore a very standard 10g ring, which seemed more for decoration than function, like Dunn's endless statement necklaces. Gambit, however, wore a heavy 6g ring, which seemed more in proportion with the club of his cock.

"Does it manifest in your Bestial Form?" Chiron asked, stroking the length of Gambit's cock as the big man sat on the edge of the hot tub.

Gambit and Dunn looked at each other for the answer.

"You've not experienced sex in your Bestial Forms?" Chiron asked.

From the other side of the hot tub, Cavalier said, "We've only hunted."

Chiron sighed. "We have more to do than I thought," he said to me. "How long before your flight home?"

"The day after tomorrow," I said.

Chiron nodded. "Then we will have mid-day meal and travel to the Magic Realm. In the meantime," he said to Dunn and Gambit, "would either of you like your foreskin back? This century has seen a horrible rise in genital mutilation -- it distresses me that it hides behind the guise of religion, but it doesn't surprise me, either."

"Wait," asked Gambit, "go back. You can regrow our foreskin?"

Chiron shrugged. "It's a simple matter," he said, standing in the hot tub, revealing his own massive cock -- uncircumsized -- in its own state of *nonischemic priapism.* "I have a salve."

****

It was this pink, slimy goo that Chiron kept in a clay jar -- gods, how it stank! He generously spread the goo along Gambit's fourteen inch cock, then wrapped it in a soft cotton bandage. "It feels funny," Gambit said. "Warm and... weird."

When Chiron turned to Dunn, the barber asked, "How soon will I be able to fuck with it?" He shrugged, saying, "I don't want to miss out on any of the action today."

"By the end of mid-day meal, I should think," Chiron said. "Unless this salve has gotten old."

Dunn opened his arms. "Slather it on," he said -- Chiron happily complied.

****

"I feel like I'm eating with a celebrity," Cavalier said during the lunch (and this from the guy who regularly fucked the Norse God of Thunder). "I mean, it's hard enough to wrap my head around the idea of living gods and mythology being real, but I'm sitting here with a being that's thousands of years old, who's lived adventures I read about as a kid -- it's mind-boggling."

Chiron smiled and sipped his wine. "There is a philosophical argument that gods don't exist until men worship them into being and when men stop worshipping that god, he/she weakens and disappears. As powerful as they are, gods only exist because of human belief and worship."

Pokey perked up. "So I reckon Jesus must be some super-god or something?"

"Never met him," Chiron said. "My understanding is he got his education in the east." That snub seemed to annoy him, but he continued. "Wherever he and his father/ other self have chosen to manifest, it isn't in any of the Realms I've visited. I've never seen either in this world. Even though the Christian cult has millions of followers, I'm still not convinced it's based on anything that actually happened." He smiled. "But the same argument could be made about mythology and, as opposed to me, lots of people have heard of the Christ."

"Wasn't that the whole point of mythology," Dunn asked, drinking his wine and gently touching his bandaged cock, "to explain things that man couldn't understand? 'How is the sun rising?' 'Um… I don't know, there must be some god pulling it on a chariot…' 'Of course, completely sensible!'"

"Tell that to Helios -- you'll save him a day's labor." Chiron chuckled as one of his serving boys made another round with the wine. "As Cavalier so cleverly said, I know it's hard to… wrap your heads around, but the basic fact is that everything's real, all myths, all gods, all origin stories. You seven have had your eyes opened to the truth behind the universe -- as overwhelming as it may seem, it's simple: everything is real and anything is possible. It all depends on belief."

"Can I ask a question?" asked Pokey.

Cav snorted. "You just did."

"What?"

Chiron cast a sidelong glance at Cavalier, smirking. "What's your question, Pokey?"

Pokey smiled broadly. "Why is Red your favorite?" he asked, like a bratty teenage girl. "And why'd you pick him to be a centaur? Why din't you pick Ajax or Hippopotamus or any of them other guys?"

We all looked at Chiron for the answer to that, myself included. Smiling, Chiron looked up at me and held my eyes throughout his answer. "Why is the sky blue, Pokey?"

"What?"

Chiron kept the eye-contact with me, even while speaking to Pokey. "You heard me -- why is the sky blue?"

Pokey shrugged. "I don't know -- it just is."

"My answer to you is the same. Why is Pholus my favorite? Because the sky is blue."

Dunn clutched his pearls. "Awww…."

There was lots of communal clinking and general support of romance when Pokey asked, "So now that he's been reborn, are you guys gonna get back together?"

"Geez, Pokey…" Cavalier said, sitting up straight suddenly. "Subtle…"

Pokey shrugged. "You want an answer, I reckon you ask a question." He glanced at me. "I don't mean to offend -- I'm just curious." Under his breath, he added, "I mean, he's fuckin' HOT for a daddy…"

"It's not him, Pokey. It's me." I tried to make eye-contact with Chiron, then Pokey, but couldn't, so I studied the ceiling as I answered, then the floor. "I drank a magic potion about a year ago that turned me into Pholus, I suddenly remember this life I had thousands of years ago -- all the adventures, the friends..." I looked at Chiron. "...the lovers. And as much as I want to embrace all that and BE Pholus, I wonder what happens to Red?"

"Who gives a fuck about Red?" asked AppleJack. "You get this jacked, incredible body, these fucking amazing superpowers... THAT COCK! And your lover knows more about sex than anyone living. Leave Red behind, my friend!"

"Plus you get to live in the Batcave," Gambit added, chuckling, playing with his wrapped cock.

"So Red was nothing more than... holding space for Pholus?" I asked AppleJack, angrily. "Thanks for the life value, oldest friend."

"Well, what did Red ever do?" AppleJack asked, downing his wine. "Anything? When you were Red you had no drive, no ambition, no *joie de' vivre* of any kind -- seems like that's all Red amounted to, anyway... holding space. Embrace who you are now, I say -- release Red -- be Pholus like you're meant to. The same way I embraced AppleJack!"

"Hey!" Pokey perked up. "I reckon I told you that!"

"You did!" AppleJack agreed. "You told me that once I embraced AppleJack, everything would change -- and you were right! It did! I accepted myself as AppleJack -- you need to accept yourself as Pholus."

Silence descended on the table until Chiron spoke. "If I may?" he asked, patting my knee.

"Of course."

Chiron stood, clearly used to teaching on his feet. "The subtleties of the reincarnation theory is not what we're here to debate. The Fates have woven you back into reality for a reason, Pholus, or you wouldn't be here at all -- you have to accept that. The longer it takes you to realize the truth of your identity, the stronger your opponent gets. And in the world of gods, there is power in a name." Chiron put his hand on my shoulder and looked me in the eye. "Whether you choose me as a lover again is secondary to why you're here. Please let me help prepare you."

I reached up and gripped the arm he held me with. "I remember loving you," I said. "I remember the joy that gave me. Let's... start with one thing and then hopefully the other will find its way."

"That is a fine place to start, *erômenos*. We will arrive at the solution together."

I stood up and hugged him -- and whatever we were thinking, our cocks were clearly having thoughts of their own. Just being this close to him got me going.

Maybe this decision wasn't as difficult as I was making it out to be.

He looked me in the eye and quietly said, "Your cock already has an answer."

"I do love you, *Erastês*."

"I know." Squeezing my ass, Chiron stepped out of our embrace and addressed the table. "My new friends and brothers, we've had sex, we've had a civilized meal, it is time to release the beast."

A small cheer around the table -- for some, this was better than sex and food.

"Let us start with the basics," Chiron said. "Traveling. Have any of you attempted to access the Magic Realm without the wine?"

"Is that possible?" Cavalier asked.

Chiron smiled. "To a magical being, everything's real and anything's possible," he said. "This is easier to do in the Realm itself, but I want you to try it here. I'm curious if anyone has a natural talent."

Cavalier again. "How do we do it?"

"Begin by closing your eyes." We all did. "Now imagine the place you wish to be -- what does it look like? Imagine its physicality -- picture it in your mind -- supply as many details as you can, no matter how arbitrary."

I pictured the meadow where we usually gathered and started our adventures. I knew it fairly well at this point -- the giant oak tree in the center, the tall grass, the random outgrowths. I could smell the mulch of the forest floor -- I could feel the slight breeze on my face, the river off to the west. The chattering family of faeries that lived in the deadfall.

"Now imagine you're there, looking back over your shoulder at..."

His voice was gone -- even with my eyes closed, I knew the light was different. The wind on my face...

****

...tells me I'm outdoors. I'm somewhere else.

I've Traveled.

And I'm not alone. Pokey and Lickety Split stand with me -- we are in our Bestial Forms.

"Well, how 'bout that shit?" Lickety says, prancing around our meadow. "I got a talent!"

I clap. "Of all of us, it should be you who's the most natural at Traveling -- the Scout, right?"

He runs into the sunny field and suddenly disappears, reappearing on the far edge of the meadow, a good two hundred yards away -- he waves, then begins to run his little Pinto body toward us. The same thing, he disappears mid-stride and suddenly reappears, a few feet from us. "Oh fuck -- this is fuckin' awesome!" he says, his smile likely to split his face in half. Suddenly, his energy changes, as if he's aware of something we don't sense. "They're coming," he says, looking to his left.

From the edge of the forest, the Herd rushes in, led by Chiron and Cavalier. Like Gambit, Chiron's bestial form is a workhorse, a Shire, the only breed large enough to support his human torso in some sort of proportion. Unlike Gambit, who is powder gray with a black tail and forelocks, Chiron's a beautiful grayish-white with a white breast and forelocks, matching the hue of his beard -- his tail is white, as well. Honestly, he is a very handsome beast -- I have to resist running into his arms and kissing him.

AppleJack, the white-fannied Appaloosa, again brings up the rear, but at least he's with the group this time -- he's getting stronger.

Chiron is enraptured. "Look at you all!" he says, tears in his eyes. "I didn't know if I'd ever look upon a herd of centaurs again! This is a joyous day! Still…" he looks around, and when he does, he pauses, as if seeing the unexpected. "Do you know where we are?" he asks.

"This is the meadow where we always meet," Cavalier says. "The very first time we came to this Realm, we appeared here. We call it Home Base."

"Incredible," Chiron says, indicating the area with a gesture, "for this is the Plain of Thessaly! This is where centaurs were said to have originated."

"How do you know that?" I ask, looking around myself.

"For the past few thousand years, I've had little to do other than explore the Magic Realm and practice sexual techniques. I know my way around both the body and the world fairly well. Look to the North," he says, and we all seem to naturally know which direction that is. "In the distance -- can you see it? The mountain peak?"

We can. Above the trees on the far horizon, mountains loom up, the peaks of the tallest hidden by the clouds.

"That's Olympus," Chiron says.

Cavalier bristles.

"Fear not -- He can't see us," Chiron informs Cav. "You're with me and I'm warded against him. But this should tell you how close to danger you are whenever you're in this Realm -- you're right under your adversary's nose…"

Cavalier smiles. "That's how I like to play it," he says.

Chiron shakes his head, then says to all of us, "If he appears, go back to the cave immediately — DO NOT ENGAGE HIM! Do you understand me?"

We all agree.

Chiron says specifically to Cav, "Do you understand me…?"

After a second, Cav says quietly, "I won't engage. I'll go to the cave."

"Good man. You'll have your chance soon enough. Don't rush." With that said, he turns to the group. "And so, back to the lesson," he says. "Traveling. It seems we have some naturals." He looks at me. "I expected you to remember," he says. "You used to be quite good at it. And you," he continues, indicating Pokey, "I would imagine it's so simple for you, you don't even know how you did it."

"I reckon I don't," Pokey says.

Chiron puts his hand on Pokey's shoulders, slightly distracted by Pokey's folded wings. Chiron opens his arms to Lickety Split. "But you," he says, "I'm delighted to find it natural to the Scout."

Lickety Split is ecstatic. "Watch this!" he says, and goes through the same performance for Chiron and the Herd as he had for us moments ago, disappearing and reappearing around the meadow, finally charging us until we thought he might trample us, then popping up behind us, skidding to a halt and then just as suddenly before us. "Ta dah!" he sings, holding his arms out presentationally, bowing on his foreleg slightly.

The herd goes wild -- even Chiron cheers him.

Cavalier shakes his head. "This whole team is a bunch of show-offs."

"Speaking of which," Chiron says, turning to Pokey, "may I see you fly before we continue our lesson? I fear I won't be able to continue until I do."

In the bright sunlight, Pokey's white, sparkle coat glimmers with tiny rainbows, his blue, cotton-candy tail flowing out like a choreographed cloud. In the moonlight, he seems to glow, but here in the sunshine, he's a disco ball.

"I need sunglasses to look at that kid," says Gambit, shading his eyes.

"He's remarkable," says Chiron, next to Gambit, while studying Pokey.

Gambit nods as Pokey takes off. "Yeah, he is," Gambit says, quietly. "He's mine."

Chiron smiles.

Pokey swoops and swirls above our heads, dancing in the sky. Laughing, he suddenly disappears and reappears three hundred feet higher in the air, upside down, then drops toward the earth as if dive-bombing. Our concern grows until, just before he crashes, he disappears again, this time reappearing directly above Gambit.

"He can Travel while he flies," Chiron says, shocked. "Who is this Pokey Dakota?"

Gambit reaches up and grabs Pokey's forelegs, intent on pulling him to the earth. But Pokey flaps his big white wings hard, lifting Gambit up about a foot off the ground. Just as it seems he's losing strength, Pokey disappears -- Gambit crashes to the earth with a thump. Pokey reappears near the other side of the meadow and waves triumphantly.

Chiron helps Gambit to his feet. "Go get him," Chiron quietly says. "Put him in his place."

Gambit snarls, drawing in a deep breath, then he disappears, immediately reappearing directly beneath Pokey on the other side of the meadow -- he reaches up and grabs the surprised boy's forelegs again, this time pulling him down before he can react. Grounded, Gambit throws himself on top of Pokey, pinning him down. He says something, then he kisses Pokey quite aggressively.

"Can we suspend the lesson while we watch them have sex?" Dunn asks, rubbing up against my bestial form. To Chiron, he adds, "I'm just as horny as ever, but I've noticed that masturbation is all but impossible in this form."

"That's why centaurs are social animals," Chiron says. "We need each other."

We walk as a herd across the meadow, toward them. Chatting away, Chiron takes us to a Watering Hole on the far side of the field, where we plop down in the shade of a giant maple, overlooking the pond. There are several dozen cattle roaming along the other bank, sloppily drinking and chewing their cud -- they're significantly bigger than cows in the real world.

"All they do is shit," says Chiron, rolling his eyes. "'Divine Cattle' -- they're kept at the Augean Stables to the west on the Alpheus River. One of Her... our adversary's labours was to clean the stables in a day -- thirty years of accumulated cattle dung. After killing all the centaurs, it wasn't nearly enough shit to punish him, in *my opinion -- but, small victory, because he got paid, this labour didn't count."*

Dunn, lying on his side next to Chiron, asks, "Is there a difference between the Day Me and the Night Me? What I mean is, when we're here at night, I feel almost compelled to hunt, like a taste for blood -- the longer I'm here, the stronger it becomes. But in the daytime, I don't feel that at all -- as a matter of fact, just the opposite, I feel ridiculously horny — I just seem to want a different kind of meat."

"Such is the difference between night and day," explains Chiron, manifesting a leather wine bag, drinking from it and passing it to Dunn. As Dunn drinks, Chiron reaches over and strokes Dunn's sheath, causing his penis to quickly emerge. Chiron spits on his hand and begins masturbating Dunn, causing the bearded man to moan.

"Oh, my…" Dunn says, breathing deeply.

"Different here, isn't it?" Chiron asks. "Everything is felt more intensely in the Magic Realm."

Gambit and Pokey, lying side by side on the grass, are already making out, Pokey leaning against Gambit's torso. It's not hard to miss Gambit's erection -- it's only slightly larger than it is in his human form -- and the Prince Albert glimmers in the sun. Breaking their kiss, Pokey disappears and reappears facing the other direction, causing Gambit to smile and kiss him again. With one hand, Pokey strokes Gambit's cock -- Gambit immediately pushes Pokey's head down until the blue-haired unicorn takes Gambit in his mouth. Gambit's breathing suddenly becomes heavy -- his moan fills the valley. Even the cattle look up.

AppleJack and Lickety Split waste no time, manifesting wine bags and getting into 69 position. I haven't yet seen them kiss, but they jerk each other off with familiarity, each knowing the other's rhythms already. Lickety laughs. "I love being a centaur!"

AppleJack looks like he's trying to make a decision -- or maybe trying to NOT make a decision, maybe just trying to be who he is -- "It doesn't matter what it means," I hear him mumble, then he bends down and takes Lickety Split's cock in his mouth, Lickety's thick dick nearly gagging him. But AppleJack is unperturbed -- he's seeking to pleasure his friend. Labels be damned.

Cav is closest to me, but he seems distracted by Mt. Olympus in the background -- I pinch his nipples to get his attention. He prances playfully around me, rubbing his flanks against mine. "You wanna play?" he asks quietly, circling me.

I glance up at Olympus, then at him. "You want him to look down here and see us fucking, don't you? That's exactly what's going on in that head of yours…"

He wraps his hand around my neck and pulls me in for a kiss. "Shut up and fuck me, Pholus. And pound me hard enough that they can hear me scream up on god-damned Olympus, get me?"

It has been a pleasure denied mounting Cavalier -- never in our civilized forms, but feeling my bestial cock slide inside him is one of the greatest physical experiences of my life. This unsheathed centaur cock is significantly more sensitive than my human one -- and I didn't think anything could feel better than fucking as a human -- each thrust elevates the level of pleasure. Cavalier moans, not to be dramatic, but to be honest.

I'm surprised -- but not surprised -- to see Pokey mounting a kneeling Gambit, Pokey's wings spread wide as he slides himself in. I've never seen Gambit submit in the real world and I love the pleasure of discovery in his expression now. If there's one thing Pokey's good at, it's ending up on top -- it's why we're all here in the first place.

I'm also not surprised to see Dunn mount Chiron -- my old Erastês probably hasn't had the pleasure to receive in centuries. I'm sure he's delighted by the talented topping of Dunn, especially with Dunn's new cock… or is Dunn's cock only new in the Real World? It doesn't matter in the moment, when they're both so clearly content.

As we start our slow pace, together -- the walk before the cantor -- thrusting in the same rhythm, connected by the same invisible rein -- I see Lickety Split mount AppleJack out of the corner of my eye and I smile.

I'm feeling nothing but pleasure and happiness, each growing exponentially as my brothers and my sons join my emotional fraternity.

As I fuck him, I see Cavalier kissing Chiron as Gambit moves to suck Chiron's nipple. The old centaur has hands of his own, stroking their rockwall abs and cupping their pecs -- he catches me looking at smiles at me. I smile back and pick up my pace. Cavalier's moans don't disappoint.

Cavalier suddenly rears up on his hind legs and shoots an unexpected load -- it streaks across Chiron's torso, a thick white line. I have to ride him to finish in him, which I'm strong enough to do, filling Cav with my centaur cum.

But there is no respite, there is no break -- I just blew my load and I'm hungry for more -- there is no such word as "sated". (Just the spirit of satyr.)

I immediately kneel before Chiron and lick the cum from his chest -- so sweet, so wild, so untamed -- and then kiss him, sharing it with him. That must be the moment Dunn shoots, for Chiron's orgasm happens while we kiss. He moans into my mouth as Dunn cums in his ass.

Pokey is the last to shoot, but he loves being the centaur of attention! He opens his wings and gently flaps as he fucks, as if he'd ever lift the deadweight of Gambit off the ground. When he finally shoots, both he and Gambit scream together, scaring the Divine Cattle at the watering hole, driving them to slink back to the stables in Augea.

We fall into different pairings and small groups -- Gambit and AppleJack, Cavalier and Chiron, Dunn and me, watching Pokey try to fly while mounted by Lickety Split, the lightest of us. It lasts for hours and hours, until the sun begins to land on the horizon -- Helios ending his ride for the day as we all began ending ours.

As a herd, we lay amongst each other, contented, watching the sun. It was a quiet moment after so much noisy lust -- I'm sure the faeries are done with us!

Until AppleJack. "I want some pot!" he whines.

Everyone laughs, cuddling a little closer knowing the end is in sight.

"My friends and brothers," Chiron says, his arms around Cavalier and myself, "this has been a remarkable day. One this old centaur has waited for a long time. This bonding moment will make some future decisions much easier, I suspect. So… I want you all to know I'm grateful -- and I'm proud of you. That you should all find each other this way…" He wipes his face and continues. "Anyway, let's head back. Traveling home is remarkably easier than traveling here -- same process though. Shut your eyes, imagine the cave -- put in all the detail you can and then…"

13. "Raptio"

Raptio *(in archaic or literary English rendered as "rape") is a Latin term for the large-scale abduction, i.e. kidnapping for the purposes of marriage, concubinage or sexual slavery. The Oxford English Dictionary gives the definition "the act of carrying away a person by force" besides the more general "the act of taking anything by force" (marked as obsolete) and the more specific "violation or ravishing of a person".*

****

I stood on the dock and watched them sail away, back to Mykonos to catch their plane to the States, shades of Penelope on the departure of Odysseus. (Emotionally, anyway -- I knew it wouldn't be twenty years before I saw them again.) Technology ruined the classics -- imagine the Odyssey with GPS! That would sure make a short ride to Ithaca…

Funny, with the exception of AppleJack, I'd only known those guys for a few months, and I felt closer and more fraternal with them than I had with my actual blood family -- none of whom I'd seen since my transformation. I had a bit of a lump in my throat as I'd said goodbye.

"Don't worry," Cav had said as they boarded the tender to the yacht. "We'll be fine -- and you got some shit to work out. We'll see you in a couple weeks." He'd kissed me. "I'll take care of the wine. And I promise I won't do anything stupid."

I'd smiled and said, "Thank you, Herd Master. Heracles has tried to get the wine before, to use as bait...."

Cav interrupted. "He won't get it from me," he said. "Don't worry."

"I'm just repeating what Chiron said."

Pokey'd butted in. "Speaking of Chiron, the next time I see you gents, you better be boyfriends again -- he's too hot for you to fuck this up."

Hugging him, I'd said, "I love you, Pokey. And frankly, you should be the one staying."

He'd cast a glance to Gambit, already on board and he'd whispered, "Well, I reckon I got something going on, too."

I'd pulled the scruff of hair on his chin. "I told you you were irresistible, Pokey."

Shrugging, smirking, he'd said, "Yeah, well...apparently I'm pretty dang powerful!"

"Get on the boat, boy…"

"*Euoi Euan!*" I called to them, as the tender pulled away from the dock.

"*Euoi Euan!*" they answered back, laughing and waving.

As I ascended the mountain, I could still see their yacht, a speck near the horizon, until it disappeared around the end of the peninsula and I could follow it no more.

Two weeks… and I'd be back home.

"*Euoi Euan*," I whispered. "Well done, sons."

****

I found Chiron in the hot tub, leaning back, his arms on the rim, and he'd helped himself to one of my joints. I stood on the stone deck and watched him, smiling -- as I began to undress, Chiron's attendants were suddenly there, submissively removing my clothes for me. (I didn't even know their names.) *"Poia eínai ta onómatá sas?"* I asked, in my sorry Greek.

Chiron smiled, exhaling a huge cloud of smoke. "They speak English," he said.

They stood before me with their heads bowed, these beautiful local boys, teens with olive skin smooth as glass. Had they even begun shaving their faces?

The taller and more muscular spoke. "I am Lucas and he is Tobias -- it is our honor to serve." The two boys bowed -- the slighter one following the lead of the larger -- and they disappeared out of the grotto.

"In the old days, the local boys would compete to be my servants." He sighed, laying his head back. "It was a different time -- join me, Pholus."

I stepped into the hot tub, grateful for the warmth of the water on my tired body. As I settled next to him, he held the joint to my lips -- I gladly inhaled.

"Your herd launched on their Odyssey?" he asked. "They understood why you stayed?"

I exhaled. "They did," I said. "And they do."

With his free hand, he reached beneath the surface of the water and stroked my swollen scrotum, squeezing the base of my cock. "They won't miss this?" he asked quietly, swiftly bringing me to erection. "They won't be angry with me for taking it from them?"

I met his dirty smile. "Not if you use it enough," I growled.

Turning to face me, he swung his leg over my cock like he was mounting a bicycle. As he straddled my hips, I felt his ass pressing against the tip. The lack of lube made for an uncomfortable entrance, for sure, but once inside, I found him smooth and firm and oh, so slippery.

He had my entire cock inside him, balls deep -- subtly, he gently rolled his hips as he looked me in the eye. Such a handsome man, my *Erastês*, with his strong features and his soft eyes. He kissed me while he fucked himself on my cock.

His own erection broke the surface, leaking it's droplets of pre-cum to float away with the churning water. I remembered the way he liked to be masturbated and instinctively began those motions. "Yes," he moaned, his tongue in my mouth. "Gods, yes!"

"Have you missed my cock, *Erastês*?" I asked, kissing the slit of his as it floated above the water like a whale attempting to get airborne. "Is this why you wanted me to stay?"

"It is not the only reason," he said, increasing his tempo. "But it's a good one!"

He brought me to orgasm with little more than his pelvic muscles, kegeling me over the edge. His load blew through the surface of the water and shot all over my beard -- I was lucky to get some in my mouth. I did love his familiar taste. We both wiped it off my beard and put it in my mouth -- then the kissing began again. He didn't move to remove my cock and I was comfortable inside him, so we just stayed there.

"In the past few days I've received more than I have in a millenium, at least!" he said. "I've forgotten how much I miss my own kind."

"Have you not had sex?"

"I didn't say that," he said, kissing me. "But humans provide no… challenge to such as us, and certainly none are as gifted in size as my *erômenos*."

"Is that why you transformed me?" I teased. "For my centaur cock?"

He chuckled. "Even if that were the only reason," he said, leaning his forehead against mine, "I would still deem you a success!"

I lifted him out of the hot tub and laid him on the edge, so I could stand on the tub's seat and fuck him more easily. He spread his legs to the sides and grabbed his own ankles so I could penetrate further -- I did not disappoint.

He was big enough that I could fuck him and suck him at the same time -- his pre-cum fueled me like a steam engine overloaded with coal. I was afraid I was gonna fuck him hard enough to break through the slate tile -- but the moment called for reckless abandonment. His noises confirmed the choice.

I hadn't noticed it before, but centaurs were masters of simultaneous orgasm. Being able to feel our partner's rhythms, perhaps, or our incredible sense of sexual empathy, whatever -- it was rare that one orgasm didn't trigger the other's, if we hadn't already cum together.

The acoustics in the cave were exceptional for moaners. We could hear our orgasm echo for nearly a full minute after we finished. Spelunkers on the other side of the mountain probably heard us for minutes after that. It was glorious.

"There is much to do other than fucking," Chiron said from beneath me. "But I'm really enjoying the fucking, too!"

"As you have so wisely said," I murmured, kissing him, "we are what we are."

He rolled his eyes playfully. "The student learns," he said, then tapped my side. "Come, let us clean up and do something with our brains next."

"You're the *Erastês*," I said, agreeing verbally, though I really did like the way my cock felt inside him.

This could last forever.

****

@AppleJack: We're HOME!

        @me: Excellent! How long did it take?

@AppleJack: The flight was a little over 12hrs
@AppleJack: Layover in London

@AppleJack: (Dunn got caught getting a blowjob
@AppleJack: from some skinhead in the loo)

@me: Hahaha! Did he get in trouble?

@AppleJack: Probably would've...
@AppleJack: if he'd been caught by a female officer.
@AppleJack: The responding officer (male) joined in.

@me: Hahahahaha!

@AppleJack: And when the chaos broke out
@AppleJack: And the orgy started
@AppleJack: Dunn just strolled onto the plane
@AppleJack: like nothing happened.

@me: We need to think up some clever title for that
@me: like, *centaursexual chaos* or something
@me: along the lines of CENTAUR FUN FACTS

@AppleJack: Speaking of CENTAUR FUN FACTS
@AppleJack: Is it cool if Lickety Split stays with us?
@AppleJack: His housemates moved out
@AppleJack: while he was in Japan.

@me: That was last month!
@me: Where's he been living since Japan?

@AppleJack: Friends' sofas -- his car.

@me: Oh, for fuck's sake!
@me: of COURSE he can move in!

@AppleJack: Thanks.
@AppleJack: I knew you'd be cool.

@me: This is almost like you having a boyfriend...

@AppleJack: LOL
@AppleJack: I figure you, Chiron, me, and Lickety Split
@AppleJack: like the Golden Girls

@AppleJack: except we'll be the Golden CORRAL!

@me: Hahahaha!
@me: You should pitch that to Netflix.

@AppleJack: So everything's good there?

@me: It is.
@me: Chiron is overjoyed to be a teacher again!
@me: (And to have a sexual partner who can keep up with him.)

@AppleJack: Is it weird?
@AppleJack: I mean, your boyfriend from a thousand years ago
@AppleJack: Literally

@me: No.
@me: Oddly enough, I feel more…
@me: content than I ever have
@me: more settled
@me: like… I don't know…
@me: like I'm where I'm supposed to be
@me: Does that make sense?

@AppleJack: absolutely
@AppleJack: (says the guy about to open his bedroom to another man)

@me: So, what's next?

@AppleJack: Cav doesn't fuck around.
@AppleJack: We have a meeting tomorrow night.
@AppleJack: He didn't say why.

@me: Ok -- dial me in

@AppleJack: I will.
@AppleJack: Gonna get high.
@AppleJack: (btw -- Our babies downstairs made it through our vacation!)
@AppleJack: Talk to you later.

@me: Cool. Give my love to Lickety Split.

@AppleJack: Will do!

@me: I'm happy for you!

@AppleJack: I'm happy for me, too!

****

"So… tell me about your parents."

Before a roaring fire, we laid on some kind of fur rug -- I couldn't identify the beast it had been, something mythological, I assumed (maybe one of those Divine Cattle) -- but it was soft and large enough to fit the two of us. Several massive pillows were strewn about and -- for a change -- we were sipping brandy. I really wanted a joint, but it was three rooms away and I was comfortable where I was, with Chiron inside me, spooning me from behind.

"You mean, Red's parents?"

"YOUR parents, yes."

"I'm sorry," I said, running my hand through my hair. "I'm still a little confused about who you want me to be. In one breath you tell me I have to accept being Pholus and in another, you want me to tell you about Red. Who am I supposed to be?"

He chuckled. "You're both." He began stroking my hair while he spoke, as he had done ages ago."People live multiple lives, *erômenos*, learning lessons, growing spiritually, until they finally ascend -- it would help a great deal if they could remember those lives, and just pick up where they left off, but discovering the reason for one's existence is part of the journey, isn't it? And Red has discovered the reason for his -- hasn't he?"

I nod slightly. "People used to say that I was… passive. Passionless. My parents -- Red's parents -- said I lacked ambition. I'm almost thirty and I haven't really done anything with my life -- that's their complaint."

"So they haven't seen you lately?"

I laughed, a bark almost. "They haven't seen me since I was six inches shorter and a hundred pounds lighter."

"What are you going to tell them?"

Sliding myself off his cock, I sat up and reached for my drink. "I don't know," I said, sipping. "The truth, I suppose. I drank a magic potion and got turned into a centaur. And I'll likely get a lecture on the dangers of drinking strange potions, how being a thoroughbred is better than being a workhorse, and how am I ever going to give them grandkids with this impossible penis?"

Chiron laughed, sitting up himself and leaning against a cushion. He stared into the fire and sipped his brandy. "Pholus' parents were very sweet and simple -- do you remember them at all?"

"She was portly and red-headed," I said. "I don't remember him at all."

He nodded and continued. "Farmers, grape-growers -- salt of the earth, as is said. They were overjoyed that you were to be my *erômenos* -- there could be no greater honor for them, for you came from nothing. You didn't have the privilege of Achilles, or Dionysus, or even Heracles, who could name-drop Zeus. Pholus was nobody."

I snorted. "Maybe I should have you talk to my parents," I said. "Red's parents."

"No thank you!" he said, holding his hand up flat. "That's on you. I do hope to meet them someday, tho."

"Yeah, right!" I laughed. "Mom... Dad... this is my former teacher, an immortal figure of myth who became my mentor and lover, transforming me into a centaur a few thousand years ago then engineering my resurrection through your womb by copping some deal with the Fates so I could return and confront the mad god that killed both myself and my brethren."

Chiron took a sip of his brandy, then said, "I'd start with Mom... Dad... this is Chiron."

We laughed together.

I crawled closer to him, on my knees beside him. "Do you think I'll be able to beat him?" I asked quietly. "Heracles? Do I stand any kind of chance at all?"

Chiron put his hands on either side of my face and looked directly into my eyes. "The Fates have brought you back for a reason," he said. "I doubt it's to fail."

****

I'd never been a good grappler. Even as Chiron awakened my memories of our early training, the familiarity of the holds and the motions of the bodies and the smells of my *Erastês'* sweat and effort. I always found wrestling to be sexualized foreplay -- even though I knew intellectually it wasn't -- it was a sport. But the contest of dominance always struck me as sexual, not athletic, and so I'd end up getting turned on.

"Battle rods" were a familiar site at wrestling matches, but mine wasn't all that easy to hide.

When I was a youth, before I'd been transformed by Chiron, when he was well over twice my weight, I used our time on the mats to fulfill domination fantasies. Knowing this, he would walk a fine line between lecturing me as a coach and giving in to the sexual play as a man.

My grappling still hadn't improved.

Worse that the tradition in those days was to wrestle nude. Gods forbid they could make it easier for me somehow!

Meeting Chiron on the mats now -- this whole week I'd been here -- it was hard to maintain a serious attitude. He was so fucking beautiful -- this massively muscular beast, mature and primed, hung like a horse -- his white beard, the scruff that covered his body, his swollen balls. This was one of those times when I knew I was bigger than him, but I was channeling the emotions of the boy he raised and I couldn't help but feel trapped in the dimensions I had then.

Gambit was watching via the mobile hookup on my laptop. He liked the way Chiron coached -- though he thought Chiron was a little too kind -- but it was clear Gambit was picking up stuff, too. Chiron was "old school" for sure, but there was nothing wrong with learning from the classics. For Gambit, it was like having a Coach Emeritus in the wrestling room. In this case, however, the old man could take down any current champion and wipe the floor with him, not some geezer who just told stories.

"For Gods' sake, Red," Gambit said, the laptop audio blue-toothed to the speakers, "do you get a fucking hard-on everytime you wrestle?"

Though I was trying to get a takedown with Chiron, gripping him round the neck, I spoke to Gambit. "So do you," I said.

"Sweep!" Gambit called, and I swung in my left foot and took out Chiron's legs. As soon as he went down, Gambit yelled, "Cover him!"

I threw myself on top of Chiron, spreading my legs and locking them into the mat to secure him while I sought to get him in a hold -- I was struggling to lock down his left arm.

"Cross him!" Gambit said. "Get on the other side of his body, Red! He's weaker defending his right side."

Chiron got his arm under me and threw me off -- I landed with an "oof!" on my back.

"Get up! Get up! Get up!"

Chiron was on top of me, throwing his weight against my torso -- he was trying to get a grip on my leg, behind the knee.

"Don't let him do that!" Gambit yelled from his side of the Atlantic. "Twist around and scissor him! C'mon, Red, use your god-damned legs!"

From my position in Chiron's hold, I gasped, "This was easier when I didn't have two coaches!"

From the dominant spot, Chiron growled, "Take as much coaching as you can -- there is no greater grappler than Heracles."

Gambit -- "Hey!"

Chiron tapped and released me -- he turned to the camera. "Speak not until you've bested Heracles in a match," he said, grabbing a towel and wiping his face. "Though I admit, I would pay good money to see that match... and the lusty sex that would follow."

Gambit chuckled. "You crack me up, old man."

"Am I at least getting better?" I asked, reaching for a towel of my own. "I feel like I'm getting better..."

"You're absolutely improving," Chiron said immediately, King of Positive Reinforcement, putting his arm around my shoulder. "Considering you've only been here a week, you're incredible!"

From the laptop, Gambit said, "You'll be better when you get home and we can train more seriously. It's time for you to start learning strikes."

Chiron sighed. "Well, that's not grappling..."

"No," said Gambit. "That's fighting. Grappling is all well and good, but this won't be a civilized battle, will it?"

Chiron nodded. "No, it won't."

"Ok, then," Gambit said, turning his attention to me. "What do you got there, another week?"

I looked at Chiron -- we hadn't really discussed my return to the States in terms of definite dates. "Yeah," I said. "I'll be home before the end of the month, anyway." Chiron absorbed that information, slowly nodding.

"Ok," Gambit said. "I gotta go -- I got clients coming in! Gimme a shout next time you roll."

"I will. Thanks, Gambit."

Chiron chimed in. "Thank you, Warrior."

"Peace, old man. Defend your right side." And he logged off.

Chiron grabbed me and we rolled around on the warm mats, playfully like otter pups. "You don't need to leave," he said. "This is your home, really -- it's in your name."

"What?"

He rolled on top of me. "While you've been here these last few days, I've had my lawyers draw up the paperwork -- I'm transferring ownership of this property to you. We'll be signing off on everything early this week before you… leave."

I shook my head. "No," I said, breaking his hold and sitting up. "That's completely unnecessary, Chiron. This is your home…"

He smiled. "I intend to live here still," he said, grabbing a water bottle and drinking from it. "And I'm hoping you'll be living here with me."

We held eye-contact for a moment before we kissed.

Gods, I was falling in love with him… again.

****

@Cavalier: Has anyone seen or heard from Dunn lately?
@Cavalier: He's not answering my texts.

@PokeyDakota: Why? Need a haircut?

@Cavalier: I'm serious.

@LicketySplit: Not since our meeting last week.

@Gambit: Two days ago -- he trimmed my comb!

@AppleJack: I can swing by the barber shop…

@Cavalier: I'm AT the barber shop.
@Cavalier: It's closed.
@Cavalier: But it looks like something happened inside
@Cavalier: a freakin' crime scene
[pic1]
[pic2]

@AppleJack: Lemme see if I can hack his security feed.
@AppleJack: I'll connect when I know more.

@Cavalier: Fuck
@Cavaler: FUCK!!!
@Cavalier: You guys need to check in with me EVERY DAY!
@Cavalier: We talked about this!

@me: Let's not worry till we know something, guys.

@me: Speculating isn't gonna help
@me: Calm down, Cav

@Cavalier: I'm standing outside a ransacked business
@Cavalier: My friend and teammate is missing
@Cavalier: I think I'm doing pretty god damn good, frankly
@Cavalier: Calm down…

****

@AppleJack: Guys, I took this off the group text chain
@AppleJack: Cuz I think you two need to see this first

@Cavalier: Understood. What you got, AppleJack?

@me: What is it, buddy?

@AppleJack: I was able to hack Dunn's security system
@AppleJack: Here's what I got
@AppleJack: It's not the clearest
@AppleJack: But it doesn't take a genius to guess
[AVI -- security]

****

The video was grainy, at best -- no sound -- it also had a slow frame-speed rate, so we only saw images that were far enough apart to convey motion, but not in any smooth way. The camera was mounted on the ceiling by the inside front door, with the cash register in the foreground, almost looking down on it, and the barber chairs in the rear.

There was Dunn -- identifiable by his build and beard, his face a blur -- walking a client toward the register. They kissed briefly and the guy handed Dunn a wad of cash, which Dunn slipped in his pocket as the guy left. Dunn did something at the register, then moved toward the front door. Suddenly, he was backing up into the shop, assertively gesturing at whoever had entered.

Whoever had entered was little more than a dark shape on the bottom of the screen, not quite in frame, but he had to have been huge because Dunn was looking up. This thing -- this shape, this dark intruder -- made some sort of motion, waved his arms perhaps

-- and suddenly, Dunn was in his bestial form, displaying his steel gray body and black legs, his finely-groomed tail, the strange white slashes on his forelocks -- I'd never seen him with my human eyes. He was a beautiful beast.

But he was terrified.

He seemed unable to comprehend where he was and it horrified him. Each thing he saw seemed to raise his level of fear a notch further, his reflection in the mirror, his clothes, the electricity, the lights. In his terror, Dunn began kicking, destroying the shop with his powerful rear legs, breaking mirrors and denting chairs. It wasn't quite a bull in a china shop, but it was hard not to draw that analogy -- it was the beast destroying the civilized.

And then I finally could see an arm extend from this intruder's dark shape, a heavily muscled arm, and it threw something at Dunn. Something that wrapped around Dunn's throat. Whatever had been fueling Dunn's hysterical reaction ceased -- Dunn completely stopped moving, standing there in his bestial form, staring off into space.

It was then that I finally saw the shape of the intruder, his thick traps and his wide back, the lion's skin draped over his shoulder. There was no mistaking him for anyone other than Heracles, even if he never revealed his face.

He reached out, grabbed the stunned Dunn, and the two of them simply disappeared.

That was where the video ended.

Horrified, I watched it twice more before I yelled, "CHIRON!"

****

"And what are you doing, exactly?" Chiron asked as I threw my clothes in the suitcase. He'd been watching the video as I frantically gathered my things.

"Packing," I said. "I've gotta get home!" I threw a bunch of jockstraps in the case -- why did I bring so many jockstraps? I never wore them...

"To do what?" he asked. "How will you help? By being another target?"

I sighed and threw my clothes down. "Chiron, this is my friend..."

"I understand -- he's my friend, too." Chiron stood and put his arm around me. "But let's take a breath and not react emotionally. Heracles is obviously trying to draw you out of hiding. You running into the line of fire is not in your best interest. This is not your battle, Pholus -- not yet."

"I'm not in hiding," I say. "How am I in hiding? I'm closer than they are! I'm right under his nose!"

"He can't 'see' you because the cave is warded against him, that's why. The reason he's striking now is because he wants to find out where you are and what you're doing. He's scared."

"But why Dunn?" I asked, pulling out my ditty-bag and retrieving a joint -- there was one last pre-rolled jammed into the groin of the little stone idol I always carried. "That doesn't make any sense -- Dunn hadn't done anything to him that would make him hit Dunn first."

Chiron shook his head, though he took the lit joint. "Dunn doesn't matter," he said, then shrugged when he saw my reaction. "Sorry, but look at it strategically. Who's the biggest threat to him in the herd?"

I released my hit. "Gambit," I said, "or Cav -- Gambit probably. Why didn't he start with Gambit?"

"He was testing out his equipment," Chiron said, indicating the computer screen. "Whatever Heracles used to put the whammy on Dunn, he had to test it, to make sure it worked. He doesn't want to confront Gambit until he's sure it does. But you can rest assured that Gambit's next."

"How did he make Dunn transform into a centaur? I thought we weren't able to do that here."

Chiron thought about it, then shook his head. "I don't know," he finally said, quietly. "It shouldn't be possible. That type of transformation has been forbidden in this realm since the triumph of science over magic, thousands of years ago. That's why Dunn freaked out when he became his Bestial self -- he couldn't comprehend the reality around him. His centaur senses didn't allow him to process what he was experiencing sensorially -- the panic of being confronted by technology -- civilization -- was more than the Bestial Dunn could take. It's a dark thing that Heracles does -- and I worry as much for him as for us."

"Then we should call Gambit? Warn him?"

Chiron snorted. "For all the good it will do."

****

Whatever evidence the police investigating Dunn's disappearance had, it wasn't made public -- so if they possessed the security film (and AppleJack was pretty sure he'd erased it), they hadn't leaked it. Nor had they spoken to any of us, so I doubt they were doing anything at all.

Our luck didn't hold, though.

Gambit's disappearance was all over the internet.

Lickety Split's business partners posted the footage to YouTube before we'd even realized Gambit had been taken. From there, it'd gone viral in a matter of hours. I saw the link trending on Twitter before I'd even heard from AppleJack.

Although still security footage, the set-up at Lickety Split's gym was vastly superior to Dunn's barber shop, and included multiple angles. (Interestingly, it was the multiple angles that the people on the Internet said made it "fake".) It had been roughly edited by the guys who'd posted it, and it also lacked sound.

"WATCH TILL THE END!" the clickbait read. "YOU WON'T BELIEVE!"

The video title was "GAMBIT v HERCULES" -- "MMA heavyweight fighter Gambit battles bodybuilder Hercules. You won't believe the ending!"

The video opened with Gambit doing clean and presses in (what I knew was) his normal corner of the gym. Wearing only square-cut spandex fight shorts and training shoes, his "GAMBIT" tattoo was easy to read across his back -- he was completely pumped, his muscles swollen, his veins out and throbbing. I was surprised he didn't have a hard-on from his own reflection, though his sac made no secret of its existence, especially in those tiny shorts, stretching the image of the knight chess pieces across his crotch. He looked magnificent.

I saw him see Heracles appear in the gym, in the mirror behind him. Gambit spun with the bar he was pressing and threw it at Heracles. Heracles caught it while stepping into frame. He was nearly a foot taller than Gambit, who knew how much heavier, though they looked proportionately the same -- Heracles just looked a size larger. He was dressed as he'd been when we'd beaten him in the Magic Realm, the short leather skirt, the lion's skin draped over his shoulder, lace-front leather sandals. Gigantic muscles covered in coarse black hair and his thick black beard, Heracles looked more a beast than sleek-skinned Gambit ever would.

Heracles swung the weight bar like a baseball bat but Gambit was able to get a grip on it and avoid taking the blow -- the two of them fought for possession until Heracles snatched it away and cast it casually aside. No weapons -- he wanted to fight man to man.

As they stepped into a formal grappling stance and the battle started, it it began to resemble some weird cross between MMA, greco-roman wrestling, and pornography. These two supreme specimens of man -- though, ironically, neither actually was a man -- hairy and muscular, slipping quickly from move to move, trying to gain an advantage. For his size, Gambit was surprisingly fast and was able to escape just about any hold Heracles tried to put him in.

More, Gambit had a powerful strike -- I'd felt his punches, and they'd hurt when he'd been holding back -- he delivered many body blows, trying to soften Heracles up a little. For all his size and advantage, Heracles was clearly not used to delicate work, attempting power moves intended to take Gambit out -- he wasn't landing anything.

And they rolled around, each finding himself on the bottom for a moment, but Gambit kicked out like it was pro-wrestling, throwing the bulk of Heracles across the mats, where he landed hard on his back. Gambit pressed the advantage, leaping onto Heracles and throwing him into a front headlock. Though he struggled with this for a moment, Heracles was able to roll his way out, but wasn't able to take Gambit with him.

They separated, sweaty and heavily breathing, when Gambit pressed another attack. Heracles, whether worried or tired, had clearly had enough -- instead of allowing Gambit to engage, he made some sort of gesture, though I couldn't hear if he'd said anything or not, and Gambit, quite against his will, transformed into his Bestial self.

Gambit was a Shire, a workhorse, nineteen hands high -- the largest of all of us -- a soft powder gray with black fetlocks, tail, and stub of mane where his human lower back met his equine withers. A strong, powerful beast -- again, I was struck by how incredibly beautiful this centaur was to my civilized eyes -- but as he transformed, his confident, arrogant expression turned to terror. At his size, he barely fit in this trash-collection of a gym, obstacles at every turn, low ceilings -- and, as I witnessed with Dunn, reality horrified him. He seemed unable to process what he looked at, raising his level of fear wherever he focused. I'd never seen Gambit look anything but confident and secure. The sheer terror of his expression hit me harder than his plight. He could've won a fair fight.

He began striking out, trying to escape -- he tried to take out the lights, the mirrors, anything he saw -- kicking, punching, utterly and completely hysterical. It looked like he was screaming.

Heracles stood and manifested his weapon -- in a way, it reminded me of the bolas Lickety Split always used, something metallic on a tether. He had to have said something, because

Gambit suddenly focused on him, and Heracles launched it. Quickly and easily, it wrapped itself around Gambit's throat and locked in place. As soon as it did, the life completely drained from Gambit's face -- his eyes emptied of emotion. His physical rage slowed to nothing, until he just stood there motionless, staring into space, drained of personality and life.

A cocky smile on his face, Heracles limped his injured body toward Gambit and grabbed the tether, which looked more like a rein. Gambit shuddered when he did. Heracles pulled it hard, jerking Gambit's neck down until Gambit knelt on his forelock…

...then the two of them completely disappeared.

****

2.7 million views
58,921 COMMENTS:

MadDog8213
FAKE!

BobCobb
Some of the CGI is good, some of it looks rushed. The whole transformation didn't work -- that's not how someone would morph into a centaur!
        Reply:
        Jonah White
        Why a centaur at all? What the f*ck did Hercules have to do with centaurs?

MichaelDrakeman
Poorly choreographed. If you're gonna spend that much money on CGI, at least lay out a better battle plan! Get a fight coach!

TimmyDrake
Hercules looked awful! Who cast this dreck?

C*cksuckerOne
The MMA guy stuffs his trunks!

KevinSorboFan
Only one Hercules in my book! And this guy is NOT IT!

NotAFan829301
Fake!!!!!!!
MMAfan4Gambit
Gambit's a legit fighter -- he's ranked. This has gotta be some kind of promotion.
>Reply:
>Randy McNally
>Isn't he gay4pay? Wasn't he one of those FOALS REBORN guys?

>MMAfan4Gabmit
>You wish!

DowntownBaxter
This is some gay-ass shit!

JohnsonDavis
That guy could turn ME into a centaur! I'd be his slave!
>Reply:
>Shirley Logan
>You're weird.

>JohnsonDavis
>Fuck you, Shirley. Ready, Hercules, for my transformation!

CGI Expert
It's good animation -- but it's fake. Way too homoerotic, too. The creators would be wise to try to expand their viewership by making it more accessible to a general audience. Perhaps the MMA character's genitals could be... edited slightly? The audience gets that he's hypermasculine -- you don't need to be so obvious. But kudos, all that body hair must've taken forever -- and then to add the sweat. Good effort, but not completely successful.

GilenLaFleur
FAKE!!!!! Nobody's balls could be that big!

****

Chiron was FaceTiming Cavalier while I did the most productive thing I was capable of at the moment: I paced around the sitting room.

"Fuck… FUCK!" shouted Cav. "Did you see that? Did you see? Gambit almost had him! That mother-fucker…"

"Let's keep it calm," Chiron said to Cav, but he was speaking just as much to me. "Everybody's reacting emotionally here and that's just what he wants -- he wants everyone upset and panicking. He's doing what he's doing to get a rise out of you, Cavalier."

"Yeah, well… surprise! It's working."

Chiron sighed and stroked his white beard with his free hand. "A leader must put emotion aside and react with calm strategy, Cavalier. Now, we've learned a lot from this video. Heracles is significantly weaker physically than he's ever been -- Gambit was nearly able to take him down. Yet even though he didn't, he wounded Heracles -- we can see that from the way Heracles is limping before they Travel."

"So you think we can beat him?"

Chiron nodded thoughtfully. "I'm starting to feel very good about our chances," he muttered.

"I'm going to fucking kill him then!"

Chiron was serious. "No," he said. "You're not."

"No, I AM! Mother-fucker has fucked with me and my brothers -- I'm going to fucking kill him… AGAIN!"

"Cavalier…"

"And again and again and however many agains it takes until that stupid fucker is DEAD! For GOOD!"

Chiron remained calm, but spoke in tones so serious I could taste their intensity. "No, Cavalier, young buck and headstrong leader, you will listen to me! You will do no such thing! Heracles' death, if required, must come from Pholus' hand -- not yours!"

I stopped pacing and turned to face him -- Chiron stood.

"When Heracles comes for you, wise Cavalier, you will surrender yourself and let him take you -- that is your only option. If you fight him, you will die -- your herd will die -- and likely, Pholus and I will die, as well." As Chiron intensified, he quieted, barely in a whisper. "We have waited thousands of years for this opportunity, Herd Master Cavalier, and we all must play our parts, yourself included. Your time will come -- I promise."

Cavalier trembled with rage. "I hate him."

"Your time will come."

****

@me: AppleJack, haven't heard from you in a hot minute.
@me: What's up, how's the basement babies?

@me: AppleJack? Please respond…
****

Oh, fuck…

****

[Musical Intro -- Theme roll. Camera dissolves to two-shot. The chyron reads "HERCULES IS BACK!"]
"Hello and welcome to TMZ Live -- Harvey Levin here!"
"Charles here."
"And the video we have today is explosive and shocking!"
"It's impossible to believe, Harvey! I've watched it a thousand times and I can't figure out how they did it."
"You and the whole internet, Charles. But, before we show it, let's set up this story. Last summer, during Pride Season, we were introduced to the PHOLUS REBORN brand, a bunch of super-hot guys who presented themselves as modern-day centaurs!"
[VIDEO -- Pride Parade Dance Choreography B-Roll]
"But it wasn't really centaurs. It was like Chippendale's -- they were dancers who displayed their… horse parts… and they became the big hit of this summer's gay scene."
"Don't forget, Charles, they caused a LOT of scandal because public sex tended to break out wherever they appeared!"
[Still shots and short vids of people in various "walks of shame" out of bars and nightclubs after orgies have been broken up -- some are escorted by police, looking disheveled and broken.]
"Yeah, but you can't say the PHOLUS REBORN guys caused that -- they were never caught at it or anything, and there were no charges brought against them."
"True enough! True enough! I'm sure it was just a crazy coincidence that wherever they went, orgies seemed to happen."
"Sure sounds coincidental to me! Happens all the time!"
"Everyday in Venice…"
[They laugh.]
"Anyhoo, Charles, they came back into the news a few days ago with this crazy… confusing… well, I don't know anything to call it other than an abduction video, 'Gambit versus Hercules'. You've

probably seen it -- it's all over the internet. It's been viewed twenty million times or something ridiculous like that. It's crazy! It's like a pro-wrestling match!"

"That's exactly what it's like, Harvey! It looks like basement-league pro-wrestling, except the guys are both superhero-types!"

[VIDEO insert window begins to play "GAMBIT V HERCULES -- we see Gambit doing clean and presses.]

"We know this Gambit guy is an actual MMA fighter and as you see, the fight between the two of them is pretty good…"

[In the video, Gambit's gonads are pixelated.]

"Although some people are saying it's kind of homoerotic and they must be promoting some kind of porn scene for this PHOLUS REBORN brand."

"And I'd buy that Charles, especially when the impossible happens and Gambit transforms into… well, into a CENTAUR as you can see! Half man -- half horse! And Centaur Gambit goes wild until Hercules subdues him with some kind of bridle or rein or something… and then they disappear. As I say, it's just crazy, whatever it is!"

[Video loops transformation moment.]

"Personally, I think the effects are amazing, but people are putting down the CGI all over the place. It's unnecessary, it's not well-done, it doesn't add anything to the scene -- most people think this Hercules guy is CGI, too. I mean, not everything's got the budget of the Marvel Universe, guys! It looks pretty real to me."

"Well, they're going to have a hard time arguing Hercules is fake when he showed up today in public! We have this exclusive NEW VIDEO, caught by TMZ's own cameraman, Mitchell -- and Hercules is in this one, too…So, let me set it up -- like I mentioned before, unlike the Gambit video, this happens in a public place -- at an outdoor food court where it's caught not only by TMZ, but by multiple cameras and phones from the public, so I don't know how they're faking this."

"I've been watching these videos all morning, Harvey. I can't figure out how they're doing it, either."

"Unless it's real…?"

[They laugh.]

"Yeah, Charles, sure. Mythological creatures have been reborn in the world and Hercules is gathering them up -- I think that's what the PHOLUS REBORN people would like us to believe for whatever their reason, whether they're making a movie or a Netflix series -- they're promoting something."

"I agree, Harvey, but let's show the video first in its entirety, then we'll come back and break it down and we'll talk to Mitchell."

"Good idea, Charles -- run it, Regan."

[VIDEO -- An outdoor eating area on a sunny mid-day. The cameraman is finishing an interview when an athletic young man with blue hair bursts from the building behind them, pushing his way through the crowd, trying to get away. People are upset and reacting loudly when the door this young man had just come through blows open out of its frame. There are screams from the crowd as a hugely muscular man, wearing a short leather skirt and a lion's skin over his shoulder emerges -- there is a scowl on his bearded face as he yells after the youth. "Stop!"

["It's Hercules!" someone in the crowd yells.

["It is!" "It's the guy from the videos!" "Hercules -- hey, HERCULES!"

[Hercules steps out of the building and leaps over the crowds' heads, landing almost in front of the blue-haired youth, who reacts -- "No! NO!" he yells -- trying to back up and spin away, only to stumble through the furniture of the eating area. The camera unsteadily moves closer to the action, circling around the rim of the patio.

[Hercules growls in his profound basso, "Thou shalt not escape! Cease this game or it will meet a swift end by my hand!"

[The blue-haired youth throws a chair at him, which Hercules easily bats aside. "Fuck you! You ain't getting me!"

[Hercules speaks his enchantment -- the words are intelligible -- and waves his arms. The impossible seems to happen -- the blue-haired youth somehow transforms into a centaur! And not just a centaur -- he's got wings! He's sparkly white, catching the light and refracting it in a strange way, in little rainbows, his hair and tail a puffy, cotton-candy blue -- the tips of his wings are blue, too, like glitter. He is magnificent and beautiful, but as he looks around, he becomes suddenly spooked, horrified -- he begins to scream, his voice curdling in terror. People in the crowd begin screaming, too, now fleeing themselves.

[Hercules seems shocked. Several phones capture him asking, "What art thou, Pokey Dakota?" as he stares at this winged creature.

[In his horror, the blue-haired centaur takes off, flapping his massive wings and rising up off the ground.

[Hercules has a lasso -- it seems to have come from nowhere. He's suddenly circling it around his head and then launches it, catching the centaur around the front foreleg. Naturally, this terrifies the centaur, who begins a somewhat lopsided tug-of-war, nearly lifting Hercules off the ground.

[Hercules, however, is having none of it. With seemingly superhuman strength, he begins pulling the centaur to earth, hand over hand, like he was landing some powerful fish on a line. The pretty centaur is struggling, screaming, a gut-wrenching sound that incites the crowd. "What you doin'?" "Leave him be!" "Let him go!" -- but this seems to sway Hercules not at all. Nobody helps, but plenty of people film.

[Again, Hercules holds a weapon that appears from nowhere -- this appears to be some metallic hook on the end of a leather leash. Like he had with the lasso, Heracles spins it around with one hand while holding the rope restraining the centaur with the other. Effortlessly, he launches it toward the beast and it easily wraps around the blue-haired youth's neck and locks in place.

[Almost immediately, the centaur stops flapping its wings, crashing loudly to the ground. Although the creature has stopped screaming, the crowd begins to scream now, again fleeing away. The cameraman catches the look on the centaur's face, now devoid of emotion and energy, but then the youth is snatched away by Hercules and lifted into the air.

[The two of them disappear, leaving confusion and panic in their wake. Several people speak, including the cameraman, who asks, "What the fuck was that?"]

****

We watched the segment (and the commentary that followed it) several times -- they seemed convinced that the whole thing had somehow been faked, so I guess that meant something, anyway. Chiron sat next to me with his hand on my knee as I tried to keep myself from crying.

"Oh, Pokey," I said, my voice wavering when his body slammed to the ground with that dead "Thud!"

Chiron tried to comfort me, his arm around my shoulder, when my cell phone began to ring. I had to break his grip to answer it -- Cavalier, FaceTiming me -- he'd obviously seen the TMZ piece, too. Now came the part where I had to keep Cavalier from going crazy when I was barely holding on myself.

I answered. "Oh my gods, Cav! Did you see the TMZ piece…?"

But it wasn't Cavalier on the other end of the line. "Hail, Pholus," this man said in his basso profundo, his bearded puss filling the screen.

"Heracles!" I said, trying to control my breathing. "How did you get this phone? Where's Cavalier?"

Heracles smiled slightly. "Be at peace, Pholus," he said. "Thou's friend is here with me, enjoying a gift given in celebration of our meeting."

He turned the camera so I could see Cavalier in the same condition as the others, an emotionless zombie, a rein wrapped tightly around his neck.

"This makes my collection complete," he said. "Though it disappointed me -- there was an expectation of combat from this one. I eagerly sought an excuse to kill it. Sadly, it did not provide that to me -- it actually surrendered!" The muscular god laughed heartily. "What a sad, pathetic lot thou hast chosen to surround thyself with, Pholus, weak playthings as centaurs and a Herd Master that lacks courage. Thou forces me to waste my time."

I tried to mask my rage. "What do you want, Heracles?"

He chuckled. "Thou knowest what I want," he said. "Give me Chiron."

Looking at Chiron, I said, "I don't know where Chiron is."

"Then thou art a worse liar than thou art a herd maker," he said. "Enough games, Pholus, let us play for real. Thou knowest what I require -- and when thou provides me the information I seek, I will release thine friends. I care not for them, Pholus -- they could be alive or dead for all this god cares. I require Chiron -- and thou whilst give him to me, or I will kill thine herd one by one until thou dost. Dost thou understand this?"

"I can't give you something I don't have."

He snorted disbelievingly. "Then thou should spend thy precious last hours of life finding it! I will give thee until Helios completes his journey on the morrow to reconsider thou's position. If not, perhaps the killing shall begin with the pretty winged pony -- thou prefers that one, dost thou not?"

"NO!" I yelled. "Do nothing! Please, Heracles, don't harm them…"

His expression became dark, unreadable. "Thou hast one day, Pholus, or I shall kill them all."

He hung up.

14. "Pederasty"

Pederasty *in ancient Greece was a socially acknowledged romantic relationship between an adult male (the **Erastês**) and a younger male (the **erômenos**) usually in his teens. Both words derive from the Greek verb erô, erân, "to love"; see also eros. The <u>Erastês</u> (ἐραστής, plural erastai) is the older sexual actor, seen as the active or dominant participant. The Erastês was responsible for the education, training in the arts and combat, and anything that would make the erômenos a more productive citizen. Usually these lessons were "paid for" with sexual favors from the <u>erômenos</u> (ἐρώμενος, plural erômenoi). Both art and other literary references show that the erômenos was at least a teen, and often an embodiment of idealized youth.*

****

I sat on the edge of Chiron's bed, contemplating the little stone icon of Heracles in my hand, the one that had come in the garden gnome that had started this whole nonsense -- my "good luck" charm -- its little jeweled eyes and massive cock. Whoever had sculpted it had clearly idealized Heracles' hypermasculinity. I sincerely doubted he was hung this well -- otherwise he wouldn't wear the skirt.

I'd been spiraling in my helplessness and frustration, now I was just shaking and angry. My herd -- my sons and my brothers -- had been taken from me… just to be bait!

Why did he hate me so much?

Chiron appeared in the doorway -- he saw what I was holding, so went to the bureau and retrieved my ditty bag himself. "Would you like me to roll a joint?" he asked, fumbling with the papers.

I snorted lightly. "No," I said.

He shook his head. "Well, you must be upset," he said quietly, "if you don't want to get high."

I laughed I was so near tears. "What am I gonna do, Chiron? How do I save them?"

He sat down next to me on the bed and put his arm around me -- he was careful not to touch the idol. "You're going to do your best," he said quietly. "That's all your friends can ask of you. That's all you can ask of yourself, my love. You're going to do your best."

I wept then -- I broke down and wept. I cried for my friends and for the Fates and for the love I felt for this man next to me, the one who held me in his strong arms and made me feel safe, even against a fearful, uncertain future. "Release this," he said, stroking my hair. "Get it out and get it gone. You must be clear-headed if we are to plot."

I wiped my eyes. "Maybe I do want that joint."

****

We were in the sitting room, smoking in the great leather chairs before the fireplace, watching Lucas start a fire. (I thought it was Lucas, but it might have been Yanni -- they looked so much alike -- I knew he was too big for Tobias, at least.) It turned out a joint was exactly what I needed -- it suppressed that crazy energy I'd been drowning in and allowed me to be calm. Calmer.

"Let's start with what we know," Chiron said, as Tobias -- yes, definitely Tobias -- appeared with a tray of snacks, vegetables and cheeses. Chiron motioned for him to leave it and go, which the boy did. "I recognized the tool he's using to keep them under control. They're called Poseidon's Bridles -- there are a dozen of them -- they were a gift from Athena to the horsemen of Thessaly, intended to be used for the taming of wild horses, to bring them under control until they could be broken by experienced riders. Who knew they could have such a dark application?"

I reached for my wine -- this was not a brandy moment -- Chiron had some incredible vintages. (I hadn't yet been to the wine cellar, but my understanding was that it was vast -- the boys could play hide and seek down there, they said.) "So these bridles simply need to be removed," I asked, as if that were some easy thing, "and the guys turn back to normal?"

Chiron shrugged and swirled his wine, thinking. "I don't see why not," he said. "That's what happens to horses. Though I've never seen these used on centaurs before, I have to assume they work the same way."

"Well, that's some good news," I said, taking the joint from him and inhaling. It was finished, so I popped the roach in my mouth and swallowed it. "Now all we gotta do is find them."

Chiron continued to stroke his beard. "That shouldn't be too difficult to figure out," he said. "There aren't many places he could go."

"Olympus?"

Chiron shook his head. "He is not held in high esteem on Olympus -- Hera alone would forbid his keeping centaurs on that sacred ground, let alone allowing them to live!"

"Does he have any other traditional home?"

"Not really. Nor would he be welcome in Thebes, nor Crete, Ormenium, Arabia, Troy, or Sparta -- he seems to be more popular in places he hasn't gone."

"That doesn't help us."

"No, it doesn't. Though we can feel sure that he's not keeping them in this reality -- where on earth would he stable six...? Wait a minute." He sat up in his chair, setting the wine down on the small lamp-stand next to it.

"What?"

"What I said, 'where on earth would he stable six horses' -- what's the operative word?"

"I don't know. 'Where'?" I guessed. He shook his head. "'Earth'?"

"No," he said. "Horses are kept..."

"...in stables!" I finished for him. "Horses are kept in stables! The AUGEAN STABLES! His fifth labor!"

Chiron clapped his hands. "Well done," he said, smiling. "It makes absolute sense, a horrible environment, avoided by almost every living thing in the Realm but the Divine Cattle and their excessive dung! The whole thing just reeks of Heracles!" He stood suddenly out of the chair. "Come, we'll go now, before the sun sets."

"To rescue them?" I asked, setting my wine down and standing myself.

"No," he said. "To scout. Let's make sure we're right and then we can plan. We're not going to just race in there headstrong -- Heracles would love that." Chiron held his hands out to me. "Come, let us prepare to Travel."

I took his outstretched hands and he quickly pulled me in and kissed me, then he winked. "Close your eyes," he said and I did. "Now imagine the place you wish to be -- picture it in your mind -- supply as many details as you can. Now imagine you're there, looking back over your shoulder at..."

"...the place where you've come." His voice isn't different, but there's a dimension to it I haven't been aware of till now -- a musicality, a playfulness. I open my eyes to see my beautiful Erastês as his Bestial self, the salt n pepper workhorse with a white belly and forelocks, the same color as his beard -- as his tail! *"Hello, beautiful,"* he says, smiling.

Even now, even amidst everything we're challenged with, I want to fuck him -- perhaps because the sun is still up. I would rather these feelings transform to bloodlust rather than lust-lust, but we'll need the moon for that. It doesn't stop me from kissing him, though -- he's my Erastês, my love. *"This place makes me so horny,"* I say.

"There'll be time for that later," he says, smiling and stepping away from me. *"For now, let's find our friends."* He pointed toward the sun. *"Do you hear to the West -- the Alpheus River? The Augean Stables are about twenty kilometers downstream. First, let's Travel to the sound of the water -- that will bring us to its banks."*

I do -- we do. I'm actually surprised that I can Travel somewhere without being able to see it.

"You can Travel with any of your senses," Chiron explains. *"Once you experience the smell of the Stables, that will be enough of a marker for you to use it to return. In the meanwhile, I know the way, so hold my hand or try to follow alone."* He holds his hand out to me and I take it -- and I can feel us move and not-move at the same time, the scenery melting by -- it reminds me of the first time I was in the Magic Realm, when I'd first heard Chiron's voice and I'd run to the edge of the sea. I must've Traveled then without being aware of it. Suddenly, Chiron and I are on the edge of a forest, about a hundred meters from the entrance of the Augean Stable.

The smell is outrageous -- the stink of ancient shit rotting beneath a layer of old shit under a spread of even newer shit. This tri-aged shit soaks into the vegetation around the massive building, built to hold hundreds of Divine Cattle, its brownness expanding like a crap-happy target. A stone building with multiple arches and gates, it's larger than a football field -- there seems to be an open-area toward the front, where shoeing or showing takes place, filled with stacks of hay bales. The rest of it seems to be rows of stalls -- filled with shit. I mumble, *"We'll never find them..."*

"They're in there," Chiron says, quietly. *"I can smell them."*

"You can smell something other than all this shit?"

"I can smell Heracles," he says. "And that's worse than all the other shit combined."

I can't tell if he's joking.

From our hiding place at the edge of the forest, I whisper, "Do we rescue them?"

"No," he says. "Not yet. We need to plan. We came to confirm their location and we've found them. That's enough. Let's head back to the cave before we're discovered and we'll figure out how to get them out of here." He's suddenly on alert. "Quiet," he orders, we squat our Bestial selves down as low as we can into the greenery.

As we settle, Heracles strolls out of the Stables and looks around, studying the forest. Is he aware of us? Does he sense our presence? Chiron motions me to remain still and silent. Standing in the final rays of the day's sun, Heracles leans against the archway of the stable and sighs heavily, seemingly exhausted. "Why is he so weak…?" Chiron whispers, scrunching his brow in thought.

He studies Heracles for a few more moments, watching the demigod's uneven breathing.

Finally, he seems to have seen enough. "Come," he whispers, taking my hand. "Let's get out of here."

Not waiting for my permission or for me to use my own powers, Chiron whisks us home. I can feel us enter the cave…

****

…and I perceived the world as I normally did.

We'd rematerialized in the grotto -- though why we'd reappear somewhere other than where we'd left surprised me for some reason. But I understood when Chiron dropped his linen skirt and stepped naked into the water. "The stink of that place stays with me," he said, quickly submerging his head. "I can't tolerate it."

I happily joined him -- I could still smell the Stable still deep in my sinuses. Although the boys appeared with soap and towels, prepared to wash their master, I dismissed them, took their soap and began lathering up Chiron myself as he stood there thinking aloud.

"We have learned much," he said as I wiped the soap across his muscular torso -- he lifted his arms so I could get into his armpits. "We know how he captured our friends. We know where he's holding them. And we know that for some reason, he's weaker than normal…?"

I wiped my hands across his wide back, working my way down to the globes of his ass. "Gambit must've inflicted more damage than we thought," I surmised, soaping up his hairy crack.

Chiron shook his head. "Heracles is a god -- a demigod, but still a god," Chiron said. "He should've recovered by now. It's something more..." He broke his train of thought and glanced down at me as I soaped his big balls, stroking them lovingly, running my slippery hands down the length of his cock. We made eye contact. "It's hard not to feel guilty, isn't it," he asked, "that our friends are in such peril yet we still feel such powerful lust for each other?"

I stood, still holding his cock, and nodded my head. "Yes," I said simply. "It is."

He wrapped his soapy arms around me and kissed me, deeply. "We are what we are, Pholus. And centaurs are made for the Bacchanalia -- you can't feel guilty about that." He gently pushed me away from him. "But that doesn't mean we need to give in to it every time — that's what supposedly separates you and I from the other centaurs. Now, finish washing me, I will wash you, and then let's get back to thinking."

It wasn't until later, after evening meal, when we were watching the video GAMBIT v HERCULES for the upteenth time, that the obvious occurred to me. "You know, they keep calling him Hercules," I said.

"Hmm?" asked Chiron, as he looked from the screen to me.

"All the comments... all the news reports... they keep calling him Hercules."

Chiron shrugged. "Heracles is the most famously misidentified god in history," he said. "I'm sure it angers him, if he's paying attention."

"No, that's my point. You've said a million times 'a god is only as powerful as his name'. A god is created by man and empowered by his worship, right? Therefore, god and man have a symbiotic relationship -- so if the humans are worshipping the wrong god, isn't the wrong god getting all the power?"

"I see your point," Chiron said, nodding slightly and smiling. "And it makes complete sense. Heracles wakes after thousands of years. He's still a god, but he's weak -- he seeks worshippers, or humans to use his name and empower him. But the humans use the wrong name, so he gains no power. Worse, he nearly meets physical defeat several times in the public view and they still acknowledge the wrong god, so his recovery slows even more. I think you've got it, Pholus -- I think that's it!"

"So how do we use that to our advantage? Do we call him 'Hercules' the whole time we're fighting him?"

Chiron chuckled. "No, that'll just enrage him. We don't want to feed that fire. You always want to engage Heracles in a battle of wits, not arms. Once he's physical, he's hard to beat."

"Gambit almost had him."

Chiron nodded. "Gambit almost had him," he agreed. "You're not Gambit."

"Thanks a lot."

Chiron put his arm around me. "It's not an insult," he said. "You have to make this battle yours, not Gambit's, not mine, not anyone's -- this is Pholus' fight, and so, you have to fight like Pholus. That means brains, wise centaur. Cleverness, outside-the-box thinking -- your specialty."

"May I ask you something?"

He acted surprised. "You may ask me anything."

"Why did you make me a centaur?" I asked plainly. "Why me? Why not Theseus, or Achilles, or any of the other *erômenoi* you've taught? Why a red-haired farm boy with no breeding? And none of this 'because the sky is blue' bullshit -- a real answer."

He smiled gently and pressed his forehead to mine, as he often did when he meant something. "Because I felt something for you that I didn't feel for them," he said, a tear in his eye. "Because I loved you so much that I didn't want to lose you." He sighed. "And then I lost you, anyway...."

"But I'm back."

He smiled through his tears. "Yes, you are," he said. "And I am as much in love with you as ever." He kissed me and held me close. "Now, listen, I have a plan. And you're not going to like it."

****

We laid together that night, but I wasn't sure either of us slept. It was enough for me to feel him next to me, the heat of his body, the steadiness of his breath, his arms around me as I used his pec for a pillow -- the same way he held me as a youth. But he pretended that he was asleep, so I pretended I was asleep, too. It was enough that we were together.

I must've drifted off a little, because I woke in the little spoon position, feeling the life of his morning wood press against the crack of my ass. I snuggled back into him, wishing we didn't have to get up, wishing we could make love in the warm sunshine instead of enacting the task before us. Either of us could die, both of us could die and maybe making love would've made facing that a little easier, but I couldn't bring myself to, knowing the condition my friends were in.

He kissed the back of my head. "Good morning," he whispered. "Did you sleep?"

"No," I said simply. "A little."

Softly, he slid his hand down my belly and wrapped it around the base of my hard cock -- he began to gently masturbate me.

"Chiron…"

"Shhh."

He was slow -- deliberate -- pressing himself against my backside as he rubbed my front. He kissed my neck until I turned my head so we could meet lip to lip. Then he rolled me on my back and laid himself down on top of me -- still kissing, he slid between my legs. In the softest, kindest way, he pressed himself into my hole -- simply magic that I could take it -- and without breaking eye-contact, he slowly began to fuck me. Thrusting in so that I felt like I was filling up with rising dough, packing me full and then sliding out again.

His eyes were an olive brown, too dark for hazel, dancing with life and mischief -- I could look into him forever and never see the depth of his love. I looked into his abyss -- and he looked into mine, his red-headed *erômenos*, the student he fell in love with.

Even when his thrusting hits a pitched-rhythm, it was a different timbre than the fucking he did for play, or relief, or power. In his moves, I felt nothing but love emit from him, nothing but desire for my pleasure.

Our centaur powers allowed us to orgasm together, but it was the first time I anally orgasmed. Ever. Even with everything weighing over us, a new experience — it was incredible. With a wide smile on his face, Chiron hugged me. "Thank you for allowing that," he said. "I would hate either of us having a regret if today went sour."

"I love you, *Erastês*," I said, holding him inside me.

"And I love you, *erômenos*," he answered, kissing me quickly. "Now let's save our friends."

****

The boys bathed us and dressed us and fed us some bread, grapes, and cheese. Only Dunn had groomed my beard before, so I wasn't completely comfortable when Yanni combed and oiled mine. Chiron and I were silent while they went about their business, occasionally making eye contact and smiling at each other.

Upon finishing, Chiron dismissed them and we walked up to the sitting room. "One more time through the plan," Chiron said, facing me and holding my hands. "I will remove the wards from the cave. When I do, Heracles will immediately sense me and he will be here within moments. Once Heracles arrives, I will Travel to the Augean Stables and release the herd. Your job is to keep Heracles occupied here, distracted. Again, I suggest you keep him talking -- he won't win a battle of wits. Don't allow it to become a fight! I only need ten minutes -- fifteen on the outside to free them -- and we will be back. Then we can attack him here, together, if we have to."

I shook my head. "Attacking him here doesn't feel right to me," I said. "It feels like we're just recreating history. This was the site of his victory last time."

Chiron took my shoulders in his hands -- he looked deeply in my eyes. "It won't be this time," he said. "We've learned from history, unlike our adversary. We will defeat him, Pholus. Together."

I sighed and shook my head. "Then let's do it and get it over with."

He gave me a peck. "Good boy," he said. "Here we go." He closed his eyes and took a deep breath, lifting his arms as if praising a god, he suddenly threw them to the side like he was tearing away a screen, heaving out his breath. "Done," he said.

Nothing felt any different.

He held up a finger. "Give it a second," he said.

Suddenly, there was a pounding on the front door -- the heavy bang of a gigantic fist.

Chiron made a "See? Told you so" motion. "Fifteen minutes," he whispered to me, kissing me for luck. "Keep him talking." With that, he closed his eyes and completely disappeared.

****

The thumping on the door grew louder until Yanni opened it and I heard a deep basso voice say, *"Páre me ston afénti sou, agóri."*

The boy led him up the few steps to the sitting room -- I didn't see him leave because my attention was drawn to Heracles, whom I hadn't seen in this reality in over a thousand years and a few dozen lifetimes. I was six-five, yet he stood a head taller than me, easily. Hugely muscled, like a comic-book character, over-exaggerated to quickly convey the visual shorthand of strength, covered in rough black hair, a thick pelt on his chest, flowing down into the grooves of his abdominals. He wore a leather battle skirt and the skin of a golden lion around his shoulders, like a Greek-themed superhero.

His footwear gave him away. Instead of his usual lace-front sandals, he wore a pair of rough, leather boots -- they were caked in dried shit that he tracked through my house, adding to his litany of sins.

He had dark, olive skin and a thick, black beard that descended all the way to the shelf of his upper pecs, blending into his chest hair. Even his eyes were so dark they appeared black. I couldn't say he wasn't handsome -- though there was something captivating about him, his looks weren't what the maidens would consider "dreamy" -- he was more an action-hero type, strong lines and blunt features, not quite rom-com material.

When he saw me, his face betrayed his disappointment. "Games," he said. "Thou playest games."

"Hello, Heracles," I said quietly. "Welcome back to Mt Pelion -- it's been a while. The last time you were here…"

"I slayed thee," he said, matching my intensity.

In the awkward silence, I nodded, then said, "Yeah, well, I've had the place fixed up since then. Like a tour?"

He smiled with the corner of his mouth, as if I were an amusing bug. "Where is he?" he asked, crossing his arms before his mammoth chest.

"Let's try something you and I have never tried before," I said, walking to the leather chairs before the fireplace. "Let's be civilized. I have information that you want. You won't be able to get that information if you put one of those bridle-things on me, and I can't tell you anything if I'm dead, so -- as I see it -- your best option right now is to play my game and talk to me."

"I have the lives of thine friends in my hands."

I remained calm. "Yes, you do, but they're not here," I said. "And as soon as you go to them, I'm going to follow you, and I'm going to try to stop you… but that still doesn't get you the information you want. Again, your best option is to play my game and I promise, I will tell you all I know."

We made eye-contact and he studied me for a moment as if testing the veracity of my statement. Silently, he strode to the leather chair and sat, legs spread, so that I could see his pouch if I chose to look. "Witness thou," he said, with open arms. "Civilized."

I took the chair opposite -- immediately, the boys were there with wine and charcuterie, delivered and gone. Heracles took the wine with suspicion, deeply sniffing it as he swirled his glass -- I suspected he was waiting for me to take the first drink, to determine if it had been poisoned, so I did.

He reacted with a satisfied sigh after drinking his entire glass at once and refilling it. "Thy vintage is exceptional," he said, as if this confession hurt him. (It didn't stop him from drinking more.)

"Dionysian," I said, sipping my own.

He snorted. "Yet another of Chiron's famous loves. How dost thou tolerate it? Hera was driven mad by far less a number."

I smiled. "I'm no jealous wife," I said. "I have one question I want you to answer, Heracles, just one. If you answer it to my satisfaction, I will tell you where Chiron is."

"A riddle?" he asked, pouring himself another glass. "I am weary of thee."

"No, nothing so trite," I said, leaning forward and putting my forearms across my knees. "I want an honest answer to a question that's been plaguing me for over a thousand years. Why do you hate me?"

He looked at me silently. "THAT is thine question? Why do I hate thee?" He snorted and laughed. "Fetch thee a scroll and a quill so we can begin a list."

I was silent while he laughed himself out. He looked at me curiously. "So begin a list," I said, making a move-it-along gesture.

"Why dost thou want to know this?" he asked, swirling. "What care have thee for my opinion?"

"This is not for me," I said, putting my hand on my heart. "This is for you -- I think you need to understand why you hate me."

He rolled his eyes. "Dreary," he mumbled. "Dost thou not know why I hate thee? It is simple: because Chiron chose thou to receive the power. Because he chose some exotic, red-headed foreigner with creamy skin and a passive disposition rather than an aggressive, olive-skinned warrior from his own country. Because I had to toil against the prejudice of the gods to gain my immortality whilst thou simply fucked thy mentor -- it was not fair! I hated thou because it was not fair! The power should have been mine!"

I was very quiet -- very careful. "It's not about power," I said. "Chiron favored me over you -- that's why you hate me. You don't hate me because I won the power, stop lying to yourself, Heracles -- you hate me because I won his heart."

"Enough!" he raged, standing suddenly with enough force to knock the chair back. "Thou goest too far! Thou rips the scabs off wounds created thousands of years ago, Pholus! He died -- Chiron died by my own hand! Dost thou even begin to comprehend the guilt that has plagued me? I killed my *Erastês*! Thousands of years torturing myself -- only to discover that he had not perished as I thought. He lived -- and he'd kept that knowledge from me! Dost thou have any idea how much my suffering could have been lessened if I had known he'd lived?"

"YOUR suffering?" I said, standing myself. "You killed me -- you slew dozens of my brethren in your rage! Yet you speak of your suffering? You have some gall, even for a god. What of Chiron's suffering?"

"Chiron?"

"You slew his lover and his children!" I said loudly, aggressive even for me. "Did you expect him to simply forgive you and reinstate you as his *erômenos*? Are you really that selfish?"

"Yes, well his lover has been reborn, has he not? And thou hast created new children. So I am not sure I understand thine strategy here. Do you rub salt in this wound simply to enrage me? Because in that way, thou hast succeeded beyond expectation. Now, I weary of this exchange. Give me what I came for! Give me Chiron!" He stomped his foot for emphasis -- it echoed through the cave.

"Oh, here it is: Heracles' famous temper!" I mocked. "Always your excuse -- always getting the better of you. Honestly, your threats aren't worth the Divine Shit on your shoes!"

He was quiet for a moment, studying me. "Thou knowest," he said quietly.

I didn't answer him -- "Shit!" I thought -- I merely held his gaze.

"This is a distraction," he said, nodding slightly. "Thou art attempting to stall me, but thou has shot thyself in the foot yet again, Pholus. Chiron is in Augea, is he not? Hoping to rescue thy little herd whilst thou provides his cover? A desperate and pathetic ploy, especially for as brilliant a strategist as Chiron -- afraid to simply face me as a man." He shook his head. "All of this death... I am tired of it, Pholus."

"No one has to die," I said.

He sighed deeply, half-laughing. Finally, he said, "Chiron does."

"How many times, Heracles?" I asked. "How many times does Chiron have to die to satisfy you? How many times do we all have to die before this is over?"

He frowned, nodding his head. "As many times as it takes," he said. "Still, thou hast given me an idea, Pholus. Instead of Death over and over again, this time we will try something new -- this time, we will try Insanity. And as thou faces thy new Fate, know that thou has done nothing to stop me from exacting my vengeance. Live with thy failure for as long as thou can comprehend it, then thou will beg for the chance of death."

He waved his hands and said something odd, something archaic, something in no language I'd ever heard, then he disappeared...

...and the world turned inside out.

****

Something is terribly wrong.

I was mixing my tenses -- *I feel like my fonts don't match!*

I'd never experienced the physical transformation before -- *Where is my Bestial Form?* -- my hips thrust and literally push my forelegs out. They grow as my lower back extended -- *lengthening vertebrae, legs bones, my toes fuse together* -- it hurt! What had always been instantaneous was now stretched out, uncomfortable -- *taking a hairy shit or growing a tail?* They touched -- I was now four legs on the ground. *My weight shifts.*

Confusing signals to my brain. I can't understand what I'm seeing, except everything I see is familiar to me. *Taste for wine -- need to run!* I knew what that... thing there was, but why did it blink?

I'm trapped!

I need to be outside! They are trying to pen me! Lock me away -- *I am for outdoors!*

The panic grew.

I kick my way out! The glass shatters -- the fire burns! Escape! I had to escape! I sought freedom -- *I can't understand...*

Where is the outside? *What are these tiny suns that glow from the roof?* How do I get out of here? No -- *NO!!! The blaring wail of sound -- kick the soundbox.* DESTROY IT ALL!

I can't -- I had to stop -- *it's all too much! My senses don't work the same way* -- they were overloaded, overstimulated, too much color, too much intensity. *Too loud! All the noise!*

I'm sobbing -- my eyes were closed -- *hands over my ears trying to shut out the everything!* Shot myself in the foot! *My friends will die!*

"NO!" I screamed -- *and even my voice sounds wrong!*

My friends will die! My lover will die!

Shot myself in the gods-damned foot -- AGAIN!

HERO! *Be a hero!*

Control -- control it, Pholus. Red -- *Pholus! Who the fuck am I???*

Who do I want to be? Where did you want to be? *Where do I want to be?*

OUTSIDE! No, the meadow -- *I want to be in the meadow.* Outside!

Screaming -- I'm screaming.

Picture the meadow. *I want to be in the meadow.* The fallen tree -- the watering hole!

I NEED to be in the meadow!

Please, gods…

I'm seeing things -- a tunnel. A golden youth standing on the other end! Is he showing me the way to the meadow, this beautiful young man, or to death…? *I don't care -- I run to him. Even as he disappears,* as I run through him, I looked behind me -- *I look back over my shoulder and see…*

****

…the Plains of Thessaly!

I'm here!

Oh, thank the gods! The madness washes away as a calmness comes over me, a release of tension and fear. My heart slows. My senses finally work together in harmony. I can see -- I can hear -- I can remember…

CHIRON!

The Alpheus River is to the west -- I Travel to it easily. And how could I forget the stink of Divine Shit that accompanied Heracles? I race blindly toward that smell, Traveling the twenty or so leagues in seconds. And with barely enough time for it to register, I'm here -- the Augean Stables.

At full gallop, I approach the main archway, hoping my entrance will be in time to help -- I don't know how long it took me to break the madness. I'm desperate, praying, until I see them.

Thank the gods -- they're still alive!

Cavalier is facing off with Heracles, screaming at him -- they are equally enraged. Chiron lies on his side, a golden arrow protruding from the breast of his beast-form -- he is hurt, but he holds himself up nobly. It is a tableau from the side of an urn -- centauromachy in relief. In the background, I see Lickety Split in the stalls, releasing the other members of the Herd from Poseidon's Bridles -- Dunn helps him.

It's then that Heracles sees me -- his rage focusing. "PHOLUS -- impossible!"

As Cavalier turns to look at me, Heracles takes advantage of his distraction, manifesting a spear and launching it. "CAV!" I scream!

And then the moment -- the moment that will be seared into my mind for the rest of eternity: as the spear speeds towards Cavalier's heart, wounded Chiron suddenly leaps in front of him -- Travels as much as leaps, appearing in the right position -- taking the spear just under his left pec, through the upper belly, sacrificing himself.

Chiron falls to the ground.

Cavalier, Heracles and I all yell, "NO!" together, for very different reasons.

I run to my fallen Erastês, spitting "KILL HIM!" to Cavalier and my herd.

"KILL HERACLES!"

15. "Liminality (Rite of Passage)"

*In anthropology, a **rite of passage** is described as a three-fold structure, made up of the following components: <u>preliminal rites</u> (or rites of separation): this stage involves a metaphorical "death", as the initiate is forced to leave something behind by breaking with previous practices and routines; <u>liminal rites</u> (or transition rites): a middle stage (when the transition takes place) implying an actual passing through the threshold that marks the boundary between the two phases -- the term **'liminality'** was introduced in order to characterize this passage. Finally, <u>postliminal rites</u> (or rites of incorporation): During this stage, the initiand is re-incorporated into society with a new identity, as a "new" being.*

****

"ATTACK!" Cavalier yells, manifesting his quarterstaff as he charges.

Heracles has made a bow and is launching a volley of golden arrows at Cavalier, who knocks them aside easily with his quarterstaff as he advances. Ultimately, Cav is too close for the bow to be an effective weapon, so Heracles discards it, manifesting his familiar club.

Cavalier takes advantage of this transition and cracks Heracles in the side of the head, the "thwack!" of the wood against Heracles' skull is glorious, even if it doesn't really do anything other than annoy him. "C'mon, Heracles," Cav says, smacking him on the other side. "What you got?"

Heracles swings his club, which Cavalier dodges easily, graceful and adept in his Bestial form -- even in all this filth, Cavalier's black coat still shines -- he smacks Heracles in the back of the head with his quarterstaff, making the demigod stumble forward.

Galloping out of the depths of the stables, Gambit leaps into the air, his huge Bestial self lifting from the ground. While he soars, he transforms into his Civilized form, his human self, and hits Heracles with a Flying Neckbreaker, flipping over the top of Heracles' head, locking his arms around demigod's neck, and using his momentum to slam Heracles to the floor, face-first into the shit that covers everything. "Fucking CHEATER!" Gambit screams. "Only way you could beat me was by cheating!" He growls, mashing Heracles' face down over and over again into the muck, repeating "Cheater" each time.

Heracles somehow stands with Gambit still riding him and flips them over, slamming them on their backs, Gambit taking the brunt of the hit, winding him slightly. Heracles stands -- they are in the open area at the front of the Stable, dirt floor, hay carts, piles of Divine Shit -- and he gets into a grappling stance. "Come then," he says, beckoning Gambit to him. "Show me."

Without hesitation, Gambit takes the challenge. The two square off.

Next to me, Chiron moans -- he's in-and-out of consciousness. He's losing so much blood -- the spear protrudes at an uncomfortable angle from his lower rib cage. He can barely breathe. "Chiron," I say, "tell me how to help you."

"There is no helping," he whispers. "Not now. The gods always require… a sacrifice."

"No," I say, my eyes welling with tears. "No…"

"Erômenos." He smiles weakly. "Don't. I've… always known," he says, trying to catch his breath. "It was… the price of... getting you back."

"No…" I hug him and cry. "It isn't worth it,"

"It… is."

Heracles crashes on the floor nearby, thrown by Gambit, but stands and heads back to the conflict, ignoring us. The others gather in a rough circle around them, a safe-enough distance back, knowing that for the moment, this is Gambit's fight. "Thou art a decent grappler," Heracles says, circling, catching his breath. "Thou should feel proud to have lasted this long against a god."

"Thou art a shit god, then," Gambit says back, mocking him, also breathing heavily. "Or art thou the god of shit? I can't remember."

They look like they've been wrestling in a mud pit, stained and filthy as they are. "This is the perfect storage place for thee and thy kind," Heracles says, smiling. "Thou blendest right in."

"Stop stalling and fight," Gambit says. "C'mon… semi-god."

As Heracles charges, he manifests his club. Gambit barely has time to make a shield before he's blocking Heracles' blow. He knees Heracles in the gut and rolls out from under him, discarding the shield and making a club of his own. "Again he cheats," Gambit says. "I'm done with this shit god -- hit him, herd! Hit him hard!"

"Ho!" Cav screams. As one, as if they'd been waiting for the cue, the herd strikes -- there seems to be chaos at first, but it's clear that Heracles is accessing who the fighters are (and who the fighters aren't). Although AppleJack gets a good hit on Heracles with his club, AppleJack is the tech guy of the group, not the fight guy, and he leaves himself open to Heracles' retaliatory blow, right in the side of his head.

AppleJack goes down.

Dunn is just as easy. The lover, not the fighter -- Dunn is the dom in any orgy scene, but weak in a battle plan. Even with his whip now, lashing painful welts into Heracles' flesh, Heracles grabs the tether unexpectedly, and easily yanks Dunn into striking distance -- holding Dunn behind the neck, little more than a few punches, mashing his nose into his face, takes him out.

Lickety Split gains the upper hand for a moment. "Hey, Ugly," he says, waiting for Heracles to turn to him and then punching Heracles in the face. Before Heracles can react, Lickety Split Travels to Heracles' other side. "Right here," he says, again punching the godling, bloodying his lip -- he Travels to another location. "Here!" he says -- punch! Travel. "Here!" Punch -- Travel. "Here!" His cadence continues to accelerate.

Annoyed, Heracles stops reacting and waits as Lickety Split continues to appear around him. Suddenly, Heracles reaches out into the empty air just as Lickety Split's throat appears in his grip -- Heracles squeezes, choking him, and then quickly brings Lickety Split in for a head butt, cracking their foreheads together.

Lickety falls to the ground, a bloody contusion already forming.

I can see them from where I cradle Chiron. "He's going through them like nothing," I whisper, distraught.

Chiron's head is against my chest. "I always... loved... when you held me," he says sincerely.

"Shh!" I say, stroking his hair. "I'm gonna get you out of here."

"No, you're not," he says. "You're going to... battle him. It's your Fate."

"Oh, fuck Fate," I say. "You need help -- I need to get you help..."

"Your friends… need you more." He smiles at me, all-wise and knowing. *"Don't… fight him on his...level… not like this… Fight like… Pholus."*

Fight like Pholus? *I think.* What the fuck does that mean?

"Everything… will be clear."

Pokey isn't able to fly well, due to the dense system of wooden rafters in the building -- he can get airborne and overhead, but he's not out of reach. He's firing arrows at Heracles, some of which bounce off Heracles' invulnerable Lion's skin -- one or two find their mark, but Heracles swats them easily aside, taking them as he would a wasp's stings. "Thou annoyest me, Pretty Freak," Heracles growls, grabbing for Pokey's forelegs. Pokey is dodging him but he's prancing on thin ice.

Protecting Pokey brings Gambit back into the fray. Still in his human form, he grabs Heracles from behind, locking him into a full-nelson. Wrapping up Heracles' arms and holding him behind his head, he exposes Heracles' torso. "Cav!" Gambit barks. "Show him the shoes!"

Cavalier spins around and kicks Heracles with his rear hooves, powerfully enough to knock both Heracles and Gambit backwards off their feet. They land on Gambit's back, who rolls out and catches his breath -- it stuns Heracles, who's shaking his head and coughing in an empty way.

Cavalier presses the attack, manifesting his quarterstaff again. As Heracles is bent over, coughing, Cav cracks him in the back of the head, dropping him to the ground. Without looking up, driven by fury, Heracles launches himself from a four-point stance and tackles Cavalier's Bestial form more easily than a professional lineman playing the pee-wee league, taking Cav's legs out from under him. Cav's body slams into the floor. Without skipping a beat, Heracles stomps Cav in the face, down into the shit-stained dirt.

Cav is only beginning to recover when Gambit takes Heracles to the ground yet again. Enraged, Heracles throws Gambit off him, into the side of one of the wooden stalls. Roaring like a lion, Heracles charges, manifesting a spear as he comes. He hits Gambit like a freight train, driving the spear through Gambit's shoulder, pinning him to the wooden frame behind him.

Gambit yells as much in frustration as pain.

On his way to confront Pokey, Heracles passes Cavalier, who nearly has his feet again. Heracles casually clubs him, putting him back down. Then he hefts Cavalier's unconscious Bestial Form over his head and throws him into the stalls on the other side of the stable, where they'd been held prisoner.

Heracles turns his attention back to Pokey. "And now, tis thou's turn, Freak," Heracles says.

"No…" Gambit moans, unable to free himself, struggling through the pain. "Leave him alone! Face me!"

Heracles reaches up and grabs one of Pokey's forelocks. "Dost thou have feelings for the freak?" Heracles asks Gambit, pulling Pokey down to the ground, hand over hand, despite the desperate way Pokey resists, kicking at Heracles' head. Heracles finally secures his grip and purposefully snaps Pokey's wing, breaking it between joints. The "crack!" is followed quickly by Pokey's scream as his body falls like deadweight to the ground.

"NOOO!" Gambit cries. "Pokey!"

Heracles examines the broken Pokey. "What's so special about it, now?" he asks, manifesting his club -- he swings at Pokey's head. "Nothing."

Pokey's cries cease and his body slumps in a pile.

"No!" Gambit wails. "NO!"

"I weary of thee, too," Heracles says. "And I believe this makes us even." Then he casually smacks Gambit with the club, leaving an unconscious Gambit to hang from the spear through his shoulder like a pin-up clipping on a bulletin board.

Heracles searches the scene, the bodies of my friends, my brothers and sons broken and slumped around him. Covered in the filth of his victory, he asks, his back to me, "Is he dead yet, Pholus?"

I don't answer him -- I stroke Chiron's cheek. "I love you," I whisper. Chiron kisses my hand.

"We have stalled this out long enough," Heracles says, turning to face me as I hold Chiron. "Hast thou had thine tender death scene?" Heracles pants, exhausted, yet he strides toward us with purpose. "I asked, is he dead yet, Pholus? Is he?" Without a single shred of empathy, he swings his club, beating Chiron's body over and over again. "Is he? IS HE?!? Then perhaps thou can find the humor in me beating a dead horse!" This causes him to laugh, a sinister chuckle.

"Stop!" I say, standing. Charging him, I morph to my human form. "STOP!" I dive at him, grabbing his neck, but sweeping his legs out from under him. He doesn't expect this from me -- surprised, he goes down.

I quickly straddle his chest, putting him in a schoolboy pin, and begin punching his face. "Killer!" I scream. "Murderer! What's wrong with you? He was your teacher -- you said you loved him! And you killed him! Beat him! Killer! Killer!" I continue the barrage until he bridges his back and throws me off him.

"Well, look at Pholus," he says, smiling, wiping the blood from his mouth with the back of his hand as he regains his footing. "Finally found thee some passion. Finally a reason to fight -- all it took was the death of thy lover."

"Fuck you!" I say, my rage blinding me, the tears searing down my cheeks. "Jealous fuck! Jealous that he gave me his power -- his love! And even then, he didn't hate you, Heracles -- he felt sorry for you! A petty god with an uncontrollable temper."

We begin to grapple in a traditional stance, but the formality is soon lost and it just devolves into a fight. Even in my anger, I know I don't stand much of a chance against him this way.

I have to change the rules of the fight.

He punches me hard enough to send me into the air, crashing into a hay cart parked just inside the door -- my back bends in a very unnatural way, adding more pain to the mix. I stand and attempt to manifest a weapon, but nothing comes. That's the moment Heracles charges, swinging his club underhanded, like he's golfing -- I'm able to make a shield before it hits, but it still sends me into the air again, landing hard in the bed of the cart. The shit-filled hay does nothing to soften my fall.

New pain -- shoulder.

Heracles is panting, catching his breath. "This is why thou hast been brought back?" he asks, sweating and bleeding and filthy. "To simply die again? What a pathetic waste of time and energy."

I try to manifest a weapon -- nothing.

Instead, I stall. "You haven't come through this unscathed," I say, trying to manifest something -- anything. "We've hurt you pretty good."

"I shall recover," he says, easily creating his spear, "but thou shalt be dead." He snorts. "And even as thou seemest to continually recover from that sorry state, I promise thee -- not this time."

He's walking toward me, a stalking, exhausted plod, as if he's holding himself together just to get the satisfaction of my death, then he'll fall himself. I'm desperate for a weapon. This is it, he's upon me -- c'mon, Pholus, something! Anything!

Suddenly, in my hand I feel the little stone idol I'd found in the garden gnome -- my "good luck" totem from my ditty bag -- the rough, hewn statue of a hypermasculine man with enormous genitals. Why do I have this? Why has this come? I need a weapon!

Still, it's familiar to me and feels oddly comforting, so my hand instinctively wraps around it -- and as my thumb touches its gigantic cock, its little jeweled eyes light up.

A change comes over Heracles.

"Thou and thy kind, just tools of the flesh," he growls, adjusting himself beneath his leather skirt. "Just constant fornication."

"What are you talking about?" I ask.

I begin to rub the idol's cock with my thumb.

"Thy kind and thine horse cocks," he says, clearly getting a hard-on, uncomfortable, though not completely trying to hide it. "It is all they speak of, thy sexual prowess."

I see what's happening here -- I rub.

"Yet thou hast never experienced the cock of a god, hast thou?" he asks, openly touching himself now -- his spear has disappeared (being replaced by another). "Perhaps before I kill you I shall give you one last pleasure -- sex with a god!"

"Get back," I say, even as I continue to rub the idol, weaving my web. I slide myself further back into the hay cart. "Don't do this…"

"What? Enjoy the spoils of war?" He strips his leather skirt off, revealing himself to me. His cock is about eight inches, thick -- a fine cock if he were a mortal -- but certainly nothing for a god to brag about, especially a god of his proportion. It extends from his hairy groin above his well-sized balls -- he's a fine choice for a virgin, or an inexperienced erômenos, otherwise, he's only impressive for his physique. "Who will stop me? Thine friends? Look around thee, Pholus. Thou art done."

I'm on my back in the cart and he slides me down to him, the rough wood splintering into my skin. I've not stopped with the idol. "Heracles, I beg of you. Stop."

"This is what thou hast been created for -- born again for, correct? Enjoy it, Pholus, for thy life ends upon my completion." He bluntly pushes his cock into me, hard and dry -- another arena of pain to contend with -- and he roughly begins to thrust.

Unfortunately, my centaur physiology doesn't discriminate between enemy and friend, lubricating me and making me able to take anyone, no matter how large (or, with Heracles, how disappointingly small) -- I feel my hole tighten, surrounding him completely.

Worst of all, regardless of my injuries and pains, I can feel my own cock harden.

Heracles moans. "Is this why Chiron chose thee?" he asks as he thrusts. "For thy whore's ass? Do not feel shame, Pholus. I can see thou likes it."

Out of the corner of my eye, I see Cavalier in his human form, quietly sneaking around the back stalls, approaching us. We make eye-contact and I hold up my hand flat -- "Wait," I think. "Not yet."

I rub the icon's cock, arms out to my sides.

He has no rhythm or skill -- nothing to enjoy about the encounter except that I do. I try not to feel guilt -- it's how I'm made, I remind myself. I am what I am. Suddenly, Heracles' hands surround my throat -- as his fucking increases intensity, he starts to choke me. "Now thou begins to understand," he says, squeezing. "My end is thine."

He's getting close -- I can't breathe.

"I actually prefer thee dying this way," he says, thrusting hard, continuing the pressure on my throat. "Quietly."

The world is starting to black out, but I'm holding on. But I can't hold the idol -- it falls from my hand.

The world seems far away -- the darkness so comfortable and near, surrounding me in a painless silence. From far away, I feel his orgasm -- and even in the state I'm in, it triggers my own. The small death. I know what I have to do -- with my last ounce of strength, I raise my hands to his heart…

…and I let the power flow.

He releases me, unsure of what's happening -- I immediately draw a huge breath, desperately sucking air in. Gasping.

It's too late -- the change has happened, I can feel it.

He can feel it, too.

"What hast thou done to me?" he asks, feeling his torso, removing his cock from me. "What hast thou done?"

"Given you your heart's desire," I say. "Congratulations -- you're a fucking centaur!"

The metamorphosis begins. First, it's his cock, growing in both length and thickness as it rises into a new erection, then the rest of him follows, his muscle, his hair. Heracles has a spectacular body, over-developed and muscular, the envy of any bodybuilder in any gym -- yet nobody would ever describe Heracles as "ripped." "Thick" for sure, but never "fat-free" or "striated" -- he's bulk, not detail.

But this new Heracles requires new adjectives. He's bigger -- it's not just the illusion of bigger given by being defined, he's gaining weight, lots of it. His muscles are surreal, unimaginably large -- impossible. He's thicker through the shoulders and thinner through the waist -- his erect cock nearly reaches his pecs.

He looks like the icon made flesh.

Heracles begins to laugh. "Fool!" he says. "Fool of a fool! Continually shooting thyself in the foot! Now that thou hast given me the power, thine death will have even less meaning!"

"This is not even the tip of the power," I say, holding my throat. "Your human form -- that's not where the power resides. The true power is in your Bestial form."

"My BESTIAL form!" he says, grabbing at his huge cock. "Yes! YES! I will be a BEAST! How? How do I become a true centaur? How do I access this Bestial form? Tell me, Pholus!"

I'm still panting from his attempt to kill me. "Just... imagine it and... let it happen. The power will do the rest."

He breathes deep, concentrating, and transforms without effort. I don't know why he wouldn't -- he's been a lion before in this Realm, many times. As a centaur, his Bestial form is unbelievably large, a warhorse, over 25 hands high, solid black with olive hues. Hypermasculine and hyper-equine, his head nearly reaches the rafters, making him around nine feet tall. I've never seen anything so beautiful, so deadly, and so dangerous. He's so excited, like a bully given his schoolyard dream, his sheath opens and his cock spills out. "Yes," he growls, flexing. "YES! Finally! After all these years..."

I shout, my throat raw, "Cav... NOW!"

From behind the closest of the stalls, Cav emerges in his human form, running but clearly injured, twirling something over his head like a lasso. He jumps and launches his weapon at Heracles -- I recognize it as one of Poseidon's Bridles -- which wraps itself neatly around Heracles' neck and locks in place before Heracles even has a chance to react.

"No," Heracles says, realizing what it is. "NO!" He reaches for the bridle, but his energy suddenly wanes, and his arms drop lifelessly to his sides. His face becomes empty and expressionless as he falls under the bridle's spell.

Cav limps up to him and takes the rein in his hand. "Got you, you fuck shit of a god!" he says. "Got you!"

I can stand, though my back is killing me -- it's easy to ignore it in this moment -- and I hug Cavalier. "We did it!" I say, collapsing against him -- though I think we're collapsing against each other. "Oh my gods, we did it..."

"We sure did," Cav says, holding my head back so we can look in each other's eyes. He kisses my forehead. "That was amazing."

"You were amazing! Oh, Cav..." I hug him again.

Cav turns us slightly and addresses Heracles. "I know you can hear me, shit god, so hear me good. You were caught by Pholus and Cavalier, defeated by our herd, but you won't get the honor of death from us. We'll see you spend eternity trapped in the form of the thing you wanted to be the most, but will never get the chance to be. Welcome to your Fate, slayer of centaurs."

From behind us, near the main door, we hear the unexpected sound of someone clapping.

We both turn our wounded bodies -- there's someone standing there, but it's hard to see him clearly because of the sunset behind him. He's a young man, I can tell that much, handsome -- he almost glows.

"Bravo!" he says, clapping his hands. "BRAVISSIMO! That was... beautifully played! What an amazing story -- it had drama and comedy and character growth, unexpected tragedy, gripping action, and even a musical number! Oh, it was just good theatre! Well done!"

He enters the Stable, somehow not getting dirty, and approaches us -- it's the Youth from the Orgy! He's lean, well built but not muscular, dressed in a little golden skirt and lace-front sandals. He carries a wand -- my memories say the word "thyrsus" to me for some reason -- wrapped in grape leaves and dripping honey. He's stunningly handsome, barely old enough to drink, but somehow worldly and wise.

Cavalier falls to his knees, recognizing the Youth immediately. "Hail, Dionysus!" he says.

Dionysus, the god of wine (and pot) smiles and says, "Hello, boys! Nice to be recognized."

16. "Theophany"

Theophany *(from Ancient Greek (ἡ) θεοφάνεια theophaneia, meaning "appearance of a deity") is the manifestation of a deity in an observable way. This term has been used to refer to appearances of the gods in ancient Greek and Near Eastern religions. While the Iliad is the earliest source for descriptions of theophanies in classical antiquity (which occur throughout Greek mythology), probably the earliest description appears in the Epic of Gilgamesh. Divine or heroic epiphanies were sometimes experienced either in dreams or as a waking vision, and frequently led to the foundation of a cult, or at least an act of worship and the dedication of a commemorative offering.*

****

He's stunned by the change in Heracles — I'd say "gobsmacked" if I were talking about anything other than a god. "Wow," says Dionysus, leaning back and looking up at the nearly nine-foot centaur that stands frozen and helpless before him -- he sighs. "Honestly, he's a little too big for the spot I have to display him," Dionysus mutters, then shakes it off. "But no matter -- I'll make it work!"

I'm confused. "What?"

He turns to me and smiles gently, stroking my cheek. "Oh, Pholus, I love you, but you can be so humorless." He pats my shoulder. "I promise to explain everything, but first -- I have a few bits of business, none the least of which is healing your herd. So let's prioritize."

"You can heal them?"

He waves me off. "Please! I've been curing hangovers for thousands of years. I learned Healing from Apollo himself -- I got this down." He looks around disapprovingly. "Still, I can't abide this filth. Indulge me for a moment."

Taking in a slow, deep breath, Dionysus faces the stalls and exhales, slowly pushing his arms away from his body in a sweeping motion. The decades of Divine Shit, ground into every nook and cranny, the smell seeping into every pore, all lifts and melts away, disappearing completely, leaving only the flaking paint, the wooden stalls, and the ancient masonry, all of it spotless. Even the hay is clean and fresh.

Dionysus smiles. "I have a vineyard that dung will be perfect for. Divine Dung makes fabulous fertilizer -- next year's vintage will have a nice deep note to it." He turns to Heracles and says to the zombie, "Notice how I did that in a matter of minutes. You had to divert a whole river and you wasted over a ton of perfectly useful fertilizer." He shakes his head. "Stupid half-god."

Cavalier quips, "We've been calling him Shit God."

Dionysus giggles. "Much better," he says, smiling. He turns to Heracles and says, "Stupid shit god." He puts his hand over his heart and turns to us, smiling. "Oh, that feels so good! You don't know -- I've waited so long for this moment." He shifts his focus too quickly for me -- his transitions are much faster than mine. Then he reaches out to me. "Now, let's get the healing started."

I grab his wrists as he reaches for my head. "I can wait," I say. "Chiron first..."

He frowns slightly and shakes his head. "Pholus," he whispers, as if I should know this.

I start to cry at his confirmation. "No... please..."

He wipes my tears gently with his fingers. "Shhh," he says. "Honey... shhh. There'll be time for that later. Right now is time for the living." He puts his hand on either side of my head and makes eye contact with me -- sparkling, purple eyes -- and then kisses me.

I feel what I can only describe as a cool wave flowing through my body, a breeze through the meadow, the smell of rain on grapevines, honey on suckle, and my pain goes away, drifting off with the wind. I am whole for the first time in forever -- I feel completely fresh and new, healthy and happy. I am as rejuvenated as an ancient vineyard, weeded, mulched, and ready for planting.

I release my breath like I've just had an orgasm.

"I love you so, Pholus, my brother erômenos and instrument of my vengeance. I knew I made the right choice in you. Thank you... for THIS!" he jokes, motioning to Heracles. "Honestly? It's absolutely the best gift I've ever gotten, and I've gotten some nice things!"

"'Instrument of your vengeance'?" I ask.

Dionysus rolls his eyes. "Healing first, expository explanations during the Feast! May I heal your herd before you inundate me with your endless plot questions, Pholus?"

I hold up my hands in surrender. "Sorry," I say. "Force of habit."

Dionysus blows me a kiss and manifests a leather wine bag on a tether. "Have some wine," he says. "Let me do my work."

He turns to Cavalier. "You!" he says, smiling broadly. "Herd Master! I'll be honest, the biggest gamble of this whole plot was whether you'd give yourself up to him or not. Did you see what it gained you? Did you learn your lesson, Cavalier?"

Cav smiles. "I did," he said. "I knew I had to trust the gods. I've read these stories over and over -- and I know what happens when people don't listen." He laughs gently. "It was the hardest fucking thing I've ever had to do in my life, tho." He snorts. "Humility…"

Dionysus smiles proudly, taking Cavalier's head in his hands. "I know," he says. "But there's so much more coming for you -- greatness! Greater even than this. GrandMaster Cavalier will be one of the names echoed throughout eternity -- this I promise!"

Cav pulls Dionysus in for a kiss, which surprises the god, because he intended to do the same thing, yet Cav beats him to the punch. I can see Cavalier being healed, so I know what he's feeling, the bliss that goes along with being remade. When the kiss breaks, Cav whispers, "Thank you."

Dionysus smiles. "The pleasure's all mine. You sure can kiss, baby!" He grabs another, then laughs.

Cav and I hug each other -- gods, how I love this man, my brother, son, and leader!

AppleJack is the closest to us, so we attend to him first. The side of his head is severely bruised, and he's barely conscious when Dionysus takes his head in his hands and whispers, "You showed us how badly you wanted it, AppleJack. Don't give up on us now." With that, he kisses AppleJack and I watch my best friend heal, his wounds fade, and his breathing becomes even.

"What's happening?" he asks as he comes back to awareness. "Why is the Pot God kissing me?"

"We won," Cavalier says, clapping AppleJack on the shoulder, "and the Pot God is healing us."

"Oh." AppleJack says, as if that's enough of an explanation. "Okay…"

Dionysus excitedly adds, "Though I'm anxious to try the hybrid you grew that everyone raves about." He looks at me. "At the Feast," he adds with humor.

I smile and shake my head.

Dionysus creates another wine bag and hands it to AppleJack. "Have some wine," he says.

"I can make those, too!" AppleJack says.

Dionysus nods. "I guarantee mine is better. Take it."

AppleJack does.

Dunn is next. His nose is broken and bloody and he's got two black eyes already. "Hello, Dunn. I'm Dionysus -- I'm going to heal you."

"By doze ith boken," Dunn tries to say.

Dionysus nods. "Sounds like your jaw is, too." Carefully, he kisses Dunn and we watch his face go through months of healing in a few moments. He's back to his normal, handsome self with his beautiful beard and silver septum ring. Once he is, he kisses Dionysus with significantly more passion.

"Holy cow!" Dunn says, when the kiss breaks. "I feel amazing! Seriously, I haven't felt this good since I was a teenager -- and I'm an old pony! Ready for pasture!"

We all laugh and Dionysus hugs him. "You are the sexual leader of this herd," Dionysus says. "As much as Cav leads in battle, you lead in seduction. You embrace your sexual powers as much as these boys embrace their enhanced athletic abilities. When you become a herd master yourself, you will generate so much sexual energy during the Bacchanalia, I…" He looks around. "I'm getting ahead of myself… again." He looks at me and gives me a cue.

"The Feast?" I ask him.

He smiles and blows me a kiss. "The Feast," he says.

Lickety Split has a double black-eye, too, as well as a contusion on his forehead that swells as large as an avocado and a bruise around his neck in the literal shape of Heracles' hand. Lickety Split is unconscious, and probably concussed. Dionysus whispers in his ear, "Okay, Scout, find your way back" and he kisses Lickety, gently, on the lips.

It takes a second, but Lickety Split suddenly sits up, coughing -- it reminds me of those people who have drowned and are given mouth-to-mouth and they suddenly breathe again on their own. "What happened?" Lickety Split asks, looking around at us all. "Who's this guy, now?"

"This is Dionysus," I say to Lickety. "He's kind of the reason we're all here -- he's the God of Wine."

"And pot," AppleJack adds.

"Oh," says Lickety Split, smiling. "Nice to meet you."

"You, too." Dionysus smiles like he knows a secret.

"What?" asks Lickety, suspicious.

Dionysus continues to smile, shaking his head -- he waves it off. "Nothing," he says. "Your potential -- this herd is nothing but potential."

AppleJack helps Lickety Split to his feet and the two hug, warming my heart.

Back in the main arena, we find Gambit -- it's hard to look at him, even if we know he's to be healed -- a spear through his upper chest, pinning him to the stable wall behind him. His body hangs there, still bleeding across his heavy torso.

"Dear God," Dunn says, putting his hand on his heart. "What happened to him…?"

"We'll recount the battle later," I say, closing in on Gambit with Dionysus and Cavalier. "Right now we have to save him."

"He'll be fine," Dionysus says to me, sensing my growing panic. "He'll be fine -- we're gonna have to slide him off the spear, though. I don't think we're gonna be able to pull it from the wall." He cast a sideways glance at Heracles. "Overcompensating Ass."

It takes the three of us to move Gambit -- as deadweight, he's heavier than he looks. Thank the gods he's not in his Bestial form -- we'd never move him! As it is, it takes work.

He reacts as we begin to slide him toward the blunt end of the spear, a gasp that, scary as it is, at least lets us know that he's still in there. We all begin our litanies of "It's okay, Gambit" "Hold on, big guy" "Almost there…"

As he comes off the spear, he falls to the ground with a thud and we roll him over on his back. He is drifting near consciousness, his eyes open a crack. Dionysus kneels beside him as we are all around him. "Hello, Warrior," Dionysus says, placing his open hand on Gambit's wounded chest, right where the pec meets the shoulder, under the collarbone. "You're right -- you would've had him if he'd followed the rules. You beat a god in fair combat. Believe me when I say everyone will know…" then he adds, loud enough for the warhorse centaur to hear, "…we will call it 'Heracles' Humiliation'."

He giggles with satisfaction, then he bends down to kiss Gambit, keeping his hand over Gambit's wound as he does. Gambit gasps in the kiss, then suddenly sits up, fully aware. "POKEY!" he yells, then he registers us around him. He looks from one to the next. "Did we win?" he asks. "Did we beat him?"

"See for yourself," Cavalier says, standing aside and revealing Heracles.

Gambit is shocked. "What the fuck?" he asks, standing and walking over to the trapped god. "What the fuck did you do to him?" he asks, admiring the trophy.

Cavalier is understated. "What he did to us," he says. "Shit God."

Gambit snorts. "God of shit, for sure." He touches his shoulder, surprised at its condition. He rolls it around and tests it. "I'm healed," he says. "Not just the shoulder, either -- old injuries, aches, war wounds. How did you heal me?"

"This is Dionysus," I say, presenting the youthful god.

Gambit is confused. "Did you just kiss me?" he asks. "I thought that was a dream."

Dionysus smiles. "It was a good kiss. Welcome back, Warrior -- thank you for your service."

Gambit isn't interested in niceties. "Where's Pokey?" he asks, looking around. "That fucker broke Pokey's wing! Right in front of me -- I never felt so fucking helpless in my life!"

"Don't worry. Don't worry," Dionysus says. "He's nowhere near the dire condition you or Lickety Split were in. He'll be fine."

Confused, Gambit -- who'd witnessed Lickety's battle with Heracles-- asks Lickety Split, "What happened to you?"

Lickety Split shrugs. "I don't know," he says. "I think I had a concussion. I don't remember."

We quickly cross to where Pokey lay in a pile of hay, his broken wing covering him like a down blanket. Dionysus sighs. "So dramatic," he says, kneeling next to the blue-haired boy. He looks up at the rest of us. "I do love this one," he admits, smiling. "Power and naivete mixed together in almost equal amounts." Dionysus shakes his head. "Oh, how he makes me laugh." He makes eye contact with Gambit and adds, "He thinks the world of you, too."

Gambit kneels next to Dionysus and says, "Please save him."

"He's fine," Dionysus says, indicating Pokey. "Melodrama, this one -- always. That's why he needs you to protect him." Dionysus tilts his head to the side, conceding. "That's why I need you to protect him. Train him. Love him."

Gambit puts his hand on Dionysus' shoulder and nods. "Please save him."

Dionysus smiles. "It's as easy as a kiss!"

As Pokey heals, his wing stretches out straight, and I can almost hear the weird, reverse snap (!panS) it makes as it mends itself. After a few seconds, Pokey draws a giant, healthy breath and, discovering himself in a kiss, gives in to the moment, and the two of them are literally making out in front of us.

Until Pokey opens his eyes and sees where he is… and who he's kissing.

He pulls back, looks in confusion at the young god and asks, "Donny?"

"Hi, Pokey!"

"What are you doin' here?"

Gambit asks the question the rest of us are thinking. "Pokey, do you know this guy?"

"Yeah! This here's Donny Isis! I knowed him from the Rodeo Circuit."

"What?"

"Yeah," Pokey says, nodding his head. "I met him in a bar one night, after I got throwed. He's the one done told me I should go to the city, seek my fortune. Ain't that funny…"

"This is Dionysus, God of Wine…" I point to AppleJack and give him his cue.

"And pot!"

Pokey puts it together. "Donny Isus," he says, smiling broadly. "Ain't that funny…"

I turn to Dionysus, who's clearly pleased with himself, and I ask, "So, you've been manipulating us…?"

He snorts. "Longer than you've been alive, honey. But again, I'll give you ALL the details…" He cues me, the same way I cued AppleJack.

"At the Feast," I say, returning his smile.

He takes my hands and becomes serious. "Now, there's one last task I have to perform." He looks toward the fallen body of Chiron, and my eyes follow him.

The tears are there again, sitting right on the edge of my lower lids -- my breathing hitches -- I'm not ready for this. I get up with Dionysus, but he turns to me and stops me. "Remember him as he was," Dionysus says, touching my arm. "Not in his current state. Let me take care of this -- you stay here with your friends."

He walks away and we watch him, huddled together, hanging on each other. Standing over Chiron, Dionysus says something. "We did it, Erastês. Your sacrifice was worth it. My humble thanks," I think he says, but I can't hear him clearly. Then he holds his arms out to the sides and looses his power one more time.

It is energy, light -- magic. The wind whips around Chiron's body, surrounding him with light. That ball of energy lifts off the ground and condenses upon itself, shooting off an explosion of silent whiteness that blinds us for a second.

"Goodbye, Chiron," I whisper, and my brothers support me.

Dionysus returns to us, his ever-present smile back in place. He approaches me and holds out a tiny glass bottle, crystal with an ornate stopper -- it's full of wine.

"What's this?" I ask, taking it from him. I already know.

He puts his hand on my shoulder. "It's Chiron's essence," he says. "I've preserved it in Dionysian Wine, his favorite vintage."

I'm confused. "What am I supposed to do with it?"

He shrugs. "Put it on a shelf, bury it in a garden gnome, I don't know. It's up to you."

"Will Chiron be reborn?"

"I don't know -- there's always a chance, I suppose, but there's no guarantee. It's different than with you. And I'll explain…"

I smile. "At the feast," I say, holding the bottle close to my heart. "Thank you."

Dionysus holds my eyes and places one of his hands over mine. "I loved him, too. He made it easy."

"Yes, he did."

Dionysus winks, then opens himself to the group. "Boys, let's head back to the cave on Mt. Pelion for a victory celebration and feast -- I think it's the least we deserve."

Everyone cheers, myself included.

He points to the massive Heracles, forever frozen in his living prison. "I have to take care of that first, then I'll meet you there."

"Wait, I reckon I was in the States when I got took!" Pokey says. "Won't I just go back there?"

Dionysus smiles. "That's not how Traveling works, Pokey. Just imagine where you want to be and you'll be there -- this Realm is the intermediary. You'll save a ton in airfare!"

I ask, "Why didn't Chiron tell me that?"

Dionysus -- always the smile. "Because he didn't want you to leave," he says. "I'll see you all at the Feast!"

And with that, he grabs Heracles' reins, and he and Heracles disappear, leaving the seven of us standing there.

They all look to me, but I'm out of words. "I love you guys," I say. "But honestly, I need a joint…"

Laughing, we hug in a big group -- and we Travel together.

****

"A toast!" Dionysus said, raising his glass -- the wine nearly splashed over the edge.

We all raised our glasses. We were at that wonderful point of drunkenness -- in touch with the Divine, the place the Followers of the Bacchanalia seek — but not lost. In our case, the Divine was sitting here at our table with us, raising his glass, so it didn't take much effort.

"To the Fates," the young god said, smiling, "who wove the seven of you together out of all the people in the world. And look what you did! To the Fates!"

"The Fates!" we agreed happily, swigging this amazing wine back.

Yanni, Lucas, and Tobias hurried to refill our glasses. It shouldn't have surprised me that the boys had a feast waiting for us upon our return, but it did -- as if they'd known. And I think by their controlled response to the news, they had. Still, Tobias cried when I'd told them what happened to Chiron, so I hugged him, and promised I was staying, which seemed to make them all feel better.

The herd had bathed before we'd eaten, scrubbing the dirt and dried blood from each other. And even if we'd been turned on enough to engage in sexual activity -- and I think everyone had been -- it didn't seem like the right moment. Not yet.

It had been easier to eat this delicious food, revel in this incredible wine, and tell the guys the parts of the story they'd been unconscious for. Gambit had been anxious to see the abduction videos, remarking on his own like he'd been the color commentator at the WWE. "And here's where the mother-fucker cheats!" he'd yelled, when Heracles had turned him Bestial. "I had that bitch." If it had been hard to watch himself go insane and get caught, watching it happen to Pokey and the cynical commentary following it -- really hit him hard. He held Pokey close.

Pokey, for his part, was excited to have appeared on TMZ. "That don't happen to rodeo guys that much, I expect."

I was a little drunk -- and happy. "Well, I think it's time for a story!" I said. "THE story!"

"Here! Here!"

"Tell us the story of Dionysus," I said, raising my glass. "Tell us everything." I drank.

He smiled and laughed. "All rightie!" he said, as the orchestra swelled behind him. "Though I wish you guys would let me do this as a musical number?"

"NO!"

He rolled his eyes, sighed, and grabbed his glass -- the band faded away. "Your loss," he joked. Another breath, to focus. "I am one of the Twelve," he began. "The Twelve Great Greek Gods. Even so, I prefer to walk among men -- I always have -- rather than sit up there on stuffy Olympus with the rest of the gods and their "thees" and their "thous" and their formal rhetoric, looking down on everything, apart from it all. I'm not exactly… disliked by them for it… but I've always felt a little bit of an outsider.

"It's their fault, in some ways, that I am as I am. When I was young, Zeus brought me to Chiron, to serve as my *Erastês* as I learned of my powers and the ways of the gods. In being *erômenos* to Chiron, I learned instead the joys of humanity, the pulse of the living, the lust of mankind -- it was a glorious time in my life. Then I assumed my godhood and Chiron became my follower, yet our relationship never seemed to change. He had that way about him.

"Chiron sponsored another dozen *erômenoi*, easily, before Pholus came along -- Heracles being one of them -- but once Pholus came into the picture, that was the end for Chiron! Oh, how he doted over that boy -- some gossiped it was Pholus' exotic red hair, his creamy skin, his… willingness." Dionysus smiled playfully at me, raising his eyebrows. "Whatever. Chiron did something he'd never done before -- he made Pholus a centaur -- then he broke a mad societal tradition of the time and declared his love for the youth, his former *erômenos*.

"Scandal!"

"I don't get it," Pokey said, right there next to Dionysus. "Why was it a scandal? Their relationship was the same."

I snorted. "No, it wasn't," I said. "Our relationship was different. It stopped being so much teacher/ student and we became… equals. Lovers."

Dionysus continued, "Which at the time was scandalous. A man was expected to have a wife and family, that's the tradition of society. But a man took on *erômenoi* to prepare the next generation to be proper citizens. It was one thing to have sex with your *erômenos* -- that was normal -- it was quite another to fall in love!"

"So we ended up living in a cave in Mt. Pelion."

Dionysus laughed. "That's a rather… blunt way of telling that part of the story," he said to me, raising his glass. "But true." He drank then, laughing to himself.

"I am the God of Wine…" he glanced at AppleJack and added, "and Pot, and when people drink -- or smoke -- they release their human limitations, the restrictions of their senses, and they begin to perceive the Divine. This state is called the Bacchanalia -- we're in it right now!"

He laughed, raising his glass. "A toast! To the Bacchanalia!"

We all yelled, "To the Bacchanalia!" and drank.

"This Bacchanalia empowers me," Dionysus explained. "The more people in this state, the more power it gives me. There were whole cults devoted to it -- AND it's the origins of modern theatre!

"Centaurs, though? Centaurs were a valuable tool of the Bacchanalia. Honestly, Centaurs quite naturally create Bacchanalia wherever they go, drinking, carousing, orgying -- it's glorious! That orgy you created at Pride last summer? Oh, my friends, I hadn't felt that good in thousands of years -- what a rush of power! That was absolutely fabulous! Well done -- that's when I knew I had a herd that was gonna win."

A confident murmur among us as we clinked glasses and drank again -- the boys immediately refilled us. I felt like I was in that place right before I was drunk -- I feel like I'd been there for hours, happy and light. AppleJack lit a joint and started sending it around the table.

Dionysus took the first hit. "Oh, that's good," he said as the smoke crept from his mouth. "Thumbs up from the Pot God."

AppleJack was elated.

"Back to the story," I said.

"Yes, yes," Dionysus said, taking another quick hit and passing the joint to Cav, on his right. "So I love centaurs. Centaurs have been very, very good to me. However, centaurs, being centaurs, often pushed the limits of what they could get away with. So, they ran afoul of the Lapith family, big, rich, fancy folks -- story had it that, drunk, the centaurs had kidnapped the King's daughter on her wedding day and raped her, ruining her for her husband. In fact, they'd kidnapped the groom and very consensually fucked him, ruining him for women, especially the aptly named Hippodamia, his bride -- but the Lapiths were rich enough to have history edit that part out.

"Regardless, the Lapiths had it out for the centaurs, and the King hired Heracles to come into town and get rid of them. Heracles had just returned from his fourth labor -- killing some boar or something -- so he was more than happy to help. Remember, Heracles was madly jealous of Pholus, especially that Pholus had been 'raised' by being transformed into a centaur, much less had become Chiron's lover."

I interrupted. "Can I tell you that I never knew that? Until he showed up at the cave that day and beat the shit out of me, leaving me for dead, I'd no idea how he'd felt."

"You remember it?" Dionysus asked me.

I nodded, taking the joint from Pokey as it came to me. "Mostly, yeah," I said, taking a hit -- a needed hit. "I remember him storming in, demanding the wine, swinging that damn club of his, wrecking everything. He beat me pretty bad -- and left me there for dead while he used the wine to attract the others. I don't remember much after that. I think I died."

Dionysus nodded. "Very close, anyway. They came to rescue you, Chiron included, but Heracles was ready for them. He had arrows dipped in the poison blood of the Hydra and he… slaughtered dozens of centaurs that day, including Chiron, who only lived because he had the medicines he needed -- even then, he nearly passed. Heracles thought he had, anyway, and apparently tortured himself publicly with the guilt of slaying his *Erastês*, to which I say, 'Fuck you. Good.' Do you have any idea how much power I lost when the centaurs all died?

"Except Chiron. But Chiron was too late to save Pholus, as much as he tried. And as every man does in his last moment of desperation, he prayed. He prayed to me.

"And even though we gods hear all the prayers that come to us, it's up to our discretion about whether we answer them or not -- but this was Chiron, my former *Erastês*, and I loved him dearly…" He looked at his wineglass and quietly said, "So I answered his prayer." He looked up at me, his smile gone. "I made a deal with the Fates, Pholus, the details of which… well, suffice to say that they cleaned out my wine cellar -- and my breweries, and my hidden stores in the Magic Realm, and their yearly percentage -- but they're sweet old gals and they deserve their wine.

"They agreed to reweave you into the Fabric of Reality, where you could help me achieve my vengeance against Heracles and reintroduce the centaurs into the world, creating new Bacchanalia and empowering me, while the rest of the Twelve sleep away on Olympus, forgotten.

"The Fates agreed -- but they required a sacrifice."

I set my wine glass on the table. "Chiron," I said.

"Chiron," Dionysus said, nodding. "Chiron chose it. But if it hadn't been him, it would've had to have been someone. Probably one of your herd -- and Chiron could never have lived with that. It made the time together after your rebirth short, for sure, but I think for him it was worth it."

I nodded, near tears. "I hope so," I whispered. "I want his sacrifice to be worth something."

Dionysus smiled at me. "It is," he said. "And it will be."

"Here's to Chiron," Cavalier said, standing. "And his sacrifice!"

"To Chiron!" the herd echoed, clinking glasses.

"To Chiron," I added, trying to smile. "My love."

"And to Pholus," Dionysus added, "inheritor of gnomes, builder of herds, and keeper of essence! And now, the wisest and justest of the centaurs!"

"TO PHOLUS!"

"To you, my brothers!" I said back, raising my glass. "*Euoi Euan* -- well done, my sons!"

"*EUOI EUAN!*"

The party went on. We sang -- we danced -- we loved each other drunkenly. The pot burned and the wine flowed, and soon, so did the spit and the lube and the cum. We were what we were, after all.

Later, nearing the sunrise, we found ourselves piled in the hot tub, smoking more pot and preparing to crawl into beds and fall asleep. Dionysus, happily hogging the joint, spoke once more. "So, gentlemen, before I take my leave, let's talk about what's next." He exhaled and offered the joint to me -- I gladly took it.

As he spoke, he went around and kissed each of us on the forehead. "When I healed you, I gave you all the ability to reproduce, to make other centaurs. My charge to you is to go out into the world and do just that, create seven mighty herds, each of you as a leader. Worship me, creating the Bacchanalia wherever and whenever you can and I will reward you beyond your wildest dreams. You also now carry my blessing, which you will find will keep you out of trouble. Mostly. I mean, you can still be killed or maimed, but you won't die of sickness or old age. And you can always pray to mo if you have to, but I'd prefer you text -- I'm more likely to answer a text."

He emerged from the tub completely dry and dressed, wearing his golden skirt, laced sandals, and carrying his thyrsus (which dripped honey on the tile). "My friends, I love you all with affection unspeakable," he said, with his ever-present smile. "And I once again give you my thanks. Go forth and multiply, centaurs! Do what you have been brought back to do! I'll see you soon!"

And just like that, he was gone, off to the next party.

It was getting to be cliche in these moments that Pokey would always break the silence and get the punchline, yet somehow he always did. "I can't believe Donny Isis is all that," he said. "I reckon he was just a happy drunk."

That allowed us to laugh and break up and move forward. Everybody found a place to crash -- Gambit didn't even make it out of the grotto, he fell asleep on the rubber-sheeted playbed (I gave Pokey a blanket for them to share), while AppleJack and Lickety Split took the guest room.

Dunn put his arm around my shoulders and asked if I wanted to be alone or with someone. I really didn't want to be alone, so Dunn and Cavalier slept with me in the Master, which comforted me -- because the sheets still smelled of Chiron.

I didn't think I'd ever fall asleep, but exhaustion won, and I finally drifted off, safe with my herd. Mad god defeated.

My dreams were full of my *Erastês'* scent.

EPILOGUE

*An **epilogue** or **epilog** (from Greek ἐπίλογος epílogos, "conclusion" from ἐπί epi, "in addition" and λόγος logos, "word") is a piece of writing at the end of a work of literature, usually used to bring closure to the work. It is presented from the perspective of within the story. An epilogue often serves to reveal the fates of the characters. They can be used to hint at a sequel or wrap up all the loose ends. They can occur at a significant period of time after the main plot has ended. In some cases, the epilogue is used to allow the main character a chance to "speak freely".*

****

My Dearest Chiron --

Winter has finally ended and spring has come to Mt. Pellon, the meadows at the base of the mountain bloom in a magnificent array of wildflowers and greenery. The sunshine is warm, but the cold wind still blows down from the mountain top to remind us that Persephone just got back from the underworld and things aren't quite settled yet. Still, I can smell the fertilizer in the air from the vineyards below, so I choose to look forward.

Gambit and Pokey frolic in the fields below me as I sit on the patio, drinking coffee and smoking a joint as I write these words. They use the excuse of throwing the football around, but they are just playing, romping, using any excuse to enjoy the outside after a winter in the cave.

They were the only ones who chose to stay, though the others visit frequently -- Traveling has become the greatest gift of our centaur abilities. Being anywhere in the world within moments? Priceless. We used to joke that our smartphones and internet made the world smaller -- take away travel-time and the world is your local neighborhood.

We all recognize Pokey's uniqueness, the outrageous amounts of power he seems to wield in so simple a manner -- it's frightening, honestly. Gambit has taken on the task of training him -- and bull-doggedly protecting him. From Gambit's perspective, the universe is Pokey-centric. I also know, from sharing a VERY non-acoustically dampened cave for half a year, that Gambit is the bottom in their sexual couplings!

Pokey pokes.

However, if he didn't, I suppose none of this would've happened in the first place. What are the chances of picking up Dionysus in a bar one night and fucking him so good that he sets a whole epic in motion around you? Only Pokey...

I'm in charge of Pokey's "formal" education -- the role of his *Erastês* without the benefits, I often joke. (Though the three of us have had an extraordinary amount of sex together, I don't consider "us" anything more than a couple, plus me.) Gambit often listens in on lessons -- though he pretends not to -- and I can see the gaps in his formal education, which he filled with sparring.

Gambit is preparing for a big fight, coming up later this spring. It will be his first time in the octagon since the viral video of him and Heracles went public -- it's already sold out.

I haven't really told you about this -- those videos -- and the clear genius of Cavalier. Everybody thought the videos were fake, even the ones featuring Pokey, filmed from multiple angles from a variety of phones -- in this cynically-minded, self-promoting age, everyone assumed we were marketing something. So here comes Cavalier -- he approaches Netflix, showing them the view numbers on the videos, and proposes the series "CENTAURS REBORN" following a gang of hot, built young studs who get transformed into modern-day centaurs. Extremely homoerotic and porn-star sexy, he's got the pictures we took before Pride last year, tons of video footage of us in action -- and, being Cavalier, he... "hired" one of the top writers in Hollywood to create a treatment and pilot script.

Netflix gave it a green light. It's now in development and casting starts next month.

Cavalier has gone LA -- and to be honest, west coast works way better for him -- embracing the celebrity lifestyle and the perks that come with it. And I know for a fact that he's been responsible for more than one Bacchanalia, for I've been in attendance. He's got a beautiful home in Orange County with this crazy infinity pool that overlooks the valley -- it's just made for orgy. And he's truly had some of the best looking men -- literally.

Cavalier is a full-on acolyte of Dionysus, worshipping the young god and following his creed. Normally, I don't cotton to the religious types, but when you have a personal relationship with your god -- when you're friends with benefits -- I think that changes things. He has a weird reverence for Dionysis that keeps them from being "buddies" -- and I know it makes Donny uncomfortable -- but Cav has been into mythology since he's been a boy, so I don't think he can help but get all star-struck when a real god is around.

I confess that Donny has become a good friend of mine. He created theatre, after all -- "Until those damn muses took over everything!" -- and he loves musicals! "Very American," he's said. "WAY better than that dreary opera our *Erastês* liked so much! I didn't think the nineteenth century would ever end." (Maybe I shouldn't tell you that, dear Chiron!) We see two or three shows a month, mostly in New York or London, though there have been those occasions where we've gone to a Fringe Fest or some experimental theatre in some hole-in-the-wall somewhere that I'd never be able to find by myself. He tends to like more frivolous things than I do, but I think that's his nature.

What a couple we make! A six-five, two-hundred ninety pound bodybuilder with red hair, beard and enormous genitals towering over a golden-haired, purple-eyed boy who looks barely more than a teen twink, even though he's thousands of years old. I'm just saying, I get recognized as "that centaur guy" more often than he gets recognized as the god of wine -- still, we go by "Red" and "Donny" in public.

Donny likes to have a drink after a show -- I prefer to smoke -- so we always visit at least one bar where Donny will inevitably get carded. He's a loud, friendly drinker, and everyone loves him! The trick is getting Donny to stop -- he can keep Bacchanalia going for days if he's in the mood (and he almost always is, especially if the show was good). Half the time, I think the only reason he brings me along is to start an orgy.

He wants me to start dating again, but every time he brings the subject up, I shut him down. "It's bad enough you stay in that cave," he says. "Don't get trapped in the past, Pholus."

I like the cave -- I feel like I'm home there, not trapped.

Gambit LOVES it! "I'm living in the batcave, man! This is fuckin' AWESOME!" He sings, "Nana nana nana nana Gambit!" With our ability to Travel, we can live where we choose, not be restricted by commute. Gambit trains in the cave's gym, but he also maintains his client load, training fighters at Lickety Split's gym, so still works out there, too. Gambit is one of the few of us that can't Travel without the Dionysian Wine -- both Pokey and I can, which annoys him -- so he carries a flask of it in his gym bag, specifically for Traveling. (Interesting observation: whatever container we pour the wine into never empties after that. We poured wine from the bottle into our centaur flasks and those flasks never completely drain. The bottle is always full, too. Glasses empty, bottles don't. How did I not notice that when you sent it to me, Chiron? Magic...)

Our Warrior also got a new tattoo across his upper left pec that says, "Gambit 2, Heracles 0" (The tattoo artist supposedly asked him if he didn't mean "HERCULES"? I was proud of Gambit because he knew the difference.)

AppleJack is still living at our old house (and probably will forever, now that they've added a pool). I'm debating giving it to him much the same way you gave me the cave, my sweet little sneak. How did you get all that legal stuff done without me knowing? I've met your properties manager, by the way, and the accountant (who sucks a mean dick) -- you've done your job well, Chiron. We are brilliantly invested. Thank you for that, too, my love.

Anyway, AppleJack is still at the house, living there with Lickety Split, who continues to own his gym, doing Ninja Warrior Guest Spots and Triathlons on the side. He's forever training -- and I love that he's gotten AppleJack into it. AppleJack is doing his first triathlon in a month -- we're all going. He's beyond excited about it. I've never in my life seen him this enthusiastic about something. (He's even put pictures of his abs on social media! Will wonders never cease?)

They've expanded the basement grow and -- perhaps because of their friendship with a certain God of Pot -- their yield is not to be believed. Lickety Split is an experimenter, and his breeds and strains and hybrids have made HIGH TIMES magazine! Mix him with a craftsman like AppleJack and it's no wonder their weed is banging -- they keep me supplied. (I call it "rent".) They call it "Centaur Stash."

Sadly, they live like they've never graduated college. The place has devolved into a freakin' frat house -- although it is hot that they hang around all day in their overstuffed jockstraps and compression wear. Whatever -- I'm glad AppleJack has found a fetish. I mean, a hobby.

He still maintains the domain, though they've been moving away from PHOLUS REBORN to CENTAURS REBORN (with PHOLUS!), then to just CENTAURS REBORN within the year. It will coincide with the release of the Netflix series. It's more of a team thing that way, and I'm not the focal point anymore, even if I am considered the "wisest and justest" now.

That was a lousy title to throw on me, my love -- wisest and justest. You've made me into their queen — and not in a fun, gay way!

But that's okay -- Cavalier is all about the pomp and circumstance. Both he and Dunn have started their own herds, as Dionysus instructed us. (I was going to write "Donny" there, but felt like I should be formal in a paragraph where I'm writing about formality.) But the herds are as different as Cavalier and Dunn themselves. Cav has created two foals -- three for Dunn. The difference? I had to be there for Cav's -- it was a whole ceremony. I mean, it was fun and dramatic and very hot, but it was Cav -- it was formal. There were recitations and oaths and such. The initiates gave up their old identities and picked centaur names from antiquity: Orneus and Dictys. As you might expect, they are both painfully beautiful young men, as I'm sure the rest of Cav's herd will be, and very polite.

They are also disciplined fighters, black belts BEFORE they'd been transformed -- Gambit's been training with them, and even he's impressed. "We're not gonna wanna fuck with that herd," Gambit has reported. "I think we should always keep an eye on Cav."

Now, take everything I said about Cav and turn it all upside down for Dunn.

Where Cav's foals are young and smooth, Dunn's men are mature and hairy. "The Leather Daddy Herd," we joke. They're these dom-top "Sir" types, straight out of the Pageant Circuit, cigar smoking, harness wearing, Tom-of-Finland throwbacks -- hot as fuck: Coach, Rimmer, and Master Fist -- very different from the stiff formality of Orneus and Dictys in Cav's tribe. Dunn's herd has at least one human slave each (Master Fist has two). Dunn claims the slaves are taken willingly -- knowing what our pheromones can do to people, I doubt him, but I'm choosing not to say anything. The slaves look happy enough -- and their Masters were willing to take a knee for me.

(I'm just wondering how we're going to seat people at Thanksgiving…? Maybe a kiddie table for the slaves?)

Dunn's barber shop is slowly morphing into an underground play place for the local leather scene. "Dunn's Dungeon" sounds better, anyway. I go there, not for the roleplay stuff -- but to get in a sling and let Dunn have his fun. Dunn's guys work the circuit, hitting all the parties. Some of the orgies have been epic and scandalous, but Dunn and his herd always seem to walk away scott free -- talk about luck!

So, Dionysus' vision has started to happen. There are now two of the seven herds of centaurs -- well, three if you count mine, but why would you do that? -- and certainly more on the way. In some ways, I feel like a proud patriarch, watching my sons create more sons, watching their families become uniquely theirs. (I promise to write you the moment AppleJack has children!)

I will be honest here because I know you will never read this, but I don't think I'll ever get over the mourning -- I don't think this loss will ever lessen. Six months later and waves of grief still crash over me with a frequency that doesn't allow me to catch my breath.

How did you wait so long?

I don't think I can.

Anyway, *Erastês*, enough of this. I am signing off on this letter. The little crystal bottle that holds your essence sits before me on the table, twinkling in the sunlight -- the same way your eyes did before you attempted something mischievous.

I have a decision to make.

All my love, forever,
Pholus

****

As I become aware, I'm running, my hooves pounding on the dirt floor of the forest. It isn't dark, but heavily shadowed, and the shapes of giant tree trunks slide by me -- I'm confident in my footing, leaping over fallen logs and rocks, but I have no idea where I am. All I know is the joy of movement... freedom... living. I have left my worries in that other world -- and now I am free to be my Bestial self.

I emerge into a meadow, but it's not the Plains of Thessaly, where we normally come. This forest is much older than that, something from antiquity, something from forever ago -- before there were names. I feel like I don't belong here. I'm searching, seeking, opening myself to the new environment. There is something... someone... over there!

I look to the west, toward the sun, already beginning to drop behind the mountains that range there. On the top of a rise, almost hidden by the glare, I see his familiar silhouette, facing away from me, his Bestial form so handsome, thick and rugged, his appearance such an irony to his nature, so gentle and soft.

I walk up the rise slowly, disbelievingly, afraid he's just a mirage, or a fever-dream to be taken from me in a blink, in a gust, in a distraction.

Still he remains there, looking into the distance -- I ache for him to be real.

It isn't until I crest the rise that he turns to acknowledge me -- my Chiron. He studies me for a second before the corner of his mouth curls up in a half-smile. "You drank the wine," he says quietly.

I nod slightly. "I did."

He nods, too, looking out over the vastness of the valley before us.

"How long has it been?" he asks.

I snort, a little embarrassed. "Six months, a little over."

He barks a laugh.

"What?"

He waves me off. "I lost a bet," he says. "Dionysus said you'd drink it within a year -- I didn't believe him."

"Are you angry?"

He smiles. "With you? Never."

I'm almost crying. "I want to touch you, but I'm afraid you won't exist."

"That would be pretty cruel, even for the Fates." He reaches over, grasping my hand. I can feel him.

He's real -- thank the gods!

I immediately throw myself into his arms, hugging him, crying. "Oh, Chiron, I've missed you so much!"

He comforts me, stroking me like a child. "Shh," he says. Shh, erômenos. I'm back now."

"Are you?" I ask, pulling back and looking him in the eye. "Are you?"

He's lighthearted. "Well… you drank me!"

We hold each other for a while, watching the sun sink behind the mountains. He breaks the silence. "I hate that my last words to you were 'Fight like Pholus.' I had a whole speech planned." He shakes his head.

I smile. "Actually, your last words to me were 'Everything will be clear' -- and it was."

"Really?" he asks, scrunching his eyebrows like he's trying to remember. Finally, he grunts, then speaks. "I take it you won."

I laugh. "I did -- I fought like Pholus. I turned him into a centaur then Cavalier caught him in one of those bridles."

Chiron winces. "Ouch," he says. "Well done -- there's some good, classic irony in that. Can't say he doesn't deserve it." He studies the sunset before he speaks again. "I guess that was why we needed Cav alive -- that makes me feel like my sacrifice was worth it."

Silence again, each lost in our thoughts, until it's my turn to break it. "When I go back, what'll happen to you?"

He shrugs. "I'll go with you, I suppose. I don't know -- I've never done this before. It looks like we'll manifest separately in the Magic Realm, but in the real world, who knows?" But this is Chiron, he loves an academic exercise, so he supposes. "I could manifest one of three ways there: either I'll be a reference for you, my memories a sort-of database you can access, or I could end up a disembodied voice that instructs and advises you, or, in the most-likely way, we'll become some sort of hybrid being. Just what you need, to accept another soul -- I guess we'll have to see."

"I guess we will." I kiss him, saying, "I love you, Chiron."

He kisses me back. "And I love you, Pholus -- I always have and I always will."

The kissing becomes more intense, and the sun is still up, stirring feelings. "I don't have to go back anytime soon," I say, as we settle down together into the tall grass of the meadow.

"We have nothing BUT time," Chiron murmurs. "We have nothing but forever."

And there, in some unidentified ancient forest in the Magic Realm, as the moon rises, we come together again. Here in a place where everything is real, and anything is possible.

Forever.

ACKNOWLEDGEMENTS

Even with writing, no one does it alone. I've been posting stories, series, and novellas online in writer's forums and differently-themed sites for decades and I have acquired a large -- and vocal -- fanbase, making some good virtual friends along the way, except I don't know anybody's real name. @BearParadox (not his real name— or maybe it is) served as my editor/ creative-consultant for PHOLUS, and a completely delightful relationship emerged. One of the few people who knows more about mythology than me, my manuscript is literally littered with his comments. This story would not exist without his valued input -- I'm extremely grateful. Also, my wonderful husband, who isn't necessarily a fan of the genre, but who loves and supports my efforts and passions, even as I forced him to sit through endless plot summaries and backstories. @pecs_to and @Rock_Creek_Werewolf also read the manuscript and gave me welcome feedback. Finally, I have to give a huge thanks to @adultjunkdrawer for the absolutely amazing cover art -- it exceeded my expectations in every possible way!

ABOUT THE AUTHOR

Austin Miller is the mainstream pseudonym of online erotic short-story author absman420, who has been publishing gay erotica since the early 90's, penning dozens of transformation-themed stories featuring muscle-growth, mind-control, and superheroes (*Cycle One, King Rex*, and the never-ending *Pollination - the Series!*), accruing a wonderfully weird fan-base along the way. Over the years, his work has appeared in multiple online magazines, forums, and archives -- most recently and unexpectedly cited in two academic publications, *Embodying Contagion*, from Univ of Chicago Press, and *Feminist and Queer Information Studies Reader*, from Litwin Books and Library. Just use The Google, you'll see. PHOLUS REBORN is absman420's second novel -- though it's Austin Miller's first. Follow @absman420 on Twitter!